ONE NIGHT WITH A ROGUE

India turned back the blankets and slid into bed. It was only when she was covered that she removed her shift, drawing it over her head and letting it fall over the side.

South's eyes followed the movement. The fabric brushed his bare calf as it drifted past. He could recall no succession of moments from his past that were filled with such eroticism as India's modest disrobing. His mouth was dry and the words came with some difficulty, hoarse and rough. "Unpin your hair."

"Yes. Of course."

He had not meant it as a command. Now he could not make his tongue and lips conform to the word "please." In the darkened bedchamber, her pale hair was its own light, and he would have it framing her face. He could make out each gold and platinum wave as it was released and sifted between her fingertips.

"It will be better if you have few expectations," she whispered.

He bent his head, brushed her mouth with his. Her lips were cool and dry. "Why is that?"

India didn't answer. Couldn't.

South dipped his head again, this time catching the corner of her mouth. The tip of his tongue teased her lips, pressing lightly, tracing the lush pink line. It was all the urging she needed. India's mouth parted. The breath that had snagged in her throat was released in a tiny sigh. This time when he kissed her, she kissed him back. . . .

Books by Jo Goodman

Published by Zebra Books

EVERYTHING
I EVER
WANTED

Jo Goodman

ZEBRA BOOKS
KENSINGTON PUBLISHING CORP.

http://www.kensingtonbooks.com

For Lisa, Beth, and Carolyn.
Just like the Compass Club, we go in different directions
and still manage to connect in so many ways.
Good stories. Great laughter. Best friends.

Prologue

Michelmas Term 1796

It was a trap.

Matthew Forrester, The Right Honorable The Viscount Southerton, had willingly, even eagerly walked into it knowing that. Where would have been the game otherwise? Now, he had assured his friends, all the elements were in place. A challenge. A dare. A wager. And finally, a trap. South refrained from naming it a battle of wits, because the wits were so obviously distributed on his side as to make the entire intrigue a bit of a yawn. Still, it was a jolly good diversion for a Sunday evening.

Only a few months past his eleventh birthday, Matthew could most kindly be described as gangly. His mother said he hadn't come into his hands and feet yet. His father was not pleased to hear it, though it explained his heir's awkwardness well enough. Upon hearing the countess's pronouncement, the earl had wryly regarded his son at the breakfast table while a servant hurriedly cleaned the upended platter of eggs and tomatoes in front of the boy. "Thought it was only his head he hadn't found. Demmed dreamy lad, your boy." His mother had merely smiled at each of them in turn, indulgently at her husband, then encouragingly at her son.

Now, in what he hoped was an attitude of casual, even insolent disregard, Matthew stretched his long frame in the chair set before the tribunal, folding his arms on his thin chest and crossing his feet at the ankles. He had someone in mind as he struck this pose. An acquaintance of his father's—and not the usual sort of young man the earl was likely to know well—Matthew's brief glimpse of the stranger in his father's library had captured his imagination. That man had also struck a pose, though Matthew had not consciously realized it was affected until he found himself in the same position. Dashing. Perhaps a bit dissolute. Daring in the raised chin. (Upon this thought Matthew lifted his chin at the appropriate angle.) And finally, the devil-may-care smile.

"He's grinning like a trout," one of the tribunal members pointed out. "I've had a trout grin like that at me before." He leaned slightly forward until his upper body cast a shadow on the table in front of him, then he looked down from his place on the dais. It was an aggressive overture, neither sly nor subtle. "Just before I filleted it."

There was appreciative laughter among the other four tribunal members, not for what was said but for its immediate effect on the young viscount. Matthew visibly gulped, the smile disappeared, and a directive went out to his arms and legs to come to attention. The chair actually slid several inches to the rear as he forcefully sat up straight and braced his shoulders and spine firmly against the ladder-back.

"Ate it then," the tribunal member went on. "Fish never stopped grinning at me."

Matthew didn't blink but stared straight ahead. This had the unfortunate effect of making his light-gray eyes, which had begun to water, seem absent of life and more fishlike than not.

The archbishop raised his hand to halt the laughter. Quiet reigned among the tribunal members as smiles faded along the length of the scarred table. It was time to reflect on the serious business before them.

"Well, Trout?" the head of the Society of Bishops demanded in bored tones.

The dais rumbled as the tribunal laughed as though with a singular voice.

"It's a good name for you," he went on when only a ripple of amusement remained among them, and the fish caught on their line began to wriggle a bit. "Do your friends call you Trout?"

Matthew finally blinked. He wanted to wipe his eyes, but he was certain the gesture would be misinterpreted. No one on the Society's tribunal would credit the abundance of lighted tallow candles in the small room as the cause for his watery eyes. He would certainly be damned for all time if they thought he was on the precipice of weeping. Better to be named a fish than a girl.

"Do they, Trout?" There was impatience now from the archbishop. At fourteen he was not older than every other member of the Society who had elected him, but he was unquestionably what they were seeking in a leader. He was a handsome young man who gave no more thought to his bred-in-the-bone confidence than he did to the color of his hair or the shape of his mouth. He was too clever to be cocky, but not wise enough not to be cruel.

"No," Matthew offered simply.

There was a faint lift to the archbishop's brow and a disapproving murmur across the tribunal. "No?"

"No, your Excellency." Matthew had no liking for the form of address the archbishop demanded. His voice quavered slightly. "That is, no, your Excellency, my friends do not call me Trout."

Albion Geoffrey Godwin, Lord Barlough, permitted himself a slim smile. "A fine response," he said after a contemplative moment. "Yet I cannot help being struck by its falseness."

Matthew stared at him, not understanding.

The archbishop prompted in carefully cajoling accents, "Are we not your friends, Trout?"

"I believe that has yet to be put to the vote, your Excellency."

Young Lord Barlough nodded approvingly. "Right enough." He looked to the pairing of friends on his right and left flank and caught their eyes, communicating a message without altering a single facial muscle. "But surely that is a mere formality. You are here before us now at our invitation. Invitations are never issued lightly; an audience is never granted as a matter of course."

It was the Society's way to couch its activities in comforting language. To say that the Viscount Southerton had been brought before them by invitation was to entirely dismiss the fact that he had been jumped by two of the Society's Praetorian-like brothers in the cobbled courtyard of Hambrick Hall and carried bound, blindfolded, and gagged to this room deep in the moist, subterranean bowels of the school. To name this an audience when in fact it was a trial was further proof of the Society's penchant for couching the truth in an innocuous phrase.

Archbishop of Canterbanter. Matthew almost smiled as the title came to his mind. Lord Barlough would not like it if he knew about the name or the scornful, irreverent way in which it was often said by those on the outside of the Society. Of course, since there were many on the outside who wanted, even yearned, to be part of the inner sanctum, and Matthew and his closest friends—the ones who did *not* call him Trout—never referred to Canterbanter where they might be overheard. The spies among them, the ones with their noses out of joint because they'd been pressed for so long to the Society's collective arse, would reveal a classmate's disrespect if they thought it would gain them entry to the exclusive and powerful cabal.

For as long as there had been a Hambrick Hall, there had been a Society of Bishops. The origins of the organization were not known to the uninitiated. Within the Society the history was passed orally from archbishop to archbishop, a tradition that was maintained for almost two hundred years and that deviated neither in the words used nor their inflection. For a communication that was so sacred as the genesis of their order, the first archbishop devised a chant, and in this manner the story flowed uninterrupted from leader to leader for generations of boys.

Southerton had never been particularly curious about the Society's beginnings, or about the Society at all. When he arrived at Hambrick Hall three years earlier for his first term, he had heard about the Bishops before he had finished unpacking his trunk. He had put them out of his mind, being much more interested in when dinner would be served and if there would be custard as his father told him there sometimes was. A trifle vague in his own approach to the world around him, neither an avid student nor an indifferent one, friendly but not gregarious, cooperative but not obsequious, Matthew fell outside the notice of the Society until late in the last term, with the arrival of Mr. Marchman.

The school break had done nothing to improve the Society's mood. Rather, Matthew suspected, they had used the time away from Hambrick Hall—while he had been swimming and sailing and studying astronomy for the pleasure of sitting up at night while the rest of the manor was abed—to devise a plan that would see him shamed, caned, and expelled from the school.

The Society of Bishops rarely meted out punishment in half measures. In truth, they rarely meted out punishment. It was their way to find others to do it.

The archbishop continued to regard Matthew with something akin to friendly derision. "You know, Trout, I do believe I have heard some of the other boys refer to you by another name. South, I think. The diminutive of your title, isn't it?"

"Yes, your Excellency."

"And those other fellows? North. East. West. I'm afraid I don't understand that."

Matthew made a mental shrug but said nothing.

"You call yourselves the Compass Club. Is that right?"

It sounded rather juvenile when Matthew heard it from the archbishop. Still, in his little group no one was addressed as his "Excellency." Oh, from time to time they called East "his Nibs," but that was all in good humor. The fact that they *were* juvenile was not a truth one could easily get around, so Matthew simply dismissed it. "Yes, your Excellency. The Compass Club." He almost added, *"Sworn Enemies of the Society of Bishops,"* but he considered it rather too dramatic and akin to playing his cards fast and loose. There was also a problem with his voice of late, and something as deeply felt as *"Sworn Enemies of the Society of Bishops"* should have some hint of the profound and ominous about it. If his vocal chords failed him, as they had been wont to do recently, it would just sound silly.

"Very well, Trout," Lord Barlough said. "And what of your allegiance to the Compass Club? Are you prepared to deny them and take the vows as a brother first among the Bishops?"

Matthew's response was solemn. "I am prepared, your Excellency."

The smile came again, just a crease in the handsome visage that was the archbishop's most animated expression. "Good. Then you have what you promised to deliver."

There was no mention of the promise being extracted by threatening the health and well-being of his best friends. This omission did not surprise the viscount. Indeed, any admission of the techniques used to coerce his cooperation would have been the real surprise. Equally expected was the restraint the archbishop showed in not revealing the exact article that was to be delivered, or the other truth: that it was not Matthew who offered it up but that it had been named as the price of his friends' safety and his admission to the Society.

"I have it."

There was a stir at the table. They all knew that Matthew, upon having all his bonds removed and secreted away, had been summarily searched by Lord Barlough. That search had turned up nothing. It was cause for confusion now because the search had been, in the smooth lexicon of Canterbanter, *thorough.*

"You will produce it now."

"Certainly." Southerton began in the carefully modulated tones of the schoolboy that he was, "The reign of Henry VIII, lasting as it did from 1509 to 1547, was perforce to have wrought many changes, especially to the role of the Catholic Church in policies of law, governance, and allegiances. Henry VIII's choice of his bride upon taking the throne—the widow of his brother—had ramifications beyond what could have been imagined at the . . ." Matthew broke off because the archbishop was on his feet.

"What the bloody hell is this?"

"What you asked for," Matthew said calmly.

"Bugger a duck," one of the Bishops said, slapping the flat of his hand on the table. The candle flames flickered wildly for a moment, then were still. "You said you could get the examination."

"Yes," said Matthew. "I did. And so I did." They simply stared at him, and he began again. "Perhaps after another you'll understand. Significant events during Henry VIII's reign were the explorations of the coasts of the Americas by the Portuguese and Spaniards, the appointment of Thomas Wolsey as Archbishop of York, the excommunication of Martin Luther in 1520 by Pope Leo X, and conferring the title of "Defender of the Faith" on Henry for the *Assertio septem sacramentorum* against Luther the following year." Matthew's voice trailed off a moment as he pondered this last. "Always thought there was a delicious historical irony there, but unappreciated by the headmaster." He looked at Lord Barlough, then the other Bishops, as though for comment. "Unappreciated by this audience as well, I see." His shrug was real this time, not mental. "Let's see, where was I? Oh. There is also the fall of Cardinal Wolsey from power and the appointment of Sir Thomas More as Lord Chancellor in 1529. A position I've often wondered if he had cause to regret. But I digress again. History is like that, don't you think? So many points of divergence and convergence that one can study the links while forgetting the chain.''

The archbishop sat down slowly, the wind quite beaten from his sails. The puff of air that had momentarily rounded his cheeks was gone, leaving his face sunken below the refined arch of those well-placed bones. ''You memorized it,'' he said as though he couldn't believe it, which he couldn't. ''You memorized the answers to the headmaster's examination!''

''Not precisely,'' Matthew said. ''Only the questions. The answers are my own.''

Now the archbishop's complexion actually mottled. ''Get him!''

But the Society was trapped on one side of the table, and Matthew had planned his escape long before he had been brought to the room. He leaped to his feet, shoved the table as hard as he could, and managed to unseat two of the Bishops and a half dozen of the candles. Hot wax and flying legs, overturned chairs and a wobbling dais, confused calls for help and ''Bugger him!'' all conspired to give the loose-limbed and fleet of foot Viscount Southerton a head start to the door. He flung open the door and ran headlong into the headmaster.

''So you *are* here,'' Glasser said mildly. He looked at young Southerton's flushed, upturned face and ignored the commotion going on behind the boy. He saw enough to know that the school wasn't going to go up in flames and, for that matter, neither were any of the Bishops. *Pity that,* came the errant thought. He suppressed it. He laid a hand on Matthew's thin shoulder, not in a protective gesture but in a calming one, and thought idly that not only had the young viscount grown like a weed since the last term, but the boy was inordinately prepossessed in spite of the flushed complexion. ''I came to see how the skull session was going. I wasn't certain you would agree to tutor them, but I know they can be persuasive.'' He raised his eyes and regarded the tribunal blandly. ''Had a bit of an accident, did you?'' Only Lord Barlough displayed the presence of mind not to gape at him. The others fell into line quickly. "Don't mind me," he said. "Pick yourselves up and pray continue with the session. The little I heard at the door has me frankly fascinated." He took a single step backward out of the room as the fallen began to rise and they peeled cooling wax from the backs of their hands. He crooked an index finger toward the boys skulking in the narrow and dank passage. "Come forward. Do not be shy. There's room enough for all of you."

The first two boys to enter the old cellar were the tribunal's two guards. They shuffled in, heads bowed to avoid the anger they knew was simmering in their archbishop's eyes. Following them, at a similarly reluctant pace, were Gabriel Whitney, Evan Marchman, and Brendan Hampton, known to each other and Southerton as East, West, and North.

"Chairs?" Mr. Glasser asked pleasantly, glancing around the room as he closed the door. "No matter, we shall make do. Place that table on the floor. Those chairs, too. Master Marchman. You and your friends sit on the dais. Master Pendrake. Lord Harte. You will sit on the table. Mind the candles don't burn your clothes. The rest of you, take your seats."

Matthew started to return to his chair, thought better of it, and politely turned back to the headmaster. "Sir?"

"Yes?" It was so very difficult not to give in to peals of laughter with the surfeit of astonishment that existed in this room, and Mr. Glasser only just managed the thing.

"What about you, sir? Would you like my chair?"

Mr. Glasser merely leaned back against the door so it clicked in place, effectively barring it until he determined it should be otherwise. "I believe I will remain here," he said. "I am intrigued that so many of you are interested in history outside the classroom. But then, these damp and moldy walls lend themselves to historical accounts, I dare-say. All of them riveting, I'm sure. Go on, Lord Southerton, I believe you were coming to the point of the king's secret marriage to Anne Boleyn."

Matthew glanced a shade guiltily at his friends and began

by way of apology, "Afterwards Thomas Cranmer became Archbishop of Canterbanter . . ." He saw their eyes light with good humor at his purposeful blunder and knew he was forgiven even while the Bishops were plotting his demise. "Canterbury, that is," he continued, "and the marriage between Henry and Catherine of Aragon was declared. . . ."

Matthew Forrester, the Viscount Southerton, warmed to his subject. He did so love an adventure.

Chapter One

September 1818

Laughter erupted from the private theatre box. Hearty. Rolling. Sustained. It came at her like a succession of wavelets and played hell with her timing. She waited for it to recede so she could speak her next line. Even before she finished, there was another ripple of laughter from the same box. Wavelets be damned. What was coming toward the stage now threatened to pitch her under and press her down.

She paused mid-phrase and pointedly stared past the candle footlights in the direction of the disruption. The four actors sharing the small Drury Lane stage with her did the same. The audience, largely male, fell silent. They turned in their seats if such was required for a clear view of the box that had stopped the players cold. It was not that the audience was as ignorant of the private box's occupants as the leading lady. Quite the opposite was true. It would have been difficult to find someone in the packed house this evening who did *not* know that the Marquess of Eastlyn and his boon companions were in attendance.

From the wings came the loud aside: "Line! *You cannot expect that I will always save you, Hortense!*"

"I know the line," she said without rancor. "What I cannot know is if I will be permitted to speak it."

This had the effect of raising sympathetic chuckles among the general audience and finally wresting quiet from the private box as those occupants realized they had become center stage.

"Now you've done it, East. I believe she is speaking to us." The Earl of Northam indicated the stage, where Miss India Parr was standing with her fists resting on the wide panniers of her gown, and her elbows cocked sharply outward. Her painted lips were pursed in a perfect bow, and her darkly drawn eyebrows were arched so high they fairly disappeared into the fringed curls of her powdered wig. This exaggerated demonstration of impatience would have been more amusing if it had not been so clearly directed at them.

The Marquess of Eastlyn turned from his friends and once again gave his attention to the figure in the footlamps. He made a good show of appearing much struck by this turn of events. "Why, so she is. Odd, that. Doesn't she have a line?" His deeply pleasant voice carried easily across the craned heads of the audience below his box.

It was Evan Marchman in the chair beside East who answered, *"You can't expect me to save you, Hortense."*

This prompt, offered as it was in dry, uninflected accents, lifted more chuckling from an appreciative audience. Looking toward the stage as almost no one else was doing now, South knew the lady was in danger of losing her support and her momentum. He shook his head as he came slowly and with some care to his feet. It remained for him to make amends. It was his ribald aside, after all, that had sent East into a paroxysm of laughter that turned out to be as contagious as it was ill-advised and ill-timed. South braced his hands on the box's balustrade, curving long fingers over the side. He leaned forward, grimacing only slightly when he realized that behind him North had made a fist in the superfine tails of his coat. Did Northam seriously think he was in danger of falling overboard? The notion was absurd. Half asleep he could still climb a ship's frosted rigging in a pitched North Sea storm. In clear, commanding tones, South announced, *"You cannot expect that I will always save you, Hortense."*

On stage, the lady's eyes narrowed. She lifted one hand to block the candlelight and peered more intently in the direction of the scrupulously modulated voice. "Thank you, my lord," she said politely. "You have it exactly. Shall you go on or must we?"

South thought she looked perfectly at her ease now and even willing to seat herself comfortably on the stage and allow him to finish all the parts if he wished it. He certainly did not wish it. "I most humbly beg your pardon," he said, inclining his head in an apologetic gesture to her, then to the audience. "For myself and my friends. Pray, continue."

The lady inclined her head in a like gesture; then she stepped back into the circle of light, lowered her hands, and covered herself in the mantle of her character. This transformation, done so expertly as to seem both instantaneous and magical, was greeted by thunderous applause. From the back of the theatre where there was only standing room, the men stomped their feet and cheered. In the Marquess of Eastlyn's box the response was equally appreciative, if more subdued.

The four friends did not leave the theatre immediately upon the play's final curtain. They remained in East's box as the audience filed out toward the street or, as was the case with many of the hopeful young Corinthians, toward the dressing room.

Marchman pointed to a small group that was headed for the stage doors. "They don't all think they can get a glimpse of her, do they? What a stiff-necked business that would be."

"Don't fancy yourself craning to view the lovely from a more agreeable distance?" asked East. He stretched his long legs in front of him and made a steeple with his fingers at the level of his midriff. A lock of chestnut hair had fallen over his forehead, and he made no effort to push it back. His eyes were heavy-lidded, their focus vaguely sleepy.

Mr. Marchman shook his head as he considered East's question. It sounded like a ridiculous effort. "I don't fancy making myself a clear target for what would surely be physical retribution on the part of the lady."

Reviewing the possibilities raised East's smile. "Polite slap, do you think? Or a blow?"

The Earl of Northam saw immediately what direction this conversation was taking. As the only one of their group who was married, albeit recently, he believed he had an advantage in determining the outcome of a confrontation of this sort. "Three shillings that it's openhanded."

"Openhanded," Marchman agreed.

East shrugged. "I was going to say the same. No wager there unless South takes an opposing view. What say you, Southerton? Will she use an open hand or a fist?"

Southerton's cool gray eyes regarded each of his friends in turn. "I'd say it depends a great deal on which one of us invites her to do it."

North held up his hands palms out, eliminating himself from consideration. "I fear I cannot be the one. Elizabeth would hear of it before the night was over, and I am not up to explanations involving actresses. It is not the kind of thing that is generally well accepted."

Marchman snorted. "You have only to say that you were with us. She knows that any manner of things can happen."

"My wife is with my mother," North said dryly. He raked back a thatch of hair the color of sunshine. "I can appease one but not both. It is the very devil of a fix when they join forces. Like Wellington and Blücher at Waterloo."

The others nodded sympathetically. It was uncharacteristic of any of them to find empathy for the defeated Napoleon, but Northam's description was not off the mark.

Eastlyn moved to extricate himself as well. "I'm afraid I must also refrain," he said. "I'm in a damnable coil as it is. No sense in tightening the spring."

Marchman grinned wickedly and a dimple appeared at

the corner of his mouth. "You're referring, I take it, to your engagement."

"I am referring to my *non*engagement, West."

The marquess's statement had no impact on Marchman's grin. It remained unwaveringly stamped on his fine features. "*Non*sense." He easily caught the playbill East tossed at his head and used it to lazily fan himself. "The announcement in the *Gazette* was pointed out to me by. . . well, by someone among my acquaintances who attends to such things. The wags have the story. There is betting at White's. There must be an engagement. Your mistress says it is so."

"My mistress—my *former* mistress—started that particular rumor." East actually felt his jaw tightening and the beginnings of a headache behind his left eye. "The only thing Mrs. Sawyer could have done to make it worse was to have named herself my fiancée."

"Then you will not mind being leg-shackled to Lady Sophia."

"There is to be no leg-shackling to anyone," East said in mildly impatient tones. "You only have to look at North to see all the reasons why I choose to avoid wedlock."

North's scowl had no real menace. He couldn't pretend that he hadn't been distracted this evening. His marriage was too new, the circumstances of it too unusual, and the nature of the alliance too uneasy to give him much comfort or confidence when he was away from his countess. Instead of being at his country estate in Hampton Cross, where he would have had a chance to court his bride, at her request they were in London, where he discovered that the fiercest competition for her attention often came from his own mother and his best friends.

"Marriage hasn't precisely put a period to my freedom," he said, feeling compelled to make that point. "If you will but recall, I was the one who suggested we go out tonight."

Marchman shook his head. "No. It was South's idea when we found you alone at home. At sixes and sevens, you were."

"Well, I had been thinking about going out," North said

somewhat defensively. He allowed his friends to enjoy a moment's laughter at his expense before he joined them. "I *am* pathetic." He started to rise. "Perhaps I should be the one to beard the lioness in her den."

South laid a hand over Northam's forearm and exerted a bit of pressure to reverse the direction of North's movement. "Sit down. If you care nothing for remaining in your wife's good graces—or your mother's—there are those of us who do. East is right. He shouldn't go. Not with a mistress and a fiancée to consider. His plate is already full. We can't send West. Have you noticed no one ever hits him anymore?"

Marchman's grin deepened and he tipped his chair back on its hind legs, balancing it carefully while he considered South's observation. "It's true, isn't it? I'll have to think on that."

Southerton used the toe of his boot to nudge West's chair back into place. "Don't exert yourself overmuch. The explanation does not strain credulity. For the Corinthian crowd it has something to do with your reputation and that blade you always carry in your boot. For the Cyprians, I believe, it has something to do with how well you wield your sword."

Marchman gave a low shout of laughter. "You flatter me."

"I do," South said dryly and without missing a beat. He stood. "Allow me a few minutes to reach her through the pandering gaggle at her door." He rubbed his jaw as if anticipating the blow. "You may as well give me your money now. No one ever pulls their punches with me."

Though she pretended not to, she saw him as soon as he reached the periphery of men crowded in and around her dressing room. She realized he could not be sure that she would know him again. Her glimpse of him in the theatre had been hindered by the candlelight in her eyes and his distance from the stage. During their brief exchange she had only an impression of dark hair, light eyes, and a mouth tipped at the corners in secret amusement. None of it may have been accurate. She could not know with any degree of certainty that it was him until she heard his voice.

But somehow she did know. There was no mistaking this small flutter beating against her rib cage. It was not her heart. That was steady, as was her breathing. She had no name for this part of her body that shifted or tensed or, in this case, fluttered when she had a certain sense of things. Just as she had no name for it, she also had no understanding of its exact workings. She only knew that it did and that she had come to trust it.

Inside her, feeling had become fact.

This man standing quietly at the back, patiently waiting his turn for admission, was someone she wanted to know. And then know better.

The flutter became a steady thrum.

India Parr smiled politely in response to what was being said to her now. It could have been praise or condemnation and she would have accepted it with the same public face. "You are very kind to say so," she whispered demurely. Then she turned her attention to another and went through the same motions, giving no hint that she wavered between exhaustion and excitement, expressing nothing so much as unflagging grace in the face of the onslaught of admirers.

While the crowd did not precisely part for the Viscount Southerton in the same way the Red Sea parted for Moses, there was some stirring and jockeying and ground was surrendered. The natural curiosity of those acquainted with him, whether familiarly or by reputation, assisted his advancement. His apology had already been made to Miss Parr and accepted by her. It seemed to many that it was unwise to raise the thing again.

South could not decide her age. Onstage she had seemed older and playing at someone who was young. Standing a few feet from him, trying to peel away the layers of powder and paint that placed her character in another century, she seemed much younger and playing at someone with considerably more years. He watched her eyes for any hint they could give him. They were dark, so deeply brown that the pupil and iris almost blended seamlessly to a shade that was very nearly black.

A shutter suddenly closed firmly across her eyes, making South blink. Had she been so aware of his scrutiny? Threatened by it? He had not meant to be obvious, and he was not sure that he had been. He glanced around for another cause or to see if anyone else had noticed this faint distancing. India Parr was farther from all of them now than she had been when she was behind the footlights. She was protected better by this invisible shield she had thrown up than she was by the transparent fourth wall of the stage. Rather than being put off, South was intrigued.

One could be forgiven for supposing that was her game.

There was a slight commotion at the back of the room as India's dresser pushed her way in. With the brisk determination of one who wants to see her duty done, she began moving the admirers aside. Her spine was stiff if slightly curved, and her shoulders sloped forward, hunched as though against her will, as if she had not yet surrendered to the realities of her age. She carried an armload of material with her, but from beneath that mound the sound of her clapping hands could be heard as she started to shoo the crowd. "Out wi' ye now," she said firmly. "Miss Parr's a rare one, it's true, but she cannot lally here. Go on wi' ye."

Tipping her head back in the direction of the door, she exhorted the squeeze of men all around her to use it. Her lips pursed tightly so that vertical creases deepened around her mouth. A large brown mole sporting three frighteningly aggressive hairs actually twitched on the corner of her right cheek. Her nostrils flared, and even the stalwarts among Miss Parr's legion of devotees shrank back in anticipation of flames roaring from those dark openings.

There was a rolling wave of bobbing heads at the door, then the hall, and very slowly the room began to thin. South stayed his ground, though he would not have been surprised if his rumpled coattails were now singed. From somewhere behind him he heard the familiar voices of his friends trading easy barbs as they worked their way against the exiting tide.

He stepped into the breach when the dresser began another harangue and his closest competitor for Miss Parr's attention was carelessly diverted.

He inclined his head toward the actress much as he had from the marquess's box. "Viscount Southerton," he said by way of introduction.

"My lord."

Her eyes were most definitely brown, he decided. Like windows at night, they had become dark mirrors, reflecting his own image back to him and hiding what was just beyond the glass.

"Your servant, Miss Parr."

She smiled slightly, and the coolness of it touched her eyes briefly. "My heckler, you mean."

He did not apologize again for it. "Aaah, so I am unmasked. It is not to be as I hoped, that I was safe from your scrutiny in the low lights."

"Safe enough," she said. "But your voice gives you away. It is unquestionably distinctive."

"Really?"

"To my ears."

South considered those ears in turn. They were small, delicate pink shells, perfectly symmetrical in their placement on either side of her head. A veritable chandelier of paste diamonds hung from each lobe and glittered brightly as she fractionally lifted her chin. "Truly wondrous, your ears."

Her lush mouth still creased with its slim smile, she casually unscrewed each earring and pressed them into her fist. "So they have been remarked upon." She regarded him patiently as he simply stared at her, and when he didn't speak, she prompted, "If there is nothing else, my lord . . ."

"What? Oh, yes. The reason I have come. Pray, do not look, but just beyond my shoulder hovering in the hall are three wholly disreputable . . ." He sighed, his voice dropping huskily as her glance shifted in the exact direction he had asked her not to look. "Don't *look*," he said, drawing her attention back to him. "They are hardly worthy of your notice."

"I believe they are your friends, my lord. I recognize their laughter."

Indeed, they were chuckling again and working out the details of another wager. This time it was the dresser whose antics had their mirth and money engaged. The old woman was none too gently using physical persuasion to remove the hangers-on from her employer's dressing room. Safe as East, West, and North were in the hallway, they were no doubt waiting for the dresser to turn her attention in his direction.

"Pretend I have given you a grave insult," South said quickly. "And chuck me on the chin."

"I beg your pardon?"

"Go on. It's all right. I'd rather not insult you, and I am not concerned a blow dealt by your hand will hurt overmuch."

India Parr said nothing for a moment. "You are a bedlamite, aren't you?" It was the only plausible explanation for his behavior. She was more curious than alarmed. One cry from her lips, and any number of the men Mrs. Garrety had herded out would simply stampede back in. She was likely to be hurt in the crush before she was harmed in any way by the oddly engaging viscount. "Is there nowhere you can go this evening? Perhaps Mrs. Garrety can arrange for a room here for one night."

He shook his head. "Just here," he said, tapping the side of his chin lightly. "There's nine shillings in it for me. I am quite willing to share my winnings."

This did nothing to clarify the situation for Miss Parr. Her dresser's voice had risen shrilly as another man was shooed from the room. "Oh, please, Mrs. Garrety," she said after a long exhale. "Put a shiv between their ribs if you must, but remove the last of them quietly. I cannot bear more caterwauling."

South's brows lifted in tandem. In the hallway the rest of the Compass Club fell silent. The last two admirers slipped out. And Mrs. Garrety's jaw clamped shut.

India Parr raised her glance to South. Her lips moved around words he could barely make out as she murmured to herself, reviewing their conversation as if she were reaching for her lines. "Now, where were we. . . ? Servant . . . heckler . . . voice . . . ears . . . grave insult . . ." She caught herself, and her expression became considering. "Yes, grave insult. Very well, though you may wish you had delivered one, you know."

Rearing back, she plowed South's jaw with her weighted fist.

The blow actually moved him off his feet. He shifted right, caught himself, and cupped the left side of his face in his palm. He felt a warm trickle of blood against his hand. His slow smile was a trifle disjointed as he worked the kinks out of his jaw. "I forgot about the earrings," he said.

India's expression was without remorse. "I thought you might have." She glanced over his shoulder toward the hall. His friends were gaping at her. Over the top of the armload of clothes she still held tight to her bosom, Mrs. Garrety was also openmouthed. "Will that be all, my lord? Or do you seek another boon?"

South's humor asserted itself. "One boon is all these bones can stand." He pulled out a handkerchief and touched it to the corner of his mouth. Even when she saw the evidence of his blood, she remained unapologetic. "You know," he said, "about our laughter during your performance. I feel compelled to point out that the play *was* a comedy."

"It wasn't *that* amusing."

He allowed her own words to sink in, let her critique serve in place of one that he might have offered, then said rather drolly, "You cannot expect that I will always save you, Miss Parr."

On his way out he dropped five shillings—the better part of his winnings—on top of the dresser's stack of clothes.

Only South did not retire to his town home straightaway. His friends did not pry when he merely said he was about the colonel's business. They had all been about the colonel's business at one time or another. Sometimes they were all engaged at once, though rarely toward the same end. It was better that way. Soldier. Sailor. Tinker. Spy. It was bound to become complicated if they were tripping over one another. East was apt to shoot someone, and Marchman always had the knife. North's affairs were apt to be tangled, and for proof of that one had to look no further than his recent marriage of convenience to Lady Elizabeth Penrose.

Deuced inconvenient, South thought, though he liked the lady well enough and had a hand in bringing the thing about. It was another of the colonel's schemes in which South had had to assume a variety of roles but was not privy to the whole of it. So he had played all his parts with industry and inspiration, though nothing like what the colonel usually required of him. No, during this summer recently past he had been Cupid, companion, and, on more than one occasion, fool. Whatever served the meeting of those two he had done, and if it did not end well and happily for North and Lady Elizabeth, he would force the colonel to explain himself. South was certain he deserved that much from the man.

Although it was late when South arrived, he was shown directly to the colonel's sitting room above stairs. The colonel had been carried there some hours earlier by two servants and cared for by his valet. Now he sat in a wheeled chair beside the hearth. A lamp burned on a table beside him and cast his thin face into harsh relief. A plaid rug covered his legs. His lap held an open book and he was running a single finger down one page as South entered. Neither man spoke until the colonel had finished reading and marked his place.

"You'll want a drink, I expect," John Blackwood said, setting the book aside. He looked South over in much the same way he read: quickly, thoroughly, with an eye to what was on the surface and what was between the lines. "In the sideboard as always. Scotch for me. There is a story that explains the swollen cheek and lip, I collect."

Matthew Forrester felt the stirrings of an old memory, one that did not often come to him. This evening's play had something to do with it, he was sure. There had been the odd moment when he had been reminded of Hambrick Hall days. Something the characters did or said pulled him back to that time; the farce of the courtroom scene was an obvious reminder. He hadn't been alone in those memories, because it was at the root of all the outrageous laughter and ill manners on display this evening in Eastlyn's box. None of them had been as foxed as they wanted to be, so there was no blaming it on drink and a thick head.

But if he had been thinking about the Society of Bishops and their silly tribunal earlier, he thought now about the first time he had seen John Blackwood. There had been that glimpse in his father's study of the pose struck just so, the one that he had adopted to such good effect for the Bishops. Insolent. Mildly challenging. Daring.

It was a posture Colonel Blackwood could no longer affect. His wasting illness had weakened the muscles of his legs, made his balance uncertain, and slowed his reflexes. This evening his hands were steady. That was not always the case. He was still a handsome man with his shock of black hair. True, it was thinning slightly at the crown and seeded with gray, but it was not what one noticed about the colonel at first glance. It was the eyes that captured attention at the outset and made one stand one's ground, not out of any sense of bravery, but because it seemed quite impossible to move until permission was granted.

From behind a pair of gold-rimmed spectacles those dark-brown eyes watched South now. Insolent. Mildly challenging. Daring South to express even a hint of pity for him. Time and illness could not change that. It made the viscount smile to realize how wrong he had been.

"Scotch, eh?" South said. "What does your doctor say?"

"He doesn't advise me in regard to my libations, and I don't call him a charlatan. We find that to be a satisfactory arrangement."

South chuckled, then winced. He touched his fingers to his lip, wondering if the small cut would scar. He opened the sideboard, withdrew a decanter of Scotch, and poured two tumblers, not stinting for either of them. Returning to where the colonel sat, he handed him one of the tumblers, took a moment to stoke the fire, then eased his long, athletic frame into the wing chair opposite him.

"I went to Drury Lane this evening," he said.

"Alone?"

"No. North needed a diversion. The dowager countess is showing her daughter-in-law off again."

The deep creases around Blackwood's mouth eased a bit. His smile was gentle. "Elizabeth." He said her name fondly. She was a blood relation, the daughter of his dear first cousin, long gone. "She deserves to be shown off, not relegated to the country or playing handmaiden and companion to Lord and Lady Battenburn. Is she well?"

"Better than well." South chose to remain quiet about the Baron and Baroness of Battenburn. Let Northam extricate his wife from their influence. There were some things a husband should be required to manage on his own.

Blackwood nodded and returned to their business. "So you and Northam went."

"Eastlyn also. It's his box. And Marchman, of course."

"No, you couldn't very well leave West behind," the colonel said wryly. "I trust you managed some discretion."

Staring at the contents of his glass, South cleared his throat. "I rather suppose that depends on one's definition."

The colonel's eyes narrowed. "My definition is widely accepted as standard: demonstrating good judgment; prudent. Above all that you were circumspect, not attracting notice."

"Aaah," South said, one dark brow kicking up as he raised his glass. "Well, there you have me. Afraid I attracted some notice."

Blackwood merely stared at him before he finally surrendered a sigh. "You might as well tell me the whole of it now. I find the application of thumbscrews so tedious these days."

Grinning, then wincing anew, South launched into his tale of his evening at the theatre, sparing himself nothing in the telling of it. His recitation was no more flattering to his character than the actual events had been. Since there was no point in taking refuge in his own embarrassment at having allowed things to get so completely out of hand, South simply acknowledged it, apologized, and went on. At the conclusion he was still stretched negligently in the wing chair, but with the tumbler of Scotch pressed lightly against his cheek and the corner of his lip. It was a small concession to his injury at the hands of Miss India Parr.

The colonel was quiet for a long time. "I suppose," he said finally, taking a moment to finish his drink, "that it could have gone worse. Though it's difficult to see how at first blush."

"I might have fallen from East's box and broken my neck."

"That would have been better, South. Not worse." The colonel waved aside any more of his protégé's attempts to be helpful. "You made her acquaintance. That is something at least. She will have no difficulty remembering you. Was there anyone left in the dressing room to witness your introduction save her dresser and the Compass Club?"

"There were loiterers in the hall. If they didn't glimpse it, they heard it. Berwin was among the last to be ejected. I believe he saw me exit, and I don't think he was alone. Grissom was there, I think. I made no attempt to hide my injury."

"Good. Because you can count on your friends not to repeat the incident."

"I know, but I think I can safely rely on Berwin and Grissom to spread the news of my comeuppance. It will soon be public record that I have alienated the affections of Miss Parr, which, indeed, I have."

"That is your own doing. I did not suggest that."

"It was a moment's inspiration."

Colonel Blackwood withheld comment. He would let South work out how to right the matter. The younger man invariably did. "I should like to hear your assessment of Miss Parr. Refrain, please, from pointing out that she delivers a considerable wallop. I see the evidence of that for myself."

"It was the earbobs," he said, pointing to the corner of

his mouth. "I quite forgot she had them in her fist. Though I cannot say the same for her."

The colonel ignored that. "Your assessment."

"She is quite magnificent on stage. Dedicated to her craft, I think, judging by the way she took us to task for our disruption. I believed at first that she stepped in and out of character with uncanny ease, but I wonder at that now. While she was entirely confident behind the footlamps, I suspect she is much less so in other circumstances. In her own dressing room, for instance, surrounded by admirers, I found her to be less certain of her ground." South raised himself a few inches by pushing up on the arms of the chair with his elbows. "An impression, nothing more, I assure you. It flies in the face of the confident blow she delivered to mine, but I find I cannot entirely dismiss the notion that, left to her own devices, she is eminently vulnerable."

Blackwood frowned. It was not precisely what he wanted to hear, though he was uncertain of what Southerton could have said that would have satisfied him. "Could she be our murderer?"

South shrugged. "I couldn't say. Is she capable? I can think of no way to answer that except by asking, who among us is not?"

"How would you assess the risk to yourself if I ask you to continue?"

"I certainly would go on more cautiously than I began." He frowned slightly. "Are you thinking of asking me to stop now? I assure you, nothing of note has been accomplished."

"I need to consider this further."

South's frown deepened. It was unlike the colonel not to have made a well-considered decision at the outset. The fact that he was reexamining caused South to wonder what he had said that was giving his mentor pause. "Is it that I referred to her vulnerability?" he asked frankly. "What does that signify?"

Rather than answer the question, Blackwood said, "Let it rest. I find I am in need of the same. I will send for you in a few days' time. I think an evening at the theatre is in order for me. Pray do not show your face there until you have heard from me. And mind your friends stay away. Northam has much to do that has nothing in common with this bit of business, and Eastlyn and West have their own affairs to consider.''

Southerton gave voice to none of the questions that occurred to him. The affairs of East and West were certainly the colonel's doing. Of North's current assignment he knew only a modest amount. That worthy had been tapped to find one rogue among the *ton* known familiarly to all as the Gentleman Thief. Northam's recent marriage had complicated the investigation, but South had no real concern that his friend would not be successful. The colonel demanded it. The members of the Compass Club therefore never delivered anything less.

South stood slowly, stretched. He tossed back the last of his drink and relieved Blackwood of the tumbler in his outstretched hand. He placed both glasses on the sideboard. ''In a few days, then,'' he said, carefully neutral.

''Yes.'' The colonel waited until South had reached the door before he spoke again. ''It was done well, Southerton.''

''Thank you, sir.'' South considered later that the colonel had only been so effusive with his praise to prompt a reaction. He hadn't disappointed, either. He had practically gaped, which in turn caused him to wince and clap his hand to the side of his face. The colonel had most definitely chuckled. The man had a decidedly twisted sense of humor.

India Parr examined her face in the mirror for remaining traces of the paint and powder. The application had been done with a particularly heavy hand for this evening's performance, and removing it had proved to be difficult. She was not inclined to spend more time on the matter. She wanted to remove herself from the theatre, away to her home, and crawl between the cool sheets of her bed. Perhaps lick her wounds.

True, there were no visible scars from tonight's altercation, but her loss of control left her feeling wounded and out of sorts. Behind her she heard Mrs. Garrety gently clucking her tongue as the dresser arranged clothes in the armoire.

"Leave it," India said. "Leave all of it."

"It's no good being cross with me, dearie. I'm not the one you're angry at."

India eyes refocused on her own reflection. She conceded the truth of what had just been said. "No, you're not."

"I've never seen the like before," the older woman continued as she straightened and fussed over the clothes and costumes. "You were . . . were . . ."

India sighed as words failed Mrs. Garrety. "I've never been so provoked. It's the sort of thing I could expect in the beginning. In the less reputable theatres. And always from the students crowding the back who thought it a good joke to pull the actors from the play and make them part of their own little dramas. It was surprisingly easy to resist then. They were obvious in their intent." She swiveled on her stool, turning away from the mirror. "I think I won their respect because I never gave in."

"I know ye did, dearie. I was there. Remember?"

A slight crease appeared between India's brows. She raised a hand and rubbed at it absently. "Yes, you were, weren't you?"

"Hmmm." Mrs. Garrety closed the armoire. "Done here. Now, let's have a look at you." She studied her employer's pale face. "What's toward? Is it a megrim? Shall I prepare something?"

"No," India said quickly, letting her hand fall away. Then more softly, with less force behind the words, she said, "No, thank you. It's nothing save reaction to the end of a very tedious day."

The dresser studied India a moment longer. "As you wish. Let me finish removing the paint from your face."

India acquiesced without any show of the reluctance she felt. What she truly wanted was the thing she couldn't have: solitude. She gave herself up to her dresser's ministrations, lifting her face and turning her head from side to side as docilely as a lamb. One of Mrs. Garrety's strong, warm hands closed over the slim stem of her throat but held it as gently as if it were a delicate crystal vase. The other made short work of the remnants of the stage powder and paint.

"There," she said upon completion. " 'Ave a look, dearie. It's your lovely face you'll be seeing. Not the French trollop's."

India turned and spared a glance for her mirror. "Do you think the critics will take notice of what happened tonight?"

Mrs. Garrety waved that concern aside. "I think you gave as good as you got. They were gentlemen behaving as louts. Well into their cups, I'd wager. For all their foolery, ye never lost your true audience." With an efficiency honed by experience, she began helping India out of her costume. The ribbons and stays did not tangle tonight. The separate pieces of the gown, bodice and skirt, then the undergarments, all fell away without a tug-of-war. The dresser whisked them to one side, draping them over a chair to be pressed later while India removed the whalebone panniers that had given her gown its classic silhouette. " 'Tis a pity, perhaps, that more didn't see you take his lordship to task right here."

India glanced at her dresser in some surprise and saw Mrs. Garrety was watching her, something shrewd in her regard. "You were particularly single-minded in your efforts to remove everyone tonight."

"Yes, well, I saw him and his friends coming this way," she said crisply. "I couldn't predict what a scene it might be. I should 'ave known you'd hold your own. Didn't expect ye'd land him a facer, though. That was a picture, I tell ye. I'm thinking now that more should have enjoyed it."

India said nothing, choosing not to reveal that Viscount Southerton had asked for the facer. She was not certain what to make of it. Perhaps it *was* part and parcel of some ridiculous wager made with his friends. Then again . . . In any event, she did not care to entertain Mrs. Garrety's opinion on the matter. "I'll finish myself," she said. "Will you ask Doobin to flag a cab?"

"Of course." Mrs. Garrety still took several minutes to

gather India's costume for the wardrobe mistress before she left the room. By the time she returned, India was reaching for her pelisse. "Ye'll be wanting company for the ride home."

"No," said India. "I am certain I'll be fine. There's really no need for you to trouble yourself."

" 'Tis no trouble at all."

India forced a smile. "Truly, Mrs. Garrety, I will be fine. As you said, I can hold my own."

Mrs. Garrety clucked her tongue gently. "Didn't mean to put that maggot in yer head. Ye need a protector. It's not the first time I've thought so. Ye have too many admirers, and I don't have enough 'ands to push them all out. And ye don't have enough 'ands to slap their faces. A protector's the answer. Just see if it isn't."

India watched the dresser go. In the quiet aloneness that followed, India felt the first wavelet of fear uncurl inside her. It was quickly followed by another. Then another. Fighting the tide was ineffective. It only left her exhausted. She drew a shaky breath instead and closed the velvet frog at the throat of the pelisse. More important to India than the question of a protector was the question of protection. The viscount's parting words returned to her now.

You cannot expect that I will always save you, Miss Parr.

If not Lord Southerton, India wondered, then who? The next wave crashed against her rib cage. Heart racing, she hurried toward the theatre's rear exit and the sanctuary and anonymity of the black hansom cab.

Lords Berwin and Grissom proved themselves reliable in repeating what they had witnessed—or almost witnessed—in Miss India Parr's dressing room. The first tidbit was dropped with even offhandedness that very night. The bored accents played well to the crowd gathered around the card table at Simon's. The story spread quickly in the gaming hell, and when members were moved the following the morning to face sunshine and hangover remedies, the tale became a delicious *on dit* to placate the stone-faced valets and disapproving mamas.

Southerton learned the scope of his success from his sister the following afternoon. Emma, he discovered, was also paying a call on their parents, and in South's estimation she was rather too cheerful in her greeting to be lightly dismissed. The mirth in her eyes spelled his certain doom. He kissed her cheek when she raised it to him.

"Emma." In her ear he whispered, "No one likes a tattle."

She beamed at him. "Oh, yes, they do." Without moving her head, she indicated the Earl and Countess of Redding with a playful slant of her eyes. She chuckled when South did not risk a glance and took his nephew from her arms instead. "He'll ruin your coat," she warned him. "He's been fussing all day."

South immediately held the baby at arm's length and considered him gravely. "Slobber, d'you mean?" Out of the corner of his eye he thought he saw a smile edge his father's mouth. His mother, though, was made of sterner stuff. Her back was up. "Plump and pretty," he said as his nephew stared back at him. "Ears are still in the right place. Not at all like that doll you had, Emma. Remember? The one that—"

She took her child back. "There will be no talk of what happened to Cassandra, South. It's not for Niles to know." She pursed her lips and added significantly, "Or anyone else, for that matter."

South smiled coolly, one brow lifting the merest fraction. "Remember that when your tongue starts wagging again."

"Beast."

"Scylla."

"Ogre."

He touched a lock of his sister's hair that had fallen past her temple, and pushed it gently back. "You are looking well," he said sincerely. "Motherhood agrees with you, I think."

"Indeed it does."

South turned to his parents. "Mother." He kissed his mother's proffered cheek and found it warm in spite of the cool mien she affected. South looked to the earl to see if there would be assistance from that quarter and saw immediately he had covert sympathy. Outright support in the face of his mother's displeasure would have been folly. It was not the sort of breach a man as circumspect as the earl committed often. "Father. You look well."

It was just the opening the Countess of Redding had been waiting for. She pounced. "Of course he is well. And why wouldn't he be? He has me to assure that he remains so. You could claim the same if you did not choose to live on your own, travel about with friends of a certain reputation, frequent places that no woman wants to acknowledge exist, least of all a mother, and behave in a most ramshackle manner, making a complete cake of yourself in the theatre, and later with an . . ." Here, her voice dropped to a pitched whisper. Southerton supposed it was all in aid of preventing his four-month-old nephew from comprehending this last, most salient point. ". . . with an *opera dancer.*"

South glanced at Niles. The infant was most definitely attentive. Emma, he noted, did not have the grace to look sheepish. Her features were almost as rapt as her son's. South rounded a nearby chair and served himself tea from the silver service. "Miss India Parr is an actress, Mother. Not an opera dancer."

"She is a . . ." The pitched whisper came again. "A *Cyprian.*"

The earl intervened, laying a hand over his wife's. "That is quite enough. You will make yourself overwrought."

"I *am* overwrought. Your son sees to it, my lord. He has neither your sense nor your compassion to have it be otherwise."

Sighing under his breath, South lowered himself into a chair, politely sipped his tea, and let his mother slowly cease to spin. He loved her dearly, but ofttimes she reminded him of a tightly wound, brightly colored child's top. He had loved that toy, too.

The countess did not linger overlong on the problem of the opera dancer. She went to the heart of the matter, a concern for which she could depend upon the full support of her husband. "It is time you marry, South. There can be no getting around it. I was speaking to Celia only yesterday about this very thing."

South noted his mother conveniently did not mention two things of import. One, that she spoke to Celia every day about this very thing, and two, that Celia was Celia Worth Hampton, the Dowager Countess of Northam. Only a few short breaths earlier, his mother had spoken of North as one of his friends "of a certain reputation." Now that same friend was no doubt about to be lauded for having had the good judgment to enter into a matrimonial state. There would also be no reference to that event as a most ramshackle affair.

South remembered with some fondness that his spinning top had had the same dizzying affect on him.

Lillian Rheems Forrester continued in this vein for several minutes, making the most of her son's good-natured forbearance. When she finally finished, she regarded her firstborn with satisfaction, certain she had mined every nugget and could not have but persuaded him with the logic of her arguments and the soundness of her advice.

Over the rim of his teacup, his eyes hooded to hide their glazed expression, Southerton nodded serenely. "I shall apply myself immediately to the matter of securing a wife."

The countess threw up her hands. "Speak to him, my lord," she said to her husband. "I find myself out of all patience. He only means to humor me."

Redding bit the inside of his lip. "Right you are, m'dear. South, you will cease to humor your mother."

"Yes, sir."

The earl looked askance at his wife. "See, it is done."

Lillian's dark-gray eyes darted between the two male loves of her life, and she surrendered. "Oh, very well. You shall each defend the other. It is always thus even when you pretend it is otherwise." Her gaze alighted briefly on her grandson, and she saw Emma's embrace tighten protectively, albeit with great care. Hah! *There* was the future of the Forresters.

South almost laughed out loud when he saw his mother's attention shift to the next generation. He might have felt sorry for Niles if he hadn't been so certain of Emma's ability to protect her son. As for Emma, it was her loose tongue that had dealt him this harangue in the first place. He had no misplaced sympathy for her.

"Since no one has any interest in my version of the events of last evening," South said, "I should like to hear how it came to your ears—and in so short a time. I am only recently risen from my bed."

Emma volunteered that she heard it first from her own husband at breakfast. He had had it from Lord Hastings during his early morning ride in the park. She could not account for the provenance of the tale, but she heard a similar story from Lady Rowena Douglass, who had come calling that morning. The earl and countess remained silent about their source, as if there was some doubt in South's mind.

"The critics say she is quite a remarkable presence on stage," Emma said. "Is that your opinion as well, South?"

"Yes, that's a fair estimation."

Emma sighed. "I do so want to see her. I did before, you know, and Welsley had agreed to take me. Now, with you at the center of this bit of business, he says it will have to wait. Just when *everyone* else will be clamoring to see her. It is too bad of you, South. But there you have it; Welsley says we cannot go, because it would cause a stir and hardly be fair to Miss Parr. He says we shall have to wait until the gossip is well behind us."

South said nothing. He reflected that if the colonel did not remove him from this assignment, the real gossip was only about to begin.

Chapter Two

Five nights later, Southerton found himself once again at the Drury Lane Theatre. The same place where the great Edmund Kean had made his debut as Shylock four years earlier was enjoying renewed interest and patronage because of one India Parr. Kean himself, never effusive in his praise of a rival, had embraced her talents rather than stand in opposition to the public clamor for more performances from their new favorite. Unlike the revered Sarah Siddons, who first trod the boards in Drury Lane more than a quarter of a century before, India Parr was not foremost a tragic actress. It was widely agreed that while her tragic heroines were most excellently realized, Miss Parr had a particular gift for the nuance of character in the comedies, and the sharp timing and physical humor of farces.

Southerton was but a face in the crowd on this occasion, purposely avoiding East's box tonight. He sat six rows back from the stage, his broad shoulders uncomfortably squeezed between a heavily perfumed matron on his left and a dandy in daffodil on his right. It was a tribute to India Parr's talents that South was able to entirely ignore the discomfort to his hunched shoulders, the musky fragrance, and so much blinding yellow until the performance was ended.

He remembered with some regret his backhanded critique of the play as not being as amusing as the company he had been keeping. South now realized he had a second apology to make to Miss Parr. It *was* amusing. This evening's crowd had done much more than politely titter at the risqué moments and ribald humor. They had laughed deeply and loudly and long, unembarrassed by the French playwright's frankly sexual themes and his assault on the secret mores of a society that was at once free to act and hopelessly repressed from doing so.

Southerton joined the patrons who had come to their feet, adding his standing approbation to the enthusiastic applause. He watched the company step forward, bow in unison, and gesture once again to their leading lady. It was hard to believe the hand-clapping could sustain itself, let alone grow louder, yet both these things occurred as India Parr came front and center and made her deep curtsy. Candlelight glowed warmly on the nape of her neck as she modestly inclined her head toward her audience and accepted their admiration.

She had won them over, and no further gesture was required, yet she did a surprising thing then that effectively secured her place in their hearts. Standing once more, Miss India Parr stepped as close to the footlamps as she dared and applauded her audience.

The house fairly erupted.

When the acting troupe disappeared into the wings, and the echoes of approval gave way to the crowd's exiting hum, Southerton moved into the aisle and no farther. He allowed anyone who desired it to precede him toward the exits. Finally, when there was no one around, he chose a seat on the end and sat, thrusting his long legs into the aisle and folding his arms across his chest. He lounged comfortably for the better part of half the hour before rising and heading in the direction of Miss Parr's dressing room.

The crowd had not thinned appreciably. South considered

the damage to the line of his wool frock coat and claw-hammer tails if he were to become part of the crush. He leaned a shoulder against the wall and smoothed one crisp corner of his white stock as he applied himself to the problem. Miss Parr's dresser, so helpful the other evening, seemed to be occupied elsewhere tonight. Perhaps she was staying away at the express orders of Miss Parr herself, or perhaps, as South suspected, she was availing herself of the medicinal properties of a dram or two of gin. He remembered the faint fragrance of alcohol wafting from the woman as she went about her business that evening. Whatever the cause of her absence, it was just as well that it was so. Southerton had no real hope that the dresser would serve to aid his cause. For that he would require an accomplice possessing a more youthful countenance.

South bided his time and was rewarded when a lad of some twelve years came hurrying down the corridor, carrying a pair of boots in each hand and another pair cradled close to his chest, secured by his crossed arms. South stopped him, laying a hand firmly on the boy's shoulder.

The young prisoner chafed at his restriction. "Oh, no, m'lord. I dare not tarry. I 'ave these boots to polish." He tried to show them off, puffing out his thin chest so all three pairs would be highly visible and the importance of his work would not go unnoticed. "You'll find someone else, won't you, sir? There's plenty here what will do your bidding."

South did not shift from his relaxed posture against the wall, nor did he loosen his grip on the boy's shoulder. He did permit himself a small smile. "How do you know what my bidding is, lad?"

"Doobin," the lad said. "I'm called Doobin, though it ain't my proper name."

"That would be Donald? Douglas?"

"No, m'lord. No one knows my proper name, so I just be called Doobin."

"I see. Enlightening."

"It's good of you to say so, sir." Doobin took a single

step forward and found himself immediately off balance because of the fingers that still clamped his bony shoulder.

South permitted Doobin to get his feet under him again. "You haven't answered my question. How do you know what my bidding is?"

Doobin shrugged. "I don't know. Not for certain. But it's likely the same as the others that waylay me here."

"Oh?"

Heaving a sigh, Doobin went on. "You want me to deliver your card to Miss Parr with a message that you would be pleased for her company at a late supper at Sarver's."

It was somewhat humbling to have the whole of his plan pointed out by the bootblacking boy. South had not considered the number of men who had already attempted this approach, thus paving the way for his failure. "I was thinking of the Cumberland."

"It doesn't matter."

"Does Miss Parr prefer Sarver's?"

"Miss Parr prefers to be left alone."

"Why don't we let her decide? There's a shilling in it for you." He could see the boy was tempted, but South was late in realizing he had baited his hook too lightly. Doobin was savvy enough to know that a single shilling was little in the way of remuneration when weighed against the continued security of his employment. South tried another tack. "You like Miss Parr?"

"I do indeed, m'lord. A fine lady, she is. And very good to me."

"What if I told you she will be disappointed if you do not deliver my message?"

Doobin shrewdly studied South's face for evidence of his sincerity or the lack of it. "I can't risk it," he said finally, reluctantly.

South decided he had one last opportunity to plead his case. "If I'm wrong, I'll take you into my own employment at double your earnings." The boy's eyes practically bulged at the notion of this fortune being laid before him. It was left for Doobin to determine whether Southerton could be trusted to keep his word. "Perhaps if you heard the whole of my message," he said. He removed a card from the gold case he carried and showed it to the boy. "Here is my name." He turned it over. "And here is my message. Can you read?"

"A little, m'lord. Miss Parr, she's teaching me my letters."

"It says, 'You cannot expect I will always save you, Hortense.' "

The boots bobbled in Doobin's arms and he almost lost his grip. He gaped up at Southerton. "That's you?"

South's dark brows creased, uncertain what the boy meant. "That's my message."

"But you're the one. From the other night. The one in the box who spoke the line."

There was really no point in denying it. "Yes, I'm afraid so."

"You should have said so straightaway, m'lord. No good circling the thing, hoping I'd stumble over it." He thrust his sharp chin toward the boots pressed against this chest. "Tuck it just there, m'lord. Under the turned-down top. I'll make certain she sees it."

South did as ordered. "Then you are in expectation that she will welcome my address?"

Doobin chuckled. His soulfully large eyes brightened with laughter. "That's a good one, m'lord." He waited for South's grip to lift. "Is there anything else?"

"Dinner," South said. "The pleasure of her company, and so forth."

"Sarver's or the Cumberland?"

"A detail for you to manage. Surprise me."

The boy's smile split his thin face. "Just see if I don't." As soon as he was free of South's restraint, he was off at a determined pace.

South expected Doobin would partially relieve himself of the burden of boots. He didn't. With the skill of the most adept sneaksman, the lad slipped between elbows and waistcoats, pockets and polished beaver top hats, and disappeared into the squeeze. From South's perspective there was no discernible movement in the crowd that allowed for the addition of another figure, no matter the slightness of the build. It suggested to the viscount that perhaps the boy's early training had been in the Covent Garden or Holborn school for thieves, and that likening him to a sneaksman was not so very off the mark.

In less time than it would have taken South to move from his position in the corridor to the bottleneck at the door, Doobin emerged from the rear of the crowd in almost the same place he had entered. He hurried over, his face revealing nothing. The boy, South thought, was learning as much from Miss Parr about acting as he was about reading. Southerton cocked an eyebrow. "Well?"

"I am to arrange for a hackney at the stage door. Miss Parr says you may await her in the cab."

"I have my own carriage."

"That is neither here nor there, my lord."

"I see," South said dryly. "Very well. I'll send my driver along directly. And what of supper?"

"In Miss Parr's home."

Now South's other brow lifted. He *was* surprised. "Very well done, young sir."

The tips of Doobin's ears reddened with this praise. He offered the truth reluctantly. "It wasn't my idea."

South chuckled and dropped several shillings into one of the open boots. "I didn't think it was." He gave Doobin an encouraging prompt on the back with the flat of his hand. "Don't count your money now. See about that hack."

"Yes, m'lord. Right away."

The cab was waiting for India in the usual place when she emerged from the theatre more than an hour later. When the driver leaped from his perch and opened the door for her, it occurred to her for the first time that perhaps Southerton had grown impatient with the wait and left. With the driver's assistance, she climbed the steps and discovered

that her concern was for naught. Southerton was indeed
inside the cab, ensconced in relative comfort in one corner—
if one ignored the odd angle of his neck—and snoring softly.

India found herself surrendering to the humor of the
moment. She glanced at the driver. "Has he been asleep
long?" she whispered.

"Can't say, but I recollect a rumble soon after he climbed
in."

She nodded, amused. "A gentle ride, then, if you will."

"Your home, Miss Parr?"

"Yes." She hesitated, eyeing the driver. It occurred to
her to inquire if she could rely on his discretion, but she
dismissed it. No matter what answer he gave, she knew the
truth: she could not. To believe otherwise was to permit
herself a sense of security that was without foundation.
Anyone could be tempted. She thought of this view as practical and realistic rather than cynical. Temptation was human
nature from the beginning of time, documented first in Genesis and every day since then. "Mind the noise," she
reminded him softly.

He nodded. "I'll see to it."

India seated herself in the bench seat corner opposite
South. The door closed and the hansom rocked slightly as
the driver climbed back aboard. The start was smooth. India
laid her reticule beside her and drew a woolen shawl around
her shoulders. The evening was cool and damp but not
uncomfortable. She tied the fringed ends in a loose knot
below her breasts and leaned her shoulder against the side
of the cab. Her eyes swiveled, not toward the street, which
was still noisy with the activities of vendors and the revelries
of the gamers, but to the viscount, who continued to sleep
through it all deeply.

The cab's exterior lanterns illuminated Lord Southerton's
face as the driver took the first turn. India renewed her first
impression of features that were both finely drawn, as though
with a careful hand, but stamped with strength, as though
by a bold one. The effect was to render his perfectly propor-
tioned face with certain intriguing opposites: a nose that was

aristocratic in its line, aggressive in its thrust; a firm yet
sensually yielding mouth; lashes that were almost silkily
feminine, and dark brows that were most decidedly not.

Sleep, she noted, when the lantern swung its pale arc of
light into the cab again, did not seem to render the viscount
particularly unprotected. India could not dismiss the conflicting appearance of complete relaxation and readiness as
she studied him. He was virtually boneless in the way his
long frame had accommodated itself to the hard angles of
the cab walls and bench seat, yet the spare lines of his body
suggested tone and vigor. She supposed that depending on
the circumstances, this was a man who awoke with a languid
stretch or an unerring pounce. It did not surprise her when
the image of a great striped, stalking tiger flickered at the
periphery of her mind's eye.

A small smile lifted the corners of her mouth as she turned
away. She wondered if he knew that he was not a merely
handsome man but a very nearly beautiful one. It was likely,
she decided. Men who were graced with much less often
thought a great deal more, provoked to find themselves so
by doting mamas and fawning matrons with daughters on
the marriage mart. India considered saying as much to him,
not necessarily as a compliment but as simply something
that must be said to remove it from further consideration.
She amused herself thinking what tone and phrasing she
might adopt to intimate such an outrageous thing. Practical:
*You are a beautiful man, my lord, but that is neither here
nor there.* Bold: *It cannot have escaped your notice, my
lord, that you are a beautiful man; however, it is of no
consequence to me.* Amused: *And how have you passed your
days, my lord, since you last posed for the great Michael-
angelo?*

She would say nothing, of course. She could not imagine
that the words would ever come properly to her mind when
she would be in need of them.

India sank more deeply into her seat, gentled by the steady
rocking of the cab and syncopated beat of the horse's hooves
on the cobbles. She closed her eyes for but a moment.

India missed the viscount's awakening, but he did not miss hers. He was turning from paying the driver when he saw her stir. He paused, waved off the cabbie, then sat back in the seat and awaited India's return to full consciousness. She came to it with an abrupt little jolt as though breaking a fall. South knew he would not like to awake so rudely. There was no peace in the sleep that came before, and usually no peace in the living immediately after.

"Miss Parr," he said, inclining his head. "May I assist you from the carriage?" He permitted himself a small smile when she stared at him blankly, though he was more troubled than amused. There was no recognition in her eyes, no sense of her surroundings. She was thoroughly unprotected in that moment and remained unconscious of it for several more.

"What?" She blinked slowly. "Oh. Oh, why, yes. I slept, didn't I? Odd, that's never happened." This last was said more to herself than to him. Her chin jerked, a small, birdlike movement as she heard the sound of her own speech as though from a distance. She fell silent, trying to orient herself.

Southerton waited no longer. He ducked out of the carriage and turned to offer his hand to her, grasping her wrist when she did not avail herself of his assistance. His pull was light but inexorable, and he drew India to her feet and then outside without a show of force or even effort. The driver flew ahead of them to the small stoop outside India's unexceptional gray stone home and applied himself to the brass knocker. The door swung open, held there by a distracted young maid in a twisted gown and skewed cap, just as South and India reached it. The driver forgot himself long enough to stare openly at the flustered maidservant before the advance of his passengers reminded him of his place. He made a slight bow and disappeared.

South noticed India lift a single brow in her maid's direction, a gesture that managed to be censorious and tolerant at the same time. She would never have any discipline among the ranks while giving those opposing orders. Mildly amused and more than a little intrigued by this lack of discipline,

South escorted India to a sitting room on the main floor. Miss Parr found wits about her enough to tell the maid to bring some light repast for them from the kitchen; then they were alone.

"Please," India said softly, "you will make yourself comfortable."

The way she phrased it, with that slight inflection at the end, South thought the invitation was more in the way of discovering if he *could* be comfortable here. Looking around, he very much decided that he could. He had not thought that he might have preconceived some notion of how the actress lived, and he realized now that this was not the case. He must have given it some fleeting thought since the moment of their first meeting, or perhaps since the colonel raised the specter of such a meeting, because this room, at least, seemed to him wholly unexpected.

It was sparely furnished with a chaise longue, a Queen Anne settee, and a single chair near the fireplace. The hearth itself was not an elaborate green-veined marble affair but plaster. The mantel gleamed whitely against light blue walls and darker wainscoting. There were two small round tables with ball and claw feet situated so they could be reached easily from wherever one was seated. One held the remnants of material that spilled over the side into a basket on the floor; the other held a stack of three books still bound with carrying string from the booksellers. The appointments were centered by the Aubusson rug. The perimeter of the room had a narrow sideboard, a window seat that overlooked the front street, and a table near the door, which held a Delft blue vase abundantly filled with hothouse flowers.

Southerton removed his hat and gloves and placed them on the table beside the vase. Miss Parr stepped toward him as he began to unfasten his coat, belatedly realizing that her flustered maid had taken no measures to secure these items from him. South waved away her concern and laid his coat over the back of the chaise. He walked slowly around the room, studying the occasional figurine, reading the spine of a book lying on its side. He was aware of India watching him but wholly unconcerned by it.

"This is a pleasant room, Miss Parr," he said.

"I am glad you find it so. I have been told it is rather too spacious a room to be so meagerly appointed, but there is nothing I wish to add."

He shrugged. "Then you should not. You enjoy the late-morning light here?"

"Yes. For reading and sketching. Sometimes I sew."

He nodded, his glance going from the books to the basket of colorful fabrics. "And for entertaining?"

"I . . . no. That is, I do not . . ." India sat down abruptly on the settee. Her shawl slipped over one shoulder, and she made no attempt to reposition it over her in spite of the fact that she was chilled. "I have only the rare visitor," she said after a moment. "I suppose it comes of being so often surrounded that I find a great deal of peace in being alone."

"But not lonely?"

"No," she said. "Not here." *Only sometimes,* she could have added but did not. It was more often that she felt as one out of step in the middle of a dressing room filled with admirers than she did in here. Standing onstage, accepting the accolades of an approving audience, was on occasion an experience of profound and disturbing loneliness. That admission was difficult enough to make to herself. It was not the sort of thing one confessed to a stranger.

And he was a stranger, no matter that he seemed oddly familiar to her. That was the stuff of fanciful dreams, she chided herself. In truth, she had taken a risk by inviting him here, though not as great a risk as it may have seemed to the uninitiated. This was more in the fashion of a calculated risk. If she was correct, then the viscount was biding his time as well, taking his direction from her. If she was wrong, then . . . then she would accustom herself to the fact that she must never see him again. It might come to that end anyway.

Southerton went to the fireplace and stoked the coals, making them give up a little more heat and light. "I was uncertain if you would accept my invitation," he said. "That I should then find myself in a position to accept yours was most unexpected."

"You were clever to send Doobin. You would not have reached me otherwise."

"My thinking exactly." Without conscious thought he moved his jaw sideways, the gesture reminiscent of working out the kink she had put there on their first encounter. He turned more fully in her direction and found her gaze had narrowed on his chin. "It no longer hurts," he told her.

"There's a faint bruise."

"Yes. But no scarring." He touched the corner of his mouth, where her earrings had cut him. "Pity, that. My sister says it would have improved my standing in society to have a scar just there."

One of India Parr's brows lifted in a perfect arch. "You did not believe her, I hope."

"Certainly not. She is my sister, after all, and given to the worst sort of encouragement and wild tales if she thinks it will serve in humbling me."

Since he said this with a certain amount of affection in his voice and a gleam in his eye, India accepted that Southerton found his sister's attempts not at all provoking. "Had she told you a scar would have improved your countenance," she said, "you may have depended upon her word. But your standing in society? I think not. It is not as if such a scar was earned at the point of a rapier. There is not much standing to be gained from an encounter with a lady's fist, especially when one expressly asked for the delivery of the very same."

Southerton stared at her. "Improve my countenance?" he said after a moment, as if it were the only part of her speech that mattered. "Do you truly think so?"

He delivered these questions with such perfect self-absorption that India found herself wondering if she had mistaken the man. She held his gaze, searching for some crack that would indicate a facade. There was none. What she saw instead was a look of keen, penetrating intelligence, unwavering in its return regard, so that she could not help but be touched by it. "Indeed," she replied in dry accents. "A scar is just the thing."

Southerton laughed. "I believe you would delight in wounding me."

"I think what I should like is making the acquaintance of your sister."

The viscount's smile faded. There was an imperceptible straightening to his figure, more an absence of the relaxed mode he had been enjoying than an alteration in his posture.

India did not fail to miss the change in her guest. She was embarrassed by the wistfulness that had crept into her own voice when she had imagined an introduction to his sister. No, that would not be possible. Not at all. "Forgive me," she said softly. "I spoke without thinking. I did not mean—"

The scratching at the door interrupted India, and supper was wheeled into the room. The larger table was cleared of fabrics, the basket moved to the side, and dishes set out. A footman appeared with two chairs and placed them at the table. The maid, looking again as if she had her wits about her, worked efficiently and quietly, and both servants took their leave at India's dismissal.

Southerton regarded the late supper with some surprise. There was a hot, clear soup for their first course, the aroma of roast lamb from under one of the covered platters, and, if he wasn't mistaken, the fragrance of fresh, crusty bread slipping out from another.

India encouraged her guest to begin. "I often eat late, though alone. The odd hours of my profession."

South knew that something of his thoughts had been related to her, and he wondered how he had given himself away. A less perceptive woman would have assumed his surprise had been only for the supper, yet India Parr sensed more than the obvious and unerringly targeted the things he had not said. He had found himself doubting the truth of her earlier statement about entertaining infrequently in her own home. Now she underscored it again.

Southerton tasted the consommé and discovered the stock was seasoned to perfection. Miss Parr had found herself a diamond of a cook. "Is it so important that I believe I am the exception to your rule?" he asked, deciding they might as well confront his doubts openly rather than delicately step around them.

India's spoon hovered a few inches above her bowl. "You are direct, my lord."

"When it suits me."

She nodded once, accepting this, and lifted the spoon to her mouth. The broth went down easily, and that struck her as odd, because she had not thought swallowing would come so simply with his clear gray eyes watching her. "I suppose I do not wish to seem a foolish woman to you, nor a promiscuous one. I know what is said about actresses. Indeed, I should have a head full of cotton otherwise. It is generally held that we are little more than Cyprians, hardly discernible from prostitutes for all that we walk behind the footlamps rather than in front of them."

South cocked one dark brow. "You are also direct, Miss Parr."

"When it suits me." Her imitation of his timbre and tone was impeccably done. She liked that he immediately recognized himself and had the capacity to find humor in her well-intentioned mockery. "There are exceptions, of course. I am referring once again to the actress-as-prostitute. Respect is hard won. The great Mrs. Siddons comes to mind."

He waited for her to expand on that theme. When she did not, he nodded in sympathy. "Society is not kind to independent women."

"It depends on the nature of their independence. Widows enjoy a certain freedom."

This was true. Southerton thought of Lady Powell and their renewed acquaintance earlier in the summer at the Battenburn estate. By all accounts, Grace had been a faithful wife to her much older husband. As a widow she conducted herself discreetly, choosing lovers with care and caution.

She did not squander her dead husband's fortune and played within society's rules by observing mourning and respecting Lord Powell's memory. It mattered to no one that she accepted all manner of gifts, if not precisely in exchange for sexual favors, then as part and parcel of her liaisons. It was expected, even when the liaison was brief, hardly more than a flirtation. No one among the *ton* thought of Lady Powell as a Cyprian. Her brothers would have demanded satisfaction.

"I take your point," South said.

"Courtesans enjoy the most freedom," India went on. "But they are prostitutes, no matter how one refines upon it."

"Governesses," South said.

"Perfectly respectable, though not necessarily respected. Remunerated hostages."

True enough, South thought. "So you accept society's characterization of your profession as the true price of your independence."

India smiled. "Something like that. But it does not mean I wish you to accept it. We will enjoy a more companionable evening together if you trust at the outset that it will not end in my bedchamber. I am cognizant of the fact that inviting you to my home could have raised the opposite expectation."

"Yes, but feeding me is an inspired diversion. The consommé is most excellent."

"You are a man of simple tastes, then."

He saluted her wordplay with a small lift of his spoon. "How is it that you became an actress?" he asked.

Her tone was positively arid. "Experience as a governess."

He chuckled as he knew she meant him to. South was enjoying her company too much to respond contrarily. There was a story here, though. It was one he decided he would hear another evening, preferably when Miss India Parr's complexion was flushed with sleep and loving and her pale hair lay soft and silky against his forearm. He could wait, would even enjoy it. The consommé might be a diversion, but Miss Parr did not seem to understand that anticipation was the real aphrodisiac.

India served the main course. South watched her manage this small intimacy with apparently no self-consciousness that it was one. His mother did not serve his father in such a manner. Nor would it have occurred to her to do so. There were servants to perform these tasks then soundlessly whisk away the platters and half-eaten remains.

"Will you tell your friends you were here this evening?" she asked.

South knew he would not. While normally circumspect, he might have done otherwise if he had not been about the colonel's business tonight. He wanted no speculation among the other members of the Compass Club. Northam had his hands full, and South was willing that it should remain so. "Tell my friends that I dined with the most lauded and applauded woman in London?" he asked. "The same woman we insulted with our inconsiderate behavior not above a week ago? I think not. Their imaginations are too constrained. They would not credit it."

"I think they would," she disagreed. "I know something about your reputation."

"As a brilliant thinker."

"As a rogue."

"Hardly."

"A rake."

"No."

"Roué?"

"My dear Miss Parr, your sources are alliterate but ill-informed. However, in keeping with your theme, let us say that I am a romantic."

"Like Byron."

Southerton was patently horrified at the thought. "Heaven help us all."

"Then you do not write poetry?"

"Only very bad rhymes. Sonnets with fewer than fourteen lines. That sort of thing."

India laughed. She wondered if he was truly a romantic or merely entertaining her with the notion. And she was entertained. Vastly so. It made her want to put off the moment of truth a while longer because, once their link was openly revealed, it would be only the nature of their business that would occupy them. It had to be that way. She would insist upon it. "So you are a romantic," she said softly. "And you admit it freely. Many of your set would rather take refuge with rakes and rogues."

He sighed. "It is the inevitable comparison with Byron that forces their hand. Better to be thought rather heartless than to have to set one's heart to paper. It is all well if one has a talent for it, but most of us do not, and the literary world is the better for that admission. So is the muslin set. If you insist on poetry, then I shall be forced to steal it. Deuced hard, that, what with you knowing most of Master Shakespeare's lines. Marlowe. Jonson. You'll have me there as well." He looked at her questioningly, and she nodded. "Shelley?" She nodded again. "Donne?"

"I'm afraid so."

"Then I would have to steal from a more obscure source, and if he is obscure, how good could he have been in the first place? It is one thing to steal the stuff and pass it as my own, but then to discover one has stolen poorly written sonnets . . .?" South cut a sliver of lamb and raised it to his mouth. "You can see why a true romantic is an adventurer, not a writer at all. Be damned with the pen, I say, and take up pistols. Dewy dawn mornings in the park. One's best friends as witnesses. Ten paces marked. The potential for blood. A real or imagined slight righted. A lady's honor served."

India's lips twitched. "I am persuaded. You have experience, I collect."

"What? With dueling?" He swallowed, waving his empty fork with a flourish. "Foolish business. Too many rules, and I dislike early risings. I find I possess a happy talent for talking my way out of difficulties."

Her smile deepened. She had no trouble believing that. "Your arguments are absurd."

"A moment ago you admitted yourself persuaded," he reminded her. "It is only when you realized I had no notion of what I was talking about that you changed your opinion. In circumstances of life and death I do not let on that I have no notion of most things. It is impossible to be convincing otherwise. One must first convince oneself."

India leaned forward and held up one hand, palm out. "Oh, please, do stop. I have lost all the threads of our conversation, but I am convinced you are in the right of everything."

"That is all that is ever important," he said wryly. "I am satisfied you are a perceptive woman." South bent his head and applied himself to his meal, pretending not to notice that this last observation had caused his hostess to gape at him. Without looking up he said, "The lamb is tender. My compliments to your cook."

India knew she should not permit herself to be baited and reeled and released so easily, but she *was* persuaded Southerton would have the last word. An entire soliloquy, if she wasn't careful. It made her wonder again what sort of man had been sent to her this time. It also crossed her mind that he hadn't been sent at all and that she had very much mistaken the matter. With some small shock, she realized she would be sorry either way.

They finished the meal in companionable, comfortable silence, a state that agreed with both of them. At the end, India rang for the table to be cleared. South afforded himself a snifter of her good brandy while India had a second glass of wine. She chose the chair near the hearth. South flanked her first at the mantel, while he poked at the fire and warmed his brandy, then on the settee.

In an absent gesture South pulled lightly on the sleeves of his jacket, returning the tailored line to his broad shoulders and doing the work of his valet and shirtmaker proud. He sat back in the corner of the settee much as he had in the hack. He would have not required much encouragement to fall asleep. The manner in which India was eyeing him suggested that she was in anticipation of its happening.

"I can sleep anywhere," he said.

"Another of your happy talents?"

South shrugged. "One learns the trick of it on his Majesty's frigates."

"You were at sea?" That made no sense to her. He was a viscount. Not a younger son, but the only son. He was the heir to the Earl of Redding's title and fortunes, and by all accounts, that fortune was considerable. The Viscount Southerton's quarterly allowance was more than India Parr could reasonably expect to earn in a lifetime spent at her craft. "You were a passenger, of course. Returning from the Continent. Displaced during the war with Boney, perhaps."

South did not correct any of her notions. They were the familiar conclusions drawn by those outside his family who knew he had been at sea as a very young man, but could not fathom the reasons or satisfy their curiosity by asking outright. His service in the Royal Navy was not at all the usual thing, the result of his romantic, adventuring nature and a father's life lesson disguised as indulging his son. Southerton had been taught something about his father by the experience, but perhaps not has much as the Earl of Redding had learned about his son.

"I was at sea," was all South said. "And I learned to catch sleep as I could. It was kind of you not to make much of that earlier."

"I made you wait in the cab rather a long time."

"It was graceless of me."

"Not at all. I found it . . ." She paused, searching for what had struck her at the time.

Southerton said, "Insulting?"

"Charming," she said. "I found it charming. Unaffected."

That could only mean he had been snoring. He wondered if he had been slack-jawed and drooling as well. There was nothing for it but to grin at this picture of himself, the would-be suitor made hapless by boredom and the necessity of sleep.

India went on, reminding him, "Circumstances being what they were, I slept also."

His grin deepened. "An odd beginning for us, wouldn't you say?"

"Oh, was that the beginning?" *"For us,"* he had said. She did not want to dwell on that, yet the idea of it enticed her. "Then I should not mention the disturbance from your box or the—"

"Eastlyn's box."

"What?"

"It is East's box. Not mine. Let us be clear on that point."

"Or the bruise on your chin," she said, knowing she must finish or he would spin her in circles yet again. In the future they would refrain from even a mention of their sleep-filled cab ride to her home or the late supper they shared. Their real beginning would start now. It only depended upon one of them to say it.

India's own safety dictated that it must come first from him. She was touched by what she perceived as his reluctance to broach the matter.

South rolled the snifter of brandy between his palms. The crystal rim reflected the warm yellow glow of the lamplight. He did not look at her. He had a picture of her in his mind— several of them, actually. India Parr on stage: bewigged and rouged and costumed, a slight, willowy figure commanding almost as much space and men with as few words as Admiral Nelson had. India Parr in her dressing room: polite now but somehow reticent, estranged from the very crowd that had come to pay homage, the woman inside the dress and paint closer to the surface. India Parr in the dimly lighted carriage: weary, without protection, pale hair secured in a few combs, and a stem of a neck that was too slender to support her. And India Parr in this room: charming and cautious by turns, gracious, fighting her natural inclination to be alone, still wearing her woolen shawl as if it were a breastplate of armor, while speaking of Cyprians and disabusing him of the notion that he might share her bed.

He looked up and met her dark eyes waiting for him— a deep, direct gaze but not without expression. He thought they hinted at sadness.

"It is the colonel, of course," he said quietly.

She nodded slowly. There, it was said. "You might have told me . . . before."

"No."

Then he had been given instructions to wait. She did not examine what reasons Blackwood might have had. The colonel's own thinking could not concern her. She never knew enough to make it her concern. The part she played in his dramas was but a small one, and she accepted that. Indeed, she would have agreed to do nothing else. "You understand I couldn't be sure," she said. "I had to hear it from you."

He nodded. "And if I had only been an ardent suitor, more fortunate than most for getting this far? What then?"

"I would have thanked you for the pleasure of your company and seen you out. You had not much time left to speak before that would have been the outcome."

South had suspected as much. "And if I were neither ally nor admirer?"

"You mean if your intention was to harm me?"

"I mean if my intention was to kill you."

India shrugged indifferently. "I considered it," she said. "More carefully than you. Doobin knows that you are here this evening. My maid and footman also. The hackney driver. I believe I can expect some discretion from them if nothing untoward happens. I cannot be persuaded that they will hold their tongues if I disappear or am murdered."

"So you assessed the risk to your life against the odds that I would be caught."

"That you would not *want* to be caught. It is a different thing."

"It is," he agreed. "And you concluded you were most likely safe this evening."

"Yes."

"And in the future?"

"There would be no future, my lord. We would never be alone again."

South mulled over what she had said. "You did indeed give this some thought."

"Yes." She frowned slightly as she watched Southerton's light-gray eyes take on a certain steely strength she had not seen before. "What is it?"

"It is only that your thinking presupposes the most obvious: that it is the colonel who sent me to kill you." He watched India's chin come up and the delicate wash of color in her cheeks disappear. "If that were the case then you know I would never be caught. There would be no witnesses. Those who are not already in my employ would simply disappear. You would do well, Miss Parr, to never suppose that you are even a half-step ahead of the colonel. Am I clear?"

"Yes." By great effort of will she held herself still. Not for anything would she have Southerton see that he had frightened her.

South set his brandy aside. "Enough of that. You are quite safe with me. My purpose here is exactly the opposite of the scenario I just proposed. I am to manage your protection. However that might best be accomplished remains to be seen."

"Manage my protection?" she asked carefully. "Offer it, you mean."

"An offer is something you can turn down. That is not what Blackwood intends."

In spite of her wish that it might be otherwise, India could feel herself shrinking back into the corner of her chair. The heels of her hands pressed whitely against the cool damask arms. Once she was aware of this posture, she forced her fingers to relax and curl lightly over the fabric. "Then Mr. Kendall has been found." Which, perforce, meant the man was dead.

South nodded. "A sennight ago. Floating in the Thames."

India did not gasp, though she couldn't say why. It felt like that inside her. What she did was breathe deeply through her nose, her nostrils flaring ever so slightly. She held the breath, this air she needed, so that she was almost light-headed with the effort; then she released it slowly and drew another, more shallow this time, until she was breathing with the even rhythms of one who had not just been delivered a blow to her midsection. "I was hoping for a different outcome," she said at last. "There was a woman, you see. Someone for whom he had a *tendre*. I thought perhaps he had gone to Gretna." Actually, she had prayed that had been the case.

Southerton stood and crossed the room to the pocket doors. He stood there a moment, listening; then he deliberately put his shoulder against the wood to jar it. No one moved on the other side. "A precaution," he told India, returning to his seat. "Nothing more. You know this woman's name?"

She shook her head. "Because of the nature of my contact with Mr. Kendall, there were few personal exchanges. I teased him once about his manner of dress. It embarrassed him, I think. He surprised both of us by admitting to an assignation following our meeting."

"An assignation? He used that word?"

"I don't remember. It was more than a month ago."

"Remember."

She tried to think back. "It's no good. I cannot recall."

"What was he wearing?"

A crease appeared between India's lightly feathered brows. "Pardon?"

South remained patient. "You said you teased him about his manner of dress. What was he wearing that caused you to comment?"

India closed her eyes and tried to picture Mr. Kendall as he had been that evening. She stood taller than many women, and he had no more than her height, perhaps an inch or so less. He did not do well in crowds, which suited his purpose admirably as he came and went largely unnoticed. That night, though, she had caught sight of his silk faille claw-hammer coat, the exact color of an orange rind, before she realized he was the man who occupied it. It was a bit like having dawn approaching as he maneuvered his way through her crowded dressing room. Mrs. Garrety relieved him of his bouquet of yellow roses before he reached her and dropped them unceremoniously on the dressing table without fetching a vase. In retrospect she thought Kendall had spared them a longing glance, and it made her consider for the first time that the flowers had not been meant for her.

With her eyes remaining closed, India described the coat. "He wore a green-and-yellow silk waistcoat beneath it. A white stock and chitterling. Pale yellow knee breeches and white hose. Brummel's influence? I think I asked him. Yes. That's what I said. And he said no, it was a woman's fine hand." A shadow of a smile briefly changed the shape of India's mouth. "Or perhaps that a fine woman had taken him in hand." She paused, thinking. "The latter. *'I've been taken in hand by a fine women, Miss Parr. I'm to see her this night and I dare not be late. She will think I am not coming and take her leave.'* "

India opened her eyes. "I inferred the idea of an assignation. He never said it in so many words. I was left with the distinct impression that it was a tryst that was arranged, because he said she would leave if he were not there. Even impatient women will wait for their lovers. Some longer than others. A fine woman with nothing to be lost might well wait forever."

"You inferred a great deal."

"Perhaps. But I am likely not wrong."

South agreed, but silently. "Had he a message for you after your performance, or you for him?"

"I had one for him." Before Southerton could ask her to recall it, India went on. "Lady Macquey-Howell had an appointment with the Spanish consul the following afternoon." She held up her hands. "I do not pretend to know the significance of such intelligence, only that I was asked to apprise Mr. Kendall of the lady's affairs."

"Your source?"

"My own."

South did not press. Her information had been correct. "There was nothing from Kendall for you?"

"No."

"The roses? A card?"

"No. Though it did not occur to me then, I now think the roses may have not been for me but for his lady. In any event, it would have been a rare thing that there was written communication. I learn lines all the time. I believe the colonel was impressed with my ability to do so. What I was asked to see or read or hear I committed to memory. Mr. Kendall had little more than instructions for me."

"He gave you those instructions in your dressing room? In front of others?"

"Often. Dismissing everyone to speak to Mr. Kendall would have raised the suspicions of my dresser, the other actors, even my loyal visitors. We managed the thing quite well."

"Just so," South said without inflection. "Right up until the moment he was murdered."

Chapter Three

The bundle of petticoats and panniers that Mrs. Garrety held blocked her complete view of India's dressing room. She tucked her chin, pressing on the folds of the crisp cottons and whalebone stays to peer over the top. Her gaze moved about sharply, alert to something amiss. Her nostrils flared as she sniffed the air. It was not a particular scent that made her frown, but the lack of an expected one.

The door was open behind her, and her shrill voice echoed in the corridor as she dropped the armload of garments on a stool. "Miss Parr? Ye be dressing still?" There was no answer from behind the silk dressing screen. The shadowy feminine form cast on the screen by the candlelight flickered, but it was a trick of the flame, Mrs. Garrety decided, no doubt caused by her own entry into the room. She scurried deliberately in that direction, her shoulders hunched aggressively forward in anticipation of what she would find.

India Parr's velvet pelisse hung from a hook on the other side of the screen. The stub of a candle on a nearby stand had almost extinguished itself. Frowning deeply, Mrs. Garrety lifted the dish and blew out the flame. A bit of hot wax dripped onto the tip of her thumb, but she paid it no heed.

"Aaah, dearie," she said softly, "what tricks are you about this night? Nothing you'll want repeating, I'll venture."

Shaking her head, the dresser pushed at the screen with the toe of her shoe, folding one panel enough to move it out of her path. She set the candle dish aside, turned up the wick on the dressing table oil lamp, and began applying herself to storing the garments she had carried into the room. She worked quickly, with more agitation in her movement than vigor, as she considered the problem of her employer's absence.

The mole on Mrs. Garrety's cheek twitched as her tightly pursed mouth moved from side to side. There had been one errand after another this evening. That cursed boy Doobin, so often underfoot when he was least needed, had managed to make himself scarce. Perhaps, Mrs. Garrety mused, all his sniffing after Miss Parr's skirt had finally landed him under them.

This last thought brought her up short. There was nothing to be gained by veering off in that direction, only something to be done. It was uncharacteristic of her to hesitate, but she did so now. Did she want to do something? Or let this evening's disappearance pass without consequence? If she said nothing . . .

Mrs. Garrety straightened, pressing her hands to the small of her back to ease the ache there. A movement in the hallway caught her attention. Her head cocked to one side. Silence. "Doobin?" She remained still, her feet firmly planted, elbows jutting outward. There were few people left in the theatre. She had seen Mr. Kent and and Ben Whipple in deep discussion on the stage earlier, and the wardrobe mistress was mending a doublet accidentally slashed at the end of the first act. As was much the case, Mrs. Garrety's own departure was among the last, planned to precede or follow Miss Parr's by but a few minutes. Except tonight she had no clear idea how long her employer had been gone.

There was movement in the hall again, and the deepening of a shadow on the far wall. Mrs. Garrety did not flinch from it. "I know rats when I hear 'em, boy. I can hear 'em wigglin' their whiskers. Let me see ye, now, or I swear I'll box yer ears when I catch ye. And I will catch ye. Depend on it."

Doobin stepped into the open door frame and regarded the dresser with a mixture of wariness and curiosity. "How'd you know I was there?"

"Same way as I know everything else." She touched the bent fingers of one hand to her temple and tapped lightly. "I use what the good Lord give me for more than to hang my ears on."

The tips of Doobin's own ears reddened at this rebuke. He shuffled uncomfortably in place. His eyes darted around the dressing room.

"She ain't here," Mrs. Garrety said. "As if you didn't know." She clucked her tongue at his feigned surprise. "Actin' ain't your strong suit, so don't bother yourself on my account. Did Miss Parr put ye up to this?"

Doobin remained loyally silent, pressing his lips together for good measure. If the truth were known, India Parr's dresser frightened him a little. She put the image of a hook in his mind, bent and barbed, ready to snag him smartly if he wandered too close. The boy made certain he remained hovering on the threshold, with an escape route at his back.

"Did she?" Mrs. Garrety asked again.

"Don't know what you mean," he said stubbornly. "I come lookin' for Miss Parr."

Mrs. Garrety made a sound deep in her throat that clearly indicated her disbelief. "Did she tell you to come around pretending you didn't know she was gone?" Though she anticipated no reply to her question, she inclined her head in Doobin's direction. She chuckled without humor when he remained mute. "I'll tell her ye did just as she asked. She won't fault ye for yer efforts."

Doobin's shoulders relaxed a tad. "She's a good 'un, Miss Parr is."

The dresser nodded. "Yer in the right of it there, Master Doobin. And it falls to me to make certain no 'arm comes

to her, what wi' so many depending on her for their bread
and butter. Aaah, I see ye hadn't thought of that. Well, think
on it and ye'll know it's the truth I'm telling. Sometimes
she gets an idea that she's no different from the rest of us,
but you and me, we know that's not the way of it. Miss Parr
is what they call a diamond of the first water.''

The boy could not disagree. India Parr *was* someone outside the ordinary. He wished he had thought to call her a
diamond.

''Did she accept an invitation this evening?'' Mrs. Garrety
asked pointedly, her eyes narrowing darkly.

Doobin's chin came up as he was jerked out of his reverie.
He was pinned back by the dresser's shrewd stare. ''I don't
know what you mean.''

She clucked her tongue as if disapproving of his answer,
but she had already divined enough to know that she had
the truth of it. ''You were pimping for her again tonight,
weren't ye, ye little maggot? I should box yer ears on principle. But I won't, if ye tell me 'is name.''

Doobin let both insults to himself pass. He minded neither
being named a maggot nor a pimp, though the former was
infinitely preferable to the latter. What raised the hair at the
back of his neck was the implication that Miss Parr was a
whore. ''Take it back,'' he said, puffing his chest out like
a banty rooster.

Mrs. Garrety merely cackled. ''You think yer 'er knight,
do ye? Come to do 'er bidding. Defend 'er honor.'' With
no warning, the old woman struck like a cobra, closing the
distance between herself and the boy in a step-and-lunge
that had speed and strength behind it. She held Doobin
against the wall, her forearm secured under his chin and
against his throat. With the slightest pressure she brought
him up on tiptoe. ''The man's name,'' she said. ''Which
one was it tonight?''

Doobin's small Adam's apple pressed sharply against his
windpipe. That, more than an unwillingness to speak,
assisted his continued silence.

''Dacre? Stanhope? Mr. Rutherford?'' She eased the pressure on his throat, but Doobin's wheeze was an inconclusive response. "Shake yer 'ead, boy. Which one of 'em put you up to it? Dacre?"

Doobin managed a small sideways movement of his head. He had not given Mrs. Garrety high enough marks for strength or agility. With the shortsightedness of his own youth, he had never considered the long hours Miss Parr's dresser spent bending, lifting, and carrying costumes that weighed twice over what she did. He hadn't thought of the time she was engaged in packing trunks, or in moving them when no one came round to assist her quickly enough to suit her.

"Then Stanhope?"

This time Doobin merely shifted his eyes in a manner that indicated the answer was no.

Mrs. Garrety sighed. "Oh, not that romantical fool Rutherford," she said under her breath. "And 'im with naught but pennies in his pockets. What's he think he can offer Miss Parr?"

Hoping the woman was caught by her own musings, Doobin simply shrugged. His strategy worked, because she slowly released him. "So it's Rutherford," she said, continuing to watch him closely.

Doobin bit his lower lip and worried it. In the small space she gave him, he managed to get his right arm up and massage his bruised throat. There was a nervousness in his movement that wasn't entirely feigned. She wasn't allowing him enough room to get the open doorway to his back again. He could feel every ridge in his spine pressed against the frame.

"I could have ye put out on the streets," Mrs. Garrety said, no particular threat in her tone. "Do ye think Miss Parr could bring ye back? Not when Mr. Kent finds she's put 'erself and the company at risk with her antics. Like as not, he won't listen to what she says in yer defense. Only cares that she doesn't come to any 'arm. If he discovers ye've been abetting her, as they say, 'e's the one that will show ye the door 'imself. Mr. Rutherford ain't for the likes of Miss Parr.''

Doobin almost surrendered then, but the dryness in his mouth had cleaved his tongue to the roof of it. He could only portray sorrow with his large ginger-colored eyes. The fact that his sorrow was in large part for his current plight and not remorse for what had brought him to it was not anything he could communicate.

Mrs. Garrety's narrow shoulders hunched in defeat. ''Next time I will box yer ears, boy. Just see if I don't. Go on wi' ye. I 'ave no more use for ye. See that Miss Parr don't find one either.''

As soon as the dresser stepped back, Doobin slipped sideways and turned to race off. He found himself abruptly snagged again, this time by the back of his breeches, and hauled into the room.

''Let me see yer pockets,'' the dresser demanded. Without waiting for him to turn them inside out, she began rooting through his jacket. He wriggled as much from the invasion to his person as the fact that her scrambling fingers tickled him. ''Here, now. What's this? Someone's left their calling card with ye, perhaps?'' Hopeful, aware that Doobin was holding his breath, she grasped it between her fingertips and tugged. She read the engraved name, turned it over, and studied the florid script. ''Bah! The man's imagination is as spare as his wit. What can she 'ave been thinking?''

Doobin tentatively held out his hand for the return of the card.

''I think not,'' Mrs. Garrety told him. ''Are ye collecting them? I'll keep this one.'' She gave his hand a light slap when he did not immediately let it fall away. ''Go on. Before I change my mind about those ears.''

This time when Doobin slipped past her he got away, but only because she permitted it.

The dresser stared at the card for a moment longer before slipping it under her sleeve at the wrist. She spoke softly to herself, her voice at once derisive and rueful. ''Rutherford. Hardly seems worth the effort.''

* * *

India held her wineglass carefully by the stem, watching the contents as she crossed the room to the window. One could be forgiven for assuming she cared about spilling Madeira on the tapestry rug, but it was only that she feared breaking the stem between her fingers or smashing the glass against hearth or wall. It was constraint she wished to show Lord Southerton, not the extent to which she could be roused to acts of temper and violence.

She freed the ties that held the heavy velvet drapes in place. They swung free and fell into place, making a silent, gentle rippling as they unfolded. She idly smoothed them with the fingertips of her free hand.

"Am I responsible, then, for Mr. Kendall's death?" she asked, turning on South again. She felt marginally more composed with the closed drapes at her back than she had with the window. Light from the interior room had made them clearly visible to those with an interest, and India thought that even with the viscount's considerable experience, she was perhaps more conscious than he that there were always those with an interest. "Are you saying that is the case?"

"Did it strike that chord with you?" he asked mildly, watching her. She was different than she had been only a few moments earlier. He had the sense she was drawing into herself, but no sense that she was acting. There was an alteration, he decided, yet he could not place his finger on what made it so. India Parr seemed to be very much a woman who confined her considerable talent to the stage. Off it, he continued to be left with the rather odd notion that she had little in the way of confidence, and that she could not adopt an air that made it appear otherwise.

India's glass hovered near her lips. "Yes," she said. "It did strike that chord."

"And do you think you are responsible?"

She had collected herself and had wits enough about her not to recoil from the question so baldly put. "No, not if your meaning is to ask if it was by my hand. I assure you, it was not. But I have often wondered at the repercussions of these intrigues. I think I am responsible to the extent I played any part at all. I was not careless in my communication with Mr. Kendall. I was not unmindful that there might be others with an interest in what passed between us. Mr. Kendall seemed likewise circumspect.''

''Still, he was found out.''

''Yes.''

''A bad end for him, then.''

India's head came up sharply and she stared at South. His tone had been too cavalier for her tastes. ''You dismiss it lightly.''

He could have told her it was done only to gauge her reaction. He shrugged instead, punctuating his offhandedness with this gesture. South did not miss the slight tightening around her mouth. India Parr was most definitely offended by this adopted manner. He wondered that he was not more relieved by this discovery, but at times he knew himself to be possessed of a perverse nature. Now was such a time. Relief was not at the forefront of what he felt. Suspicion was.

''What of your own feelings for Mr. Kendall?'' he asked. It was appalling, really, that he should put the question so frankly to her, but he did not back away from it. Perhaps he would apologize later.

''My feelings?'' she asked, something of her incredulity revealed in her voice. He could not be seriously asking if she had developed a *tendre* of her own for the man. No, of course not. That Southerton would be interested in such a thing was too absurd to credit. ''I had nothing in the way of feeling for him that I do not have for most men of my acquaintance.''

One corner of South's lips twitched. ''That, Miss Parr, is no answer at all, but I will accept it because your feelings are your own and I have no right to pry.''

''Indeed, you do not.''

South did not disabuse her of the notion that it would

always be thus. He drained his brandy and set the snifter aside. "There is no proof that Kendall's murder is related to his work for the Foreign Office, although that is the suspicion under which we must proceed." He regretted the necessity of further blunt speech. "The condition of his body when it was discovered made it difficult to know certain details about his manner of death. That he was beaten is clear, though whether he faced one or more attackers is not. It cannot be determined if he was restrained at the time of his injuries, either by other assailants or by mechanical means."

India paled a little. "Mechanical means?"

"Ropes."

"Why did you not simply say that he may have been bound?" she asked, a measure of color returning.

"Irons," he continued as if she had not spoken. "Leather straps."

India lowered herself onto the window seat. "You are speaking of torture," she said on a thread of sound. "Why?"

"Why do I speak of it to you?" he asked. "Or why must I speak of it at all?"

"Both," she said. "Either."

"Your protection and the necessity of seeing that it is done."

"I—I think—" India fell silent, aware that she had no coherent thoughts of any kind.

"It has happened before," he continued. He cautioned himself against adopting a gentler tone or softening his expression to reassure her. Creating false confidences, especially where none were warranted, would lead to precisely the opposite outcome from the one he wished. "If it is how Mr. Kendall met his end, then he would not be the first."

"But you do not know . . ."

"No," he admitted. "We cannot be certain."

"It may have been footpads."

He nodded slightly, allowing this could have been the case, then added, "It may have been that Mr. Kendall had too much grog at the Keg and Kettle and fell repeatedly on his face, but I do not believe that.'' South paused. ''And neither do you.''

''I do not know what to believe.'' India finished her wine. It was uncharacteristic of her to indulge in a third glass, but she did so now. Standing at the sideboard, she said, ''It does not necessarily follow that I am in danger. Or at least no more than I have ever accepted as a reasonable risk.''

Southerton doubted she knew how to assess the risk to herself. Her idea that any was reasonable chilled his marrow. Like the sailor he had been, he changed tack in the face of her wind. ''Tell me what else you remember from your last conversation with Mr. Kendall.''

India did not immediately answer, thinking on the exchange. ''As I said, I gently teased him about his manner of dress; then we spoke of a recent musicale to which he had been invited. I asked him several questions. Who played. Who attended. What was his favorite piece. Our discourse was brief because there were others waiting for my attention and those politely listening to our conversation in anticipation of having their own with me.''

''Then the musicale was no imagined affair. It truly occurred.''

''I've always assumed so. It afforded him the opportunity to speak of Lady Macquey-Howell and allowed me to inquire about the Spanish consul.''

''And you gave him the information he was seeking in this fashion?''

''Yes. Always. I can assure you, our exchanges were unexceptional.''

Unless the musicale had never occurred and someone overhearing knew that to be so. Would Kendall have been so careless? No, South told himself. He knew little of the man's character, but he knew a great deal of the colonel's. John Blackwood did not suffer fools, and there were precious few he selected to work for him—fewer still he entrusted with the diplomatic tinkering that was Kendall's forte. Eastlyn was one such as Kendall. South suspected that solving Kendall's murder and protecting India Parr was ultimately in the service of shielding the Marquess of Eastlyn. East only admitted to being embroiled in one coil—with two women, true—but no one among the Compass Club believed their good friend was not engaged in something requiring his other, less remarked upon talents.

Southerton determined to investigate the musicale. As a starting place it was likely without promise, but he had no other at the ready.

"I take it you have met the colonel, Miss Parr," South said.

"Only once."

It was extraordinary that they would have met at all, though India Parr had no reason to know that. "And how did he impress you upon that occasion?"

She smiled slightly and her answer came without hesitation. "Persuasive," she said. "He impressed me as persuasive." Her eyes widened as South gave an unexpected but appreciative shout of laughter.

"I have not heard him called such before," he said. "Tenacious, yes. Like the veriest starving cur on the scent of a bone long buried. That is our colonel. But persuasive? That is putting too fine a touch on it."

"Perhaps it is because I am not a bone," she said with some dignity.

"What?" Belatedly he collected himself. His eyes, gleaming with an amused silver light now, regarded India most openly. "No," he said at length, pretending not to notice she only suffered his study and was not flattered by it. "Not a bone at all."

India could not help but notice that the gleam in his eyes remained. She could divine the thought even when he did not deign to utter it aloud. "Though not a great deal of meat to recommend me," she said.

It was surprise that touched his expression, though not entirely because she had said it. It was more interesting to South that she appeared to believe *he* had been thinking it when quite the opposite was true. Her lush mouth suggested to him that all of her was as exquisitely curved, and he could still find no reason to think otherwise. Indeed, *tender morsel* had immediately come to his mind. Miss India Parr was long of limb, with a slender, creamy neck all that was exposed by her gown, but South had an eye for feminine proportions and had won his fair share of wagers on the same. Until it was proved otherwise, he remained more confident in his own judgment than in Miss Parr's.

South chose not to make a gallant reply to her comment, and permit her to think as she would. He imagined he had not much time left with her. He sensed her impatience and suspected she would be asking him to quit himself from her house soon.

Returning to matters of importance, South said, "The colonel remains desirous of your assistance, Miss Parr. I take it you have been of no small help to him."

India shrugged. "It was little enough that was asked of me."

"Your continued well-being is of the uppermost concern to him."

Her smile did not quite touch her eyes. "I doubt that," she said softly. India placed her unfinished wine on the sideboard and let her arms fall to her sides. "There is no need to puff the thing up. What happens to me cannot be of so great a consequence. I can accept that the colonel feels some sense of responsibility for me, but it is largely misplaced. He owes me nothing, nor I him. My arrangement with the colonel was never quid pro quo, and I would not have him make it such now."

South wondered what manner of persuasion Blackwood had used to engage India Parr's help in the first place. She was not easily moved from a position once taken. Bloody intractable was what she was. "Then you are refusing his protection."

India hesitated, but only the space of a heartbeat. "Yes," she said. "There is no need for it."

"Mr. Kendall's murder is not proof to the contrary?"

"No. You said as much yourself. You may suspect his death is linked to his association with the colonel, but you have not the facts of the matter yet. In the event the evidence is presented to you, I believe there is infinitely more risk to others than to me.''

South's neutral tone belied his concern. ''What others?''

''Well . . . you, for one. And the colonel, of course.'' She stopped. ''What? Did you think I might know of any others? I hope you are disabused of that notion. Until you spoke plainly this evening, I could not be certain you were sent by the colonel. I could not even be certain he would send someone. It did not necessarily follow that Mr. Kendall's long absence meant he was dead, only that the colonel had no need of me. No, my lord, I pose no threat to anyone seeking information, because I have little enough to offer.''

''It can take as long to discover someone has nothing useful to give as it does to discover they do,'' South said. ''Do you take my meaning, Miss Parr?''

She did. He was saying that in the end it could be the same. She might well be dead for what she didn't know as for the things she did. Sighing, India returned to her chair by the hearth and sat on the edge, her hands folded quietly in her lap. ''I hope you will relate my appreciation to the colonel for his concern, but frankly it surprises me. I had not expected this consideration, nor even to come to his notice. If he insists on pressing me in this manner, then perhaps it is time for me to put a period to our arrangement.''

Southerton's expression gave nothing of his thoughts away. In any event, they had little to do with Miss India Parr. The colonel, he was thinking, could begin doing his own negotiations when females were involved. ''You are quite set on this matter, then,'' South said.

''I am.''

He nodded. ''I will make your wishes known to him.''

''I would have you convince him, my lord.''

''I would have to be convinced myself, Miss Parr, and I assure you, I am not. What the colonel proposes is not an unreasonable precaution.''

The line of India's mouth, while not precisely mutinous,

remained unwavering. She continued to regard Southerton calmly, giving not a fraction of an inch.

"Very well," he said at length. He stood slowly and thanked her for the supper and the pleasure of her company. "There is no need to see me out. I can find my way."

India stood, watching his progress to the door. His movements were accompanied by only a whisper of sound. He stopped for his coat, folding it over his arm; then he picked up his hat and gloves. Her eyes followed the lift of his arm as his fingers went to rest on the brass handle. She felt a small tug inside her that began as he lifted the handle. This feeling was at odds with the urgency she felt for him to be gone.

Southerton's hand paused and his grip loosened fractionally. He turned a few degrees toward India, so that he was not addressing her over his shoulder but neither was he confronting her directly. "There is someone, is there not?"

There were so many possible responses she could have given that at first India could say nothing at all. Finally, she gave the one that would cause her the least explanation for the nonce. "Yes," she said. "There is someone."

South merely nodded, thoughtful. His fingers renewed their grip on the handle, and this time he twisted it fully. "Good evening."

Then he was gone.

"That's my trick, I believe," Northam said, pulling the cards toward him. "You haven't been attending the play tonight, South."

Frowning at the mention of his name, South looked up distractedly. "Haven't been to the theatre for a fortnight. What's that to do with anything?" His expression became one of annoyance when his friends exchanged telling looks and brief chuckles that he knew were at his expense. He was aware of heads turning in their direction from other corners of the gentlemen's club. "What did I say?"

Mr. Marchman shook his head. "It is of no consequence as long as you continue to entertain us in this fashion."

Eastlyn nodded. "It's just as West indicates. You are vastly entertaining tonight."

Northam's amusement was slightly less than the others by virtue of the fact that South was his partner in the card game. He felt compelled to point this out to everyone as there was a hefty wager at stake on the outcome. If South did not become more agreeable and attentive, they would both be out an entire quid. He tapped the edges of the cards he had collected into place. "I was speaking of the card play," he told Southerton. "You apparently were not."

"Still at Drury Lane?" Marchman asked. His green eyes narrowed faintly as he looked askance at Southerton. "No sign of new bruises. Nor any cuts. You have not been in the company of Miss Parr of late, have you?"

"Or at least he has not offended her," Eastlyn said.

South lifted his chin in Northam's direction, indicating he should lead his next card. He did not respond to the gentle gibes of West and East. They were correct in their assumptions, after a fashion. The truth was that he had seen a great deal of India Parr of late but that she was unaware of it. Her ignorance was all that kept her from taking offense, and saved South from physically having to defend himself.

It was Southerton's own uncharacteristic quiet that silenced the others. This time they did not exchange a single glance but went back to their play, mutually agreed to follow their friend's lead no matter where it took them. In the case of Northam there was a price to be paid in the form of a pound sterling. He paid his debt alongside South, gathered the cards, and motioned to a footman for a round of drinks to be brought to their table.

"And where is your wife this evening?" Eastlyn asked. "The dowager countess has her again?"

North shook his head, some of his displeasure visible in the set of his mouth. Though he could not say why it should be so, he would have preferred his wife were in the company of his mother rather than where he knew her to be. "She's sitting with Lady Battenburn. The baroness sent a servant around saying she was not feeling at all the thing, and Elizabeth elected to go to her.''

"Then it is fortunate for you that we're in town to provide a diversion.''

"Yes,'' North said wryly. "Isn't it?'' The truth was that Northam had hoped to conclude his assignment with the colonel quickly and still get his wife to the country before October was out. Success on all fronts was eluding him. He glanced at Southerton. Judging by the expression on that worthy, the fates were being similarly unkind.

Mr. Marchman was of the opinion there was no amusement to be gained from Eastlyn's line of inquiry. He changed the subject. "I have it on good authority that Rutherford has exiled himself to the other side of the Atlantic.''

"More debts called in?'' asked East.

"So it was intimated.''

North drew the recently placed snifter of brandy in front of him toward his mouth. "Interesting, that. The first I heard of the man's considerable debt was this summer past at the Battenburn estate. The country gala. South was still there when Madame Fortuna revealed it to Lady Battenburn's guests.''

"Saw it in her cards, did she?'' Marchman said.

It was South who answered. "I would never malign the fortune teller's reputation, but I would not be surprised if she wasn't privy to certain information provided by our host and hostess. If you recall, it was that same evening Madame accused North of being the Gentleman Thief. In that we know she was wrong.''

North remembered it somewhat differently. "She said I had certain stolen articles in my possession, which I did, no matter that I had no knowledge of how they came to be there.''

Eastlyn tasted his brandy. "How I wish I had been witness to that, culminating as it did in Lady Elizabeth's valiant though ill-considered defense of you. Brought you forthwith to the altar, it did.''

One of North's brows kicked up. "Such can be arranged for you, East. You have but to name your poison. Lady Sophia or Mrs. Sawyer."

Eastlyn quickly set down his snifter and threw up his hands, surrendering. He looked elsewhere for a timely rescue. "You were saying about Rutherford, West?"

Marchman laughed, a dimple appearing at the corner of his mouth. "Only that he's disappeared. Since he hasn't turned up leg-shackled to an heiress, there is speculation that he embarked for America to make his fortune."

"Or marry one," North said.

South tapped the stem of his glass with a fingernail. A small crease had appeared between his dark brows. "What part of his destination is speculation and what part is fact?"

Mr. Marchman shrugged. "I overheard the talk at Simon's two nights past. Why? Is it important?"

"I doubt it," South said easily. It had been South's experience that oft-repeated gossip eventually became fact. "I saw him not long ago. He was laying siege on that occasion. It rather flies in the face of his plans to take himself off to America."

"Laying siege?" asked East. "A renewed interest in Lady Powell?"

"No." He felt three pairs of eyes boring into him. Lest they mistake the matter and he find himself and Grace Powell once again the subject of speculation, Southerton gave up the truth. "Miss India Parr."

Marchman leaned back in his chair. He was thoughtful. "That explains why it must needs be a siege, but is she possessed of a fortune? I certainly have never heard of such."

"Neither have I," South said. He had given no small amount of thought to the possible sources of Miss Parr's income since the evening he had been invited to her home. It had, in part, prompted his final question to her as he was about to leave. While she did not live lavishly, she certainly lived in a style supported by more than an actress's wage. He considered the gifts that were sent her way by the hopefuls—as he called them now—as one wellspring of funds. While he was able to learn that on any evening she was offered at least one truly spectacular piece of jewelry, he had also learned these were never the pieces she accepted. Miss Parr kept the trifles and incidentals: the small stones and settings that had not cost a man his fortune or even his quarterly allowance, the ones that arrived with no expectation of a favor in return but were given merely as tokens of esteem and acknowledgment of her fine performance.

No quid pro quo.

He recalled her saying that no such arrangement existed between her and the colonel. It was apparently a matter of importance to her in her dealings with all men.

It did not help him explain the existence of the house, the number of servants in her employ, the expensive but simple furnishings, or the extent of her wardrobe. He had created an opportunity for himself to visit her home when she was not in residence and once when she was. No one, least of all Miss Parr, had suspected his presence. During the day he had chosen a time when most of the servants were out on errands and the ones remaining could be easily avoided. At night, everyone was soundly sleeping. South still did not count himself as an accomplished sneaksman. Gaining entry to her home had required more in the way of good planning than expert climbing skills or quick reflexes. He was possessed of the latter, but they were not needed. More to the point, he had taken nothing during his visits, nor had he forced his way into those few rooms that were locked. His purpose was to make observations, not to inadvertently bring notice to himself.

"There is someone, is there not?" He had put the question to her that evening because all of his instincts told him it was so. She had answered in the affirmative yet given nothing away. He still had no real answer to the question of the man's identity. Who provided for her? Kept her? Someone made certain she did not have to accept a position as any man's mistress, by seeing to it that she was adequately cared for.

The more South learned, the more questions that were raised in his own mind. Of answers, there were precious few. The colonel denied that he was India Parr's benefactor, but he was clearly intrigued by South's assurance that such a person existed. It left South with a very long list of possibilities.

Eastlyn caught the attention of North and Marchman and rolled his eyes in South's direction. "Wool-gathering again," he said in hushed accents of the type that were meant to be overheard. "I should be offended if I thought it was in any way a personal slight. It appears, though, to be a defect of character."

"Amusing," South said dryly. But he had been wool-gathering, so nothing but ridicule would come of denying it. "Another round of cards? North?"

"With you as my partner a second time? Not bloody likely. I should have the duns at my door and no way to pay them. Before you can say 'Philadelphia,' the Compass Club will have become a threesome and I will be fleeing with the clothes on my back and Elizabeth in tow to points west of Land's End."

This speech was met with hoots of laughter, as well it should have been. The wagers among the four friends, while many in number, were notorious for their miserliness. They wagered no more money now than they had when they had been together at Hambrick Hall and their allowances were dear.

"West?" Southerton asked, picking up the deck and flicking through it with his thumb. "You will take a risk, won't . . ." He broke off, looking up as a liveried footman approached. The man carried a small silver tray absent of libation. "Yes?" South asked, for clearly the man had been approaching him.

"This arrived for you, my lord. Only moments ago. I was instructed to give it to you directly." He lowered the tray so the viscount could remove the card.

South opened the envelope, glanced at the card without removing it, then placed it in the inside pocket of his frock coat. "No reply," he informed the footman. When the man had backed away and was out of hearing, South made his apologies to his friends. "I regret I must leave your fine company, but there you have it."

To their credit they did not ask questions. In the guise of farewells, these friends offered words of caution and good luck. It was always thus when one was summoned on the colonel's affairs.

South arrived at the house shortly before one in the morning. It was an absurd hour to conduct business of any nature, but South complied because he was intrigued. He knew his friends thought it was Blackwood who had taken him away from their evening at the club, but it was not so. At least not directly. The card he carried in his pocket was from Miss India Parr.

He was on the point of stepping down from the hired hack when he saw the cloaked figure coming toward him. He was not entirely certain it was Miss Parr until she was almost upon him and ordering him back inside the cab. Bemused, he ducked his head and lowered himself onto the uncomfortable leather seat. She followed quickly, seating herself opposite him. Her voice was husky—deliberately so, he thought, as she rapped out a destination to the driver. "Drury Lane," she said.

There was no interior lamp in the cab. India lowered the blinds over the windows on either side of her before they had gone more than a few feet. Had she not been so earnestly efficient, South could have been moved to amusement by her antics. The hooded cloak, at the very least, put him in mind of the Society of Bishops. Was she abducting him? It was a tantalizing thought.

"We are going to the theatre?" he asked with polite interest.

"Yes . . . no . . . that is, it was said merely in aid of giving the driver a direction."

"Then you have no purpose there?"

"At this hour? Do not be absurd."

"Then, pray endeavor to think of one when we arrive. A forgotten article, perhaps. Clothing. The lines of the new play you're rehearsing. Nothing piques the curious observer more than a destination without design." South leaned back and removed his brushed beaver hat, placing it on the seat beside him. He folded his arms casually across his chest and waited. A slim beam of moonlight slipped past the blind as the cab swayed on poorly maintained springs. The blue-gray light illuminated India's pale hair as she lowered her hood. Strands that were like corn silk in the sunshine had the appearance of rare and precious metals now, platinum and silver worked in a delicate filigree against her scalp.

"It was wise of you to hire a cab," she said at last. "I confess to some concern that you would arrive in your own carriage."

"I was at my club. I accompanied my friends there, so it was as much by necessity that I arrived in this manner as it was good sense."

"Your club," she said slowly. "I had not realized. How did my card find you, then? Doobin was to take it straight-away to your home."

"I am certain he did. He must have impressed someone there with the urgency of conveying it to me. He struck me as an enterprising fellow. I do not think you have to worry on his account." South's eyes narrowed as he attempted to make out the features of her face. The slanted, shifting beam of moonshine fell over her shoulder and the back of one hand she had raised to her throat. The effect was that of a finely honed blade laid sharply against her neck. It was not a pleasant image. "Perhaps you could begin by telling me why I've been summoned," he said. "At such an hour and in such a fashion. You did not go about reaching Mr. Kendall in this havey-cavey manner, I hope."

"No," she said quickly. "I never . . ." She paused. "You think this is havey-cavey?"

"Mayhap I have used the adjective prematurely," he said. "But I continue to wait for an explanation."

"You never told me how I might contact you if I had something to recount."

"That is because you should not."

"Not contact you?" she asked. "Or make no report?"

"Both. There is no expectation on the colonel's part that you will continue to provide him with intelligence, since you have refused his protection." It did not mean that she had been unprotected of late, though she should not have suspected as much. It also did not mean that the colonel would not use whatever bit of information she was turning over to him. South tried to glimpse her features again, make out the set of her mouth to see if it was stubborn, or the slant of her eyes to gauge their apprehension. "Something has happened to cause you to change your mind?" he asked.

There was a slight hesitation. "No," she said. "It is concern for another."

"Tell me." Acutely aware of her presence in the small cab, South heard her draw in a long breath before she spoke.

"It is just that I believe something unfortunate may be in the offing for Lady Macquey-Howell."

"Lady Macquey-Howell?" he asked. "Not the Spanish consul?"

"Yes."

"What are your suspicions?"

"There is some scheme of finance between them," she said. "I do not know the particulars, nor do I care to, but I gather the countess has perhaps overreached herself."

In all likelihood she had, South thought. "And the unfortunate circumstances which may befall her? What do you know of them?

"Nothing."

"Is her life in danger?

"I have not heard such. It has only been intimated that she may be exposed."

"Perhaps she should be," South said frankly.

"I cannot say. I have made no judgment about her affair with Señor Cruz. It is not my place. I only thought there would be interest in knowing that the business between them is no longer entirely their secret.''

South nodded. "Your source for this information?" he asked.

"My own."

He recalled this was what she had said once before. South did not press. Instead, he inclined his head slightly and thanked her. "I will be certain to relate what you have told me."

"Thank you."

South inclined his head again, his mood thoughtful. More than a minute passed before he said, "There is something I would discuss with you, Miss Parr."

"Of course."

Speaking as if his question were of no consequence, he asked, "What do know of Mr. Rutherford?"

India frowned. The purpose of his question, coming as if from nowhere, confounded her. "Rutherford? Mr. William Rutherford?"

"Yes. Do you know him?"

"We are acquainted only."

"He is one of your admirers, I believe." South could divine no reason to explain that he knew it for a fact. He waited to hear her response.

"He comes often to my dressing room after a performance," she said modestly. "He is always most complimentary."

"I see. And he has stopped his nightly sojourns?"

"Hardly nightly. He attended the theatre perhaps two or three times each week."

South did not disabuse her of the assumption she made regarding Rutherford's attendance. He had observed Rutherford arriving at the Drury Lane Theatre just as the evening's performance was ending, then joining the throng outside India's dressing room.

"May I inquire as to your interest in Mr. Rutherford?" asked India.

South considered what he wanted to tell her. "As it hap-

pens, I have learned only this evening that Mr. Rutherford
has fled the country to escape his creditors.''

''Indeed. It does not surprise.''

''You knew of his debt?''

''It had been brought to my attention. But why do you
mention it?''

''Merely to satisfy a curiosity,'' he said.

That was no answer at all, India thought. ''And have
you?''

''Not entirely,'' he said. ''I am wondering if you evinced
some feeling toward Mr. Rutherford?''

''If I . . . ?'' India wished she could see Southerton more
clearly and perhaps know better the bent of his mind. ''I
assure, I have not. He comes to my dressing room, pays his
compliments, and often leaves his card with me. I have never
responded to any of his overtures. In point of fact, I give
the cards to Doobin. If you can credit such a thing, he
collects all cards left with me.''

''My card also?''

She shook her head. ''No. I did not give him yours.'' In
fact, she had burned it. ''Do you not believe that Mr. Rutherford has fled?''

''My mind is not set on the matter.''

''I see.''

''He was very attentive toward you.''

''Was he? I'm afraid I did not realize such was the case.''
South's chuckle was rueful. Poor Mr. Rutherford.

India pressed on. ''Am I to understand from what you
have said that you suspect Rutherford's disappearance is in
some manner connected to me?''

''I admit that when you lay it out before me in such plain
terms it appears to warrant no such conclusion.''

''I should say so,'' she said coolly. ''There is nothing at
all flattering about your suspicions.''

''My dear Miss Parr,'' South drawled, ''it was certainly
not my intention to flatter you.'' He could sense her drawing
herself up, spine stiff, chin thrust forward, challenging. South
supposed it was a good thing that the wandering sliver of

moonlight did not flash itself across the half-smile playing about his mouth or the amusement he could not check in his eyes.

"That is just as well," India said. "I am certain that upon further investigation you will discover Mr. Rutherford is precisely where the *on dit* places him."

"No doubt you are correct," South said neutrally. He found one corner of the window blind and moved it a fraction with the tip of his index finger. He peered out through the crack. The theatre district would soon be upon them. Letting the blind fall back into place, he casually raised one leg and extended it to the opposite seat, effectively blocking the exit by hitching his boot heel on the edge. "However," he began quietly, "in the event you are not correct, will you reconsider the colonel's offer of protection?"

"No. I will not. I remain quite firm in that regard."

Her words were certainly firm, South thought, yet he could not shake the sense that her resolve might be wavering. Her head was turned at a slight angle away from him, as if even in the darkened carriage she did not want to risk meeting his eye. "Do you resist the idea because of me?"

"I do not know what you mean."

He felt quite certain she did. Her knee brushed his foot as she turned slightly toward the door. Though he did not suspect she was a coward, he was glad of his foresight to block the exit. "Well, Miss Parr?"

The carriage began to slow. The cadence of the horse's hooves changed and the cab ceased to rock. "The theatre," she announced.

"Yes." South did not move. "Be so kind as to answer the question."

She started to rise. For the first time she realized he was in her way. "You said I must make a pretense of some errand. I am prepared now to do that."

"I will go with you."

India sat down quickly. "No."

"Very well. Answer the question I put to you."

The carriage bobbled as the driver climbed down. India

threw up her hood, tucking a wayward strand of pale hair inside. She made certain the frog at her throat was secure. "He will open the door," she said urgently. "Let me pass."

"You are concerned someone will see us together."

"Please," she said huskily. "Remove your leg."

"Miss Parr." There was an absence of patience in his tone. The door rattled slightly.

India fumbled for the handle from the inside. "My lord, sit back. I will return quickly."

It occurred to him that she might not return at all. For all that she had been anxious to relate her information this evening, she had taken considerable pains not to be seen with him.

What would be the consequences, he wondered, if he were to make certain exactly the opposite happened? South prepared himself to find out. Leaning forward, he pulled India Parr onto his lap and used her openmouthed surprise to press his lips to hers.

The carriage door swung open.

Chapter Four

Her lips were cool at first touch. South imagined the condition had much to do with the blood draining from her face. She had no reason to anticipate that he would treat her with so little regard, and indeed, he had no liking for breaking her trust. For all that he had pulled her abruptly into his arms, he managed to hold her carefully, supporting her weight in a cradle of his arms and thighs, protecting the back of her head by cupping it in one hand. Strands of her silky hair sifted through his fingertips. He was met by the faint scents of soap and lilac as his fingers delved more deeply to rest firmly against her scalp.

South did not press his first advantage of surprise. He did not change the slant of his mouth over hers or run his tongue along the line of her lips as he was wont to do. His eyes were not entirely closed. He kept the merest fraction of his hooded glance on the opening, where the driver was still fumbling to shut the door that had been flung to one side.

This was finally accomplished with a considerable degree of force, some rending of material, and several embarrassed, apologetic utterances. None of it was done, however, before the pair of men walking past the carriage had halted and taken their fill of the interior tableau.

The cab was thrust into darkness again by the closing of the door. South lifted his head slowly, but not far. "Have a care what you say or do," he whispered. "There is an audience still attending our performance, whether they can see it or not."

India did nothing. She neither struggled to get up—a response she thought undignified at this juncture—nor permitted herself the luxury of relaxing against him, a response she considered too revealing in nature. She remained precisely where she was, trying not to think forward to the consequences of his actions.

"Have you swooned, Miss Parr?" South asked with polite interest.

Her tone was a trifle acerbic. "No, my lord. You can be quite certain that is not the case."

"Oh."

India wondered at his capacity to derive humor from the situation and, in turn, make her find the same. She felt the corners of her mouth edging upward and was glad for the darkness that kept him from being witness to it. "Was it your intent to provoke such a response?"

"No," he admitted. "It would have been deuced inconvenient."

"You have no smelling salts at the ready, I take it."

"None."

She stared up at him, trying to make out his fine, handsome features. She had to rely on her memory instead to find the quicksilver smile she knew was flickering about his mouth and lending his eyes a certain roguish glint. Why had he come so late to her life? she wondered. It was a thought that required rigorous suppression and received her full attention so that it was immediately accomplished. What she said was, "You, my lord, are a complete hand."

South made no reply for a moment, and still, when he spoke, he could not shake the husky timbre from his voice. "And you, Miss Parr, are a handful."

He helped her move then, as he knew he must. When she was seated on the opposite bench once more, he found the blind and snapped it. Its fluttering intruded loudly on the silence they had only imagined surrounded them. Moonshine lighted the interior of the hackney and tinted India's complexion in a pale blue wash. She was perfectly composed, though he suspected composure was not at all what she felt.

"You will explain yourself, won't you?" she asked softly, her voice barely carrying across the small space separating them.

Aware that the driver had not moved, nor had the two men who had been raptly attentive to their brief intimacy, Southerton leaned forward and raised India's hood again. "Soon enough," he said. "You will go into the theatre now on whatever errand you have devised."

India nodded. She could still feel his fingers touching her hair, tucking flyaway strands around her ears, sliding along the back of her neck from the base of her skull to her shoulders. It didn't seem to matter that he was already reaching for the door, prepared to open it. The gentle, concerned touch of him was still upon her as she accepted the driver's assistance and climbed down.

"Good evening, India." James Kent separated himself from the man at his side and stepped forward. He did not directly block India's path, but his intention to gain her notice was clear.

She stopped and lifted her bowed head. "Mr. Kent." There was no need to inject a note of surprise in her voice. It was her natural reaction to be confronted by the theatre's manager and occasional director at this hour. "You are rather late leaving tonight, are you not?"

"Tallying receipts," he explained. "A tiresome but necessary business."

"And the totals?"

James Kent was not given to effusive displays of emotion. Although he demanded something different from the actors under his direction and care, he wasted little effort demonstrating the same. "Satisfying," he said levelly. "A happy consequence when you take the lead, India."

She did not think he sounded particularly happy, but she refrained from pointing this out. "It is kind of you to say so." India inclined her head in a parting nod and made to pass. Kent fell into step beside her instead. "There is no need for you to accompany me," she told him. "I have a key. You gave it to me, if you would but recall. I can show myself in."

"It is no trouble." He glanced toward his companion and motioned for him to wait. "I will only be a moment."

India did not hear the other man's reply. She supposed he merely nodded. It took a measure of self-control not to turn and identify Kent's companion. It was no one from the troupe or he would have made himself known as Kent had. "Really," India said, "there is no need."

"And really," Kent countered, "it is no trouble."

She did not press further objection to his company. "Then thank you. I will be but a moment. I have only come for the script you distributed tonight." She felt rather than saw Kent glance back toward her rented hack.

"You are, perhaps, giving a private performance this evening, India?"

She did not stiffen, because his question was not unexpected. "Not so private as I might have wished," she admitted without any hint of embarrassment.

James Kent was possessed of a thin, angular frame that barely filled out his skin, let alone his black frock coat. It hung from his shoulders with no regard for where the seams were placed. Pressing one hand to his chin, Kent rubbed the bony point with his thumb and forefinger as India opened the rear entrance to the theatre he had locked but minutes before. His mild tone couched the import of his words. "Have I reason to be concerned, India?"

She felt an all too familiar tightening in her throat. India had known James Kent too long to be deceived by his offhanded interest. "I cannot say if you should be concerned," she told him. "Only that I am not."

He said nothing, helping her light the lantern hanging just inside the door instead. Kent took it from her hands and raised it, studying India's face. "I've worked too long with actors to have any particular fondness for them. In the main, I find them a means to an end."

India had heard this blunt speech before. "So you have said." She began to walk away from him and toward her dressing room.

"It is always troubling when one such as yourself is placed in so prominent a position. The public clamors for your work, and I, perforce, must accede to their demands or accept their disapproval. I find their dictates tiresome, yet cannot dismiss their interest for my own." He paused, allowing silence to underscore his words. "I put the question to you again, India. Do I have reason to be concerned?"

She rounded on him. "How am I to answer that when you cannot decide if your life would be improved with my presence or the lack of the same? If your concern were for me, Mr. Kent, I should be glad of it, but it is only for yourself, and I find it intrusive in the extreme."

The director was not deterred. "And what of the troupe? I speak for all of them."

Because there was truth to that, India relented. "I have no intention of leaving the theatre," she said. "You are making too much of what you saw or think you saw."

"Oh, I know what I saw, India. It is the Viscount Southerton, is it not?"

India turned and began walking again, taking pains not to rush her steps.

"Is it an affair of long standing?" he asked. It was difficult to believe that such was the case. There was little that India Parr did that did not come to his attention. Quickly. "I had heard Rutherford."

"Really," she said, giving neither credence nor lie to the rumor. "How odd." India entered her dressing room, found the script of Morton's comedy *Speed the Plough* on the table among her pots of rouge and paint, and picked it up. She waved it in front of Kent. "You cannot fault my dedication."

"No, not that." The words were offered reluctantly, as though it pained him to admit it, which it very nearly did. He regarded her gravely, his next offering nearly choking him. "Have a care, India. Whatever Southerton's interest, it can only be in passing. And until it passes, it is bound to cause difficulties for you."

"Why, Mr. Kent, I believe you are evincing some concern for me after all."

The sound he made came from deep at the back of his throat and could be taken as gruff denial or simply a need to clear it. He held up the lantern as she passed again, and followed her back into the corridor. "I hasten to add it will cause difficulties for all of us. Southerton is the Earl of Redding's heir, you know."

"Yes."

"You shouldn't have clobbered him on the chin."

So Mr. Kent had heard about that, also. There was no point in telling him the viscount had invited that action. "He and his friends behaved boorishly, and his apology was without sincerity."

"Mrs. Garrety related you delivered a facer that would have done a Corinthian proud."

India shrugged.

"I fear it is what has piqued his interest in you."

"You are assuming he is my companion," she said. "I would remind you that I have not said the same." They walked the remainder of the way to the exit without a word passing between them. The hack was waiting for her. Kent's companion was gone. "Your friend appears to have deserted you."

"No particular friend, India. An investor, I had hoped."

The faint smile that had softened her features vanished, and she turned sharply to look at Kent. "I hope you made no promises to him on my behalf, Mr. Kent."

There was no change in Kent's grave and gaunt visage, no indication that he was in the least offended. "I am no pimp."

"As a man who allows that his actors are but a means

to an end," she said without inflection, "it is the very definition of what you are." India did not pause as Kent was stopped in his tracks by her unaffected riposte. The driver came to attention as she approached the hack, and opened the door for her. She climbed in, ignoring the hand Southerton extended to her, and sat down. "Oh, do let us be off," she said wearily. "I am for the comfort of my own bed." And lest Southerton mistake this for an invitation, she added, "Alone."

South's chuckle rumbled pleasantly. He rapped on the communicating door with the driver, and the hack rolled forward. "That was Kent, wasn't it? The manager?"

India felt certain South knew the answer to his own question, but she answered anyway. "Yes. He also happens to be the director of our current production and our next." Her thumbnail flicked the loosely bound pages of script. "Morton's *Speed the Plough.*"

"A good choice."

"Yes. He is not to be faulted for his talent in choosing promising material." India sat, gave her head a small toss, and let the hood fall away again. When she realized she was sitting uncomfortably on the back of her cloak, India merely unfastened the heavily embroidered frog at the base of her throat rather than move and right the material. "He saw you, just as you intended he should. I did not confirm it, though he put the question to me often enough. I cannot say why I left him wondering, except to suppose it is because I dislike being the subject of his interrogation as much as I dislike your using me."

South made no response to this. He asked instead, "And the other man?"

"An investor, Mr. Kent told me. Or at least he was in anticipation of such a coup. I collect I was to have figured in some way in the man's interest. You might have dashed his hopes."

Southerton's dark brow creased as he considered what she was telling him. It was not only the content that troubled him but the disinterest with which she related it. "What are you saying, Miss Parr? That Kent holds out the promise of your affections to these plump-pocketed asses?''

"Better to be the carrot than the stick," she said philosophically. When this quiet rejoinder was met by silence, she went on. "Never say you mean to be high in the instep about it, not after you made me a pawn in your own game. My value to the company has always been more than my onstage performance. A public liaison with any one man diminishes the hope that I will be another's.''

"You have no say in the matter?"

"On the contrary, I have a great deal to say, and none of it that matters. Mr. Kent does as he will. You do as you will. As for me, my lord, I am no whore but merely play at one at the behest of those who would have it so.''

There was a faint ringing in South's ears as if they had been thoroughly boxed. The dressing-down she delivered smarted at least as much and humbled him more. "In the future," he said sardonically, "you will simply clap me smartly on either side of the head and have done with it.''

"As you wish."

He did not think he had mistaken a slight change in the shape of her mouth as she let her head rest against the side of the carriage. "Tell me, Miss Parr, could Mr. Kent be moved to murder?''

She cocked one brow but did not raise her drooping eyelids. The script she had in her hands was allowed to slide to a place on the bench beside her. "Only if an actor forgets his lines, or the receipts fall short of expectations.''

"I am serious."

"As am I." India roused herself to more industry when Southerton said nothing. She reminded herself that she did not know the well of this man's patience. Mayhap she had plumbed those depths already. "I cannot say what Mr. Kent could be moved to do if he perceived his company was threatened. But you will make a practice of looking over your shoulder, won't you? Contrary to my cautions, you deliberately brought attention to yourself this evening. By tomorrow your name may well be linked with mine, and

the exact nature of our exchange will not go unremarked."
India pushed herself upright and regarded him as frankly as
the veil of moonlight would allow. "How do you propose
to proceed, my lord?"

South did not mistake her meaning. "I intend to draw
out Kendall's murderer," he said. "Whether it is the colonel's affairs or your own that provided someone with motive
. . ." He shrugged. "You must see you are the common link,
Miss Parr. I believe that more time in your company, not
less, is the proper response."

"I see." She had suspected this would be his answer.
"What is it you expect of me? I told you there was
someone."

"I know what you told me."

"You do not believe me?"

"It is not that exactly," he admitted. "Only that I have
been unable to discover his identity."

"Aaah," she mocked him gently. "How frustrating for
you."

Southerton wondered at the ease with which she accepted
his declaration of failure. Was she truly so confident that
the identity of such a person could not be found? "Not so
much frustrating," he denied, "as challenging."

"Did you inquire of the colonel?"

"He was the first person I asked."

"And?"

"He was unaware of any romantic liaison."

She smiled, but no part of it touched her dark eyes. Her
gaze remained level. "You would do well to turn your
attentions elsewhere, my lord."

He raised one eyebrow. "You are threatening me, perhaps?"

"Hardly. I merely wish to point you in a direction where
something might be accomplished. If I were to tell you that
your probing into my affairs—and I do not use that word
in the same loose manner as you are prone to do—places
me at more risk than anything I have undertaken on the

colonel's behalf, could you be persuaded to put a period to it?"

"Are you telling me that?"

Now it was India who hesitated. "Yes," she said at last. "If it is your desire to protect me, then you must know your inquiries may kindle quite a different flame."

Where was the threat? South wondered. Mr. Kent? The lover she would not name? Who was it she feared? "Consider it done," he said.

She did not insult him by asking if she could depend upon his word. "Very well. Then we have arrived at the matter of how to proceed."

"How to—"

India held up one hand, stopping him as the carriage slowed in front of her house. "Can we not simply agree on arrangements that will allow me to assist the colonel without necessitating you living in my pockets? That is what you had in mind, is it not? To become my very public protector?"

"It had occurred to me," he admitted.

"Then mayhap I am protecting you, my lord, by refusing such, for surely we would not suit."

South was not certain of that at all. Still, he felt compelled to point out, "It would have been for appearances only."

"Of course," she said dryly. "An arrangement of convenience."

South was moved to laughter. "Very well," he admitted. "You have me there." He was unused to being cornered so neatly. And this notion that she was somehow protecting him? It was intriguing. Though she had not issued a challenge, South thought he might be of a mind to disprove her notion that they would not suit.

"Well, my lord?" India prompted when South made no further reply. "You are musing rather overlong."

"What? Hmmm, yes. So I was." He brought himself fully to the present. "Our mutual protection, then. Let us agree." South was unprepared for the breadth of smile this small concession raised. India's lips parted, showing the white ridges of her teeth and tiniest slip of tongue pressed between them. It struck him that he had witnessed this animation in her before, but only from the distance of Eastlyn's box or his seat in the audience. He could be a fool for a smile such as the one she shared with him now. Onstage that smile made the lights redundant. Here, in the shadowed confines of a rented hack, India Parr had done the same with the moon.

"Where do you go?" she asked softly, her smile slipping away and her features returning to their naturally cool composure.

Torture could not have wrung the admission from him that he had just been to the moon and back. Though if she had smiled again he might have confessed all. "I just wander off," he said. "I have been advised that it is a most annoying and impolite custom of mine. I beg your pardon if I have given offense."

She shrugged lightly, shaking her head. Far from giving offense, she found his introspection appealed to her. These brief unguarded moments allowed her to study him without fear of discovery or consequence. If he were her lover she might watch him in the same manner while he slept lightly beside her, his breathing softly drawn through slightly parted lips, his lashes laid down in a perfect dark arc beneath his eyes. "I do not mind."

"You would be the first who did not."

"Then you are acquainted with far too many intolerant people, my lord."

Southerton grinned. "I believe you are in the right of it there, Miss Parr. I will tell them." When India leaned forward and extended her hand, Southerton first thought she meant to touch him. The jolt he felt at the thought of it was in direct proportion to the disappointment he knew when she did not. Her slim fingers curled around the door handle instead.

"The driver," she said, "is taking his cue from us this time." She raised the handle but did not open the door. "Will you be accompanying me inside, my lord?"

Southerton very much wanted to do just that. Caution

made him hesitate. "Let us see what Mr. Kent and his investor make of our carriage tryst," he said. "I am not convinced the wags will have the tale on the morrow. Kent will have his own selfish reasons for not carrying tales. He could prevail upon his investor to do the same. If there is no nine-days wonder, then perhaps we may attend to the matter of our mutual protection in secrecy. That is what you wanted from the beginning, is it not?"

She had. India refused herself the weakness of being contrary now. Protecting Southerton from things he did not understand—because she could not explain—gave her only three choices that she could immediately determine. She must cut him from her life entirely or allow him to live in her pockets. The third alternative was to proceed with such secrecy that it appeared he had no significance in her life.

Which he did not, she reminded herself. Even for the colonel, Southerton could have no wish to align himself with an actress, who by virtue of her profession was already possessed of a certain reputation. Oh, she knew the viscount's own repute would not be harmed by a public liaison with her. In truth, among his own set it might well be enhanced, if such a thing were possible. She was the one with much to lose by so public a connection to any man. For all that Mr. Kent might hold out the promise of companionship to an interested investor, she had never allowed herself to be compromised. No man who sought favor with her in the crowded confines of her dressing room had ever been granted private moments to do the same.

London society was slowly discovering that India Parr did not comfortably fit the mold cast for her. Even in the rarified air of the *ton,* where haughty noses were often raised so they would not whiff their own stench, allowances were being made for her. Yes, she had much to lose.

"You are frowning, Miss Parr," South said, watching her closely. "Has my question overset you?"

India felt the tension around her mouth and brow only after South brought it to mind. Not only was she frowning, she had the first inklings of a headache. It did not bode well for the sleep she deserved. "Explain to me how we may meet again with no attention coming to us. If that can be accomplished, my lord, then we are done hiring hacks between us."

South's laughter was a deep, pleasant rumble. "An uncertain arrangement at best, was it not? Very well, Miss Parr. You have but to place a notice in the *Gazette*. Most any sort will do. What name do you fancy for yourself?"

She thought a moment. "Hortense?"

Since Hortense was not a character she played but one her character addressed in the course of the play, South decided it could be employed for the time being. "And I will use the initials T. C. S."

"T. C. S?"

"The Colonel's Servant, if you will."

"And then?" she asked.

"And then I shall come to you," he told her. "Never the other way around."

"But . . ."

"It must be so, Miss Parr."

She acquiesced because she could identify no other choice. "As you wish."

"Not a wish," he said firmly. "An imperative."

Though it chafed a bit to take his direction, India nodded. "I understand."

"Good." South realized there was no longer any reason to linger in her company. He quelled the desire to raise her hand to his lips. "Farewell."

She nodded once, unwittingly pressing the knuckles he would have kissed to her mouth as she did so. She returned them to the handle and swung the door open. "Farewell, my lord."

Then she was gone. A few moments later, so was he.

It was a good parting, Southerton reflected later. They did not come to the attention of the wags and thus were free of public scrutiny. Their terms were set. They had agreement on how they meant to go on. India would continue to apprise him of such matters as she knew to be of interest to the colonel, and he would tread carefully where her private affairs were concerned. He related as much to Blackwood and was given the colonel's cautious approval to proceed.

To that end, South made no further inquiries into the identity of India's protector. He did not, however, cease to remain fully aware of her routine. In deference to her concerns, this was accomplished in the main through trusted individuals in his employ.

Because he knew everything had been done with discretion, it was all the more difficult to comprehend when the first intelligence he had of India Parr arrived in the *Times,* not the *Gazette,* and the import of it had the kick of a cannon's recoil.

> *London's diamond of the stage has caught the eye of one Lord M, recently returned to town from the Continent. It is said she has accepted his attentions exclusive of all others. It only remains to be seen how long a mourning period her defection will inspire in her devoted following.*

Lord M? Who the bloody devil was Lord M? India had not seen anyone this fortnight past that she had not seen regularly. The visitors to her dressing room had not changed. The same hopefuls came to her with the same praise and pledges. At home she received only her dresser, the wardrobe mistress, Mr. Kent, and the lad Doobin. Her existence when she wasn't onstage was private, even insular.

Southerton tossed his carefully creased copy of the *Times* to the foot of his bed. His breakfast tray wobbled across his lap. What had he missed? he wondered. How had he allowed himself to be shilly-shallied down this primrose path? What M's did he know? Montrose. Milbourne. Matthews. Macquey-Howell. Morris.

"Darrow!"

South's valet appeared on the threshold between the dressing room and the bedchamber. "My lord?" He gave no indication, either by inflection or raised brow, that he was unused to being called in such peremptory tones.

"I want you to place a notice in the *Gazette*," South said. "Anything you like will do. Only use the initials T. C. S. somewhere in the bloody thing." That would serve as notice that he intended to seek her out. Miss Parr could wonder and worry when it would happen. South did not feel compelled to ease her mind with specifics.

"T. C. S., my lord. Of course." He hovered for a moment, regarding his employer through a dark gaze that had perceptibly narrowed. Southerton had arrived home late last night or early this morning, depending on one's view of such things. It was of no concern to Darrow, merely a detail. The viscount's vaguely ashen complexion, the thick, wayward cross-hatching of black hair, and the rigid line about the mouth and jaw were what drew Darrow's attention. "It was Lady Calumet's gala last evening, was it not?"

Distracted, South simply nodded.

"I will fetch the remedy," Darrow said. He turned to go only to be brought up short as Southerton recovered his wits.

"The hell you will," South countered sharply. "I have no need for it."

"Begging your pardon, my lord, but you always say that and then you drink it and are the better for it. It is the salt and tomato seeds, you know. They purge the poisons."

Some color returned to South's complexion. The problem was that it was gray. "Have done, man. Your talk alone curdles the contents of my stomach. In any event, you mistake the cause of my foul mood." He made a dismissive, impatient gesture. "The dowager duchess's fete was unexceptional." Actually, the evening had been highly diverting, and in another frame of mind South would have humored his valet with the finer points.

His companion to the duchess's home had been North's lovely wife, a circumstance which made the night's affair exceptional from the outset. Northam, chafing a bit that his

countess had helped hatch the scheme, was left at home to
twiddle his thumbs with East and Marchman as his amiable
alibis. It had all been in aid of helping North apprehend the
notorious Gentleman Thief, and Southerton had not had a
moment's hesitation in volunteering his services. An evening
in the company of North's countess was infinitely preferable
to the prospect of yet another performance of French farce
in Drury Lane. Still more important was that no wretched
disguise was required to attend her grace's ball.

He had come close to catching his man. Or North's man,
he reminded himself. He had come upon evidence the thief
had done his work again, only to lose sight of his quarry
on the duchess's rooftop. He might have given chase, but
his responsibility to Elizabeth forced him back to the squeeze
downstairs. He allowed his friends to tease that he'd been
more concerned with rending a sleeve or staining the velvet
collar of his coat than he had been with stopping the thief.
Elizabeth was the only one who found his response to stay
off the rooftops at all sensible.

South wondered what she would say if she knew how he
regretted it. He hadn't been thinking entirely of her, though
he was gentleman enough not to admit it. His responsibility
to India Parr had also been on his mind. He would be no
good to her if a single misstep plummeted him headlong
into the duchess's rosebushes.

But then again, he had not known last night that she had
made another arrangement with her mysterious protector.

Out of the corner of his eye, Southerton saw that his valet
was still hovering in the doorway. "The announcement,
Darrow," he repeated, pressing three fingertips to his temple.
"The *Gazette*. That is all I require at the moment. See to it
yourself. I don't want it bumbled."

"Right away, my lord."

"And Darrow?"

"Yes, m'lord?"

"If there is no improvement to my head within the hour,
I believe I will try that remedy."

Darrow said nothing. The morning was bound to improve if the viscount came around to thinking it was his own idea.

India pressed a linen napkin to her mouth. For a moment she thought she would be sick. A copy of the *Times* lay beside her plate, folded so the column she had been told to read was front and center. She did not look up until she had some control over her speech. There was no predicting when color would return to her blanched features.

At the opposite end of the breakfast table, the Earl of Margrave made a steeple of his long, elegantly shaped fingers and rested his chin on the points. It was not an attitude of prayer but of stern contemplation. His eyes were dark: the color of coffee without cream, bitter chocolate without milk. He watched her narrowly, with the flat, still, unnerving gaze of a predator. His smile, though, when India lifted her eyes to his, was pleasant enough. He had been told he had a beautiful smile, and if he were to judge by its effect on the women of his acquaintance, then it was no mere flattery.

At birth he had received the title Viscount Newland and the Christian name Allen. His mother was the only one to address him familiarly as Allen. To his father and his schoolmates at Hambrick he was Newland. Upon the death of his father seven years ago, Newland became Margrave, and almost without exception was addressed as such by his peers. India Parr fell outside all the neatly drawn boundaries, and he made allowance for this. He preferred that she address him as Margrave but did not refine too much upon it if she forgot and called him Newland.

They had known each other long enough that such could be brushed aside, provided she did not do it to provoke him. He had never pretended there was no end to his patience with her. She must be sensing that she had finally reached it.

He was twenty-eight years old, five years India's senior, but the attitude and tone he adopted toward her was as often parental, even proprietary, as it was intimate.

"This was unnecessary," India said, lowering her napkin. "I wish you had not done it." She smoothed it across her lap, hiding fingers that trembled slightly. She was angry, to be sure, but she also wondered at the emotion that made it surge inside her. Fear? Hurt? The prospect of further loneliness? "I thought we were agreed it need not come to this."

"That was your opinion, India. One I never shared."

India felt her stomach lurch again. If she were sick in front of him, she would never forgive herself and he would never forget. He was watching her closely, as though looking for some sign that she was injured or, more than that, suffering. If she were a cricket in a cage, he'd have just finished wrenching a leg free. Never the cage alone to trap his quarry. Must needs have crippled the creature as well. "You might have told me of your intention to do this."

Margrave did not lift his chin from where it rested on the points of his fingertips, but his smile deepened. "And listen to all your arguments to the contrary? I think not." Now he straightened his slim frame and sat back comfortably in his chair. His hair curled naturally close to his scalp, giving definition to the shape of his head and framing his brow and temples. He wore it in the common mode of consciously crafted carelessness and was never bothered by the paradox of such fashions. When a lock of gold and ginger fell forward, he did not raise a hand to rake it into place, but gave his head a toss instead, like a restless colt would fling his mane. "Have done with your pouting," he told her. "It is unseemly and changes nothing. I am set on the matter."

"For how long?"

"I have not decided." While his eyes continued to study India carefully, his shrug communicated indifference. "I suppose until your company ceases to amuse me. It is perhaps unfortunate, my dear India, that you have never had the least notion of what I find entertaining." He gave her an arch look as he picked up his fork. "One could even deduce from this that I am agreeably diverted by your very ignorance."

"And one would be wrong," she said flatly. "It is never so simple as that."

He laughed. "You see? You have amused me already and we are only at breakfast. It bodes well for a promising day." Margrave carefully cut a wedge from a slice of tomato and placed it in his mouth. "Eat, Dini. You will feel the better for it."

"India," she said.

"My pet has no use for pet names? Is that what you're telling me?"

India did not deign to respond to his assertion that she was his pet. It was too uncomfortably close to the truth. Denial might do more than merely amuse him; it might challenge him to prove it. Above all things she did not want that. "My name is India," she said with some dignity. "I have given you leave to use it. I would not take it upon myself to tell you more than that."

Margrave's chuckle was melodious. "Oh, yes, you would," he countered. "But I can see you are making an effort not to be entirely disagreeable. Now, do worry less about biting your tongue and apply those delicate buds to breaking your fast."

India stared at her plate. She thought she might manage the soft-cooked egg, but the sausages and toast and tomato would certainly remain uneaten. Picking up her spoon, she tapped the crown of her egg and began peeling away the shell. "I have rehearsal this morning," she said.

"I know. *Speed the Plough.*"

"You suggested the play to Kent, didn't you?"

"Of course."

"When?"

"I couldn't say. A few months back, I suppose. It cannot be important. I am in regular correspondence with him, as well you know."

She did. She also knew it was a correspondence that went in one direction only. Margrave would not have supplied Kent with the means to make a reply. That might have suggested there was some equal footing in their partnership.

India was clear in her own mind, even if James Kent was not, that the Earl of Margrave always maintained the high ground.

"I care very much about your success," Margrave said suddenly.

India glanced up in time to catch the earnestness she'd only heard in his voice just fading from his features. It would have been a mistake to suppose such a moment was unguarded or marked by weakness. Some observers might have found Margrave's countenance stamped with certain effeminate characteristics—the delicately pared nose, for example, or the well-defined, sensual mouth. His expression might be described as boyish or a shade wistful. This, too, would have been an error in judgment. What India glimpsed in his face and mien was not youthfulness but immaturity, the desire for approval giving way quickly to the demand for the same. He was a boy, not boyish, without heart but without consciousness of the lack of it.

It made him a predator without peer.

"I know my success is important to you," India said. It was not quite as he had stated, but her words were more the truth than his own.

A shadow flickered across Margrave's features as he considered taking issue with her. He let it pass. "You will forgive me for the *Times* entry, will you not? It will be tiresome for you to continue to refine upon it. How will you learn your lines if your thoughts are drifting elsewhere?"

"I know my lines."

Margrave continued to apply himself to his breakfast, his appetite undiminished by her contrariness. "Will Southerton see the announcement, do you think?"

"I cannot possibly say."

"He will hear of it, though."

"That seems likely." A chill ran under her skin, raising gooseflesh along the length of her arms. She would have risen and gone to the hearth to warm herself if Margrave would not have derived satisfaction from it.

"He was there last night, you know."

"At Lady Calumet's?"

Margrave nodded. "It was a decent piece of luck I found my own invitation. Being so long from this country as I was, it is remarkable the disagreeable old bitch had the presence of mind to place me on her guest list." He shrugged. "But then, she counts my mother as one of her many dearest friends. That seems to be more important than the fact that she and my mother actually share some ancestor. A grandmother? Great-grandmother?" He pondered this a moment, then dismissed the tenuous blood connection from his mind. "It signifies nothing. It is more to the point that she has such a large number of dearest friends. Curious, that. Is it always that way when one arrives at a certain age, do you think?"

"I do not know."

"Perhaps it will be so with us," Margrave said. "By virtue of the fact that we survive into old age together, you and I shall be the dearest of friends." He regarded her with a slight smile twisting his lips but was not in anticipation of a reply. He continued in the same rhetorical bent. "Who else will be part of our dearest circle? I can think of no one now."

India spooned a bit of soft egg into her mouth. It had little taste, but it went down easily enough and it helped her swallow the ache at the back of her throat. She managed to keep threatening tears at bay.

"Aaah, India, you are not going to play, are you? That is very bad of you, you know. Will you ask nothing at all about him? I can tell you whatever you'd like."

She dipped her spoon once more into the bowl of her egg.

"I shall tell you anyway," he said. "Because it pleases me to do so. But first, about the evening." Margrave set his fork down and traced the flourished edges of the silver stem with two carefully manicured nails. "It was every bit the crush I predicted. I was reacquainted with any number of people I could have wished never to see again, which is always the hellish side of an evening such as it was. Though

I did see Barlough and several others from my misspent Hambrick youth; therefore, it was also not without reward."

Margrave picked up his coffee cup and sipped. "At the moment I thought the evening had grown especially wearing, we were entertained by the appearance of the Gentleman Thief." He nodded toward the newspaper beside India's plate. "You can read an account of it there. I can tell you it caused a stir. Thank God. We might have expired for lack of fresh air otherwise."

"You saw the Gentleman?"

"No. More's the pity. What a coup it would have been to have captured the fellow." He briefly contemplated the laurels that would have been his to wear, then dismissed it from his mind. "The vandal apparently made free with the dowager's jewelry; a sapphire and diamond necklace is the missing piece. It is an intriguing notion that he was one of the invited guests, is it not? I suppose it is why his identity is a constant source of such delicious speculation. Why, India, it may have even been your viscount. I lost sight of him not long before the act of the theft was revealed."

Keeping her voice carefully neutral, she said, "I have heard the Earl of Northam's name linked to the Gentleman."

"Northam? He was not present. That will remove his name from the *ton*'s collective dance card." He paused a beat, placed his cup back in its saucer. "His wife was there, though. On the arm of Southerton."

India blinked. A touch of color returned to her cheeks.

Margrave lifted his eyes heavenward. "Finally," he said. "She evinces some measure of surprise." He regarded India again. "I began to despair that I could move you from that forced expression of serenity. That it should require something so mundane as a hint of another woman, it is not well done of you, India. Jealousy is quite beneath you. Lady Northam is in no way your equal, and if she is an example of what Southerton finds to his liking, the sooner he is displaced in your affections, the better." His smile teased her. "I believe I have arrived in time to save you from yourself."

India said evenly, "She is the Countess of Northam and the daughter of the Earl of Rosemont, and I am in no way *her* equal, though I suspect it was your intent to remind me. Your concern that I aspire to something beyond my station is entirely misplaced, my lord. I have found the position to which I am best suited."

"Better than being a governess, eh?"

"Infinitely."

"God, what a debacle that was. Olmstead trying to poke you at every turn. Except for what relief he could give himself, the man's cock was in a perpetual state of hardness." Margrave saw that he could not use crudity to rouse India to reveal more emotion. He sighed and put the Olmstead business behind him. "I meant precisely what I said about Lady Northam," he told her. "Though I imagine she is a decent enough sort, she has none of your presence. For years she's gone about in society as the companion of Lady Battenburn. Can you imagine playing companion to the baroness when you are the daughter of an earl? It would be like you preferring the role of the nurse to Juliet."

"Not everyone wants to command the center of the stage."

"Bah! That is only because they *cannot* command it. She has a limp, you know. She is utterly without grace."

Trust Margrave to regard Lady Northam's physical infirmity as a character flaw. If he felt anything at all toward the countess, it was contempt, not sympathy. "You learned a great deal about her," India said.

"She was there with Southerton, as I said. You must allow I was curious. They seemed to find pleasure in each other's company." He leaned back in his chair. "I know South and his friends from Hambrick." Margrave saw by the almost imperceptible inclining of India's head that he had caught her interest. "Not well. They were older than I by three . . . no, four years. They stayed often to themselves. I remember they had some ridiculous name for their quartet." He waited to see if India would offer it up but she remained determinedly silent. "The Compass Club, I think it was. Yes, that was it. Never understood then. Oh, South was easy enough to explain. He had inherited the title Viscount Southerton by the time I knew him, so there was one point on the compass. But the others? Northam had an older brother and was not in expectation of becoming an earl. And Gabriel Whitney? God knows what roundaboutation happened to make him Marquess of Eastlyn. Marchman is still Marchman, though. Moreover, he's a bastard.''

A little of India's color faded again. She would not let Margrave dwell on Mr. Marchman's illegitimacy to poke his finger at her. With credible indifference she said, ''Perhaps he was called West so he could be included by them.''

''Perhaps. They excluded everyone else. I don't know why they would make an exception for Marchman.''

''Did you want to be a member of their club, Newland?''

Margrave's head came up sharply and his eyes darkened. ''No! I was years younger, I told you. They would have taken no notice of me.''

Which was not precisely an answer to the question she'd asked. There was a hint of ruddy color in the high arch of Margrave's cheeks. Why, he had! India realized with some small shock. It was such an astonishing notion that she did not know what to make of it. She had thought of him always as such an insular, solitary figure, so much like herself in that regard that she never suspected he might also share her secret yearning to belong. India cautioned herself against this gentling she felt toward him.

''My God,'' he said brusquely. ''You don't imagine you feel sorry for me, do you?'' That she might was untenable to him, more so because he had not planned that she should.

''Not at all,'' she said. That quickly he had shifted his vulnerability to her. All that was left to her was denial.

''Good.'' He warmed the coffee in his cup and drew another sip. ''Lest some doubt linger, Dini, that I wanted to be part of their little clutch, you should know I was a member of a much more influential group at Hambrick.''

''Oh? And what did you call yourselves?''

Margrave smiled. ''The Society of Bishops.''

Chapter Five

From his position in the park across the street, Southerton was free to observe India Parr's residence without fear of being identified himself. He had taken the precaution of graying his dark hair with a sprinkling of powder and wearing worn garments that were suited to a vendor of roasted chestnuts. He staked out his territory between a young girl offering bouquets of fresh flowers, and a puppeteer. His pockets jingled with the proof of a good morning's work. He was benefiting from the puppeteer's skill and the flower girl's comely looks.

Every Wednesday from eight until noon, the small park took on the atmosphere of a fairgrounds. The goods and services that were available changed according to the season; there were entertainments for the children and their nannies and a sampling of oddities for the curious seekers among the gentry. Servants came from the nearby residences to spend their coppers on treats for themselves. The park hummed with the gentle noise of commerce and the occasional squeal of a delighted child.

Southerton watched a footman leave India Parr's home by a side exit and take off on some errand for his mistress.

The servant returned shortly, followed not long afterward by a hackney. The driver pulled directly in front of the house, blocking South's view no matter how he tried to angle his head to improve his perspective. He knew the probable destination was the theatre at Drury Lane. India went nowhere else. South's frustration was that he could not see if she was finally alone.

He had known at the outset he would not follow her. Abandoning his place suddenly in the park would bring notice to him, and he did not want that. His hope had been to catch a glimpse of her with the mysterious Lord M. In the two days since the tease in the *Times,* there had been only speculation on the man's identity. The man himself remained elusive, at least in the presence of India Parr. Lord Macquey-Howell and Baron Montrose were the leaders in this tight horse race. The betting books at White's and other gentlemen's clubs were busy tracking the favorites, most of them setting odds at two to one. Lords Morris, Mapple, and Milbourne were also in the running. Sir Anthony Matthews was dismissed for never having been to the Continent in his lifetime, nor far from his country home near Gloucester. An interesting dark horse was Lord Embley, recently returned from the West Indies, or so the *on dit* had it.

There was no admission or denial from any of the men named in public or, as far as South knew, in private. This was not terribly surprising, since for some of them the speculation of a connection with Miss Parr had momentarily raised their standing among others of their set. Even Macquey-Howell, the only married candidate, was close-lipped. South suspected it had something to do with his wife, who was not likely to thank him for any behavior that held their marriage up to public scrutiny.

Lady Macquey-Howell had her bit of intrigue with the Spanish consul, after all.

South sold several more sacks of roasted chestnuts as a new group of children crowded around the puppeteer. He hawked his wares with no less enthusiasm than the flower girl sold her bunches of violets, all the while counting the

number of servants that passed in and out of the side entrance
to India's home, and looking for a face that perhaps didn't
belong. He recognized footmen and maids by sight now;
the cook, the cook's helper, even the seamstresses who came
and went from Madame Fournier's dress shop were known
to him. Mrs. Garrety sometimes arrived with costumes or
what looked to be sketchbooks of the same. The lad Doobin
was the most frequent visitor from the outside. South had
considered how he might gain the boy's cooperation to further his own ends but had not made any move to do so. He
suspected Doobin's first loyalties were to India Parr and that
bribery alone would not bring the boy to his side.

As though South's thoughts had the power to conjure an
image of the lad, Doobin appeared at street level, swung
wide around the lamppost near India's front door, and walked
jauntily along the narrow sidewalk, his hands dug deeply
into the pockets of his coat. It was the fact that Doobin had
set off in a direction opposite the one India had taken that
piqued South's interest. Looking at the few sacks of chestnuts he had remaining, Southerton determined he could
finally quit his area without comment. He turned over his
inventory to a grateful flower girl and told her to do with
it what she would; then he set himself off at a pace befitting
the older man he pretended to be.

It was not so much a merry chase as a meandering one.
Doobin took a circuitous route to his final destination, sometimes crossing the same street two or three times or ducking
suddenly into an alley, almost as if he anticipated someone
was interested in his movements. It caused South to look
around himself, wondering if the boy was acting less as
messenger for India Parr and more as bait. As much as the
latter thought niggled at him, he could find no evidence to
support it.

It was only when Doobin slowed in front of the town-
houses on Carrick Street that South realized where the boy
was most likely headed. This time it was Southerton who
disappeared into an alley. There were things he had to do
to prepare for the arrival of his young guest.

After giving orders that the boy be admitted and served pastries in the kitchen while he cooled his heels, South headed for his bedchamber, followed closely by his valet. Darrow helped him make short work of the ill-fitting tradesman clothes and powdered hair. In far less time than was their usual ritual, the valet had South turned out in buff nankeen breeches and riding boots. The shirt was from Firth's, the only establishment Southerton approved for his linens. The stock was neatly tied above a pale-blue silk waistcoat, and the chitterlings fell in a gentle wave on either side. Darrow assisted South into his double-breasted coat, smoothed the shoulders and back, fixing the tailored line, and pronounced his employer all of one piece.

Southerton was seated casually at a fine cherry-wood desk in his study when Doobin was admitted. After his name was announced in stentorian and important tones as Master Doobin, the boy required more in the way of urging from South's butler to enter the room. This consisted of the long-faced Mr. Parker placing two hands firmly between Doobin's bony shoulder blades and pushing, then quickly closing the pocket doors before escape was possible. The boy stood rooted in the exact spot where he had skidded to a halt, until South looked up from his feigned examination of some papers.

South did not rise. He looked the boy over, careful not to smile when he saw evidence in the powdered-sugar-and-chocolate smears that Doobin had availed himself heartily of the offered pastries. Southerton's tone hovered between mildly curious and complete indifference as he asked, "You have business with me, young sir?"

"Mmm, yes, m'lord."

"What's that? You'll have to speak up." South waved the boy over with a brusque gesture. "Come closer. I have no desire to strain my ears on your behalf."

Doobin quickly shuffled half the distance, then ground to a halt. His eyes were overlarge in his narrow face, and it was a struggle not to gawk at the surroundings in which he'd found himself thrust. "It's me from the theatre," he said by way of renewing his acquaintance. "Doobin. You gave me your card once to pass to Miss Parr. Mayhap it confused you when his nibs called me Master Doobin."

Southerton bit the inside of his cheek, but nothing about his outward countenance was altered. He continued to regard the boy with scant interest.

Doobin braced his slight shoulders as heat colored his cheeks. " 'Twas me that carried a message to yer club from Miss Parr not long ago."

"An impressive résumé," South said in dry accents. "If I have need of a go-between again I shall certainly inquire after your services." He watched the boy's color deepen even as his chin came up. "Was there something else?"

Doobin's weight shifted, but he held fast. "I have words from Miss Parr," he said.

"Is that so? From Miss Parr?" South leaned back in his chair and crossed his booted feet. "How novel. Words from her very lips?"

"Yes, m'lord. As God and Mrs. G. are my witnesses."

Mrs. G.? South wondered. Who would that be? God's wife? Then he remembered Mrs. Garrety and surmised she was Doobin's reference. God and Mrs. Garrety. Now there were a pair to hear India Parr's confessions. "Very well," he said, letting none of his irritation show. Could India not be trusted to communicate using the means they had established? "Let me hear these words."

"I'm to say she is desirous of your company. This evening, if you will. After 'er performance."

"At the theatre?"

Doobin shook his head adamantly. "She'll take a hack as usual and cross paths with you in the park across the way."

"I see." But he didn't, of course. South was beginning to think that, much against his will, he had been assigned a role in one of India's farces, penned by one Colonel John Blackwood. "She will simply . . . umm, cross paths with me."

"Yes, m'lord. That's what she said. Exactly."

South regarded the boy keenly. "There was no pressure brought to bear?"

Doobin's brow creased. "Don't rightly know what you mean, m'lord."

"No one else around to put these words in Miss Parr's mouth? Mr. Kent, for instance. Lord Macquey-Howell?"

"Mr. Kent? Oh, no. Miss Parr, she was at home when she gave me this message. Getting ready to go out for rehearsal, she was. I come by this morning to tell her it was called early, and it was a rush all around, I can tell you. Mrs. Garrety complaining and clucking about Miss Parr never getting enough sleep. Miss Parr apologizing that there wouldn't be enough time for my lesson. I stood back while everyone was fluttering, hopin' I'd be invited to ride with the hack; only then Miss Parr remembered she had this message for you." Doobin shrugged. "So here I am."

"So you are. You came here straightaway?"

Doobin considered that a moment before answering. "As straightaway as served, m'lord."

South recalled Doobin's meandering route and wondered at the instructions India had given the boy. "Miss Parr must trust you a great deal."

Doobin's chest puffed a little. "Indeed she does, m'lord."

"Does she often engage you in this manner?"

"As she needs, I suppose. It's not so easy for one like her to get about without notice. She's particular about her privacy, I think you'd say. Doesn't want me to attach a shadow to myself, if you know what I mean."

"I think I do," South said with a certain wryness. "And did you attach such a shadow when you came here?"

"No. Oh, there was one bloke I thought was matching my steps, but I rid myself of him easily enough."

Southerton only narrowly managed not to choke. Was the boy talking about him? He merely raised an eyebrow to encourage Doobin's elaboration.

"It was simple enough to avoid him, m'lord. Even if it was the old fellow's game, he couldn't keep up."

This time South had to clear his throat. Wouldn't his friends and the colonel like to know he'd been nearly caught out by this cunning, crafty lad? "You do very well by Miss Parr."

"Yes, m'lord. An' she does well by me."

If Doobin's blush was any indication—and South had to believe it was—the boy was deep in the throes of his first unrequited passion. He hoped India had the good sense to tread carefully around this child's heart. "What of her protector?"

"M'lord?"

Southerton leaned forward, dropping his forearms to his knees and addressing Doobin as a familiar and equal. "Let us be frank. You have heard the rumors, have you not? Miss Parr has accepted the attentions of a certain lord."

Doobin's chin came up. The sudden change in his host's demeanor from lord to confidant, and his need to defend India, conspired to make Doobin forget to hold his tongue. "I know what's being said. All the whispering about 'er . . . that she's taken a lover. It ain't true."

Since Southerton was of a similar inclination, he recognized he was predisposed to believe the boy. "How can you be so certain?"

"Because I ain't seen the like."

"None of them? Macquey-Howell? Embley? Montrose?"

Doobin shook his head fiercely. "I don't know them, m'lord."

"What makes you think you would? You cannot be privy to all of Miss Parr's intimates."

"I know you, don't I?" Doobin said with irrefutable logic.

"Morris? Mapple?"

"I heard their names, same as you, m'lord. Never from Miss Parr, though. I never had words for them, like I had for you and . . ."

"And?" Southerton prompted after a moment. He gauged Doobin's reluctance to say more and saw the boy was considering the consequences. He cautioned himself to be patient.

The reply, when it finally came, was barely audible, and Southerton had to strain to hear it.

"Well, there was a Mr. Kendall."

India put down her book at the first soft sound of footfalls in the carpeted hallway. Flames flickered in the hearth as her bedchamber door was quietly opened. Margrave entered without waiting for an invitation to do so.

"He was not there," he announced without preamble. "You warned him."

She shook her head. "You know that is not possible."

"Then the boy did."

"No!" India could not keep the alarm out of her voice. "He could not have. Think, Margrave. What suspicions could Doobin have that it was naught but a ruse? I did precisely as you instructed. If Southerton was not in the park, then it is because he does not trust me. You will do *nothing* to the boy. It must be clear between us on that count. Do you hear, my lord?"

He closed the distance between them and took India's chin in his hand, raising her face. Margrave did not mind that she regarded him stubbornly. It was more to the point that her mouth was firmly closed. The mutinous line of her sensual lips did not bother him in the least. Quiet was what he wanted from her. "I hear you," he said. "And so would your servants if you spoke but a whit more loudly. Have a care, India. I grow weary of taking your orders."

She could not have laughed at the absurdity of that statement even if she had been free to do so. India kept her chin still in the pocket of his palm and waited for Margrave to release her. In spite of the welcome news that nothing untoward had befallen Lord Southerton, India found herself chilled. It was always thus when Margrave held her.

The earl allowed his fingers to slip along the length of India's jaw before he released her. He saw that she was careful not to draw back. He had taught her that, taught her how it displeased him to be shown any proof that she merely suffered even his casual embrace. Stepping back, he regarded the pale sweep of her hair where it lay over one shoulder. She must have braided it earlier, he realized, then unwound it. Perhaps the process had been repeated a dozen times over the course of the evening, for the gold and platinum strands were faintly rippled. "It is a crime the current fashion is to wear the hair so high and full on the forehead. What man would not gladly give his fortune to look on yours as it is now? Unbound. Floating. You must tempt them all with the promise of it."

"I am sure you mistake the matter."

"Why do you say so?"

"I am surrounded by idle flatterers, and no man has ever intimated as much."

Margrave's laughter was low. He sat on the wide arm of the chair opposite India's and folded his arms across his chest. "Do you think I detect no insult in your words?"

"I meant none."

"*I* am a man." He waited to see if she would dare take issue with him. She did not. "And no idle flatterer. Is my observation about your hair of no account?"

"Forgive me," she said gravely. "Again, I meant no offense."

"Then give none. Wear your hair down for me. I find it soothing to look upon."

"Yes. Of course."

One of his brows kicked up. "So meekly compliant of a sudden? You must feel more for Southerton than I first suspected. Are you so relieved he remains unharmed?" Before she could answer, he went on. "Tell me, India, if it were put to you that the little maggot Doobin or the supremely arrogant viscount must go, whom would you choose?"

She said nothing. Her palms were damp, and a bead of moisture formed on her upper lip. India recognized the signs of the same sick feeling she sometimes encountered when she was about to step onstage. The difference was that she could not lose herself in this role. This was her life.

"That is unfair of me, is it not?" he said amiably. "Let us hope it does not come to that."

India reached behind her and dragged the shawl folded over the back of her chair across her lap. There was a glimpse of bare white calf as she adjusted it and inadvertently lifted her nightgown at the same time. When she looked up, she saw Margrave was watching her closely, his eyes fixed on the point where her leg had been uncovered. She could not name exactly what she saw in his expression. Desire? Regret? A fair amount of frustration? Perhaps it was all these things, she thought, and more besides. All of it confused by the heat of anger, so there was no peeling back a single layer of emotion. So often she thought of Margrave as having no emotion, it was odd to think that he might be possessed of too many.

Margrave looked up suddenly, caught India's eyes, and pinned her back in her chair. "I have decided to put a period to the speculation, India. I cannot abide the likes of Macquey-Howell and Mapple riding my coattails."

"Lord Macquey-Howell has sufficient coattails of his own."

"Hah! His wife's the well-connected one. It is unfortunate that her ambition exceeds her husband's ability. The countess seems to have no sense that she has overreached herself." He made a dismissive gesture, unwilling to pursue the topic with India. "Lord Mapple, though. Now, there is a toady. You should be embarrassed, Dini, that his name is linked to yours in the betting books."

"I am embarrassed by all of it," India said quietly. She drew a shallow breath. "How is it that your name has escaped the attention of the *ton,* my lord?"

"I imagine because I intimated to Lady Calumet that I was withdrawing immediately to the country to visit my mother. Such devotion to one's mother rather flies in the face of simultaneously securing a mistress. I confess I also like the idea of confounding the oddsmakers, for there is money to be wagered and won there when my name appears." He paused when India's mouth pressed itself in a tight line. "But I see talk of it merely causes you further distress. For that I am sorry."

India did not think he sounded in the least sorry. He merely mouthed the words. "How will you make yourself known?" she asked. "Shall you attend a performance? Greet me openly backstage? Am I to expect jewelry?"

"All of those things, I think." He smiled, his eyes darkening. "And something more besides."

She would not think on what he meant by that last, and yet she was afraid she would think of nothing else. "When?"

He shook his head. "I favor your genuine response to my attentions. Let us agree that surprise will add to the flavor."

She would be sick with the anticipation of it, and well Margrave knew it. "As you will."

"Yes," he said after a long moment. "As *I* will." He came to his feet and held out his hand. "Come. I would have you naked now."

The headache that was forming behind India's eyes was quite real. Mrs. Garrety glanced at her with concern. "A megrim, is it?" the dresser asked.

It hurt to nod. India did it anyway.

"Let me turn down the lamps." Mrs. Garrety moved quickly about the dressing room, turning back the wicks on each of the oil lamps and removing one out of the reflective line of the mirror. "There. Better, isn't it? Shall I pour a spoonful of laudanum for you?"

"No. I want to go home."

"In a moment. I have but a few things to finish—"

"I want to leave now."

The dresser's wiry brows jumped nearly to her graying hairline. The mole on her cheek twitched. "I'll flag a cab for ye."

"Please." India did not turn as Mrs. Garrety fled the dressing room. She sat very still on the stool, her head in her hands, and watched the glaze of pain shutter her expression until she was unrecognizable to herself. The eyes that stared back at her were Margrave's.

India drew back sharply, unnerved by what she glimpsed in the mirror. She was unaware that any sound had escaped her lips, until Doobin, always hovering nearby, appeared in the open doorway.

"Is everything all right, miss?" he asked. "I saw Mrs. Garrety hurry away."

"She's getting a hack for me."

"Then she'll be going home with ye tonight?"

"Yes. I have a megrim."

Doobin nodded. "Is there naught that I—"

"Leave," she said curtly.

The boy was too young to hide his hurt. He stared at her dumbly, eyes wide.

"For God's sake, take yourself off." India's voice rose in pitch. The taste of of her tone was like acid on her tongue. "Away!" Out of the corner of her eye she saw him take flight. Her eyes burned and her throat ached. She deserved a moment's respite, some peace from all the eyes that watched her. Hadn't she earned this small thing? "Aaah, Doobin," she whispered, allowing her eyelids to flutter closed. "You are too easily wounded."

By the time Mrs. Garrety returned, India was standing, her heavy velvet pelisse in hand. The dresser helped her into it, fussing over the brass buttons first, then the fit of the simple velvet hat that complimented the dark-emerald coat.

"You will not credit what I have just learned," Mrs. Garrety said.

India was in no mood to guess and did not attempt to do so.

"Mr. Kent has only this minute past informed me of a most interesting occurrence. The Duke of Westphal has curled up his toes this evening."

"Dukes die, don't they?" India asked wearily. She bent to pick up her reticule, feeling light-headed and a bit wobbly as she did so. "Surely they cannot be so high in the instep they think an exception will be made."

Mrs. Garrety made a clucking sound with her tongue. "Aren't you just the one?" She wound her arm through India's and let the younger woman lean against her. "This way. The hack's here for you."

India merely murmured her understanding.

"Poor dearie." Mrs. Garrety patted India's hand. "It was the footlamps tonight, was it not? They make fearsome fumes when the oil is poor quality. I shall speak to Mr. Kent about it directly and see that it's changed. He won't be thankin' us if ye pass out on the stage at yer next performance. And 'im with pockets as deep as the North Sea, thanks to you." The dresser kept up her monologue all the way to where the cab was waiting at the theatre exit.

The driver stepped lively at India's approach, peeling himself away from where he lounged against the wheel of the hack. He opened the door, assisted her entry, and accepted the directions offered by Mrs. Garrety.

India roused herself to peer out the carriage window. "You're not coming with me?"

"I'll be along directly."

Had India's pounding head not dulled her wits, she would have wondered at this change in their routine. She only knew that she was not entirely relieved by it and could not fathom the reason this should be so. Pressing her hand to her temple, she nodded agreement, then leaned back in her seat. The cab rocked as the driver quickly ascended, and then they were rolling forward. India closed her eyes and prayed that sleep would overtake her before sickness did.

The inn at King's Crossing was owned by a warmhearted and expansive fellow named Thaddeus Brinker. It was managed by his more practical and, some would say, tightfisted daughter. Mr. Brinker met the carriages and coaches. Miss Brinker oversaw everything else.

"Here, now," Brinker said as he held the carriage door

open. "She's not feeling at all well, is she? Poor thing. Have a care with her, m'lord. You're bound to bump her head going about it in that fashion." Even as he said it, the emerald velvet hat was knocked askew and tumbled to the ground. Brinker swept it up and backed away, giving his lordship a wide berth with the young lady. "She's not drugged, is she? You wouldn't be taking advantage of her?" Brinker had seen the like before, and he wouldn't have it said that King's Crossing welcomed such goings-on. "This isn't the road to Gretna, m'lord." His daughter might only care for the color of this man's coin, but Thaddeus Brinker was not such a fool that he didn't ask the important questions.

Southerton struggled with India's dead weight. She was not uncooperative in his arms, merely insensible of them. "No drugs," he said. "And no need for Gretna. The lady is my wife." He hoped that sidestepped the question as to whether he intended to take advantage of her. Once he maneuvered her through the carriage door and took the step to the ground, he was able to settle her more comfortably against his chest. Mr. Brinker hovered with his lantern in one hand and India's velvet hat in the other. "Lead on," South told him. "You would not have me take a graceless fall, would you? My man will see to our trunks."

From the driver's box, Darrow could be heard to mutter an oath, the exact nature of which could not be distinguished from the snuffling of the horses. Southerton had commandeered his valet to act as driver and attendant once the switch from hackney to South's own carriage was made. Darrow remained consistently disapproving of the scheme, though this was more from habit than from any moral, practical, or philosophical position. He never once considered actually refusing to take part in it, even if it meant doing things for which he was ill prepared or had little liking.

The innkeeper raised his lantern so a circle of light preceded Southerton and his lady into the inn. "Right this way," he encouraged as they passed through the door. There were only a few patrons at the tables at this late hour, all of them locals. They fell silent, in some cases with mouths slightly agape, as South crossed the room to the narrow stairs. They averted their eyes quickly when Brinker shot them a quelling look. "They ain't used to the likes of a lady such as you have there," he told South in an aside.

Southerton was uncertain of the exact meaning the inn-keeper attached to his words, but he didn't ask for further explanation. The narrow, winding staircase and steep steps loomed in front of him, and India had not once stirred in his arms. He needed to save his breath for what was going to be a difficult climb. He knew of only one way to get her above stairs without banging her about and causing her injury. With no apology, South hefted India over his shoulder and began the ascent.

The room was small but clean. Mr. Brinker quickly turned down the bed, commenting that the sheets had been recently washed and the blankets aired. His daughter appeared with fresh water for the basin as South was setting India down. Miss Annie Brinker took in an eyeful of the scene but refrained from comment.

"She ain't dead or drugged," Brinker told his daughter. Though it was meant to be a whisper, Brinker had never mastered the way of it. His words were quite audible to Southerton. Even Darrow, who was struggling in the stair-well with one of the smaller trunks, heard him. "An' she's his wife."

Annie merely shrugged and placed the pitcher she carried on the nightstand. She stoked the fire in the hearth, added coals, then inquired rather stiffly as to whether anything else was needed.

South wanted to see the last of them for the night, but he thought of what India might require upon regaining her senses. He asked that tea or a light broth be brought up and some repast prepared for his driver. Annie Brinker appeared as though she might object to this last request; then Darrow entered the room, looking pitifully overburdened by the weight of a valise on his shoulder and the trunk he dragged behind him, and she relented with nothing more than a heavy, much put-upon sigh.

"I believe you have made a conquest," South told his valet once the door was closed.

"What?" Darrow asked. "Do you mean the innkeeper's daughter?"

"Is she his daughter? I didn't know. It did not take you long to be apprised of the particulars. Now you only have to apply to her father for her hand."

Darrow's mouth flattened, unamused. He mumbled something about the locals giving him an earful, then applied himself to unpacking South's trunk and valise. He placed scented soap and a brush on the nightstand, along with other amenities his employer might find himself in want of during their brief stay at the inn.

South shrugged out of his greatcoat and tossed it over a chair. Darrow promptly hung it on a peg near the door, then waited patiently for Southerton to divest India of her velvet pelisse.

"Do you know," South asked in conversational accents, "I had expected some small skirmish from Miss Parr. As abductions go, this one is altogether unexceptional." He unfastened the brass buttons closing the bodice of her pelisse, unhooked the slim belt beneath her breasts, then parted the velvet over her shoulders. His fingers worked with economic efficiency.

Darrow's expression showed more interest than the coolly detached features of his employer. The realization that this was so was enough to edge the corners of the valet's mouth upward. "You have a great many abductions to your credit, then," Darrow said dryly. "I was unaware that such was the case."

"One hears stories," South said. He gingerly worked the sleeves of the pelisse off India's arms and pulled it out from under her. He held it out to Darrow for the taking. "And I have never heard of one that remarked on such a smooth beginning."

"The calm before the storm?"

"Perhaps." South laid the back of his hand against India's cheek. His palm appeared flushed with color compared to

India's pale complexion. He touched her forehead with his fingertips, then the shallow pulse beating in her temple. Her skin was cool. Violet shadows filled the faint hollows beneath her eyes. Her lashes lay in a dark arc just above. They didn't so much as flutter as South shifted his own weight to bring the blankets across her and up to her shoulders.

Uncomfortable with the intimacy he observed, Darrow cleared his throat.

South glanced at him, one brow arched in question. "You have something to say?"

"A tickle." The valet cleared his throat a second time, pressing his forefinger against his Adam's apple to emphasize the offending passage. He turned away quickly and hung India's pelisse beside South's caped greatcoat.

Southerton did not press Darrow for his opinion. It was not that South had no respect for it, but that it was ultimately of no account. South was already set on the course he had determined was necessary.

The bed creaked as South came to his feet. He went to the basin, found a suitable cloth, and dampened it.

"Is she sickening for something?" Darrow asked.

Southerton shook his head. "Exhausted, I think." He had seen the like before, battle-weary sailors and officers in the service of His Majesty, bodies flung limply into hammocks, arms lying loosely at their sides or angled oddly across their sweat-and-smoke-stained shirts, no longer sensible of the roll of the ocean or the rock of the ship except as a comfort and a cradle. "She's been unconscionably used, Darrow. By Kent. By her public. Her suitors." Silently he added the colonel's name and his own.

"Then mayhap you have not abducted her," Darrow said.

"What do you mean?" Southerton sat down again and carefully applied the damp cloth to India's forehead. There was a streak of powder at her hairline, a hint of paint just below her right ear. South removed these with the gentleness of brushing velvet. "You're not suggesting she's going to thank me for this?"

Darrow shrugged. "Who's to say what notions a woman will take in her head? But it seems to me this is more a rescue that an abduction."

South's lips quirked. "I'll remember that in the event Miss Parr makes no such distinction."

"Hmmpf."

"Wise counsel," South said. He glanced over his shoulder and observed that Darrow was close to finishing with his tasks. "Leave it. Seek your repast belowstairs. Seek the innkeeper's daughter, if you've a mind to. I am for bed and have no need of your help in getting there."

Darrow could have made a successful argument in pointing out that Southerton did not often deign to remove even his frock coat and stock without assistance, but the matter of South negotiating his own voluminous nightshirt left the valet quite without words.

"I know," South offered, his lips twisting sardonically. "It defies your imagination. Good evening, Darrow."

"Good evening, m'lord." He slipped out of the room, making sure the door clicked audibly into place behind him.

South braced one arm on the mattress beside India's shoulder and continued his ministrations. He pressed the damp cloth to either side of her jaw, loosened then removed the ruffled betsy at her neck, and ran the cloth along the slender stem of her throat. "How long has it been since you slept?" he asked, his voice but a whisper in the quiet room. "Truly slept?" Southerton had no difficulty seeing India in a restless doze with a script in her lap and lines running through her head, or nodding off between acts while Mrs. Garrety reapplied paint to her cheeks and rice powder to her nose. She made herself available for fittings and rehearsals, suitors and patrons, for performances, and finally for her protector.

South only wondered about the last. Was there truly such a person in her life, or had she created him to carve some few moments for herself? And had she come to be convinced of his existence when no evidence supported the claim, or was it simply that he could not find the evidence? Enough time had passed since the brief notice in the *Times* for her protector to come forward. In public she remained unattached save for Kent, Master Doobin, and that crusty old barnacle Mrs. Garrety. In private it appeared her company was much the same.

Southerton had not been able to find the source of the *Times* gossip. He had to consider India Parr had somehow managed to plant that seed herself. She had an entire alphabet of letters at her disposal, any of which could have fulfilled the attentive role of Lord —. *M* might have no more significance than that it was one of twenty-six of its kind.

Strands of corn silk hair darkened at her temple where they were brushed by the wet cloth. South combed them back with his fingertips. The faint scent of lilac attached itself to his skin and made his nostrils flare. He stood abruptly, tossing the cloth aside in the same motion. It splashed heavily in the basin. Droplets of water spattered the floor.

After turning back the single lamp on the small bedside table, South removed his jacket and waistcoat and loosened the stock at his neck. Not for anything would he admit that Darrow's help would have been welcome in ridding himself of his riding boots. They thumped hard to the floor when he was finally divested of them. His stockings, breeches, and linen drawers he managed well enough. He exchanged his frilled muslin and stock for the calf-length nightshirt and did not lose himself long in the latter before he found the opening for his head.

He was on the point of turning his attentions to the matter of India's dress, or rather, to the contemplation of her undress, when the knock at the door announced the return of Miss Annie Brinker. South found his robe, loosely tied the sash, and padded barefoot to the door. He opened it only wide enough to take the wooden serving tray from her hands, blocking her attempts to see past his shoulder to where India lay. He thanked her brusquely and firmly closed the door with his toes.

The tray fit neatly on the seat of a ladder-back chair. South moved the chair closer to the fire to keep the contents

of the pot warm for as long as possible. When he returned
to India's side and sat down, he tapped her lightly on the
cheek with the flat of his hand and spoke her name.

"Miss Parr? India?" She remained unresponsive. South
tapped as lightly the second time, but his tone sharpened.
"India." This time she tried to avoid the touch of his hand.
A small crease appeared between her brows, and her dry
lips parted. There was a flutter of movement behind her
closed lids, then nothing. South gave up.

He drew back the blankets and turned India on her side
so that he could unfasten the back of her dress. When he
saw the complicated lacing he had to negotiate, he understood why Mrs. Garrety was attached, limpetlike, to her
employer. Southerton was no stranger to a female's more
intimate apparel, but playing lady's maid in preparation of
the act of intimacy had always been done, well, by a lady's
maid. For demanding women who were impatient for their
pleasure, it required no particular skill to throw up their
skirts and petticoats and have at it, but the particular garment
India was wearing looked as if it had been knotted by a first
rate bos'n.

South smiled to himself. Here was something else to be
said for his time in the Royal Navy. He'd learned a thing
or two about knots that would come in handy now.

Once having freed her of her gown, Southerton removed
India's shoes, tights, and underskirt. He peeled away the
slim corselet she wore around her midriff, and unthreaded
the pink ribbon that kept the delicate batiste chemise fitted
snugly just beneath her breasts. Finally, he removed the pins
that anchored her splendid hair so tightly to her scalp, and
deposited them on the table. When he turned to her again
she was already on her side, knees drawn up, one hand
beneath her pillow, the other resting in a loose fist against
her mouth. Each one of her breaths was without sound, but
there was a gentling to the rise and fall of her chest that had
not been there before.

"The calm before the storm, indeed," Southerton said
quietly. He turned back the lamp so the room's only light

came from the fire, then raised the blankets, carefully crawled over India's curved body, and settled himself on the other side of her.

He could not have imagined it would be so simple to fall asleep.

India Parr eased into wakefulness. She was aware of several things at once: rain pressing hard against the windowpanes; a meager fire in the hearth; and the comfort of heat all along the length of her spine, around the curve of her bottom and thighs, and at the back of her calves.

It was at once so very right and all wrong.

She started to rise and discovered it was not so simple as willing herself to do so. The band of heat at her back slithered around her waist and over her knees. She stretched slowly, more as an experiment, testing the strength and limits of her bonds, and found there was little give. She arched, pushed hard, and finally clawed in her panic and uncertainty.

Southerton shifted his arm from India's waist to her shoulder, pressed firmly until she was on her back, and raised himself over her. His voice was gentle. "India. Miss Parr."

She stilled, the dark centers of her eyes slowly focusing on the face above her. There was barely any sound to her voice; it was more a parting of her lips that suggested the word. "You."

"Hmmm. Me."

"I . . . ummm . . . how did . . . ?"

"In good time," he told her. "Are you all of a piece?"

She took inventory. It was confusing with his hand still on her shoulder, his leg across both of hers. His hip was resting intimately against her thigh. The ache in her head had been replaced by thick cobwebs she could not easily clear, and there was a lethargy to her limbs that at once eased and alarmed her. She was all of a piece, she supposed, even if all the pieces were not hers. "Yes," she said finally. "I think so." At his cocked brow she roused herself to answer with more certainty. "Yes."

"Good." Southerton did not move at once. "Do you know I won't harm you?"

Did she? "Yes."

"Then you know there is no need to cry out or act in any manner that will bring an audience." Southerton measured India's hesitation more by the fractional narrowing of her eyes than in the passage of time. He waited her out, wanting her to be sure before she answered, wanting her to be honest with herself and with him.

"Yes," she said. "I know that."

He nodded. A moment passed, and then he eased away from her and fell onto his back. Beneath the blankets he had a full and heavy erection. He'd rather it had remained snugly against the cleft of India's bottom. It was good of her to extend so much trust to him when he was markedly less confident himself.

India pushed herself up on her elbows first, then eased herself higher, sliding upward against the headboard. She pressed a pillow to the small of her back and glanced at Southerton. He was staring at the ceiling, his eyes partially hooded, a grim tightness about his mouth. She had felt him hard against her buttocks, later against her hip. He probably did not suspect that she was stirred by his response to her or that she felt it still. It was perhaps not so obvious that her breasts were slightly swollen, the nipples puckered and sensitive. She would have liked to run her hands over them, press the ache she felt there into the heart of her palms. She wanted to arch her back, lift her hips a fraction, and stretch her arms. The freedom to simply feel the slow undulation of her body, the rise of her breasts, and the scraping of the hard points of her nipples against the fabric of her chemise was something she refused herself.

India understood the denial that pulled South's beautiful features taut and lent him the momentary stillness of a Greek god fixed forever in marble.

"Is there tea in that pot?" she asked for want of any other words.

South nodded. "It will be cold."

"I don't mind." She slipped free of the blankets. The floor was cool beneath her bare feet, and she shivered lightly, then hurried forward, first to raise a fire in the hearth and then to take a cup of tea for herself. She glanced over her shoulder toward the bed. "Will you have some?"

"Yes, please." It was an absurd exchange to be having with her, South reflected. It was not merely polite, but infinitely civilized. They might have been in her salon or his drawing room. South found himself grinning suddenly, struck not only by the novelty of these moments but finding himself appreciative of them.

"What is it?" she asked, approaching the bed. "Pray, if there is some amusement to be enjoyed in our existing circumstances, I should very much like to hear it."

Her butter-wouldn't-melt tone merely caused the grooves around South's lips to deepen. It was no good trying to present her with a straight face, not when he felt so very much like laughing. "I am afraid it is you, Miss Parr."

"Me?" She withdrew the cup she was holding out to him just as he would have reached for it. "You will have to explain yourself."

"It is just that you are outside the common mode."

India considered what he said. "You mean it as a compliment."

"Yes."

She held out his cup again and permitted him to take it.

Watching India, finding in her undisturbed expression and silence the first inklings of introspection and withdrawal, South's smile faded. "I've offended you."

She shook her head. Her hair swung loosely over her shoulders, and she pushed it back self-consciously when his eyes fell to it. India saw the pins South had plucked from her hair lying on the bedside table. She set her teacup down and picked up the pins, holding some between her lips as she deftly wound and twisted her hair and finally anchored it in place.

South averted his eyes as she worked, though he wanted to watch, and more than that, wanted to ask her why. Why she did it when it was not entirely comfortable for her. Why his brief admiring glance prompted it.

It touched her that he looked away, that he gave her this moment of privacy to dress her hair. She did not explain that to him, for she had little doubt it would amuse him. It was not his laughter she minded. Indeed, it was rich and deep and without affectation, but when she roused it because of who she was and not who she was pretending to be, it also had the capacity to hurt her. India had spoken the truth when she said he had not offended her; she hadn't told him that she had never known joy being outside the common mode.

South held up the blankets for her so she could slip easily back into the bed. "Come," he said. "You're shivering, and the fire provides meager heat at best."

Nodding once, India sat on the mattress's edge and drew up her knees. She swiveled into the bed and tucked the blankets around her when South lowered them. Rubbing the icy soles of her feet against the warmer sheet, she picked up her teacup and sipped. It was strong, with a hint of tang in the aftertaste, and not nearly as cold as she expected.

Outside, lightning flashed in a brilliant arc. It was followed by thunder with enough rolling force to rumble the window-panes. India let her head fall back so it rested comfortably against the scarred oak headboard. She did not find the storm unsettling, rather the opposite. "Has it been raining long?"

"I don't know. It wasn't raining when we arrived."

"When was that?"

He didn't answer her. She could use the knowledge to gauge their distance from London.

"I see," she said, comprehending the meaning of his silence. "Then there is no use in asking directly where we are."

"None."

"Someone might tell me."

"Someone might. I hope to be under way soon, and then it will not matter."

"You would travel in this downpour?"

"If it does not let up, yes."

India sipped tea again. "Am I your prisoner, then?"

South turned his head and regarded her frankly. She was staring at the far wall, her thoughts already moving beyond it. In three-quarter profile her expression was less troubled than resigned. "I would prefer you considered yourself my guest."

She smiled gently. "I'm certain you would, but that cannot make it so."

He said nothing. She was right, of course. India Parr was no longer free to come and go. South watched her smile slip slowly away. "What are you thinking?" he asked.

"That however it is gilt, one cage cannot be so very different from another."

Chapter Six

South continued to study India's profile because it would have been cowardly to look away. His actions were responsible for the ineffable sadness he saw shadowing her gentle smile. She did not turn on him angrily or offer any condemnation. Now that he had done as he had, she merely seemed to accept it. Mayhap, he thought, she would find the words to accuse him later, even fight him, but he did not think so. He did not believe she was in expectation of stirring his sympathy with her quiet reflection. He had simply asked what she was thinking, and she had told him. *"That however it is gilt, one cage cannot be so very different from another."*

"You know something about cages, then, Miss Parr?" he asked.

"I know a great deal." She did not glance in his direction.

He waited, thinking she might expound on these few words. She sipped her tea instead, her hands steady. South observed this. He also observed the fingertips she pressed to her cup, and that they were white.

"India." She spoke her name without explanation or inflection.

South tore his gaze away from her elegantly expressive

hands and returned it to her face. She was watching him now, her dark eyes shielding from him what her bloodless fingertips had just revealed. He frowned slightly, not able to follow what she was telling him.

"India," she repeated. "It is nonsensical, is it not, to continue to extend me the small respect of calling me Miss Parr?"

He understood it was not truly an invitation but rather her way of forcing him to acknowledge the full measure of disrespect he had already shown her. "India," he repeated. "Once again you demonstrate your unique gift for chastising me."

Above the rim of her cup a slim smile edged the corners of her mouth. "I take it you would rather I cuff you on the chin a second time."

"I should welcome it."

India did not doubt that he was in earnest. The proof of it was in the alacrity of his wry response and quirk of a single dark brow. "You are a most vexing individual," she said at last.

"So my mother tells me. And my sister. My father, also, on occasion. My friends, often."

She did not think he sounded particularly displeased. "It is not a compliment, you know."

"Aaah, well, there you have me. I had not comprehended that."

India surrendered to her urge to laugh. Seemingly without effort, he made it quite impossible for her to do otherwise. "Vexing," she said again, softly this time, slightly bemused. Even to her own ears it had the mild lilt of an endearment. She looked away quickly and pressed her cup to her lips.

As if tossing back a dram of liquor, South finished his tea in a single swallow. He passed the cup to her to place on the table; then he swept his long legs over the side of the bed and stood. His dressing robe was lying at the foot of the bed. He put it on and belted it. Darrow had set his slippers out. South ignored them, heartily glad for the cold floor against his feet. As a substitute for opening the window and allowing the icy rain to drench him, it was imperfect. It was also less likely to cause India alarm.

"What do you recall of last evening?" he asked, his tone clipped.

Both of India's brows came up, but she did not take issue with his abrupt accents. She understood the necessity of them. "My head ached abominably," she told him, sifting through her recollections and finding them disjointed. "I took some laudanum . . . no, perhaps I did not. Mrs. Garrety offered it, I think. Yes. And I refused. The dressing room was too warm. The light bothered my eyes. Doobin came and asked . . . no, I don't know what he wanted. I sent him away. Mrs. Garrety . . ." India paused, her fingers tightening once again on her cup while her eyes remained darkly impenetrable.

"Mrs. Garrety . . ." he prompted.

"She found a hack for me. I . . . I wanted to go home."

He nodded. "She escorted you to the hack."

"How did you . . . oh, it was you standing there. I hadn't realized."

"I know. I imagine you would have raised a hue and cry if you had."

India did not deny it. "Mrs. Garrety came to no harm? You did not hurt her?"

"No. Of course not." South watched India's grip relax.

"Then she suspected nothing."

"Nothing. Aaah, I see. You are saying my true fight would have been with her. A lioness protecting her cub. Then I am happy to say it did not come to that. She handed you over easily enough, though I confess I was prepared to take her as well, for at least the first leg of our journey."

India set her tea aside. Chilled, she drew the blankets higher. "She was going to accompany me home. Something . . ." She frowned slightly as she tried to catch the elusive memory. "Something happened, I think. Something to change her mind. I cannot remember. Things to do, I believe she told me. There is always . . . she has so many things to occupy her."

"It does not matter," South said, dismissing India's absorption with her dresser out of hand. "It is fortunate Mrs. Garrety takes her responsibilities so seriously. I should not have liked to distress her."

"No, indeed," India said quietly. "That would not do." Her chin came up, and a measure of spirit that had been absent in her voice returned. "It is heartening to know that you can entertain some remorse at the thought of distressing my dresser."

"And none at all at the thought of distressing you? Is that what you are saying?" South went to the hearth and added the last of the available coals to the fire. "Forgive me, India, but I remain uncertain that you *are* distressed. I sense more in the way of resignation to your fate than in you railing against it."

"You would prefer I spit and claw and scratch?" she asked. "I shall rally directly."

South grinned at her ironic accents. "Perhaps after a decent breakfast."

India blanched at the thought of food.

"Perhaps not," South said, watching her complexion pale. "You are still unwell. I had not realized. What can I do?"

"You have done quite enough." She let her head fall back gently again and closed her eyes. "I remember nothing after entering the hack. Did you give me some drug?"

"No."

She smiled faintly, without humor. "I collect I simply fell asleep."

"I believe so. You were sleeping soundly when I met Darrow and exchanged the hack for a more comfortable carriage."

India realized she had gone to him like a lamb to the slaughter. It was not an image of herself she found pleasure in entertaining. "Darrow?"

"You will meet him shortly. He is my Mrs. Garrety."

"I doubt that."

South shrugged. He poked the fire again and then sat down. "Do you often have these megrims?"

"They have seemed to come regularly of late. I think it is the footlamps on the stage. The light flickers so sharply at times. I try not to look at it, but it is difficult to look away. Then there is the smell of the oil. It all conspires to bring me to this state." It was with visible effort that India raised her head again and regarded South. "You would not have had so easy a time of it otherwise."

Though he was beginning to have some doubts this was true, South accepted it as such. He wondered if Darrow had not been closer to the mark when he'd put forth the notion they had rescued India Parr more than crafted her abduction.

"What are your intentions?" India asked. "I may ask you that, may I not? You have some plan, I collect."

"If you are asking how long you will be away from the stage, I cannot say. You will be safe; of that have no doubt."

"I will be safe until you satisfy yourself that I should not be. Do you imagine I think you have done this to me solely for my protection? A fortnight ago I might have believed such was the case. No longer, my lord. You suspect me of something. I would have you make the accusation and allow me the right of my own defense."

South shook his head. "In due time," he said. "When you are able to mount that defense with more vigor than you show me now."

She smiled weakly. "You will regret those words."

"I expect I shall. But I would not take advantage."

"That is most handsome of you."

Watching her, South saw the toll even this small bit of sparring was taking on her. She might be resolved to understand his purpose, but she was in no condition to take issue with it. "Lie down," he said. "I am going to find Darrow. He will know just what to do. My valet has a remedy for every conceivable affliction." Somewhat to his surprise, India did as she was told, easing herself deeply under the covers until she was chin deep in their folds.

South slid his feet into his slippers and went directly to the door. "I will be but a moment." He paused on the threshold and cautioned her. ''I hope you are not playing false with me.''

''That is a very fine compliment,'' India whispered on a thread of sound. ''But I am not so accomplished an actress.'' She could have saved herself the breath of that reply. South had not waited to hear it.

Minutes passed. India fell into a light doze. An arm slipped under her shoulders; a hand gently cradled the back of her head. She felt something being pressed to her lips. An urging, ''Swallow.'' Of its own accord, her mouth opened. What passed between her lips was smooth and warm and liquid. She touched her tongue to the roof of her mouth. Licorice. Something else. But mostly sweet licorice. There was an exchange of voices above her. She could make them out, though they seemed to come to her from a great distance.

''It will quiet her.''

''Will she sleep?''

''Yes. For some time.''

''Then we should leave.''

''I'll arrange it.''

There was some movement in the room. A long pause as she was lowered back to the bed. Then, ''I did not know she was suffering.''

''That goes without saying, m'lord.''

''It would have changed nothing.''

''No, m'lord.''

Rain pelted the carriage as it moved in a steady northeast direction from the inn at King's Crossing. The twin grays kicked up great clods of mud as they were driven ahead with a speed few other pairs could have matched in such conditions. The carriage, though snugly made and appointed for the comfort of its passengers, was not proof against the damp and icy November air slipping under the door.

South leaned down and lifted India's feet onto the leather seat, removing them from the direct path of the cold. He tucked her pelisse around her again before he sank back himself. Without urging, she slipped into the natural cradle he had made for her against his body. Her head lay in the curve of his shoulder. One arm was flung across his chest, covered by his heavy caped greatcoat.

He knew the moment she woke. Even with the jouncing of the carriage, it was not difficult to sense that something had changed. It was more than the slight stiffening of her slender frame. He had been holding her for much of the journey. Suddenly, briefly, she was holding onto him. He waited, wondering if she would move away, and knew himself oddly content when she did not. He felt her relax, and then he was holding her again.

"You're awake," he said.

"Yes." India did not open her eyes. She did not want to invite further realities. "Have I slept long?"

"As long as you needed to."

The corners of her mouth edged upward, and she discovered the effort no longer caused her any pain. "You had a nanny who said that to you."

"A succession of them," he confessed. "All with very practical natures."

"A requirement for the position."

"My mother and father thought so. I gather from the beginning they were disposed to believe I would require a firm hand. Every nanny came with two—and a sharp tongue besides."

"A paltry arsenal to pit against your roguish wiles. They were all roundly defeated, I take it."

"Each one in turn," he admitted without compunction. "Though I do not think you can properly blame me. One does what one must to survive."

"They spoiled you horribly."

"Eventually. Then they were let go, of course. As soon as one of my parents caught a whiff of it."

"They were honing you for greatness."

He chuckled. "They still are. My father hopes I will affect political aspirations. My mother hopes I will aspire to marriage and grandchildren, and I am not so certain the order is at all relevant any longer.''

"You cannot believe that. No one wants the stain of illegitimacy in their family line, least of all a countess. You would do well not to present your mother with any bastards, m'lord. She will not thank you for it, and you might find at last the limits to which you can beguile the feminine sex.''

South laughed outright. ''My mother cannot be beguiled. And the truth be told, the very same can be said of you.''

That piqued her interest. "How can you be sure it is so of me?''

He did not answer immediately. When he spoke, his voice was deeper, not less warm, but without its former hint of self-deprecating humor. "Are you certain you want to know?''

She wasn't at all, but she had asked the question and would not back away from it now. ''Yes.''

"It is surprisingly simple,'' he said. "I would not find myself drawn to you otherwise. A woman moved by a simpleton's smile, a handsome face, or pretty words does not hold herself much in esteem. I would not want such as her.''

India's eyes were opened now, and she felt a vague tension in the line of her body. She remained where she was, not because she was becalmed but because she knew herself to be thoroughly beguiled. "And do you want me?''

"Very much.''

"Oh.''

Southerton gave her shoulders a small squeeze. "Yes, well, there you have it.''

Indeed. India felt the pressure of tears at the back of her eyes, but they remained curiously dry. Swallowing was more difficult. An ache filled her throat. She barely understood her own reaction to his words. She was not even certain she believed him, but then, perhaps he did not expect her to. At once beguiled and suspicious of the same, India knew herself to be at the center of a most provoking paradox. "Vexing,'' she whispered.

"Yes. And I make no apology for it.''

India sat up slowly. She brushed absently at a few loose

strands of hair that had been caught between her cheek and his shoulder, tucking them behind her ear. South reached toward her and adjusted the slant of her velvet hat. She let her feet slide to the floor and immediately felt the cold air seep through the seams of her thin leather shoes. A shiver shook her from shoulder to toe.

"You were fine where you were," South told her.

She was tempted to correct him. She had been warm, not fine. "Where are we going?" India asked. "Surely you can reveal our destination now."

"A cottage at Ambermede."

"You could have said as much to me at any time, m'lord. It means nothing to me."

"I did not want to concern myself that you might speak of it to others."

"Yes, of course. You would think of that."

"A precaution."

She understood. Lord Southerton was a cautious man, the colonel's man. "Have you been in the colonel's employ long?"

"Longer than you."

India supposed that enigmatic response was the best she could expect. "Did you serve with him?"

"No, he was in the regiments. I was at sea, remember?"

"How did your paths cross?"

One of South's brows kicked up, and he regarded India askance. "Are you interrogating me, India?"

"Does it seem so? I assure you, I am merely curious. I met the colonel but once, five years ago. In all that time I have not been in communication with him, nor talked about him to another soul except as it had to do with a specific request for my services."

"With Mr. Kendall, for instance."

"Yes. He was one."

"How many others over the years?"

She thought back. "A half dozen, I would say. My contributions were sporadic and limited. With the exception of Mr. Kendall, my contact with others was brief."

"I understand from the colonel that until recently you traveled a great deal."

India nodded. "With the troupe. France. Italy. Belgium. Spain. We were welcomed in many places in spite of the war with Napoleon. I imagine it is that very thing that suggested my usefulness to the colonel in the first place."

"Why you?" he asked. "And not someone else in the troupe?"

"I have no idea. I should be interested to know the reason myself. I wish you would ask him."

"I did. I only wondered if you knew. As you told me once, there was no quid pro quo. He said he chose you because you were resourceful."

She smiled to herself. "And nothing else?"

"No. He is not given to long discourse or to explaining himself."

"The colonel was being disingenuous," she said. "He observed a performance of *Much Ado About Nothing* in which our courtyard fountain collapsed, a painted backdrop was split by a wayward sword, potted trees fell, and I was much set upon by a drunken Don Pedro and an overly amorous Claudio."

"You were Beatrice or Hero?"

"Oh, no. A much smaller role. I was Ursula." At his frown, she explained, "A gentlewoman attending on Hero. The gropings of Don Pedro and Claudio made it difficult for Hero to sustain their attention. I spoke many lines that night not penned by Master Shakespeare, including, *'Nay, sir, do not show me your Cupid's arrow for I have had my quiver full.'* India waited for her audience of one to stop laughing. "That was when Claudio was trying to lift my skirt," she said primly. "Something had to be done."

"Would it explain the fountain's collapse?" asked South.

"My foot in his hindquarters would explain that. He went head over bucket."

"And the backdrop?"

"Don Pedro's sword, I'm afraid. I was forced to defend my virtue."

"You disarmed him?"

She nodded. "I am told I gave a good account of myself, the backdrop notwithstanding."

South's lips quirked. "The fallen trees?"

"Hero threw one at my head," she admitted after a moment.

"I've always thought of Hero as a delicate sort. Not one to heft potted plants and toss them at her maidservant's head."

"She thought I was trampling her lines and purposely bringing the audience's attention around to me. That arouses passion in an actress."

South had reason to know that was true. He clearly remembered India's challenge from the stage. "You avoided the tree?"

"Oh, yes. I was able to take refuge behind Claudio. Did I mention he was felled by one of them?"

"No. You omitted that part."

"Well, now you have the whole of it."

He only wished he had been witness to it. "Resourceful," he said finally. "Yes, I understand why he chose you."

The carriage hit a deep rut in the road, was stalled momentarily by the suck of the mud, then surged forward. India and South were both lifted from their seats, but it was India who would have fallen to the floor if South had not caught her. He pulled her back by the waist and sat her firmly down. "Are you all right?"

"Yes."

South rapped hard on the roof of the carriage. "Have a care, Darrow," he called loudly. If there was a reply, South could not hear it.

"We are in a hurry?" India asked.

"Not so much that we should risk arriving in pieces." As he slipped his arm from under her back, South felt the rumble of her stomach. "You are hungry."

Since it was more of an observation than a question, India could not very well deny it. She nodded.

"Then I think we should avail ourselves of the repast the good Miss Brinker prepared for us."

"Miss Brinker?"

"The innkeeper's daughter." He pointed to the basket sitting between the twin valises on the opposite seat. "Darrow promises me we will not be disappointed. He supervised the packing himself." Southerton plucked the basket free and set it on his lap. He opened the lid and investigated the contents. "Bread. Cheese. Fruit. A pint of ale."

"The ale," India said and held out her hand.

She was indeed outside the common mode, South thought, and hoped he did not fall in love with her. That rather vague and pensive wish made his thoughts turn suddenly to his friend Northam. He wondered if North had been of a similar mind concerning Elizabeth before he dropped like a stone at her feet and proposed marriage.

India opened the pint jar and raised it to her lips. She drank deeply and was almost immediately warmed from the inside out. Without a word she passed the jar back to South and rooted through the basket until she had a wedge of bread and cheese in hand. She sank back against the leather squabs and began to eat. "Perhaps you think I should not reveal my appetite so openly," she said. "It is not the done thing."

It was not, but South didn't mind in the least. He had seen sailors fall ravenously on crusts of mealy bread and it had never turned his stomach. He had been one of them once. "When did you last eat?" he asked.

India swallowed a bite of cheese. "Yesterday. A soft-cooked egg, I think. In the morning." She tore off a smaller wedge of bread from the one she'd taken and put it in her mouth. "Mayhap I had the first hints of a megrim even then. It was no easy thing to keep that small nourishment in its place."

"Delicately put."

She flushed. "Forgive me. I fear the ale has gone to my head. I should not speak of such things."

South found a crisp apple in the basket. He gave it a little toss before he palmed and polished it on the cuffed sleeve of his greatcoat. He offered it to India, but she shook her head, satisfied with cheese and bread for the moment. South bit into it himself. The sweet-tart taste of the apple puckered his mouth.

India did not want to watch him so openly or greedily. She recognized that her need to do so made her the vulnerable one. Knowing this did not make her strong enough to avert her eyes. His lips were damp with the apple's juice, and she simply stared at them as they parted around a second bite. It was only when he paused midbite, looking at her over the apple's polished horizon, that embarrassment made her eyes dart away.

India said the first thing that came to her mind, or at least the first thing that would not embarrass her further. "Tell me about Ambermede. Is it yours?"

"No. It belongs to a friend."

"The Marquess of Eastlyn?" she asked. "The one who has the box at the theatre?"

"No. Not that friend."

"Then your friend Lord Northam? He was with you that first night also, wasn't he?"

South nodded. "You've made inquiries."

"If it pleases you to think so." India was not willing to tell him who had come forward eagerly to fill her ears with particulars about South and his friends.

"It belongs to Mr. Marchman," he said after a moment. "The one we call West." He stayed her next question by taking another bite of his apple; then he went on. "Now you will want to know why. People who are not acquainted with Marchman generally do. The fact is, we do not satisfy their curiosity on this account, as it is his place to do so."

"I see. You are right, of course."

"However, exceptions are made." He laughed at her reproachful look. She appeared to be a novice at being teased, having the knowledge neither of how to accept or initiate it. It made South suspect she had grown up without the benefit of brothers or sisters, who would have certainly filled that void. "Among the *ton* they tend to believe it has to do with the fact there is already a North, East, and South. They assume—incorrectly, as it happens—that Mr. Marchman is West by default. In point of fact, the idea for it all came from Marchman, and it had its inception when we were still quite directionless at Hambrick Hall.''

India listened attentively, taking small bites from her bread as she did so. It seemed that Margrave had not told her falsely about Hambrick Hall, and it surprised her that he would have been forthcoming.

South's head tilted to the side as he continued his reminiscence. ''Marchman had this notion everyone we knew could lay claim to some title if only those with a better claim were to die first. To prove his point he showed us how in the right circumstances of luck—or misfortune—we could come by titles ourselves. I was not yet known as South. My father was the younger son of an earl and not in expectation of inheriting the title. I was simply Mr. Forrester in those very early days.''

India regarded him questioningly.

''Matthew,'' South said. ''Matthew Forrester.''

A faint smile touched her lips as she let the name settle in her mind. She did not try to speak it aloud. ''Go on,'' she said instead.

''But Marchman's argument was compelling,'' South told her. ''Indeed, if my father's older brother were to die, and he being without sons of his own, and entailment being what it is, then my father stood to inherit the lands and title. As the only son of my father, I would acquire the dubious distinction of being the Viscount Southerton. Such was also the case with Northam. He came into his title much later than I did, years after we left Hambrick Hall, while he was serving with the colonel. Marchman showed us that Eastlyn stood to inherit in some distant fashion as well. When we realized there was also the odd connection of North, East, and South to our names, we took to calling each other by them. Marchman had already worked it out, of course. Said we were the Compass Club.''

''But what about Mr. Marchman?'' asked India.

Southerton grinned. "Marchman stood closer to a title than any of the rest of us, and much further away."

A small crease appeared between India's brows. "You like to present a puzzle, I think. Wait. I shall work it out." In moments she did. Her face was cleared instantly of its contemplative lines. "Your friend Mr. Marchman is the elder son of a ..." She paused while she considered the possibility of rank among the peerage. "A viscount? An earl?"

"A duke," South told her.

"A duke," she repeated. "I see. And as the elder son he would naturally have had a lesser title, even at the time you knew him at Hambrick. If he did not—and it appears that is so—then it can only be because he is the illegitimate offspring of a duke."

"That is just the case."

"It must have been difficult for him," she said quietly.

South watched India's eyes shutter, her countenance grow expressionless. He wondered if she knew how much she revealed when she revealed nothing at all. He was beginning to understand these moments of withdrawal, the reflective silences. "Why do you think so?"

She shrugged lightly. "It is only that it is never an easy thing to be a known bastard."

"That is true."

"And young boys can be quite cruel to one another. Heartless, really."

"Also true," said South. "But they can also come together and become fast friends. That is what the Compass Club did."

"It was just the four of you?"

"Yes. *North. South. East. West. Friends for life, we have confessed. All other truths, we'll deny. For we are soldier, sailor, tinker, spy.*"

India laughed softly. "That is your work?"

He nodded. "Our charter. I told you I wrote bad poetry, did I not?"

"You did indeed. I had no notion you showed such promise at so early an age."

"A prodigy," he allowed simply.

India was grateful she had nothing in her mouth, for surely she would have choked on it. "Modest also."

"To a fault, I'm afraid."

She laughed again. The sound of it still had the capacity to startle her, and she struggled with it. India was used to hearing it swell and crash in upon her from an audience. That was a very separate experience from having it well up inside her. South's manner was gently coaxing but not deliberately so. She would have resisted had it been an effort for him. She sensed it was not. India wondered if he would not turn out to be the most dangerous of men she had known.

"Your club," she said, sobered by this last thought. "You did not include others?"

"What makes you think so?"

"There are but four directions, and they were all already named."

"A compass has three hundred sixty degrees and many possibilities. The truth is, we were friends before we had a name. Rather than excluding others, we were excluded by them."

"That cannot be."

"Why?"

"Because I heard you all laughing in the marquess's box," she said without guile, unaware of the poignancy in her own voice. "Who could listen to that joyful noise and not want to be one of the degrees in your circle?"

South gave her a wry look. "I recall being taken publicly to task for all that noise."

"Yes, well, it remains true that it was ill timed and had nothing at all to do with what was happening on the stage. And I fear you are missing my point."

"No, I assure you, I am not. You must understand, however, that when we gather as adults we become not so much as we were as boys but rather how we wished we might be. We did our share of mischief, to be sure. Some would say—

my father certainly—that we did more than our share. The fact that we came together at all, though, is because we were not a proper fit anywhere else.

"Evan—Mr. Marchman—was a bastard. Brendan Hampton, now Earl of Northam, was too serious by half. Eastlyn? Gabriel Whitney was a chubby one, always getting the best baked goods from home and hoarding them in his room. He was a thrasher. Broke North's nose once in defense of his hot-crossed buns and his reputation. Or mayhap that was Marchman. It doesn't matter. North's nose needed a proper tweaking."

"And you?" India asked, smiling. "What set you apart from others yet drew you to these three?"

"I am wounded. Have I not given you ample evidence of my wit?"

"They allow fools in any circle," she said. "You would not be excluded by others for such as that." Her dark eyes narrowed when he merely flashed his easy grin in her direction. "But if you played the fool because at the heart of things you were acknowledged to be quite brilliant, then I can imagine there would be those who would turn you away. That is more the truth, is it not? You were a student much coveted by your housemasters and despised by your classmates."

Though he continued to regard India steadily, South's smile had vanished. He nodded once. "Yes. No one knew what was to be made of me."

"Except Marchman, Hampton, and Whitney."

"Oh, they did not know what was to be made of me, either. They simply knew they were in for a devil of a good time when I was around."

Yes, India thought, that would have been the way of it. It was probably still true, judging by what she had observed of the four friends at the theatre. Her own experience was much the same, and that it ran counter to all common sense did not seem to matter. Things would be changed, she knew, when they reached Ambermede and he lay the purpose of his abduction before her. His accusations, when made clear, could not be taken back. However brilliant he was, he was not omniscient, and he was engaged in an activity even now that had consequences he could not have fully appreciated.

"A devil of a good time," she repeated quietly. "I understand."

South considered asking her what she meant, then thought better of it. Instead, he offered her the basket and the pint of ale while he opened the door just enough to discard his apple core. Shards of rain pelted the back of his hand before he quickly withdrew it. "Will you have more?" he asked, indicating the basket.

India nodded and found an apple for herself. She let South give it a thorough polish and accepted it back. He finished the ale, replaced the jar, and wedged the basket between the valises so it wouldn't easily take flight when they hit the next deep puddle.

"There is still the matter of Mr. Marchman," said India. "I cannot say that I know yet why you call him West."

"I thought I said . . . no, I suppose I didn't. Marchman's father is the Duke of Westphal."

India frowned deeply. A memory that had been previously elusive began to take shape. She tried to hold it.

"What is it?"

"I am not certain," she said slowly. "Something . . . something Mrs. Garrety said to me when she was escorting me to the hack." India pressed three fingers to her temple trying to recall her dresser's exact words. "The most extraordinary thing, I think she said Mr. Kent had just informed her." Of a sudden it came to her, and her expression changed from one of confusion to one of concern. She realized it was unlikely that Southerton knew anything of what she was about to say. He was going to learn of it for the first time from her. "Mrs. Garrety told me the Duke of Westphal was dead."

Southerton went perfectly still. "Dead? When?"

"Last evening. She had just been told such."

When he had been planning India's abduction, South thought. Even if West had sent word round, Southerton had informed his staff he was not to be disturbed. He had probably been gone from the house anyway, engaged in making the initial preparations.

"I am sorry," India said. "It meant nothing to me at the time. Indeed, I would not have remembered it at all if you had not explained the connection to Mr. Marchman."

"There was no love lost between West and his father. Marchman was illegitimate. Westphal was a bloody bastard."

India pressed her lips together and did not make the mistake of speaking again. Southerton's response had been tersely framed, as if he resented her intrusion into his thoughts. That he was displeased by this news was clear. A muscle worked in his cheek. There was a tightness about his eyes and mouth, a change that made her no longer think of features polished smoothly in marble but of the kind of hard, angular shapes that might be quarried from granite.

South leaned forward, opened the carriage door with a single jerk, and then stood, his weight precariously balanced on the edge of the jolting, rocking threshold. "Darrow! Hold there!"

India braced herself for the carriage's abrupt halt. Darrow made a kinder stop than that, manipulating the traces with considerable skill to slow the horses first, then bring them to a stand.

South leaped down, landing softly on the muddy ground. He started to shut the door, but India stayed the movement and passed him his beaver hat. He thanked her tersely, and this time when he pushed the door she did not resist his effort.

She sat back. It was difficult to hear the exchange over the steady beat of the rain. Had this changed his plans for her, she wondered, or only for himself? She had been cooperative from the outset, in part because she had hardly been aware of what was being done to her, then later because resistance served no purpose. India did not believe she was in any danger; he had made her admit as much to him. Her resignation must have surprised him. He could not have

anticipated she would make it so easy for him to ferry her
away from London. After all, she had a performance this
very evening, a rehearsal she would be missing in a few
hours. She had said nothing of these things to him.

It would have meant explaining her antipathy toward these
events, revealing how little she cared. It would have meant
exposing the numbness she had come to embrace, making
herself vulnerable in a way that would expose her to life.

The door opened again and Southerton put only his head
inside. "My man will be taking you on to Ambermede,"
he said, his tone brooking no argument. "I am returning to
London. I will be gone two days. Three at the most. You
will not make any attempt to return on your own, India. It
would be foolish. Darrow will do whatever is necessary to
assure you remain at Ambermede, and he will always be
acting on my instructions. Do you understand?"

She certainly understood the words. His motive still
escaped her. "Yes," she said. Before she could offer more
in the way of a reply, the door was abruptly closed.

How was he going to get to London? she wondered. Walk?
She pushed open the door and peered out. Southerton was
standing toward the rear of the carriage, untethering a great
black stallion. India had been unaware that such an animal
had been accompanying them on their journey.

"Have a care, miss," came the call to her from above.

Although rain sheeted her face and inhibited her vision,
India could see the movements of a man on the carriage
top. He was loosening the oilcloth that covered the trunks
and bags.

"For God's sake, India," South told her as he brought
his mount around. "Get back inside."

She didn't. There were limits to the orders she was willing
to accept. As a rebellion, this should have been beneath his
notice. She stared at the magnificent beast South was holding
in place. "You're going to ride him?" He did not have the
look of an animal that any man should ride. He stood seventeen hands high, long and leggy but still with massive shoulders and chest. His large black head tossed upward, exposing

the powerful neck. He threw his damp, dark mane to one side. South stood his ground, unconcerned by the posturing and preening of the great stallion. Rain made the animal's dark coat look slick and glistening, and he continued to show it off, bunching his muscles, dancing in place.

"Here you are, m'lord," Darrow called again from above.

This time India ducked back inside as Darrow dropped the saddle into South's waiting arms. She stayed there until Darrow climbed down and proceeded to assist in saddling the animal; then she poked her head out and watched, fascinated by the unleashed power of South's mount. Water pooled on the brim of her velvet hat and fell as if from the eaves when she tipped her head forward. "What is he called?"

"Griffin."

The name of the mythological beast suited him. Part eagle, part lion, this stallion looked as if, once given his head, he would be equally at ease flying over the ground or prowling for prey across it. "He is aptly named."

"This?" South shook his head. "He is performing for you. His usual temperament is that of a lamb."

Darrow rolled his eyes. "Don't you believe him, Miss Parr. This beast is an Irish thoroughbred that should have been gelded before he left the isle."

As if understanding the valet's words, Griffin lowered his head and pushed at Darrow's backside. It was no gentle nuzzle the stallion offered, but a thrust hard enough to make Darrow lose his balance. The valet stumbled forward, splashed through the mud, and came close to crumpling to his knees in the middle of a puddle.

India began to descend to help the man, but South blocked her path. The warning in his eyes said that Darrow would not thank her for it. South lent his aid instead.

"When are you going to learn he understands you, Darrow?" South asked. "Talk of making him a gelding is not—"

"Aaach!" Eschewing South's outstretched arm, Darrow clambered out of the deep, water-filled rut on his own and gave the stallion a wide berth. "Leg up, m'lord?"

"And get heaved over the other side of my mount? I'll manage, thank you." He pulled Griffin away from the carriage, placed one hand on the pommel and a foot in the tread, and without visible effort put himself in the saddle. From India's vantage point it seemed the horse accommodated South's feat by leaning forward and lowering himself ever so slightly. Surely not, she thought. She must have imagined that.

South pointed to her. "Inside, India. You are still hours from Ambermede and the day is cold. I would not have you catch your death."

"That *would* be inconvenient," she mocked.

He ignored India, turning Griffin swiftly. The curtain of rain was enough to hide his grim smile from her.

The day was merely gray when Darrow finally announced they had reached Ambermede. India accepted his strong, sharply knuckled hand when she descended the carriage step. She came to rest on a cobbled path. Small tufts of damp grass appeared between narrow gaps in the smoothly worn stones. The path parted a neatly trimmed hedgerow, widening slightly on its gently curving path to the cottage.

There had been rain here as well, India saw. Drops of it still glazed the cobblestones and fell intermittently from the emerald hedge. She breathed deeply, drawing the damp into her lungs but recognizing something more than the vestiges of rainfall in the air. She smelled a hint of the sea in that breath and tasted it on the tip of her tongue. Once more she wondered where South had sent her. And surely *sent* was the proper word. Once he left her with Darrow, she no longer felt as if she were being accompanied to a particular destination, but rather that she was being delivered to one.

"You go on up, Miss Parr," Darrow told her. "I'll see to these trunks and bags."

"In a moment."

It did not matter that the cottage was framed by pale gray skies that were darkening by the minute, or that the sharp wind was pressing her pelisse to her legs. She wanted to stand just as she was and indulge in the utter foolishness that she had come home.

The cottage sat back some twenty yards from the road, separated from the hedgerow by a thicket of flowers that had ceased to bloom in the absence of the summer sun. The roof sloped steeply and overhung the threshold, creating a deep shadow that was an invitation to India because of its mystery. The twin chimneys were smokeless, but she did not think of that as a cold welcome, merely one that could be made to embrace her when the fires were burning hotly in the hearths. Rough-hewn timbers and pale golden walls defined the outside of the cottage. The windows were small, but their placement suggested they could be used to good effect when the sun was out and a warm breeze was upon them.

"It's lovely," she said, glancing over her shoulder at Darrow. "Don't you agree, Mr. Darrow? It is Mr. Marchman's property. Is that correct?"

"Aye." He hefted a trunk onto his shoulder. "You can lead or follow, Miss Parr, but either way, I'm taking myself to yonder door."

"I'll lead." She hurried up the walk, ducking her head against the buffeting wind as she went.

Darrow set the trunk inside the door and returned to the carriage while India began exploring. With the exception of the cheerless fireplaces, the cottage had been made ready for their arrival. The furniture was uncovered and freshly polished. Though sparsely appointed with rockers, spindle-legged chairs, and a settee, all of it was of good quality. The striped damask upholstery, where such provided a covering, was gold and green. The woodwork was painted white, and the walls were awash in the palest of yellow hues.

India swept through the small kitchen at the back, sat at the window seat in the receiving room, and tripped lightly up the stairs to the bedchambers. There were two, almost identical in the simplicity of their appointments. "I shall take the sage room," India called down to Darrow when she heard him stomp his feet at the entrance. "Will that suit you? You shall have the blue."

"Begging your pardon, Miss Parr, but there's quarters that do for me above. I'll happily be staying there once his lordship returns. Until then I'll make a pallet for myself down here."

India came to the top of the stairs and peered down. "But there is no need of that. You'll be so much more comfortable . . ." She stopped because he was shaking his head firmly. "Oh, I see. You are afraid I will attempt to quit this place."

"I'm not afraid of it, Miss Parr. He is. Though I can't properly explain it. The way I'm told, the ladies like it here."

"The ladies?" India asked.

His head bobbed once. Normally one to keep his own counsel or make the briefest of replies, Darrow was nonetheless weary and wet and a little in awe of his present company. India Parr was someone he had seen onstage, and her position at the top of the stairs made him think of that again. She had glowed then. In his eyes, she glowed now. His tongue simply could not stop working. "I think I heard of one that was moved to say it was enchanting."

"Enchanting," she echoed.

"Devil of a time getting any of them to leave it behind. The last mistress cozied here was so put out by her marching orders that she's done nothing but make his lordship's life a bloody hell."

"I see. Well, we would not want to be so tiring as to repeat that effort." India started grandly down the stairs. "Take the trunks back to the carriage, Mr. Darrow. We shall be leaving at once."

That was when the steady, reliable Mr. Darrow dropped in a dead faint at her feet.

Chapter Seven

It was a somber group that gathered at the club that evening. They could not rouse themselves to humor or find the wherewithal to make a wager of no consequence. They sat for long periods without trading conversation. They drank little. No one disturbed them.

West eyed his companions over the steepled points of his fingers. Stretched out as he was in the high-backed chair, his posture was not one of prayer but rather of lazy contemplation. The subdued air of their group was giving rise to glances in their direction, and talk among the other members of the club. People acquainted with the news of his father's death would also understand he was not in deep mourning. "We're causing a stir, you know."

Eastlyn glanced around and saw it was so. He shrugged. "Must be South. He is looking rather disheveled this evening. Bound to cause talk."

South roused himself enough to ask, "You are referring, perhaps, to the flecks of mud on my boots?"

The marquess could have named a number of other things that contributed to Southerton's less-than-tidy person, but he settled for the mud-flecked boots. "That's right. Never say Darrow has left you."

"It is more to the point that I have left him," South said. His head rested against the back of his chair. Through half-closed eyes he regarded the tips of his offending boots. It had been a hard ride from the middle of nowhere back to the center of London. "It is a temporary state of affairs." He added this in the event East had some notion that he might tempt Darrow with an offer to come into his employ. "He is not available to you."

"Pity." Eastlyn sipped his port, and in due time his attention swiveled to Northam. "You are particularly introspective this evening," he said. "It cannot be solely on account of West's father."

Northam absently raked back his hair. "It's not." His slim smile communicated his apology to West.

"Elizabeth, then," Eastlyn said. He held up his hand, staying North's reply. "No, don't answer. I should not have asked. It is none of my affair."

There was a visible change in the set of Northam's shoulders as he relaxed his guard. He did not mind that the others knew things were not at all as they should be in his marriage, but he had no desire to share the blow-by-blow. Just as they had all come together for West, he knew his friends would rally if he required anything of them. He had only to look at Southerton to see the effort that would be made if necessary.

North inclined his head slightly in South's direction and caught his friend's eye. "Where were you when you heard the news?" he asked.

South wondered that he had tried not to let the strain of his journey show. Perhaps a stranger would not have recognized his taut expression for the deep weariness that it was, but these men were his boon companions. They knew him too well to suppose that he had been merely indisposed when he was apprised of the old duke's death. West, in particular, had reason to understand the pains South had taken to return to London, for he had made the arrangements to ready the cottage at Ambermede.

A small smile eased the lines of tension about Southerton's mouth. "More than halfway there," he said quietly. "I was more than halfway there."

North's own expression was wryly appreciative of the enigmatic response. "So far."

"Indeed." South pushed himself upright in his chair. "I suspect the return will take somewhat longer."

Eastlyn chuckled softly, the first any of them had laughed since coming together. "Especially if your intention is to arrive at some end. You cannot travel halfway and halfway again and expect to get there, South. Or did they teach you something different on board His Majesty's vessels? If they did, I should like to know." He raised his glass of port, his expression sobering. "How long will you remain in London?"

"Another day," said South. "Two at the most."

East nodded. His voice dropped so that it could not be heard beyond their small circle. "You will call on us, will you not?" he asked. "If there is a need."

"If there is a need," Southerton repeated in the same grave intonation. "I would not have any of you compromised."

One of Eastlyn's chestnut-colored brows rose in a perfect arch. "So that's the way of it." He needed to hear nothing else to know that South was engaged in ferreting out a spy. It was the sort of work the colonel often laid in his own lap or assigned to West, but he did not question Blackwood's judgment in using South on this occasion. It said something about the nature of the trap if South's talents were being put to good advantage. "You won't have to recount the entire history of Henry VIII's reign, will you?" Eastlyn asked. "If you have to extricate yourself from some exceptional coil, I mean. I don't think I could sit through that again."

North nodded. "I am with East there. You cannot expect so much of us this time, South."

"No matter that it was a score of years ago," West said. "The memory resides painfully in my arse." That comment immediately drew three pairs of amused glances. He returned their gaze, his own innocent. "What? Cannot a duke speak of arses?"

"A duke may speak of anything he wishes," South said. "Especially one so recently acquiring the title, the lands, and the fortune."

"You mean some allowance will be made for a bastard son suddenly acquiring legitimacy," West said.

Southerton continued as if his friend had not spoken. "But unless you want others to hang on your every word and have the same come back to you, it is usually a thing better done quietly."

"Bloody hell," West said under his breath. "Bloody, bloody hell."

His disconsolate manner first raised identical grins from all of his friends, then their rousing laughter. They fell into the moment without examining it too closely, letting their laughter speak for them when they could find no other words that would do so well.

The following afternoon, Southerton found himself wishing there might be some cause for amusement. He stood beside the green-veined marble mantel in West's drawing room, giving a good account of himself as someone who was politely interested in the conversations humming nearby, even though he took no part in them himself. His eyes slid surreptitiously toward the clock. It was disheartening to realize he had looked in that direction only minutes earlier. It had seemed to him that half the hour had passed.

He managed not to sigh, but the urge to do so was sharp. The service for West's father had been interminable by anyone's reckoning. The fact that the old duke was not particularly well liked made it an onerous duty for most of the gathering. South looked over at his friend, who was engaged in a rather one-sided conversation with Lady Benton-Reade. West seemed to be holding up well in spite of the fact that he had in no way come to terms with the altered circumstances of his life.

It was Northam and Elizabeth who rescued West from the lady at his side. South realized they were offering their condolences and preparing to take their leave. If North's manner had been slightly aloof last evening, it was positively chilly now. South had no sense that it was directed in any way toward West, or indeed that it had anything at all to do with this place and time. Although North remained close to his wife's side, Southerton could not help but think it was Elizabeth he was freezing out. Her complexion was pale. Her solemn countenance, while appropriate for the occasion, could barely contain her pain. Feeling like an intruder on their private grief, wondering at what he had done in having a hand in bringing them together, South turned away.

He waited until they quit the room before he excused himself from those closest to him and went to find the colonel. Blackwood had not attended Westphal's service, but he had come to West's home to pay his respects. South found the colonel sitting alone in West's study, a rug pulled over his thin legs, his expression every bit as pained as Elizabeth's.

The colonel did not look up when South closed the door behind him. He rolled himself closer to the fire and warmed his hands. "You have something to say." It was not a question.

"You, sir, are a bloody bastard."

A ghost of a smile touched the colonel's features. "If this is a revelation, then I have vastly overstated your intuition and sound judgment to others." He glanced at South, one brow arched. "Or is it only that you have found the courage to say so?"

Southerton ignored him. "Elizabeth and North have just taken their leave. I cannot imagine a more unhappy pair, and I can find no pleasure in having had even a small part in helping the thing come about."

The tension in Blackwood's face eased. "Then you must

be thankful it was only a small part, though I have no doubt that, should I be proved right, you will want congratulating that it was all your idea.''

"Admit to having a hand on Cupid's bow?'' South snorted. "You may rely on my discretion never to avow such a thing. The fact that they came together at all has much to do with you. What they make of the marriage has everything to do with them.''

"Just so. You are well out of it.''

Southerton sat down on an upholstered bench not far from the colonel. He did not feel well out of it, not when North was his friend and he had such regard for Elizabeth. "I saw Elizabeth escort you to this room earlier. A private audience?''

"Something like that. She wants me to remove Northam from his assignment. I refused, of course. Northam would not have brooked her interference if he had known what she was about.''

"So he is still to find the Gentleman Thief.''

"Yes.''

Southerton nodded. It was not a complete picture of what had occurred in West's study, but it was encouraging to know that perhaps the rift between North and his countess did not yawn so widely as he first suspected. "Have I truly never called you a bloody bastard before?'' he asked absently.

The colonel's chuckle was low. "Not to my face.''

"I cannot imagine why not,'' South said with perfect candor. "I've thought it often enough.''

Blackwood accepted this without rebuke. "I should be far more concerned if it had never crossed your mind. And do not worry that I will demand satisfaction for the slight, though if you had called me crippled I should have had to run you through.'' He was gratified to see the shock on South's face. Blackwood liked it that he still had the capacity to turn the preternaturally self-possessed Southerton on his ear. Chuckling more deeply, he adjusted the blanket over his legs and angled his chair away from the fire so he could face South squarely. "Now tell me what you have done with Miss Parr. She *is* with you, is she not?"

"She is with my man. And she is safe."

"You might have told me." There was disapproval in his tone. "Who else knows?"

"West knows only that I wished to use the cottage at Ambermede, and assured me everything would be in readiness. If he had suspicions as to the identity of my companion, he did not give voice to them."

"He would have wondered at your judgment, the same as I. You escorted her there yourself?"

"No. I learned of Westphal's death and returned immediately. Darrow has my instructions. Miss Parr was not entertaining notions of running off when I left her. I cannot think anything has happened to make her change her mind."

"If she's been cooperative it is because you have not yet confronted her."

Trust the colonel to present the facts plainly. South nodded.

"It is just as well. Do you know what you are about?"

He wasn't entirely sure, but he wasn't about to reveal that. "How did you know she was with me?"

"There was your striking absence after West sent a note around about his father's death, then Miss Parr's missed performance soon after. You returned but she did not. I am given to understand the audience rather loudly expressed its disappointment but stopped short of burning down the theatre. It may be more difficult to contain them this evening or the next."

Since India Parr would be gone from Drury Lane much longer than a few nights, Southerton supposed her admirers would have to contrive some other means of entertaining themselves. "They're a fickle lot, though I doubt she will be entirely displaced in their hearts."

Watching South carefully, the colonel asked, "Would it be the same, do you think, if they knew she had committed treason?"

"We do not know that she's done it either."

"The evidence is mounting. Some of it you have gathered yourself these last weeks. There is Kendall. And the business with Macquey-Howell and the Spanish consul. Last year there was the attempt on the life of the Prince Regent after the opening of Parliament. I am concerned that Miss Parr figures rather largely in these things."

Southerton said nothing. His expression remained neutral.

The colonel went on. "She knows something, South. Something she is not telling because she is afraid or because she is involved. Either may be true. Perhaps it is both those things, but you would do well to find out. I have no wish to learn that your body has been pulled from the Thames."

"I can assure you, Colonel, I have no wish to come to the same end as Mr. Kendall."

"Then see to it that you do not come to the same end as Mr. Rutherford."

"Rutherford?" South's eyes narrowed. "Rutherford took the *Cato* to the United States. I spoke to witnesses who saw him board. An agent remembers him purchasing his passage. He fled to escape his creditors."

The colonel nodded. "And in spite of that his body was recovered evening last, also from the Thames. He had been weighed down with blocks, but the mooring line was eaten through and he floated to the surface. What was left of him, that is."

"Is there any doubt as to his identity?"

"None. He had some papers on his person that were still legible once they dried. I came to this news late and only by happenstance. I have since confirmed it beyond question. It is Rutherford."

South took this in, remembering how he had questioned India after learning of Rutherford's disappearance. He thought she had been genuinely concerned, not only for Rutherford's well-being but his own. Could she have truly had a hand in his murder?

"There is one other thing," the colonel said slowly, "about his manner of death."

"Yes?"

"It was not the same as Kendall's."

"Then he wasn't beaten?"

"No. Not beaten. His heart was cut from his chest."

India placed a steaming bowl of chicken broth in front of Darrow. She bit back her smile when he regarded the offering with more resignation than appreciation. "Do you find you have no stomach for the broth?" she asked.

"Some meat in it wouldn't be amiss," he said.

"Then you are feeling more the thing? After so much difficulty with your porridge this morning, I did not think you could possibly accept even the smallest of tender slivers. Poor Mr. Darrow. You smelled it cooking in the pot and it has whetted your appetite." She sniffed the air. "Why, I can smell it still. The aroma rises nicely above stairs, does it not? Well, if you are quite certain you can manage a bit of chicken meat . . ." Her voice trailed off as she made an assessment of the ruddy color returning to the valet's thin face. It accompanied the growling and grumbling of his stomach.

Darrow's jaw clamped tightly shut, and he pressed his hands to his sunken middle as if it would stave off the noises. A bit of chicken meat? He could devour the entire hen, including the neck and the giblets and the part of her that went over the garden fence last. India Parr, dark-eyed witch that she was, was starving him and finding a great deal of satisfaction in it, if he was any judge. She was diabolical. That was the word he had been in search of these past nine days. *Diabolical.* If he said he was feeling stronger, she immediately began making noises about returning to London. That forced him to find another complaint to keep himself bedfast and to keep her tending to his failing health. It was an intricate set he had been dancing with her, but Darrow did not fool himself into thinking he was yet in the lead. He may have invited her onto the floor, but she'd been twirling him in dizzying circles ever since.

"Mayhap a drumstick," he said, striving to keep his voice at a pathetically quavering pitch.

India remained skeptical. "Well . . . I suppose it could not hurt you overmuch. Mrs. Simon said it should be only the broth until you can stomach the porridge, but it may be that she is wrong."

Mrs. Simon, a widow from the village who had been the cottage's caretaker for more than ten years, came daily to assist with chores and the necessary cooking and baking and laundering. She arrived the morning after Darrow had been struck down by his mysterious illness, to find that all had been taken well in hand. After discovering that the new mistress of the house had risen early, drawn her own water for washing, and already found the store of oats, she took over stirring the thick porridge bubbling in the hearth pot.

They might have been fast friends, Darrow remembered gloomily, instead of newly met strangers. From his bed he could hear them chattering. Plotting. It did not take India long to engage Mrs. Simon in her conspiracy. The widow was ever so helpful in recommending poultices and herbal remedies that would draw the sickness from him. What one of them did not think of, the other did. He was grateful for his own knowledge about such things, as it was his only assurance they weren't poisoning him in carefully calculated increments.

India gently laid the back of her hand across Darrow's furrowed brow. "You are warm, Mr. Darrow. Shall I prepare a cool compress?"

The problem was, Darrow thought, if one simply discounted the fact that she was diabolical, India Parr was also tender, calming, and kind. She did not bristle when his mood soured, and she had never once complained about caring for him. He couldn't think of many who would have done the same. In point of fact, when he refined upon it further, he couldn't think of any.

"Yes," Darrow said weakly, his resolve crumbling in the face of her gentle ministrations. There were worse things in life than having India Parr's exquisite hands fussing over you. "A compress would be just the thing."

"And the drumstick?"

"Perhaps later." His stomach rumbled in revolt, but Darrow manfully ignored it. For now he would settle his hunger with broth and bread and appreciate these moments when India sat on the edge of his bed and cared for him with charity—and a bit of cunning—in her heart.

India laid a cloth in the basin and allowed it to absorb the cool water. Below stairs she heard the cottage door open. She glanced at Darrow and saw that he had also heard the sound. In anticipation of the widow Simon's strident call that she had returned from the village, his mouth had flattened in a thin line. "You needn't fear," India told him. "I shall not allow her to prepare a single poultice for you this afternoon." Seeing him relax slightly, she added, "If such is needed, I shall do the thing myself."

Diabolical. The bowl of broth wobbled on his tray as Darrow leaned back against a stack of pillows.

India squeezed water from the cloth, folded it, and laid it lightly across the valet's forehead. "Tilt your head," she instructed. "Never mind the broth. I shall feed you." She sat on the edge of the bed, careful not to dislodge the tray, and picked up the spoon. "Good. It is still hot. I was afraid it would not be after our discussion about—"

She stopped. Darrow was no longer giving her the least attention. His eyes were riveted to a point past her shoulder, and judging by the deep flush rising from his chest, it was not Mrs. Simon who was standing on the threshold. India's fingers tightened on the spoon. It was more out of habit than conscious thought that she pressed it to Darrow's mouth. "Here. You must eat." It was her voice, though she had no sense of the words. "It will not do for you to lose more strength. I should like to think that—"

"A touching scene." Southerton had heard and seen enough. He stepped out of the doorway and unfastened his greatcoat with abrupt, impatient motions. Tossing it on the trunk at the foot of the bed, he came closer. The spoon India had removed from his valet's mouth still hovered in the air. Darrow had not yet shown the presence of mind to swallow. South supposed that in their place he would be equally surprised by his sudden appearance. After all, it had been two days and a full sennight since he'd left them behind. India would have had cause to wonder if he had abandoned her. Darrow, who would have known better, had contrived to follow South's instructions and had landed himself flat on his back and under India's thumb.

"For God's sake," South said, removing his hat, "swallow whatever it is, Darrow, or spit it out. Put down the spoon, India. I am quite certain Mr. Darrow can manage eating on his own. You *are* all of a piece, aren't you, Darrow?"

The valet straightened, pushing himself to attention. The cloth on his forehead fell onto his tray, narrowly missing his soup. He swallowed and nodded at the same time.

"Good." South stared at India's back. She had not yet deigned to turn away from her patient. He knew that when she did so she would already have composed her expression. Whatever opportunity there had been to see naked emotion in her darkly mirrored eyes had now passed. "You will come with me, India."

Very much aware of Darrow's guilty but watchful glance, India set the spoon down carefully. She came to her feet and smoothed the apron pinned to her unbleached muslin gown. Turning, her features perfectly schooled, she merely inclined her head in South's direction. "As you wish."

As soon as they were gone from the room, Darrow removed the tray from his lap, threw off his covers, and dressed. He took his leave of the cottage by tiptoeing down the stairs, and when he met Mrs. Simon on the cobblestone walk he invited her to leave her parcels outside and join him for a meal in the village tavern. Nonplussed, she hesitated at first. It was when her eyes fixed on the great black stallion tethered nearby that she understood.

Mrs. Simon set her things down precisely where she stood. She folded her plump arms across her chest and stared at the cottage, her head cocked to one side. There were no raised voices, but then not everyone engaged in a row that could be heard by all and sundry. Mr. Simon had been one to bluster like a stormy north wind, and for the eight years they were married, she had given as good as she got. "So he's returned, has he?" she said plainly.

"He has."

She nodded once, her bow mouth screwed to one side as she mulled the consequences of this over. "I shouldn't be surprised if there's a murder to be done."

"I was thinking much the same thing. She doesn't easily ruffle, that Miss Parr, but his lordship has a way about him, you might say, that will surely test her mettle."

Her decision made, the widow Simon eyed Darrow with more interest than she had shown on any previous occasion. "You must be weak in the knees with hunger."

"Aye." He crooked his arm for her to take. "Didn't know if I could survive your curative powders much longer."

Slipping her arm into his, Mrs. Simon had the grace to smile apologetically. She glanced at him, a bit taken aback when she had to tilt her head so far. "My, but you're a tall one," she said softly.

Too hungry to wonder if he'd leaped from the frying pan into the fire, Mr. Darrow led the widow away. Behind him the cottage remained eerily quiet.

India followed South into the hall but hesitated when he turned toward her bedchamber rather than taking the stairs. Laying his hand flat on her door, he shot her a look that was at once impatient and challenging. It was enough. With impeccable timing, she swept past him just as he pushed the door open.

India was halfway across the room before she realized she was no longer advancing, but in retreat. She turned to make her stand. "I will not be bullied, m'lord." In contrast to her words and her posture, there were her eyes, drinking him in. The proof that these last nine days had cost him sleep and peace of mind was laid open on his face. It was drawn, the skin pulled taut. His fine features stood out in sharp relief. India did not want to notice these things, yet she found that once noticed, she could not pretend otherwise. Neither could she pretend she was unaffected by them. That he could stir compassion in her so easily filled her with a sick kind of dread, yet hadn't she spent every one of these last nights praying that he had not already come to harm? It was only because she retained some small measure of pride that she persevered. "You cannot simply snap your fingers and expect—"

"Have off, India," he said wearily. South leaned against the door. In the stillness that had settled over the room, its jarring closure was loud and discordant. He pulled off his riding gloves and looked around for some place to put them. India, as if moved by a force outside herself, stepped forward and took them out of his hands. Her fingers brushed his. It was the briefest of glancing touches, and yet they both drew back from it. She was able to hold on to only one of the gloves. The other fell to the floor between them.

India stooped to pick it up. She remained there unmoving when South's hand came to rest lightly on her shoulder and his fingertips grazed the bare nape of her neck. Tendrils of hair shifted against her skin. A shiver exposed her vulnerability.

She let the glove lie there and dropped the other beside it. The symbolism of the gesture was not lost on her. Two gauntlets thrown. No matter that it had been by accident, not design. No matter there had been no formal challenge. Something existed between them that was perhaps better left unstated, wanting only to be acted upon.

India stood. His palm made light and momentary contact with her upper arm, then her breast. He did not look away from her face, nor she from his. Tears made her dark eyes luminescent and spiked her thick lashes. "You will ease yourself with me," she said, taking his hand. "And I with you."

So simply said.

South's breath caught at the back of his throat. His lips parted around an unexpressed thought. There was much he needed to say and none of it that he wanted to. He suspected it was the same with her. So they would ease themselves first, just as she said. One in the other. The rest could wait.

India led South to the bed and pressed him without words to sit. She knelt at his feet and removed his boots. He could not tear his eyes away from her hands. They were slim and strong and exquisitely feminine, entirely capable. She pushed the boots aside, rose, and turned to the window. The curtains were drawn back by silken cords, and she ran her fingers slowly across one before she loosed it from its mooring.

"Leave it."

There was the briefest of pauses before she let the other one fall. Save for the thin, transparent flames from the fireplace, the room was shuttered in shadow. India smoothed the folds in the material, quieting their waving motion. She closed the small separation between them so even a slim beam of setting sunlight could not enter.

Turning to him again, her manner neither defiant nor yielding, India began to undress. After a moment, South stood and did the same. They were silent as they attended to this task, their eyes averted. Discarded clothing pooled around their feet. South stepped back as India approached the bed wearing only her muslin shift. She moved like a wraith, weightless, insubstantial. The urge to fall on her, to tear the shift from her body and feel the shape and heat of her flesh, was upon him so strongly that he dug his nails into his palms to stay his hands.

India turned back the blankets and slid into bed. It was only when she was covered that she removed her shift, drawing it over her head and letting it fall over the side.

South's eyes followed the movement. The fabric brushed his bare calf as it drifted past. His cock was hard, his balls heavy. He could recall no succession of moments from his past that were filled with such eroticism as India's modest disrobing. His mouth was dry and the words came with some difficulty, hoarse and rough. "Unpin your hair."

"Yes. Of course."

He had not meant it as a command. Now he could not make his tongue and lips conform to the word "please." In the darkened bedchamber, her pale hair was its own light, and he would have it framing her face. He could make out each gold and platinum wave as it was released and sifted between her fingertips. "Lie down."

India did. She stared at the ceiling while South shrugged out of his shirt and finally his drawers. She raised the covers only high enough to permit him to slip beneath. His body was close, not yet touching hers, just close. She could feel heat fill the space that separated them and caress her skin. For a moment it was difficult to catch her breath. India felt him turn, rise on one elbow, and she knew he was watching her, searching her features. She wished that it might be darker still.

"It will be better if you have few expectations," she whispered.

He bent his head, brushed her mouth with his. Her lips were cool and dry. "Why is that?"

India didn't answer. Couldn't.

South dipped his head again, this time catching the corner of her mouth. The tip of his tongue teased her lips, pressing lightly, tracing the lush pink line. It was all the urging she needed. India's mouth parted. The breath that had snagged in her throat was released in a tiny sigh. This time when he kissed her, she kissed him back.

The shape of her mouth changed, meeting the slant of his. She surged upward under him, lifting her face when he would have broken away. He pressed harder, tasting, raking. His tongue swept the ridge of her teeth, and she caught it and bit gently. He groaned, and it was as if she could taste the sound of that hoarse vibration.

One of India's hands lifted to South's shoulder. His muscles bunched under her touch, and more heat exploded against her palm. Her nostrils were filled with the scent of him. Man. Sweat. Lust. Leather. She found herself breathing deeply and still wanting more. He gave her that, subtly altering the rhythm of his stroking mouth and tongue, each brush slower and more deliberate than the last. The kiss was heavy and thick, his tongue like honey in her mouth, swirling about hers so that it felt as if she were drinking from his lips.

"Again," she said against his mouth.

"Greedy wench."

"I think I must be."

South twisted so that he lay partially over her. He cupped her face in his large hands and sunk his fingers into her hair. His erection pulsed hard and hot against her flat belly. One of his legs trapped her beneath him. For a moment he thought she might speak; her lips parted as if she meant to. Her body stirred under his. Restless, he thought. Needy and eager.

It was no different for him. When he felt her lift, her back arching, her heels digging into the mattress, he pressed back. He kissed her again, her mouth first, then the curve of her neck, the hollow beneath her ear, her temples. She moaned softly when he sipped the skin at the base of her throat. He made her do it again. And again.

India clutched his shoulders until the dizzying need to hold on to him passed. Tentatively her fingers slipped down his back, not stopping until they curved over her taut buttocks. His hips ground against her. She sucked in a sharp breath, her abdomen retracting, and she held on again, this time squeezing the firm flesh. South surged upward, her name on his lips. He buried his face against her hair. Soft threads clung to his cheek, his mouth. There was the fragrance of her. Of lavender. Of musk.

He wanted to be so deeply inside her that he was afraid he would hurt her. More frightening still was the knowledge that there was some part of him that wanted to.

With considerable effort he pushed himself away and fell onto his back beside her. He was breathing hard. She was holding hers.

India's heart hammered in her chest. Her breasts ached

for the crush of his body, the sliding of his sweat-slick skin over her nipples. Her nostrils flared slightly as she released her breath and slowly drew another. She let her head fall to the side in his direction. Her eyes followed the line of his strong profile, now made a silhouette by the glowing embers in the fireplace. "What is it?" she asked, tentative and uncertain.

The silence stretched, and she began to think he would not answer. Then, "I thought if I touched you a moment longer I would hurt you."

His candor deserved honesty in return, and she surrendered that much of herself to him. "I think it will hurt still more if you do not."

South turned on his side. He laid the back of one hand against her cheek and drew his fingers across it. "What are we doing, India?" He sensed rather than saw her smile. Somehow he knew the shape of it was at once tender and sad. "Will it ease either of us, do you think? Or complicate our lives beyond reason?"

"Both."

He suspected she was right. South traced the shape of her mouth with his fingertip. Her lips were faintly swollen and no longer dry. They had been made wet by his kisses, by the damp edge of his tongue sweeping across them. "I would have you say my name," he said.

She had been prepared to let him have the use of her body, yet using his name struck her as somehow more intimate. India hesitated. "Please, m'lord. I do not . . ."

South's hand fell away from her face but not away from her body. His fingers traced the sensitive cord of her neck and then trailed lightly along her collarbone. His hand slipped lower and slowly began bunching the sheet that still covered her breasts. Each clutch gathered more of the sheet in his fist, dragging the softly abrasive fabric across her tender skin.

He stopped suddenly. His curled fingers rested between her breasts, over the beating of her heart.

She actually whimpered.

"My name," he urged.

Frustrated, India squirmed.

South lifted his fist and the sheet away from her body. She moved against nothing but the air, and it was not enough. Not nearly enough.

"Southerton," she said, the sound coming harshly from the back of her throat.

He cocked an eyebrow and waited.

"South." She took hold of his wrist and brought his hand back to the valley between her breasts.

"That will do," he whispered. "For now." South drew his knuckles along the center of her belly, and she gradually loosened her grip on his wrist. He lowered his mouth to her nipple, brushing it first with his lips, then his tongue. He drew it into his mouth and sucked.

The sensation was like slim fingers of fire that left no scar. Here was pleasure so intense she wanted to withdraw from it like pain. India cried out, and the sound of it was naked and raw and yearning. She did not hear it as coming from herself at first. It had to echo softly in her mind for her to make it her own, and when she understood that he had wrested that cry from her, she pressed her lips together.

South lifted his head slowly. He nudged her mouth with his own. "Let me hear you," he said. "I want to hear you."

"No." Not that sound, she thought. Not the one that he made erupt from her soul.

He kissed her again. Warmly. Deeply. She hummed her pleasure this time, and the vibration tickled his lips. Her fingers plowed into his hair. She held him still and kissed him back, running her tongue along his lower lip, suckling him. His hand slipped from her hip to her breast, cupped the lower curve, and squeezed gently. His thumb brushed her nipple, then brushed it a second time. India moaned against his mouth, and he swallowed the sound. His thumbnail scraped her nipple. The small of her back lifted off the mattress, and her fingers tightened against his scalp.

But she didn't cry out.

India felt the shape of his smile against her skin and found she did not mind that at all. He had a beautiful smile, she remembered, and now that she was branded with it, there would be that part of her that was beautiful, too. Her hands slipped from his dark hair, fingertips trailing over the planes of his face. She felt his knee nudging hers apart as he made a cradle for himself between her thighs. He moved over her, his erection pressing again. She was not so aware of her raised legs but of the space he had created between them.

South's hand slipped between their bodies. She made room for him by drawing in her breath. His palm grazed the concave curve of her belly, her hip, and came to rest on her mons. She held herself quiet now, aware of nothing so much as the heaviness of his hand and the stillness of his fingers.

"Shall I give you ease now, India?" he whispered.

She averted her head, her eyes closed. He kissed the curve of her neck and pressed his question again. This time she answered him and did not mistake the voice for any but her own. "Yes," she said. "Yes, please."

It was the "please" that did him in. So softly spoken as to be more an expulsion of air than entreaty, it still moved him powerfully. He was aware of her again as not just any woman in his arms, but as this particular woman. She of the corn-silk hair and sloe eyes, the fragile smile and steely spine. The one who challenged him from the stage. The colonel's spy. Perhaps a traitor. She was India Parr, much admired, often offered for, always watched.

Profoundly alone.

The first movement of his fingers was a caress between the damp folds of her flesh. He went slowly. Inexorable. Insistent. She shifted restlessly, no longer able to remain quiet under him. He stroked her. Pressing. Finding a rhythm with his hand that complimented the breathy little sighs that came to the back of her throat. He felt the rise in her bottom, her hips, the arch of her back, the lift of her shoulders as she was pulled taut by sensation and then released from it, never quite coming to ground, but resting each time on a slightly higher plane until she was lifted again.

India sucked in a breath, held it, and felt herself shatter anyway. Her hands had moved to stay his but had only ended up resting on his shoulders. A flush washed over her skin from her breasts to her face. She felt the slow and heavy throb of her body as sweet lethargy replaced excitement. The normal cadence of her breathing was returned to her in time. She opened her eyes and turned her head. He was raised on his forearms above her, watching. India wished that she might see his face better, but the price was that he would have seen hers.

How would she have explained her tears?

She lifted her hand to his cheek. "You will have me now." There was a moment's hesitation, no longer than it took her to draw another breath; then she felt him nod. His lips grazed her palm as she let her hand fall away. On either side of her hips, her fingers bunched in the sheet.

South pushed himself back. His hands curved around her bottom, and she lifted for him without urging or pressure. His cock pulsed heavily against her, and his hips made an involuntarily grinding movement. He knew again the almost violent need to be inside her before he spent himself on her belly and thighs.

He took her deeply with his very first thrust.

India reared back, her heels pressing hard into the mattress again, her hips bucking once to remove his weight from her. The unexpected force of his entry stole her breath. The pressure of him inside her, the need to accommodate the heat and hardness of him, made her clamp her jaw. There was the metallic taste of blood on the tip of her tongue.

Every line of tension South felt in India was matched in his own taut frame. He held himself very still, not daring to move even once, because he knew he would not be able to stop himself then.

"India?" His voice was low, hoarse. He asked all manner of questions in this use of her name. Was she all right? Had he hurt her beyond bearing? Did she forgive him?

"It is . . . surprising, is all," she said quietly. At her sides her fingers slowly loosed their grip on the sheets. "I did not

think there would be so much of you . . . or so much of you
so quickly.''

The sound that escaped his throat was something between
a groan and a chuckle. He carefully stretched out over her,
bracing his weight once again on his forearms. Her body
cradled his. Her thighs pressed against the curve of his
buttocks. Deeper, she held his erection in a velvet fist.
''Don't move,'' he said. She contracted around him. ''No.
Not even there.''

Glad for the darkness that hid the heated color in her
cheeks, India made herself go still. She listened to his breathing, then her own. She felt the thudding of his heart and the
same in her. She considered the shape of his body as it was
defined by hers, the breadth of his shoulders filling her arms,
the slim, hard hips between her thighs. He had a flat and
narrow waist. His legs were long and lean, sleekly muscled.
Even against hers they were shapely, making as fine a line
without breeches as they did in them.

She was unaware at first that he had begun to move in
her. Somehow, he had waited her out, and in waiting had
been rewarded. Here, most intimately, she felt the leashed
strength of him, the power he would not press on her again
so violently.

She did not need him to tell her that she could move now.
Her hips rose and fell with little direction from her head
that it should be done. In the beginning the rhythm was his;
then it became theirs. Her thighs tightened; her calves curved
around him. She ran her hands along his back, up his arms,
and she would have had more of him if such a thing were
possible. He held her with the slow, deep thrusts of his body,
and she never thought a second time of trying to leave him.

South kissed her openmouthed, his tongue sliding over
hers with the same deliberate plunge as his hips. He felt
himself near climax and tore his mouth away, lifting his
head to draw in a draught of air and hearing her do the
same. Of its own accord the rhythm of their coupling changed
as each thrust came more shallowly and quickly. Her fingertips pressed whitely into his shoulders. He rocked her, urging

up and forward with his hips. He felt her watching him as he threw back his head and surged one last time.

India embraced the shudder that was his release and drew it into her. She accepted his seed, the huskily whispered sound of her name on his lips, and the last tremors of his pleasure. When he made to remove himself from her, she bade him stay because the entwined intimacy was comforting. It was only after some minutes had passed that he made to leave her again. This time she let him.

He rolled on his side away from her. She lay on her back. At first it was only that they pretended to sleep. Neither of them could have said when pretense became the reality, just that it came to pass.

The gush of something wet spilling from between her legs woke India. Eyes opening wide, afraid to move at first, she simply squeezed her thighs together to hold back the pulsing flow of blood and semen. Her bedchamber was darker than before, and she realized though it might not be late, night had certainly come upon them while they slept. Beside her, South's breathing was even and easy. He didn't stir as she carefully lifted the blankets and slid out of bed. She tentatively touched herself between her legs. Her thighs were smeared with her own blood.

India stole a glance at South as she silently rounded the bed. There was no dressing screen in the room, no place for her to go to steal a moment of privacy. Feeling her way, she found her discarded clothes and finally her shift. She slipped it over her head and held it loosely just at the level of her hips until she could clean herself. The water in the pitcher was cold, but she poured it into the basin on the washstand anyway. She dampened a cloth, then pressed it between her thighs.

India sucked in her breath sharply at the chill of it and stole another glance at South. She wished he were not so quiet. The occasional soft snore would have done much to ease India's mind as she completed her ablutions. She worked quickly, letting her shift drop to her ankles only when she was finished. Afterward she poured fresh water on the cloth and scrubbed it hard against itself, removing the pink stain she was certain would be there. She wrung it out, placed it on the washstand, then gingerly parted the curtains and opened the window. She pitched the water outside, closed the window, and let the curtains fall back.

It was then that she turned back to the bed and found herself taking root where she stood. Southerton was sitting up now, hunched on the edge of the mattress, a sheet pulled across his hips and legs. She did not have to see his eyes to know they were watching her closely or that they had gone from gray to steel. India's nerveless fingers could no longer hold the basin. It fell directly at her feet but did not break. It was odd, that. It should have been the bowl, she thought, instead of her.

South said nothing. He stood, wrapped the sheet around him, and went directly to the hearth. He stoked the fire, added coals, then lighted the candles on the mantel. India knew what he was about and she didn't try to stop him. She watched him carry one of the candlesticks back to the bed and hold it out over the disturbed tangle of blankets. He remained there, unmoving for a moment, then pulled the edge of one quilt back. Even from her disadvantaged angle several feet away, India could clearly see the smear of blood on the sheet that had been under her.

He would have liked to believe she had simply started her courses, but what he would have liked was not what was true. South lowered the candle. He turned slowly on his heel to India.

"You might have told me," he said quietly.

She shrugged.

"Do not do that. Do not act as if it were unimportant."

India lifted her chin. It had only been because she had no words. She found them now. "It was a detail. Do not assign it more significance than it deserves."

"You were a virgin. I think that has significance of its own accord."

"I told you once I was no whore."

"It is not the same thing as speaking plainly about the other."

"It cannot matter so much to you, m'lord. Someone must be first."

"So there can be a second?" he asked. "I think not, India."

Chapter Eight

India made no reply. She stooped and began to pick up the remainder of her discarded clothes.

"I mean it, India. You will take no other lovers."

She did not look up. She regarded the creased state of her gown and regretted she had not taken more care with it a few hours earlier. It was in want of ironing now. She laid it over her arm, smoothing the wrinkled folds as best she could.

Southerton was not accustomed to being so utterly disregarded. Quite without knowing how it happened, he heard his father's voice. The intonation, the lofty accents, even the deeply felt sense of injury were all there. What was a mystery was how it came to spill from his lips. "I will not be ignored."

India glanced up, both of her brows raised in response to his high-handedness. "Then you must not make such outrageous statements, my lord. When you have recovered yourself, you will know for a certainty that you are deserving of no reply." She bent her head again, concentrating on her task.

"Leave them."

"I would not abuse your generosity in providing a wardrobe for me."

"I don't care about that."

She laid the last articles carefully over her arm and straightened slowly. "I care, my lord. Save what I wore when Darrow brought me here, none of this clothing is my own. I imagined you took some pains to see to my comfort, and I would not slight your efforts."

He waved that aside. "It was nothing."

India placed the clothing over the back of a chair, then opened the doors of the large armoire. She removed a silken dressing gown and slipped it on. It added a much needed layer of warmth to the chill she was feeling so deeply. "I wish you would not dismiss it lightly," she said. "It was kind of you." She turned around, belting the robe. "You will perhaps understand that I did not have that opinion at the outset. I am quite aware of the other women who have preceded me here."

South stared at her. "How—"

"Mr. Darrow has apprised me of the use of this cottage as a trysting place. I collect there has been a veritable parade of mistresses."

One of his dark brows kicked up. "A veritable parade?"

"I do not think I overstate," she said without rancor. "It was irksome to realize the clothing you provided for me belonged first to another."

"Irksome."

She nodded. "I thought at first it might be jealousy," she said. "But upon careful reflection it was merely irksome. It cannot be important that you set mistresses in this place before me, and it must not be important that another will come after. You see, my lord, I will care for what you have given me now, because it is not only a measure of your generosity, but also because I would not begrudge someone else the use of it later."

Southerton was glad for the bed immediately at his back. He sat down slowly. Candlelight flickered over his face, illuminating the lines of weariness at the corners of his eyes.

"You speak of yourself now," he said quietly. "And of me."

"If you say so."

"It is an imperfect metaphor."

"But you take my point."

He nodded. He set the candlestick on the bedside table. In a gesture that bespoke quietly of his frustration, South's fingers raked his dark hair. "Things have indeed become complicated," he said at last.

India remembered his words clearly. *Will it ease either of us, do you think? Or complicate our lives beyond reason?* "I believe you had some foreknowledge of that coming to pass." The faint smile that had briefly touched her lips vanished. "Do you entertain regrets?"

Did he? South wondered. There was no single-word answer he could give, nothing so simple as yes or no. Because there was more truth in it, he said instead, "Perhaps I should."

India's eyes closed briefly and she nodded, understanding. "Perhaps I should also." She quietly crossed the room to the vanity and sat on the padded stool. The mirror reflected South's still figure on the bed. He was not watching her. Though she doubted it was anything in the fireplace that held his attention, that was the direction of his gaze. She picked up a brush and ran it through her hair several times before she began to loosely plait it. "Shall I prepare you something to eat?" she asked. "It is not so late."

"Is there no housekeeper to do that?"

"There is Mrs. Simon."

"The widow," South said, vaguely recalling that West had told him there was such a person to care for the cottage. "So that is her name."

India regarded him oddly. "Yes, well, it appears she has not returned from the village. Or if she did, then she has taken herself off again. Have you not noticed how quiet the house is? I suspect Mr. Darrow has also beaten a hasty retreat."

The vision of Darrow's swift exit had the power to raise

South's smile. "He looked like a man in need of rescuing. How long had he been abed?"

"Almost from the moment we arrived. All of the trunks had not yet been removed from the carriage when he collapsed in the doorway." India saw South's brow crease as he tried to sort out what could have happened so quickly to bring the thing about. "Do not trouble yourself to feign concern on your valet's behalf, my lord. After all, it was at your command that he played the invalid, and I beg you not to say it was otherwise. You must allow it is not cotton wool packed between these ears. I have some notion of the lengths he was prepared to go in order to keep me here."

India tied the end of her long plait with a black grosgrain ribbon and let it fall over her shoulder. She turned on the stool and faced South directly. There was a measure of satisfaction in seeing that he had been rendered quite speechless. "In an odd way, it was a compliment to my character that you believed I would remain at Ambermede to care for Mr. Darrow. I tried to keep that at the forefront of my mind, else I should have put him down that very first day. He fainted at my feet, you know. That is, he pretended to. I brought him around directly and managed to get him to the bedchamber, where you found him. He had had some idea of sleeping on a pallet below stairs until you returned. That was, quite naturally, unacceptable."

"Quite naturally," South repeated faintly.

India went on as if he had not spoken. "It would have been uncomfortable for him in the extreme, especially since your return was not so swift as was your intention."

South did not want to be moved off course by explaining himself now. He said simply, "There were . . . events."

"Of course," she said. "There always are." She rose and began collecting South's discarded clothing. "I contrived to care for your carriage and your grays and bring the remainder of the trunks inside. I found the cottage had adequate stores of food, and set about preparing something for Mr. Darrow and myself. It was a light repast only. I admit to some weariness by then, and I did not think Mr. Darrow should have more. He was complaining of an unsettled stomach and muzzy head.''

Symptoms South shared at the moment. "Go on," he said, fascinated.

"As I said, I prepared a light supper only. Still, you can imagine that it gave me quite a start to come upon Mr. Darrow helping himself from the larder much later that night. When I confronted him, he dropped like a felled tree at my feet for the second time. Upon my reviving him, he swore he did not know what he had been about. He would have had me believe he had been walking in his sleep.''

"Sleepwalking," South murmured.

India finished collecting his clothes and placed them on the bed beside him. "Cannot I prepare something for you?" she asked again. The lines of weariness had eased about his mouth, but she knew it was only because she had successfully distracted him with her discourse.

He caught her wrist as she would have moved away. "In a moment," he said. "First I would hear the rest of this story."

She looked down at his hand. His long fingers were like a loosely coiled bracelet around her wrist. She was tugged gently and moved to stand in front of him. The sheet that covered his lap was pulled taut as he hitched his heels on the bed frame and opened his thighs so that she could be inched to come between them. He took her other wrist and held it just as loosely as the first. He turned her arms lightly and brushed the faint blue web of veins with his thumbs.

India took a shallow breath. She felt her breasts swell, grow heavy, and begin to ache. She glanced away from his hand but did not meet his eyes. "I . . . that is, Mr. Darrow . . ." It was no good. She could not pick up the threads of what she had been saying.

"Sleepwalking," South prompted her.

"Oh . . . yes." To her own ears her voice sounded vague and distracted. She pressed on. "That is what . . . what he told me. I knew then what he was about and that it was all in aid of keeping me here. I determined I would also play his game. I helped him back to his bed, and each time he made noises about feeling more the thing, I made noises about returning to London.''

''I see,'' he said, though he was still trying to work the puzzle out. His caress of India's wrists was more absent now than deliberate. ''So you passed nine days in this fashion. Extraordinary.''

''Mrs. Simon was inordinately helpful,'' India said. ''She knows a great many remedies for what ailed poor Mr. Darrow.''

''You said nothing was wrong with him.''

''Precisely. But he was not without complaints.''

South regarded her serene smile with new appreciation. ''Therefore, you were not without cures.''

''Just so.''

He laughed outright then, not so much at what she said but in her ability to persuade him at once of both her wicked intent and innocence of the same. ''I perceive Mr. Darrow was no match for you.''

''I did have help,'' she reminded him.

South nodded. ''Yes, you did.''

She thought he would release her then, but he did not. He continued to hold her wrists, rubbing his thumbs idly across the sensitive undersides. She looked at him more directly when he remained quiet. A faint line had appeared between his brows, and she recognized the expression as one of careful deliberation.

''There is one part I am not certain I comprehend,'' he said slowly. ''You had only arrived when you decided you wanted to go again. You gave no indication when I left you with Darrow that your intention was to immediately leave. Indeed, had you wanted to do that you could have made a better attempt at escape while you were still on the road.''

India's weight shifted from one leg to the other. ''I changed my mind.''

Had he not been holding her wrists, he might have missed the subtle shift in her stance. Nothing changed in her expression. The clues were rarely there, he realized, unless she wanted them to be or simply could not help herself. "Yes," he said. "But why? Had you done so after two or three days when I did not return, your decision would have been understandable, but this choice you made to leave so quickly seems impulsive."

"Does it?"

"India." There was a mild reproof in his tone. "I shall hear it from Darrow if not from you. I would rather hear it from you."

She sighed. "Oh, very well. It is as I mentioned before. It was irksome learning about the other women."

"Aaah, yes," South said, taking that in. "The veritable parade."

"I had not yet made peace with it."

South's glance was wry. "Then it certainly was provoking."

"Yes." India gave her wrists a tug. She should have been able to easily break free from South's light clasp, but his fingers tightened and he held her fast. It seemed to her the bracelets had become shackles.

"I am teasing you, India." He gave her arms a small shake to impress the point.

"I know." It did not change what she felt. "Let me go, please."

He did. South watched her take a few steps backward. Her features remained shuttered, but she was rubbing her wrists, erasing what lingered of the pressure of his fingers on her skin. He frowned. "Let me see, India. Did I hurt you?"

"What?" Her eyes followed his and she saw what she was doing. She let her hands fall to her side. "No. It is nothing. You didn't hurt me."

He studied her a moment longer, then drew in a breath and released it slowly. "May I still accept your offer to prepare a supper?"

India did not hesitate. The distraction would be welcome. "Yes, of course." She took a pair of soft kid slippers from the base of the armoire and put them on. "It will not take long. I made soup earlier today.'' She went to the door, pausing to look at him over her shoulder just as she made to step into the hallway. "After you eat, you will tell me why I am here, my lord.'' She closed the door on Southerton's implacably grim smile.

The soup was heartier fare than what India had served Darrow. There were large pieces of chicken floating in the broth. It was thick with carrots, potatoes, and celery. She had also warmed a loaf of bread Mrs. Simon had made only that morning. She set it out along with sweet cream butter and honey just as South came in from tending to Griffin and his grays. He was carrying an armload of parcels.

"Was Mr. Darrow out there?'' she asked.

Southerton nodded. "At sixes and sevens. Not knowing whether to come or go.''

She looked behind South to see if his valet was following. When she didn't see him she said, "You might have invited him in for a proper meal.''

"He says he had one at the village tavern. With the widow Simon, I might add.'' Southerton set the parcels on the table. "I stumbled on these outside. Darrow said something about Mrs. Simon and a delivery and I don't know what else. He's had his fill of grog with his supper and will be very happy to make his bed with the cattle tonight.''

"Oh, surely not.''

"It is not a punishment, India. He was set on it.''

"Very well.'' She began unwrapping one of the packages. "Will you not sit down? I only want to examine this fabric. I have been contemplating a new wardrobe for Katherine. I have ideas in my mind's eye that I have not yet been able to put to paper.'' India unfolded a crimson length of cloth and held it up to her torso, letting it drape loosely between her arms. "What do you think, my lord? Does it suit?''

South took his seat and picked up his spoon. "Katherine? What Katherine do you mean? Surely not the shrew.'' Before she could answer him, South took his cue and spoke Petruchio's lines, memorized years earlier at Hambrick Hall:

> *"For you are call'd plain Kate,*
> *And bonny Kate and sometimes Kate the curst;*
> *But Kate the prettiest Kate in Christendom,*
> *Kate of Kate Hall, my super-dainty Kate,*
> *For dainties are all Kates, and therefore, Kate,*
> *Take this of me, Kate of my consolation;*
> *Hearing thy mildness praised in every town,*
> *Thy virtues spoke of, and thy beauty sounded,*
> *Yet not so deeply as to thee belongs,*
> *Myself am moved to woo thee for my wife."*

There was a faint whoosh in the air as India sat down hard, stunned.

"Your mouth is open," South pointed out, waggling his spoon at her. "Shall I feed you? Or perhaps I should call upon Darrow. He will be wanting to get some of his own back after the trick you played him. A trick, by the way, of his own doing. My instructions to him were far simpler. I told him to lock you in your room. If you supposed there was some compliment to your character because you stayed to tend him, it was Darrow's compliment, not mine. I would have thought, given the chance, that you'd have left him facedown in the doorway and driven the carriage back to London yourself."

India blinked at him. It was rather a lot to take in all at once.

South tasted his first spoonful of soup. He did not think it was only hunger that made it so welcome. There was something equally satisfying in seeing India's owlish expression. "As for the veritable parade of mistresses . . ." He thought he heard her make a small choking sound, but he was skimming for a medallion of carrot and could not be bothered to look up. "They are not mine. I do not deny that I have had such, I am three and thirty after all, but I have never set one up here at Ambermede. Darrow was not speaking of me when he said whatever it was that he said that you found so . . ."

"Irksome?" India's voice was almost without sound.

"Yes. Irksome." He swallowed another mouthful of soup. "Do we have those things settled between us?"

She nodded.

South's eyes narrowed. "I would hear it from you."

"Yes." Again it was more an expulsion of air than a word.

Now it was South who nodded. He turned his attention back to the meal India had prepared. "Your soup is growing cold."

She stared at the bowl in front of her but made no move to pick up her spoon.

"You may want to put your fabric away." His suggestion might have been meant helpfully save for the decidedly wicked smile edging his mouth. "Bonny Kate." He thought she said something that sounded like "vexing" under her breath, but he couldn't be sure.

India refolded the material and moved it and the other parcels into the adjoining room. She returned to the table without sparing South a glance and began eating. He had two bowls to her one and ate a good portion of the bread besides. They did not speak again until she stood to clear the table.

"Thank you," he said. "It was very good."

"You were hungry."

He bent his head to catch her eye when she reached for his bowl. "It was very good, India," he said again. "I am not flattering you."

"Then thank you." In spite of her effort that it be otherwise, her response remained stiff. She flushed and tried a second time. "Thank you." She was rewarded by South's easy smile, the one that touched his gray eyes and turned them smoky. India quickly gathered the bowls and utensils and placed them in the washing basin.

"Leave them," South said. "Mrs. Simon can attend to it in the morning."

India nodded, her stomach clenching. Without direction from him, she followed South into the drawing room and took a seat on the window bench. He handed her a woolen shawl, and she wrapped it around her shoulders. Outwardly, she remained calm while South stoked the fire. Her fingers worked over the fringed ends of the shawl, making small knots, then plucking them free. She followed his every movement until he chose a chair opposite her and sat. It was then that she found herself looking away.

The act of averting her glance made India understand how very apprehensive she was. For nine days she had been largely successful in pretending this moment would not arrive, and yet it was upon her now. It required feeling like a coward to not act as one. Her dark eyes swiveled back to South, and she regarded him directly.

"It was not only Westphal's death that kept me gone from here," South said. "I should have returned in the time planned had it been all that required my attention. There were also personal matters."

India nodded. It was unexpected that he would explain his long absence to her. She had the sense that he was apologizing, and she felt her stomach slowly begin to uncurl. Perhaps there would be no shattering news.

"Then there was the colonel's business," he said.

"I understand." The fist tightening her midsection was back.

"Mr. Rutherford is dead, India."

Shock held her still while the reactions she could not help spoke for her. India's face drained of all color until her complexion equaled the bleached whiteness of her knuckles. Her last breath sat heavily in her lungs, the pressure building as she could seem neither to expel it nor draw another, and her eyes darkened, the pupils dilating to the degree that the focus was removed from her gaze.

South rose from his chair and went to the sideboard. He found several decanters of liquor and chose the brandy. He splashed some in a glass and carried it to India. She did not lift a hand to accept it. "Here," he said. "Drink." When she still made no move to take it, South moved to press it to her lips. She shied back immediately, ducking under his arm and lurching to her feet. She was out the front door almost before he knew what she was about.

India made it to the cottage's far side before she dropped to her knees and vomited. She did not hear South's approach over the sound of her own retching. His hands on her shoulder and midriff, holding back her braid and the tails of her shawl, gave her a start. Her attempt to shrug him off came to nothing, and it was left to her to finish emptying the contents of her stomach while he held her.

South helped India to her feet and handed her his handkerchief. She accepted it without a word, as she did his escort back into the cottage. When he offered her the brandy a second time she took the glass in both hands, pressed it to her lips, and drank deeply. It was like swallowing fire, and India gasped in reaction. Moments later it lay gently in her stomach, warming her from the inside out. When the glow was upon her she held out the empty glass to him. "Another."

He didn't argue. He filled the glass with less than half as much as he had given her before, then bade her sit again before he handed it over. Under South's watchful eye she sipped gingerly this time. He prepared himself a drink and returned to his seat. The weariness he'd felt these last days was upon him tenfold.

India watched South stretch his lean, athletic frame in the chair until he was almost in a recline. His long legs were extended toward her. His arms rested casually against his abdomen, the glass of brandy held loosely between his fingers. The crown of his head lay darkly against the green and gold damask fabric. His heavily lashed lids hovered at half-mast, shielding his eyes but not the sense of his watchfulness.

"You told me Mr. Rutherford had abandoned this country for America," India said. "To escape his creditors."

"I believe I also related I had some doubts."

"You have none now?"

He shook his head. "None."

"How did you come by this knowledge?"

"The colonel."

"It is not known about London?"

"No. His family was informed, of course, but they are not eager to have the manner of his death spread about. They believe it was gaming debts that brought him to such a bad end."

"It is a reasonable supposition, surely?"

South roused himself enough to give her an arch look. Reasonable, he thought, if one did not have the larger view. He wondered at India's ability to deny or conceal the truth from herself. "Rutherford's relations have no wish for others to know the extent of his debts or the consequences they have had on the family. They have contented themselves so well with the story that he is abroad, even one who knows better would find it difficult to disbelieve them."

"You speak of yourself now."

"Yes. One of the matters that kept me in London was spending time in the company of Rutherford's sister and his brother-in-law, reviewing what they remembered of his last days. Though they understood quite well why I was there, and that I was in full comprehension of the truth of things, they were reluctant to admit that he was dead."

"So it is now a family secret."

"Yes, I suppose it is. Those few outside the family who know the truth will not speak of it."

India's fingertips tightened on her glass. "Who mourns for Mr. Rutherford, then?"

South said nothing. He watched her eyes become luminescent with tears that never fell. She bent her head and stared at her drink. It trembled slightly in her hands.

"I would know how he died," she said at last.

"As Kendall did," he lied. If she knew the truth, then there was nothing served by repeating it. If she did not, then he could spare her some detail. "There was a better effort made to dispose of his body." He told her about the mooring line and the bricks meant to keep Rutherford from surfacing.

"He was identified by some papers found on his person. A relative, his brother-in-law, confirmed that it was he."

India took this in. "You learned of this when you returned to London," she said. "Did you not?"

"Yes."

"But you had already taken me from the theatre, so it does not follow that one has something to do with the other."

"I did not say that it did."

"Then why am I here, my lord?"

"You are aware of the attempt on Prinny's life last year after the opening of Parliament."

India frowned. "Yes. You must know that I am."

"Why must I know that?"

"Because I—" She stopped. "No. If you are truly the colonel's man, then you will know the answer. He would have told you."

South was not entirely surprised that she was beginning to have some doubts. She must be wondering at this moment if a trap had been set for her. He gave her full marks for not leaping with both feet. "You provided Kendall with the first particulars that helped uncover the assassination plot."

"Yes."

"The Prince Regent was one of your earlier admirers, I believe."

India's posture became rigid. "I would not describe him as an admirer. The troupe performed for the king and queen. Other members of the royal family were present, including the Prince Regent."

"But Prinny took a particular interest in you." He did not wait for her to confirm or deny his statement. He had amassed a great deal of information these past days. When not engaged in the personal matters that had taken him from London to Battenburn on North's behalf, his waking hours and sleepless nights had been spent in learning particulars about India Parr that even the colonel had not been privy to. "He invited you to dine with him privately."

"Yes." She set her empty glass aside and held the knotted tails of her shawl in a bloodless fist. "Not then," she said stonily. "He did not invite me to dine then. His invitation came later. It was discreetly offered."

"And you accepted."

"It would be more to the point that I did not know how to decline."

"There were several offers, I believe."

"I dined with the Prince Regent four times."

South nodded. "It is unusual that it did not come to light. One cannot always rely on Prinny to conduct his affairs so quietly. He enjoys the notoriety, I think. It would have been a coup for him to have entertained you openly, and done more to bring the public's attention to you. You were not yet as well known then as you are now."

"I begged him." Her lips moved around the words, but there was no sound.

South used his elbows to hoist himself higher in his chair. He leaned forward. "How is that again?"

"I begged him," she whispered. Then again, more loudly this time, pushing the words past the ache deep in her throat, "I *begged* him."

It was as though his chest were being squeezed. South felt India's humiliation as keenly as if it were his own. He stayed where he was, stoic in the face of her pain, unmoving because he knew she would not accept any manner of consoling from him. He was the one who had pushed her to this pass; why trust him to lead her from it?

India stood and went to the fireplace. The chill she felt was in her marrow, but she held her hands out anyway, accepting what poor relief the red-orange flames could offer. "I did not want to be the Prince Regent's courtesan," she said at length. "Nor any other man's. I have never wanted success in the theatre at the price some were wont to demand of me. That I have allowed Mr. Kent to use me as he does, to promise my favors without regard to my own feelings, is as much as I can properly bear. He never asks how I will turn the suitors away. It is truer that he does not care. He never inquires after them once he has lightened their pockets. If one of them tries to press himself most insistently, it is left to me to ensure his pride is not unduly trampled and his money is not withdrawn.''

Short of self-immolation, India did not think she would ever be warm again. Her back to South, she hugged herself. ''The Prince Regent was one of those who were most insistent. What he considered charming was often ham-handed and coarse. It required every diplomatic skill at my disposal to turn him away without giving offense and then to keep it all quiet. His wounded pride might easily have turned to revenge. In the end there was nothing for it but that I beg him not to dishonor me in fact or in fiction. So I did. It struck him finally that he might make a magnanimous gesture. I think he was quite taken with his power to grant this simple favor.''

India waited for Southerton's response. When it was long in coming, she eventually turned around and set her back to the fireplace. He was regarding her steadily, his eyes faintly narrowed, his features thoughtfully set.

''He gave you reason enough to dislike him,'' he said.

''He is still the Prince Regent. And someday he will be king. It matters not whether I like or dislike the man. I respect that we are all in his service and that he is in the service of England.''

''Still,'' South said after a moment, ''it would have been understandable if you had withheld information about the plot on his life.''

India stared at him, incredulous. ''I would never do such a thing.'' Her hands dropped to her sides, and her fingers curled into fists. ''Do you think that I did?''

''I don't know.''

It may as well have been an accusation. His doubt was like a blow to her midriff. It came so hard, it drove the breath from her lungs and weakened her knees. India actually thought she might buckle to the floor. It was the knowledge that Southerton would treat her with much less sympathy than she had shown poor Darrow that kept her upright. ''I told Mr. Kendall all that I knew,'' she said.

South's voice was grim, implacable. "You did not tell him how you knew it."

India experienced a moment's relief when his eyes dropped away from her face to her hands. "He did not ask."

South watched her fingers twist in the folds of her silk dressing gown. "Is that so?"

"Yes."

Although he knew differently, he let it pass. "Tell me about the Spanish consul. Señor Cruz." He saw her fingers twist again. When he raised his eyes to her face, her complexion was pale but her expression was now closed to him. "You were reporting to Kendall about his liaison with Lady Macquey-Howell."

India returned to the window bench and sat down. "How could you lie with me?" she asked quietly. "You brought me here with these suspicions in your pocket, all these uncertainties about my character, and yet you were able to lie with me."

"Perhaps I was the one beguiled."

She drew in a breath and released it slowly. Her voice remained polite, her dignity at full measure. "Go to hell, my lord."

"South," he said, smiling faintly. "You agreed to use my name."

India rose and headed for the stairs. "Good night."

Southerton did not come to his feet. "We are not finished, India."

She continued climbing and did not look back. He did not follow.

It was the fragrance of baking bread that woke India the next morning. It wafted from below stairs. She was usually closer to the source of it than she was now. On any other morning she would have risen before Mrs. Simon arrived and been shaping the dough in the pans. Her fingers and face would have been sprinkled with flour, her apron marked by water and a smear of butter. If she had been thinking of

Southerton, worried about his continued absence, she would not have let the widow see it. For Mrs. Simon she was entirely good-natured, some part of her glad of the woman's company even when she wished it might not last so long each day. In Mr. Darrow's presence she was equally cheerful, though not without mischief, rousing his suspicions that she was always on the verge of taking flight on her own, then allaying them by making enough noise no matter where she was so that he would know she had not.

India heard Darrow now, his voice coming to her from the bedchamber he had occupied until last night. She could not make out any single word, only muffled staccato bursts. In between them came Southerton's deeper drawl, equally hushed by the wall separating them.

She stretched slowly, her muscles protesting because she had ill-used them the night before, confining herself to the winged chair in her room rather than sleep on the bed she had so recently shared with South. India completed her morning rituals without much thought. She washed, dressed her hair in a loose knot at the crown of her head, and chose a simple long-sleeved muslin day dress from her wardrobe. Lacking ornamentation on the sleeves or closely fitting collar, it was banded near the hem by two parallel rows of sky blue satin ribbon. The silken shawl she chose to wrap lightly about her shoulders matched the bands of ribbon almost perfectly.

She was on the point of leaving the room when she remembered what she had been too tired to do the previous night. With almost violent motions, India stripped the bed of its sheets and the offending stain of her virginity. Arms full, she went back to the door, grasped the knob, and pulled.

The door did not open.

She turned the knob again, rattled the door, and was met with the same end. Over the top of the sheets she stared at the door, genuinely puzzled at first. When the truth of her circumstances was borne home, India did not know whether to laugh, cry, or indulge in a tantrum.

Southerton had actually locked her in. It was medieval.

India considered what she might do to attract his attention. She could wait for him to come to her, of course, but that did not settle well with her. There was nothing pleasant about being his lady-in-waiting. It occurred to her to knock on her door or the wall, but some time had passed since she'd heard anyone in the other room, and she suspected that South and Mr. Darrow were already below stairs. She could simply call for someone, drop a chair on the floor, or pound her feet, but none of those seemed a proper response in light of what he'd done.

India shifted the sheets in her arms as she thought. Then she found herself staring at them, a frown creasing her brow as the first vague notions of a plan began to unfold in her mind. Turning slowly on her heel, India faced the window. She regarded the sheets again.

Did she dare?

She did. She would.

It was medieval.

India tied the sheets together and pulled the knot tight. She wedged the ladder-back chair under the window frame and attached one end of her makeshift rope to the uppermost rung. Upon pushing the window open, India was first struck by the cold bluster of the wind she was facing. It swirled into the room, causing the curtains to strain against the silken cords that secured them. Flames stirred in the fireplace, and her shawl beat against her shoulders. She leaned around the chair and thrust her head out. Then she looked down.

Juliet's balcony was not so high.

India reconsidered her plan, wondered at the recklessness of it, and realized that her need to do this had little to do with Lord Southerton and everything to do with herself.

She threw out the sheet and was gratified to see that it did not dangle terribly far above the ground. Once she reached the end, it would not be a long drop. The likelihood of serious injury was small. At least that was her hope.

India bunched handfuls of her day dress and chemise around her waist, effectively raising each hem to the height of her knees, then secured the material by making a belt of her shawl. She climbed onto the slim window ledge and sat there a moment, letting her legs dangle over the side while she contemplated whether she had sufficient courage.

He must needs go whom the devil drives.

The old proverb seemed inordinately appropriate to her. India grasped the sheet, twisting it around one hand and holding it more loosely in the other, and tested the strength of it one last time. The chair creaked a bit as it was wedged tightly under the window, but it held its place as did the knots.

There was little grace in the way she eased off the ledge and suspended herself above the ground. Her stockinged legs flailed awkwardly, her elbows jutted out at odd angles, and her head knocked the windowsill with rather more force than she allowed was good for her. Still, after what seemed an eternity but in reality was only the passing of a few pounding heartbeats, her calves found purchase around the sheet, her elbows were pulled in to increase her strength, and the first wave of dizziness passed.

India began lowering herself to the ground. She reached the literal end of her rope in a very short time and dangled a moment longer before making her release. She was in free fall for less than two feet when her body was plucked in midair by two strong arms and brought to rest hard against a broad expanse of chest.

India stared up at Southerton as he eased her slowly to a standing position. He was grinning at her, not at all put out by what she had done, but as one who was genuinely entertained. Her toes settled on the ground, then her soles, and finally her heels. He gave her no choice about stepping back from the circle of his arms. She was struck by the odd thought that he had not faltered once when he caught her. Not a stumble or misstep. And now he was amused. If Southerton was not precisely the devil, then neither was he entirely human.

She was on the point of telling him that, but he spoke first.

''The colonel was in the right of things,'' South said. ''You are resourceful.''

A compliment? she wondered. Or merely an observation? He still had made no move to release her. His hands rested lightly on the small of her back, and her toes had settled closely to his. India realized she had not quite caught her breath, but she was no longer certain that the activity of her descent was responsible.

''As are we all when necessity demands,'' she told him.

South glanced up at the open window. The twisted sheet was unwinding slowly, the tail of it flapping against the house. ''You are better than most, I think.'' He regarded her again, his smile fading as one dark eyebrow was lifted. ''You have some particular destination in mind, I collect.''

''The kitchen, m'lord. Unless you mean to starve me, I would have breakfast.'' She saw his skeptical regard. ''What? Never say you thought it was my intention to leave.''

''It occurred to me.''

''Then let me apprise you of a particular fact you seem to be in want of. I do not ride and have never done so. I am quite afraid of horses. Your grays severely tested my mettle when I was forced to care for them, but now that your great Irish beast is stabled nearby, nothing could compel me to go within a stone's throw of their stalls. Furthermore, as much as I would enjoy a bracing walk this morning, I find the idea of going to London on foot rather daunting. So you see, it is only that I came for breakfast.''

At some point during India's persuasive little speech, South's eyes had dropped to her mouth. Once, as a youth, he had dared East to place his tongue on a frozen metal pail to prove that it would be caught fast. He'd been right, of course, and had cheerfully collected his winnings from North and West before he helped Eastlyn removed the pail from his face. Now South was moved to wonder if, upon kissing India, he might find his tongue wedded to her lips in just such a fashion. Her manner was half again as cold as that pail had been.

It required only a few steps to back her against the wall of the cottage.

"My lord?" India's hands had been resting lightly on Southerton's upper arms. Now her fingers curled and clutched the brushed woolen sleeves of his frock coat. "South?"

She was not frozen at all, he thought, but frightened. While it was not there for him to see in her face, he felt the truth of it in her fingertips and heard the same in her voice. She would not have acquiesced so easily to calling him South had she not felt some pressure to do so. The knowledge made him cool his heels.

He released her abruptly and stepped back. South felt the tug of her fingers on his coat, almost as if she meant to keep him close. He reminded himself that it was only that she was slow to react to her release, not that she was urging him to remain as he was.

"Mrs. Simon was preparing a tray for you," he said. "Which Darrow was going to deliver. The widow knows nothing about you being locked in your room, only that you complained of not feeling well last night and again this morning. It is up to you to explain to her as little or as much as you wish. I would not look to her for help, India. She is well compensated for her services here. It would only cause her great discomfort if you attempted to compromise her loyalties to West by slighting one of his friends."

"I should do a great deal more than slight you," India said. "If I were possessed of such a nature. I am not, however, so I shall make you this promise: I will not leave this place without your permission, but neither will I have further conversation with you if you shut me away again."

"It seems less a promise than ultimatum."

"It matters not what you name it. Do you accept?"

He studied her face, wondering how to gauge her sincerity. She regarded him candidly, but without real hope. A tendril of hair had escaped her topknot and was fluttering against her cheek. She brushed it away in an absent gesture, her concentration entirely on him. "Yes," he said of a sudden. "I accept."

India nodded. Without a word, she stepped around him and began walking on a path that would take her to the front of the cottage.

"India?"

She turned slightly, a single eyebrow raised. "Yes, my lord?"

South indicated her attire with a sideways lift of his open palm and a glint of humor in his eyes. "I can only imagine what conclusions Mrs. Simon will draw if you do not repair your dress." He cocked his head to the side to bring her attention to the sheet unfurling in the wind. "Or remove this bloody flag."

For a moment she stood as if rooted. Slowly her lips parted in a silent O as her glance took in first the state of her rucked-up muslin gown and exposed calves, then the dangling, flapping sheets and the dark smear of her blood on the lower one. "Oh!" She spun on her heels and began running, tearing at the shawl around her waist as she did so.

South watched her disappear around the corner of the cottage and welcomed the sound of his own laughter, even though he knew she would not. He was still smiling to himself as he continued on the path to where the horses were stabled.

India slipped inside the cottage's front door, looking little worse for wear. Her hope that she might manage to reach the upstairs without being seen came to naught. She was immediately confronted by Mr. Darrow, whose hands were balancing a tray laden heavily with a full breakfast. Surprise made him bobble the tray, but he recovered himself quickly enough to maintain his hold. Mrs. Simon's approach from the kitchen saved him the necessity of speaking.

"Ah! You have been for a walk, I see. And all this time I thought you were still abed. At least I thought that's what his lordship said." She wiped her damp hands on her apron.

"No matter. You are feeling more the thing, I suspect. Is that the way of it?"

"Yes," India said, although a trifle more weakly than was her intention. Relief, not ill feeling, was taking its toll.

The widow's cheerful smile faltered a bit as she came closer and gave India a thorough inspection. She noted the glow of perspiration on India's forehead and upper lip, and every strand of hair that was no longer in place. The day dress was possessed of an inordinate amount of wrinkles for having only been taken that morning from the armoire. "Though mayhap not as well as you would have us believe. You lost yourself in the morning and walked too far. You will forgive me if I say you look a trifle overwrought."

India seized the explanation the housekeeper presented her and agreed to it readily. "Just so," she said. "I had thought to improve my health and find myself still in wanting of it."

"I think 'tis likely you were afraid I'd allow Mr. Darrow to serve you the same gruel and broth we served him." She made a *tsk*ing sound with her tongue as she indicated the tray Darrow was holding. "This is rather more than you will want, I know, but I would not be stingy."

"And she wanted to rub my nose in it," Darrow muttered.

Mrs. Simon rolled her eyes. "Will you take your meal here or in your room?" she asked India.

"In my room, if you please."

"Oh, it pleases me," the housekeeper said. "Since it's Mr. Darrow who will have to mount the stairs with that great load." Chuckling to herself, she returned to the kitchen.

India avoided Darrow's pointed glance and preceded him up the stairs. Outside the door to her room, she paused while Darrow balanced the tray in one hand and retrieved the key from the top of the door frame with the other. He unlocked the door and pocketed the key.

"You will not lock me in," she said quietly as they entered the bedchamber. "I have it from his lordship that such will not be done again."

Darrow made no reply. He was staring at the chair wedged

under the open window, and the sheet knotted to its upper rung. After a moment he turned and fixed his sharp gaze on India. His smile was slow in forming but deeply admiring upon its arrival.

"Never seen the like before," he said, shaking his head, appreciative of not just her effort but of her. Then, as if he thought he'd said too much, Darrow set the tray down quickly and hurried from the room.

India stared at the door he'd closed behind him. Closed but not locked. It made her smile, and she considered what he'd said to her. *Never seen the like before.* It was high praise indeed from Southerton's man, given the fact his lordship was up to every trick—and Darrow had likely witnessed most or seen the aftermath. No doubt there was exaggeration there, but she was nonetheless warmed by it.

As India slowly walked toward the window to retrieve the sheets, she reluctantly acknowledged that had the words come from South, the warmth would have been much deeper. That same sentiment from his lips would have at last chased the chill from the marrow of her bones.

Chapter Nine

Southerton rapped twice on India's door and waited for her invitation to enter. When none was issued, he let himself into the room without regard for it. His immediate fear, that she had somehow contrived to leave Ambermede in spite of her promise, was relieved when he saw she was lying on the bed. He approached quietly, standing to one side until he was satisfied that she was indeed sleeping.

She lay curled in the middle of the bed, her back to him, one arm flung outward, the other buried deeply under her pillow. Her breathing was soft and even. She had removed her gown and slept on top of the bedcovers in her soft batiste chemise. The light-blue shawl that he had last seen wrapped around her waist was now lying across her shoulders. South leaned over India and adjusted it so that it covered her to her hip.

He had hoped to have some time alone with her this afternoon, away from the widow's keen hearing and Darrow's disapproving eye. Toward that end he had found errands enough to keep them both occupied in the village for a few hours. Mrs. Simon was happy to take herself off. South could see that she had fashioned some romantic tale for

herself, which explained his early absence from Ambermede.
Now that he was reunited with India, she thought he wanted
to be alone with his mistress for the same reason any gentleman might. The knowing glances South had observed her
exchanging with Darrow as they left confirmed this was the
bent of her mind.

Mrs. Simon's reasoned thinking, no matter how wrong it
was, was at least easy enough to understand. It troubled
South not in the least. The same could not be said of Darrow's position. What his manservant thought carried some
weight with South. They had been long together, and there
were times when Darrow had performed the functions of
confidant and confessor, advisor and friend. Always careful
of overstepping himself, it was rare that Darrow expressed
an opinion not asked for, yet he had done so this morning
when South informed him that he had locked India in her
room. Darrow had offered no less than three full sentences
to challenge South's actions and come to India's aid. When
South had dismissed them all, Darrow had merely inclined
his head and said, "As you wish." The fact that he had
proceeded with the rest of his tasks with equally reserved
and polite exchanges said far more to South than if he had
remained stonily silent.

Whether or not she had intended such a thing, India had
found a champion in Darrow.

Loath to wake her from her nap, South turned to go. His
toe nudged something on the floor that had been mostly
hidden under the bed. Curious, he gave the thing another
tap and stepped back to see what he had found. It was a
sketchbook. South bent, picked it up, and carried it to the
window to view it in a better light.

There were not many illustrations in the book, and all of
them were concentrated in the first few pages. It came to
him that what he was holding was one of the items he had
carried inside last evening. It had been wrapped in brown
paper then, slipped between parcels containing fabric and
who knew what else. India had mentioned having ideas for

a new wardrobe for the shrewish Katherine; here she had begun to realize the vision that had rested in her imagination.

South glanced to the place under the bed where he had found the sketchbook. Now he saw the pencils and charcoals she had used to make her illustrations. As he reviewed the sketches a second time, he realized that India was possessed of no small talent. With surprisingly few lines, she had been able to demonstrate the sweeping drape of a gown, the manner in which it might be shown to great advantage on stage. He recognized what he thought would become the saucy red dress, the one that bonny Kate would be wearing when Petruchio determined he would woo and wed her. India's sketch showed only a faceless woman's form wearing the gown, but South knew the lines of that slender frame were India's own. She was suggested there in the bold curve of a hip thrust forward and arms that were set impudently akimbo. The shoulders were held back, the chin lifted in an all too familiar angle. A hint of lively impatience was conveyed in the foot that peeked out from under the skirt. Raised slightly as it was, it seemed to be caught in mid-tap. As always, it was India's body that spoke for her while the face remained a mask.

"What are you doing?"

Absorbed by his study, South had not glimpsed India's movement on the bed. He did not look up immediately. "I am appreciating another of your talents," he said casually, refusing to be made to feel guilty. He turned the page and examined another illustration. "These are quite good, you know. They suggest that with discipline and study, your gift might indeed be extraordinary."

India pushed herself slowly into a sitting position. It was not so easy to throw off the dregs of sleep. She had meant only to close her eyes briefly and catch up on what she had sorely missed the night before. Now she realized she had missed her mark, and rather than waking refreshed, she felt only a kind of drugged torpor. She let her legs fall over the side of the bed and pushed ineffectually at her shift to cover them.

"I should like to have it," she said. As an afterthought she added, "Please."

"Of course." South closed the book, then the distance between them, and gravely presented it to her.

India did not look at it. Without a word she slipped it under one of her pillows. Her fingers groped for the shawl that had fallen off her shoulders, and found it behind her. She draped it across her back and around her upper arms. "Why are you here?"

"I said last night we were not finished, India. I came to talk."

"To interrogate."

"If you like."

She did not like, but there was no point in telling him so. He knew it well enough. She remained perched on the edge of the bed, making herself very still in the face of his silent regard.

South backed away from the bed and sought his seat in the wing chair. "How do you do that?" he asked. "How do you disappear in front of my eyes and become as wanting of features as your own illustrations?"

"You are ridiculous," she said in mild reproof. "I am here." One of her hands was raised, and she touched her nose, the corner of her mouth, and her chins with her fingertips. "My face parts as well."

South shook his head and sought a better word. "Detach," he said finally. "It is as though you detach yourself from the present, not drifting away on some flight of thought as I have often been accused of doing, but that you are so thoroughly withdrawn from what is before you that you cease to exist."

"I don't know what you mean."

Perhaps she didn't, South thought. Perhaps it came so naturally to her that it was accomplished without consciousness of it. A hedgehog rolled into a ball and presented its spines when threatened. All things considered, that response was not so different from India's.

"Why are you smiling?" she asked.

"Was I? I hadn't realized." South's mouth relaxed, his finely drawn features becoming solemn. "You haven't asked me about the theatre, India. Either last night or this morning. Are you not in the least curious?"

"You must allow there hasn't been time."

"Darrow says, in all the hours you cared for him, the subject of the theatre was never broached. Do you not miss it, India?"

She was long in answering. "I miss the freedom it afforded me," she said at last.

South considered that but made no comment. "And what of the people? Darrow told me you never evinced any concern for them."

"What could Mr. Darrow have told me about how they fared?" she asked practically. "He was here with me at the outset. You are accusing me of some ill feeling toward them, or perhaps of having no feelings at all. And you say this simply because I did not chatter to Mr. Darrow. That is a poor ruler by which you measure my concern."

"I make no accusation, India. I am only curious."

"Hang your curiosity, then."

In other circumstances he might have smiled at her vehemence. But not now. He would not have India thinking he was laughing at her when he only meant to be appreciative. He waited a few moments to see if she would raise any questions now. She did not. "Is there no one you wish to know about? Mr. Kent? The lad Doobin? Mrs. Garrety?"

"You have seen them?"

"Kent and the boy," he said. "Your dresser has been dismissed in your absence."

India closed her eyes briefly. Her mouth was dry. "Mrs. Garrety could often be . . . difficult. Mr. Kent tolerated her because I insisted. Do you know where she has gone?"

"No. I did not inquire. But she is bound to show herself when you return to London."

"Why do you say that?"

South shrugged. "For no reason save she seems to be devoted to you." India gave him no indication whether he had made a correct assumption. South watched as she contemplated her folded hands for a moment and then smoothed her shift over her knees. The detachment she affected was absolutely maddening. "Doobin fares well," he said.

Now a glimmer of a smile touched her lips. "I should expect nothing less of him."

"Mr. Kent first let it about that you were ill. He has followed that tale with another that you have retired to the country to rest and recover."

"I care nothing at all for what Mr. Kent has made of my absence."

"I mention it only because it strikes me as odd that he has made no private effort to find you. He seems to be satisfied with his own story, though I cannot think that he truly believes it."

"No doubt he is glad to be rid of me. I, too, could be difficult."

"It strains the imagination," he said wryly.

India lifted her head. Her smile complimented the ironic twist South had injected into his tone. "You shall be glad to be rid of me, too, m'lord."

South did not disagree with her, but it was not because she was in the right of it. He continued in a casual, conversational manner. "The wags have it that you fled first to the country estate of your lover and are now quite possibly touring the Continent with him."

This, at least, got some hard reaction from India, South saw. Her complexion paled and her fingers rethreaded themselves into a fist in her lap. He went on as she finally met his eyes with a bleakness she was incapable of containing.

"I do not think I am wrong in supposing this is what Kent truly believes has happened to you. His reluctance to confirm this latest gossip only means that he has no wish to cut off his nose to spite his face. He remains hopeful that you will return and that he can continue to promise your favors in exchange for the financial favors of others. I suspect that even now he is denying the rumors in order to squeeze a few more shillings from the hopefuls who will not credit that you are lost to them."

India's heels slid off the bed frame and dropped to the floor. She rose and padded quietly to the window. The curtains were drawn back. She stared out the window, hugging herself. "Do the wags have the name of my lover?" she asked.

"Only that it is Lord M."

She nodded once.

"The one that was mentioned not long ago in the *Times,*" South said. "The list of suspects grows short, I'm afraid. Most Lord M's have been accounted for, much to their regret. They had enjoyed a certain notoriety when their names were attached to yours."

"Then they were quite foolish."

"Mapple. Macquey-Howell. Matthews. Milsop. Embley."

She twisted and looked at him over her shoulder, frowning. "Embley? Oh, I see. I had not considered that possibility. That is clever of them to think so. Are there those among the *ton* answering to names like Emmerth, Emerson, and Emlenton?"

"Perhaps," South said. "I have not heard of such. There is also Montrose. Morris. Milbourne. A late entry has been the Earl of Margrave. He has recently returned from the Continent but almost immediately took himself off to his estate at Marlhaven. It must be that sojourn that kept his name well out of it in the beginning. Now, after paying a duty call on his mother, he is back in London and in fine form. He might have been the front runner for the title of your consort if it were not for the fact that he is out and about and you are not."

India turned back to the window. This time she pressed her forehead against a cool pane of glass. "Has society really so little to occupy itself?"

"Apparently so."

"And you, my lord? Is this the personal business that kept you away? I confess I had not considered that your absence was in aid of gathering every loose thread of town gossip. It amused you, perhaps, to know where I was while you listened to all the tales to the contrary.''

''None of it amuses me,'' he said.

She ignored him, straightening slowly. ''It is not to be borne.''

''And yet you do.'' South's voice gentled. ''Who is he, India? The one who has been your protector but never your lover. The one who has provided for your clothes and shelter and the small things you desire but could have never managed on your own. The one you fear. Milbourne? Montrose?''

''I will not listen to this.'' She placed her hands flat over her ears.

''You will listen, India.'' South came up behind her and grasped her wrists. She offered no real resistance as he drew her hands away. He brought them to her sides and held them there. He bent his head. His mouth hovered near her ear. ''I would have his name.''

A chill tapped her spine, sending a frisson down the length of her that she could not hide from South. ''I cannot,'' she whispered.

''Are you afraid of him?''

She remained silent.

''I will protect you.''

She shook her head. The movement made her cheek brush his lips. They were both still. Then the shape of his mouth changed against her skin, and his breathing hitched. Tendrils of hair were moved aside by fingertips as gentle in their flutter as a butterfly's wing. He kissed the hollow below her ear. ''No,'' she said, her mouth merely framing the word. Tears welled in her eyes. ''No.''

South lifted his head slowly, reluctantly. His chin rested against the soft crown of her hair. His own eyes were momentarily closed. ''*Does* he exist, India?'' he asked quietly. ''I have begun to wonder.''

She was glad he could not see her watery smile, or the regret that she was certain filled her eyes. He could not know, must never know, how close she came to telling him the truth just then.

"Will you tell me nothing at all?" he asked her.

"I cannot."

South released her wrists and raised his chin. "Even for your country?"

There was little space for India to turn, trapped as she was between the window and South, but she managed the thing—even managed to wedge her arms between them and place her palms flat on his chest. Then she pushed with all the strength anger afforded her. Surprised, South rocked on his heels, but he did not give ground. Instead, it was India whose feet slid backward until her spine was pressed firmly against the window.

India stared at her braced arms, extended as they were against South's hard chest. She could feel the steady beat of his heart under her palms.

"It hardly seems fair, does it?" South asked in gentle accents.

India allowed her arms to fall to her sides. She shook her head.

South cupped her chin and lifted it. "Do you want so badly to hurt me? Shall I invite one of your stinging jabs?"

"Do not be patronizing."

He sighed. "India, I must have some cooperation on your part."

She tore her chin away and slipped past him, knowing that he could stop her if he wanted to. He did not attempt to do so, and for that she was grateful. She put some distance between them. "My cooperation? Was it not enough that I came with you? I offered no resistance at the inn. None at all to Darrow. None even yesterday when you . . . when I . . ." Her eyes darted toward the bed, and she did not finish that thought. "What is it that I stand accused of that you would have cause to question my loyalty?"

"The plot to kill Prinny," South said flatly. "Kendall's murder. Rutherford's. There have been questions raised concerning the affair of Lady Macquey-Howell and Señor Cruz.

And now there is rumor of a conspiracy against the cabinet ministers, some of whom are known to be supporters of your theatre—and particular admirers of yours.''

India's legs actually trembled, but she remained standing. "You cannot truly believe . . .'' The words died in her throat. She swallowed hard and tried again. "You cannot believe I am responsible for even one of those things. I would not . . . I would never . . . how can you think it of me?''

South did not answer immediately. His weight shifted. He raked back his dark hair. Finally, he released a long-held breath. "I don't know that I do,'' he said quietly. "You confound me, India Parr. At every turn.''

Her knees would have buckled then, but South caught her by the elbow and eased her down on the stiff ladder-back chair.

"Head down,'' he said. He placed one hand at the nape of India's neck and pressed lightly until her head was at the level of her knees. "You need a moment for the blood to flow properly.''

She would need to stand on her head to accomplish that, she thought. South had done nothing but turn her world on end since she'd met him. She had no sense of up and down any longer. She was head over bucket now, and it seemed perfectly right that she should be so.

At South's instruction, India took slow and even breaths. The pressure on her nape eased, and she was gradually allowed to rise.

"Better?'' he asked.

She nodded.

"I want to help you, India. You asked why I brought you here, and that is the answer. The simplest, truest answer. Because I think you need help and don't know how to ask for it, or even that you believe you might be deserving of it.''

"The colonel . . .''

"He knows you are with me.''

"Then he approves of—''

South's brows drew together as he dropped to his

haunches beside India's chair. "Not precisely. I did not tell him what I intended. . . . He learned of it after the fact."

"After the . . . ?"

"When he heard that you missed a performance—you, who have not missed a performance in well over a year— and when he could not immediately find me . . ." South shrugged. "I have settled with him since I returned for Westphal's funeral. He is allowing me this time to learn the truth."

India understood what South did not say. "Because you have given him no choice."

South merely shrugged.

"You are defying him."

This observation raised his grin. "No. Nothing so alarming as that. It is merely that I am taking a different course than he would, but that is often the very reason he calls upon me."

"I don't understand."

"He cannot surround himself only with lackeys who never question what he says. Events . . . people . . . circumstances . . . they often look different from where he is sitting. He has information—facts—at his fingertips that are certainly useful, but he would be the first to admit he does not always have the sense of the fit of things."

"And you do?"

"Sometimes. Not always. But the colonel would never deny me the use of my own judgment in these matters. I must never substitute my judgment for his. If I am not at liberty to do what I think is right, then I am of no real use to him." South came to his feet. He poured India a glass of water from the pitcher on the washstand and carried it to her. "Here. You appear in want of something to remove your tongue from the roof of your mouth."

Smiling weakly, she accepted the glass and drank. "He thinks I'm guilty, doesn't he?"

"It would be truer to say that he is still willing to be convinced otherwise."

The laughter that bubbled to India's lips held not a whit

of good humor. She glanced at South uneasily. "There is not very much difference there."

"There is enough, India. Help me prove where your innocence lies."

She did not know what to say to that. Had there ever been a time she could lay claim to innocence? Yes, of course there had, but it was so very long ago that it seemed more often another person's life. The glass in her hand was cool, and she held it against her temple for a moment, easing the growing ache just behind her eye.

"Is it a megrim?" asked South.

India shook her head and lowered the glass. "Nothing so wicked as that." She looked up at him and asked frankly, "Why would you want to help me? If you are honest, you know you are only a little less certain of my guilt than the colonel. How can that be enough for you to want to do anything on my behalf?"

He hesitated. It was not merely that he wondered what she was prepared to hear, but that there were those things he was not necessarily prepared to admit. "Quid pro quo," he said finally.

"What?"

"You may call it quid pro quo."

"I don't understand."

"You extended your trust to me once," he reminded her. "I would offer the same to you."

"I see." Was she disappointed? India didn't know.

"You sent Doobin to my home with a message that we should meet in the park," South went on. "You did this after we had already arrived at an agreement about how we would communicate."

"That hardly speaks well of me."

"My first thought, also," he admitted. "But the more I considered your actions, the more I was able to entertain the notion that perhaps you had not acted without provocation." South returned to the wing chair and sat. Leaning forward, he rested his forearms on his knees. "Was that the way of it, India? Did someone demand you lay a trap for me?"

She said nothing.

"I asked Doobin who was with you when you gave the message to him. He told me it was only he and Mrs. Garrety who were present. Is that correct?"

India's mouth flattened briefly as she pressed her lips together. She nodded once.

"Then you received direction from someone else at an earlier time." It was not a question that he posed to her now but a fact as he saw it. "It puzzles me still *when* this might have happened, because so much time was spent observing your daily routine."

India stopped rolling the glass between her palms. Her fingers pressed hard on it instead. "You were watching me?"

"Yes." He did not tell her that he had not done so alone. She would not like to know how many people in his employ had assisted in the effort, Darrow among them.

"But you promised you—"

He held up his hand, stopping her. "I promised I would cease to make inquiries regarding you. That is all I agreed to. And I kept that promise until I had you safely here. As for what my observations revealed ... the truth is, very little. If you find any peace in it, India, you have guarded your secrets well."

Mayhap she should have felt, if not some measure of peace, then at least a modicum of relief. She experienced neither. What India felt was the sensation of one being driven inexorably toward a corner. Most frustratingly, she was allowed to glimpse each exit, every escape, along the way, yet never shown properly how to reach one.

South went on. "Is there anyone who knows about the occasional work you do for the colonel?"

"No!" More quietly she added, "No one." India set her glass on a nearby table. "I promise you that is the truth."

"I'm inclined to believe you."

India felt a measure of hope mingling with her surprise. "You are?"

He nodded. "I reasoned that if you had wanted to set a

trap for me yourself in the park that night, you would have placed such a message in the *Gazette* as would get me there. If you had informed someone else—your protector, for instance—of your arrangement with me, he would have also used that same means of communication. The fact that Doobin came round with the message suggested to me finally that you had spoken to no one.'' South regarded India with one brow raised. ''I seems to me that you are in the habit of keeping secrets on all fronts.''

''I suppose that's true.''

''It is time for you to give some of them up, India.''

''I . . . I don't—''

''Do you trust me now?''

She hesitated. ''I'm afraid for you.''

''That is not what I asked. Do you trust me?''

''I . . . yes. I do.''

''Tell me his name, India.''

India's arms clutched her middle.

''Your protector.''

She bent forward at the waist.

''Who is he, India?''

''Lady Margrave.'' Her voice came as a mere thread of sound. ''She is the Dowager Countess of Margrave.''

South stared at her. She had rendered him quite mute. It was not a thing done often, and normally his sense of humor would have asserted itself. Such was not the case this time. He simply had no response for what she had just revealed, and no means at his disposal to shield India from the pain the confession caused her. As though trying to recover from the aftermath of a blow, India remained bent forward in her chair.

South had not expected that her answer would have such physical repercussions, or raise so many more questions in turn. ''India. Tell me what I can do for you.''

''Leave.''

''I meant what can I—''

''You can leave me,'' she said, her voice stronger now. ''I want nothing so much as to be alone.''

South came to his feet. "Very well." He quit the room without another word.

"There's snow coming," Mrs. Simon said, assessing the sky from the drawing room window. "Mark my words, it will be nigh to knee deep by morning light."

South looked up from the meal the housekeeper had put before him. He ate alone because India remained in her room and neither Darrow nor the widow would have supposed he might welcome their company at the table. "Then you must remain at home tomorrow," South said. "I can think of nothing that requires your attention here."

"Oh, but there is Miss Parr. If she is not well, then you and Mr. Darrow will have to—"

"Fend for ourselves?" He chuckled. "I assure you, Darrow and I have been doing that for more years than we care to measure. Isn't that the way of it, Darrow?"

From his place on a stool near the hearth, Darrow paused in his whittling. "Aye."

"There you have it."

Mrs. Simon looked from one man to the other, each seeming to be perfectly at his ease, and wondered why she continued to suspect it was otherwise. Certainly it was nothing she could make her concern. "And Miss Parr? She has been abed all this day and looking not a whit better than when I saw her this morning. What if she has need of a physic?"

"Darrow will know what to do."

Now Mrs. Simon frowned deeply. "Oh, my lord, if you will allow me to speak plainly."

South was unaware that the widow had ever done anything to the contrary. "By all means," he said. "You may say whatever you wish."

Darrow contributed a low utterance that was somewhere between a grumble and growl. He was ignored.

She pointed to Darrow. "Do not set this man and his remedies upon poor Miss Parr. She deserves not the like. She was everything kindhearted while he lay abed."

"Diabolical," Darrow muttered. "That's what she was."

"Oh, shush," Mrs. Simon said, turning on him. "You act as if it were a hardship having one such as she care for you. After that first night, she never said a word about you tiptoeing down the stairs to take your meal from the larder." She glanced back at South a shade guiltily, her bow mouth turned down at the corners. "It were just a game, you see, my lord. She pretended one thing. He pretended another. Only I don't know that Mr. Darrow here knew how much pretending there was. She's a right good actress, that Miss Parr. I can't say that I've seen the like since our vicar played Falstaff at the village fair three summers past."

South managed not to choke, but it was a narrow thing. "High praise, indeed. Have you shared this observation with Miss Parr?"

"Oh, yes, m'lord. I complimented her several times on the same. She allowed that Falstaff is a very difficult role and Mr. Dumfrey, our vicar, is to be commended. Gracious to a fault, she is." She gave Darrow another pointed look. "In spite of what some people might say."

Darrow kicked a small pile of wood shavings at his feet into the fire. They burned brightly, sparking red and orange and finally yellow. "Have off, woman," he said. "I'm not likely to hurt Miss Parr. I've been looking after his lordship with my remedies, and you can see for yourself he's none the worse for it."

The cottage was too small, South decided. "Do you know, Darrow, Mrs. Simon might like the pleasure of arguing that point with you on her way home. I believe you should escort her back to the village."

"Oh, but that's not necessary," Mrs. Simon said, flushing deeply. "It's not so very far."

Darrow, who had been rising above his stool, sat back down.

"I insist," South said.

Darrow started to rise again, hovered when it looked as

if the widow would mount another protest, then straightened completely at South's quick nod.

There was a bit more tit for tat as Darrow and Mrs. Simon bundled up for the walk into the village, but South found he could enjoy it, knowing it was going to be short-lived. He found a moment to press some coins into Darrow's gloved hand. "In the event the snowfall keeps you in the village," he said with a significant look, "and the widow doesn't see to your comfort for the night."

"How long will you not be needing me?"

"A few days. Mrs. Simon, too."

Darrow nodded. "Have a care, m'lord," he said under his breath. "Miss Parr's tenderhearted."

South blinked. "I am becoming convinced the same can be said of you."

"Hmmpf." Darrow stepped outside, where Mrs. Simon was waiting for him, and took the widow's arm. Behind them the door closed.

The widow patted Darrow's sleeve. "Cheer yourself, Mr. Darrow. Didn't I say his lordship could be induced to send us along directly? What need does he have of us, anyway? I've never known the like before. Most times when the cottage has been occupied, my services are only required for a few hours each day, lovebirds being what they are and all, but Mr. Marchman—well, his grace now—was particular that once I made the cottage ready I should also make myself useful all the day long."

Darrow looked at her askance. "Those were West's instructions?"

She nodded.

"I think he meant to have some fun with his lordship."

"I was wondering if that might not be the way of it. A shame, too. What with Lord Southerton and Miss Parr deserving to be alone more than most. I probably shouldn't say so, but his grace has always had a bit of the devil in him."

Darrow hunched his shoulders against the cold and moved

toward the widow protectively. "The viscount also," said Darrow. "But what a dull business serving them would be if it were otherwise."

She laughed. "Exactly so, Mr. Darrow. Exactly so."

India heard South climbing the stairs. He bypassed his own room and came to stand outside hers. She held her breath, wondering not only what he would do, but what she wanted him to do.

The rap on the door came lightly. If she had not been alert for it, she might not have heard. Still, she hesitated. There was no second knock, and the knob did not turn. A moment later she heard his faint footsteps in retreat.

India pushed her sketchbook off her lap and ran to the door. She opened it just as South would have stepped into his room. They both hovered on their respective thresholds, half in, half out, their glances locked, questions traded at first without words.

"I . . . I thought I . . ." India heard herself falter and fell silent.

"I saw the candlelight under your door. Forgive me if I woke you. It was not my intention to disturb you." He started to go in.

"No! Wait. You did not disturb me. That is . . . I was making sketches, not sleeping."

"Then I will let you return to your work. I only meant to assure myself that you were all of a piece."

She nodded slowly. "Yes. I am. Thank you for . . ." India stopped. She did not know why she felt compelled to thank him for anything. "Did I hear Mrs. Simon leave?" she asked.

"That was some hours ago."

"Hours?" With her sketchbook for refuge, she had lost all sense of time. "I hadn't realized."

"Darrow escorted her to the village."

"That was kind of him."

"It has started to snow."

India looked over her shoulder, but the candlelight near the window simply reflected the room back to her. "Will there be a lot, do you think?"

"Mrs. Simon says knee high by morning."

"Oh." There didn't seem anything more to be said. India could not make out what he was thinking; the thin curve of his mouth seemed more impatient now than amused. "Good night, then."

"Good night, India."

She ducked back into her room, closed the door with a quick jerk, and leaned against it. Then she was struck by the realization that her heart was beating rapidly and that her breathing was shallow. Her stomach fluttered uneasily in a way that was familiar to her. Onstage, this tangle of anticipation and excitement was not entirely unwelcome. It made her acutely aware of her performance.

Here at Ambermede, it served only to remind her how acutely aware she was of him.

India crawled into bed when she hoped she had exhausted herself. She tossed and turned, then slept fitfully. Once she got up and sat at her window, watching the snow fall. The steady drift of white-lace flakes across the glass made her eyelids grow satisfyingly heavy. She stumbled back to bed and lay there again, wide-eyed and alert to every creak of the floorboards and rush of wintry wind through the eaves.

When she rose a second time, it was not to go to the window. She stepped into the hallway instead, barefoot and without her robe. The light fabric of her nightshift floated about her as she hurried to South's door. She did not knock, because she did not want to give him a chance to refuse her. Pushing open the door just enough to slip inside, India did so.

Firelight cast his still form into relief. In spite of the cold, he slept only partially covered. One arm and leg lay outside the blankets, limned in orange and gold by the flames, long and sleekly muscled, astonishingly beautiful, and perfectly naked.

India approached the bed on the side closer to him. She

remembered how he had been the first time she had seen him sleeping in the hackney, and again only yesterday. She had been right to suppose that sleep did not render him unprotected, for here once more was the conflicting appearance of complete relaxation and readiness. She had learned firsthand that he could awake with a languid stretch or prepared to pounce.

Wary of which it would be this time, India touched his naked shoulder lightly. "My lord?" she whispered.

There was no response.

She tapped again, bending at the waist to lean over him. "Southerton."

He did not stir.

India eased herself carefully onto the edge of the bed and hitched the heels of her cold feet on the bed frame. A light shiver passed through her. She looked longingly at the heavy tangle of blankets around him and wondered if she could pull the corner of just one across her lap. "South?"

His breathing did not change.

India nudged his arm aside so she might have the benefit of one small part of the uppermost quilt. "Matthew?"

"What is it, India?"

So startled was she by the husky, rumbling timbre of his voice, India thought that, save for his quick reflexes, she might have come out of her skin. His arm snaked around her waist just as she would have leaped to her feet. He easily hauled her back to the bed, and she sat in the space made by the curve of his body on its side, his arm still tucked securely about her.

She was out of breath again. He was inordinately calm. "What is it you want, India?"

She had to wait until her heartbeat slowed to answer. "It is what I don't want," she whispered. "I do not want to be alone any longer."

"You only had to say so." South raised his arm and adjusted his position so that she might lie beside him. He pulled the blankets over her and up to her shoulders. She quickly made a nest of his offerings, curling close, rubbing the icy soles of her feet in a depression he'd made warm with his body. "Better?" he asked.

She nodded; then, because she wasn't certain he could see her clearly, she answered him. "Yes. Better."

South rubbed her arm lightly. He could feel the small bumps of her raised flesh under his palm. "You're still cold. Let me warm you."

India could have told him that the prickles he felt were not entirely caused by the cold. She did not. Instead, she allowed herself to be turned on her side, and inched closer to him, her head tucked neatly under his chin, her back to his chest, her bottom against his groin. "You were awake, weren't you?" she asked quietly. "When I came into your room, I mean."

He'd been awake far longer than that. What he was willing to admit to was, "Since you opened your door."

"You could hear me?" She thought she had been excessively quiet.

"Yes. And your scampering in the hallway."

India smiled. "I meant to be stealthy, you know."

South's chuckle came from deep at the back of his throat. "To what purpose?" he asked. "When you intended to wake me in any event."

Her smile faded. About her waist, she felt South's arm tighten fractionally. India did not know if he meant to force the words from her on her next breath, or simply sensed the change in her and offered this small comfort. She lay her arm across his and stared at the leaping, licking tongues of fire in the hearth. "I thought you might turn me away in the hall," she said. "Or at the door. I thought if I were here, at your side, it might be . . ."

"Impossible?"

"More difficult," she said. "I did not want you to say no."

"This afternoon you wanted to be alone," he reminded her.

"Yes."

"And I left you."

She nodded.

"Now you want to be with me."

"I do."

"And I let you."

India nodded again. Her hair rubbed the underside of his chin.

"Do you understand what I'm saying, India? In these things it will be your choice. Always."

"You cannot say that," she told him softly. "It is generous of you, but it cannot always be thus. You must allow that you will tire of me or grow impatient with my disagreeable ways."

"Then you do not know my mind," he said. "Because even if these things came to pass, I would not turn you away if you had need of me."

She smiled again, albeit with more poignancy than humor. Her mind flew back to some of the first words they had exchanged. She twisted them slightly to suit her purpose now. "Then I can expect that you shall always save me, my lord."

"Matthew."

"Matthew," she whispered.

"Yes," he told her. "You can expect that I shall always save you."

"Even from myself?"

He moved his head so his lips could brush the crown of hers. "Especially then."

India's fingers insinuated themselves between his. "We are safe here."

Not a statement, South realized, but a question. The tiniest inflection at the end made it so. "Yes," he told her. "We are safe." He felt her nod. India made no demands on him to explain how he could be certain. Her trust in him was implicit. "Will you not sleep now, India?"

His voice was so gentling, like the first soft strains of a lullaby, that tears came to India's eyes. She pressed the side of her face against the pillow to catch them.

"Sssh," he whispered.

She closed her eyes.

He absorbed her small shudder.

She slept. In time, so did he.

The muted light of a gray dawn was pressing at the window when India woke. She raised her face just enough to allow her nose and mouth to appear over the edge of the blankets. There were frost flowers on the panes of glass, and the fire had gone out. She could see her breath. Like a turtle, India ducked back inside.

Once under the covers, she was met by a muffled chuckle with certain lascivious undertones. "Cold, is it?" South asked.

"Mmmm."

"I could build a fire for you."

"Yes, please."

South found India's slim shoulder and pressed her onto her back. He moved so that one of his long legs partially covered both of hers. His erection pressed her hip. South lowered his head, found her mouth, and nudged it open with his lips. He kissed her once, twice, tugging lightly on her lower lip as he pulled away. He kissed her cheek, the line of her jaw. His fingers sifted through her hair, and he kissed the corners of her eyes.

His breath stirred tendrils of hair near her temple, then her ear. He whispered, "Warmer?"

"Mmmm."

South smiled. His teeth caught the tip of her earlobe, and he worried it gently. She moved under him sinuously, her fingertips sliding along his shoulders, then his upper arms, the sole of her foot rubbing his calf. He nuzzled the curve of her neck and felt the vibration of her small cry against his lips.

India helped him with her shift, raising it first above her knees, then lifting her bottom so that it slid easily to her waist. She spread her legs for him, cradling his hips with her thighs. He did not enter her but slid lower instead, and dragged his mouth along the curved neckline of her shift, then over the thin batiste until he found her nipple. His tongue laved the puckered aureole. The fabric clung to her breast, gently abrading it as she moved under him.

She felt a heaviness steal over her that had nothing to do with South's weight on her body. It was there in her breasts, her belly, her arms and legs. It squeezed her heart and kept her eyes closed. It was there, especially between her thighs, where she was wet and warm.

That would change later. She knew that now. South would change it for her, making her light with his touch, making her feel as if she were no longer grounded but required his weight to keep her so.

India's throat arched as South's attentions moved to her other breast. He suckled her through the gown, drawing the fabric and her flesh into his mouth, drawing deeply until she sipped air to catch her breath.

She was not withdrawn from him now, South realized. That he should think of it at this moment struck him as both odd and ill-timed, but it was there at the periphery of his mind and would not be put away easily. It made him smile, this peculiar notion, because he embraced the idea that she could come to him so honestly in this manner, without guile or fear, and that he could have her heart laid open to him, if not her thoughts.

When he kissed India again, she tasted the sweetness of his smile against her lips. It started thus, she remembered. He would clear her mind of everything but the wanting of his touch. She kissed him back, drawing in the taste of him with her lips and teeth and tongue, and felt the lightness come upon her gradually as the dawn. It began with her smile.

India's arms slipped around South's shoulders, and she whispered against his mouth, "Shall you love me now, Matthew?"

Chapter Ten

India heard the words with a kind of horror. Had she been able to look anywhere else, she would have, but South's fingers had threaded into her thick hair and cradled her head, preventing any sideways movement. Her mouth remained slightly parted; her eyes remained open. "I am sorry, my lord. I did not mean . . . that is, I . . ."

South bent his head and nudged her lips with his. "You don't want me to love you?"

"No . . . not . . ." Even as she said it, her thighs were parting wider for him and his hips were lifting and settling, and then he was easing himself inside her. Slowly. With infinite care. So unlike the first time he had come into her that nothing about it was anticipated. Here was gentleness. And cautious attention. For a moment she allowed herself to do nothing but feel. Toward that end India closed her eyes briefly and pressed her lips together. Instead of a sigh, there was a hum of pleasure.

"Are you sorry?" South searched her face. "I hope you are not. I want to love you, India."

"I only meant . . ."

He kissed her again. "I know what you meant." He could

feel her accommodating his entry, conforming to the intimate pressure he brought to bear. She held him snugly, hot and tight. Her body pulsed around him, yet she remained motionless, her dark eyes fixed on his. "Let me," he said against her mouth. "Let me love you."

At first there was only her faint nod; then he began to move, withdrawing once before he sank himself deeply inside her, and that was when she said, "Yes, Matthew."

He groaned softly, aware that she caught the sound of it with her lips. Her arms tightened around him; her hips lifted. He thrust, and then he thrust again. India rose to meet him. South buried his face in the curve of her neck and breathed deeply of the fragrance that was her skin and her hair. Her nails made tracks along his spine and down his arms. His muscles bunched under her touch. She left fire in her wake so that he knew the path her fingers had traveled long after they had moved on.

India let him love her. With his mouth. His hands. His cock. She did not think of what it meant to him, or even of what it meant to her. She did not think at all. These were moments like no other, with the lightness of pleasure upon her, and the sense that nothing mattered so much as giving herself up to them.

When she made small inarticulate sounds at the back of her throat, he pressed her to give them full voice. "I want to hear you," he said. "Let me hear."

When she closed her eyes and would have disappeared into herself, he called her back. "Look at us," he said. "See what you do to me."

When she arched under him, her body lifting and tensing and straining for release, he countered with his own. "Yes," he said. "Yes."

India felt as if she might be lost if not for South's body covering hers. He kept her in place, the warmth of him there on her skin, at her hip, her shoulder, her breast. He made her aware of the limits of her *self,* separate from him yet intrinsically, powerfully of his flesh.

Pleasure uncoiled in her, and moments later it was the

same for him. They shared a single shudder and sought the same breath. Their bodies surged a final time before they lay quiet. There were occasional aftershocks between them, rippling contractions of muscle and sinew and skin, where memories of pleasure were suddenly triggered and fired. India felt such a frisson slip under her skin as South removed himself and turned to lie on his back. Embarrassed that she could still experience his touch so deeply, she burrowed under the covers as if it were a mere chill she felt.

South was having none of it. He reached for India and made a place beside him where she could nest, her head on his shoulder, her hip touching his. His encouragement to join him was all she required. She did not resist. South bent his head and brushed her silky hair with his lips. It was like kissing sunlight.

"I would not have you far from me just yet," he said. "Unless you wish it. Do you?"

India shook her head.

"Good."

She closed her eyes. "I have had this dream," she said quietly. "The deep warmth of a bed. This precise embrace. My heart . . . my heart at ease." India said nothing for a moment, waiting for the ache in her throat to pass. "The reality is more profoundly satisfying than the dream, my lord."

"My lord?"

"South."

He gave her shoulder a light squeeze.

"Matthew," she said. The vibration of his chuckle against her ear was pleasant. "I confess my dreams made no allowance for you."

His smile was wryly tender. "You cut me to the quick."

"The fault lies with my imagination. You were outside of it."

"And now?" he asked.

India's quiet response came at length. "And now you fill it." She turned on him quickly, rising up on one elbow. "Forgive me," she said. "I should not have—"

South placed two fingers over her lips. "You must always say whatever you like," he said. "And make no apology for rendering me quite speechless. It is not a thing often done. My friends and family would pay you well to learn the trick of it." Behind his fingers, her smile was tremulous. "I have never thought myself lacking in imagination, India. I once passed eight months aboard a French prison barge, certain it was only my imaginings that kept me alive, and never once in all that time did I arrive at this place in my mind."

He let his hand fall away from her mouth. "I do not mean this cottage, this bed, or even this embrace. I knew them all on cold nights when I lay huddled on a damp deck, chained to men fore and aft, befouled by waste, and craving something other than stale air to fill my lungs. It was a simple thing to lose myself in dreams of what had once been familiar, perhaps even taken for granted. Friends. Family. Lovers. It all came easily. Some men despaired when those memories were brought to mind. Others found peace."

India could only stare at him. She had never once suspected that they might share this thing.

South went on. "I found hope, India, and yet, even then, I did not find you. I had not the capacity for it. If I have been outside your imaginings, then you have also been well beyond mine."

She nodded slowly and lay her head once more on his shoulder. "Is it Providence, do you think? That we should come together, I mean, and have some sense of the rightness of it."

"Providence?" South asked dryly. "Only if God is using the colonel as his prophet."

India jabbed him lightly with her elbow and ignored his grunt of pain. "That is blasphemous."

South did not apologize. He rubbed his side instead. "I had forgotten you were a governess once. You are very quick to correct one's smallest indiscretions."

"Hardly. I make many allowances for you. You should be a single bruise otherwise."

He sighed. No doubt she was right. "How long were you a governess?" he asked.

"A few months."

"It did not suit?"

She shook her head and started to rise. South's hand on her shoulder stopped her. "The fire . . ." she said for want of a better excuse to leave the bed. "It has . . ."

"I will take care of it."

"But the last time you—"

South gave her a splendidly arch look, and India's mouth snapped closed. "Good," he said. Unconcerned by his nakedness, he rose from the bed while India immediately slid into the warm depression he vacated. "Do not make yourself too comfortable there. I will not be gone from it long."

Her reply was muffled as she pulled the quilt up to her nose. "I'm keeping it warm for you."

Grinning, he grabbed his nightshirt from inside the armoire and slipped it on over his head. By the time he finished setting the fire, South was shivering. He did not wait nearby to take advantage of its heat but dove back into bed and unceremoniously pushed India to one side. In spite of that, she rolled close again to lend her heat.

"Where were you a governess?" South asked.

India raised her head. "Is there no moving you from your course once it is set?" she asked.

"Let us say it is not easily done," he told her. "I was a navigator. Even once moved I can plot my way back."

Though he said it matter-of-factly, India thought he looked rather too pleased with himself. "Vexing," she said under her breath.

"I believe you have said so."

"Well, it is no less true now than it was then." She laid her arm across his chest and then lowered her head. "I was employed by Mr. Robert Olmstead." Before South asked, she added, "He is a wool merchant in the Cotswold Hills, near Chipping Campden."

"A widower?"

"No. Why do you think so?"

"Because it is difficult to understand why Mrs. Olmstead would agree to have you in her home."

"Mayhap because she trusted her husband," India said tartly.

South was not fooled. "Did she?"

"No," India admitted after a moment. "But she trusted me. I was also possessed of more patience for the children. They minded me in a way they would not often do for her."

He made a point of rubbing the spot where she had jabbed him earlier. "She had not your touch for discipline, I collect."

India's lips twitched when she saw what he was doing. "Oh, you have certainly been sorely abused, my lord."

South gathered he could expect no sympathy from her. "What happened to make you leave Cotswold?"

She sighed. "It is much as you suspected. Mr. Olmstead was . . . unpleasant. It was better that I left."

"Did he hurt you, India?"

"You know he did not."

"I know he did not rape you."

India considered her words carefully before she finally said, "I gave as good as I got, my lord. On occasion I gave better. Mr. Olmstead was happy to see the last of me."

Which was no straightforward answer to his question, South thought. "How long ago was this, India?"

"Six . . . no, almost seven years ago."

South's brows rose. "You must have been a child yourself."

"I was almost seventeen. Hardly in need of a governess."

"Then you were sixteen and barely out of the schoolroom."

"I was prepared."

South could not help think about his sister Emma at that same age. She had talked of little more than her upcoming Season, still a year in the future. Emma would not have been prepared for such a position. But then, he thought, she had been raised from birth to expect something different

from life. What had been India Parr's expectations? he wondered. "Were you employed as a governess again?"

"No."

"Because you were given no character or because you
wanted none of it?"

"Both."

He started to ask another question, but she forestalled
him, sitting up and dragging a good number of blankets with
her. He watched with some amusement as she allowed one
bare leg to slide outside the covers and over the edge of the
bed and then used it to fish for her discarded nightshift.
South did not miss the moment she snagged it with her toes.
Her smile was as triumphant as that of any angler with a
trout on his line. She gave her leg a sprightly kick, and the
nightshift sailed upward. India caught it midair and pulled
it under the blankets. What followed involved considerable
wriggling and the occasional epithet. South's gallant offer
to assist her was met with skepticism. When India finally
emerged, covered in her batiste nightshift, it was an accom-
plishment of some merit, and she accepted his mocking
smile and marked applause as her due.

India pushed the blankets in South's direction and hopped
out of bed. "I would have my breakfast, my lord. If you
mean to question me without cease, then you must also feed
me." She eluded the hand he put out to catch her, neatly
dancing out of the way. She did not miss the darkening of
his eyes or the way they grazed her face and then took in
all of her. Her cheeks flushed, and her palms came up of
their own accord to cover the color. "I must dress," she
said quickly, not looking at him. Then she hurried from the
room before South made a second attempt to draw her back
into his arms.

South sat up in bed and leaned back against the headboard.
He stared at the closed door. His first thought was that she
had been embarrassed by his open regard, but the more he
considered it, the more it did not settle right in his mind.
Embarrassment was not quite the right word to capture what
he had seen in her face. He was not entirely certain that her

maneuverings under the covers had been as playful as she was wont to have him believe.

South glanced toward the window and realized how much daylight had finally spilled into the room. There was no longer any shadow play to conceal her. He had not closed the curtains last evening, and she had had no reason to do so when she came upon him in the middle of the night. But morning brought a different reality. One that South did not think was to India's liking.

Was she ashamed? he wondered. Was such a thing possible? She had no secrets from his hands and mouth. He had touched her everywhere, tasted her. She was all smooth skin and long, slowly curving lines. Her breasts had filled the cup of his palms. He had suckled her. He had pressed himself between her thighs and taken her mouth with his. His tongue had laved her nipples and flicked the hollow beneath her ear. It had traced the line of her collarbone and the sensitive underside of her wrist. She had let him do exactly as he wished. Touching. Tasting. Mounting her.

All of it under the covers, he realized. Or under the cover of darkness. He could do anything he wanted to her as long as he could not see. He could touch her in any manner except with his eyes.

South rose slowly from the bed. The room was warmer now, and he washed and dressed without hurrying. Long before he finished, he heard India leave her room and trip lightly down the stairs on her way to the kitchen. When he finally followed her, he once again had more questions than when she had left him.

As soon as his feet touched the bottom step, she handed him a long wooden spoon to stir the porridge. "Have a care not to let it burn, my lord. There is nothing so vile as scorched oats."

"If that is the worst you have tasted," South told her, "then you have eaten well." He accepted the spoon and bent to his task at the hearth while she used a large paddle to lift a loaf of bread from the hearth oven and check its underside. With an expert economy of motion, she tipped the paddle just enough to permit the loaf to slide neatly back into place and closed the iron door. Watching her, South realized he was shaking his head again, something he seemed to do a great deal when he was in her presence. Just when he thought he had some sense of who she was or who she had been, she showed him an unexpected facet. He could not have pictured her so comfortably contented at a cottage hearth.

"What is it?" she asked, straightening. She brushed at her cheek. "Have I a smudge on my face?"

"No."

"Then why are you looking at me like that?"

"Like what?"

"Like I have a smudge on my face." India was a perfect mimic, and she effortlessly mirrored South's expression back to him.

For his part, South could only stare. He knew that expression and didn't wonder that she had gotten it right. He *was* thoroughly beguiled.

"Well?" she demanded.

South raised his hand. "Here," he said, brushing her opposite cheek with his fingertips. "You have a smudge."

Now it was India who shook her head, bemused. She ducked out from under his arm. "The porridge," she told him when she felt his eyes following her. "Mind it carefully."

It helped to focus South's attention when a thick bubble of porridge burst and splashed the back of his hand. He thought he heard India's light laughter as he nursed the burn, though when he glanced in her direction she was simply setting bowls on the table and humming tunelessly to herself. If there was a smile playing about the line of her mouth, then she only meant to tease him with the hope of glimpsing it.

South thought he had a better chance of seeing the porridge smile, and was still thinking the same when they sat down to eat a few minutes later. "Do you mean to be Miss Butter-wouldn't-melt for the rest of the day?"

"I do not want to encourage you," she said primly. "India."

She raised her head then and gave him the fullness of her lushly curved mouth. It almost set South back in his chair. "Mayhap you are right to use it with discretion," he said after he recovered. "Otherwise, I will be moved to take you here at the table."

India's smile vanished as quickly as it appeared. "That is what I thought," India said in precise, cool accents. "It takes little enough to start you and so much effort to rein you in." She waggled her spoon at him. "Eat your porridge, my lord, while your mouth is open for it."

His mouth was indeed open. He filled it with a spoonful of hot oats before she literally had him eating out of her hand.

India sliced a heel of warm bread for herself and added a spoonful of jam. She was quiet as she spread it across the heel, her thoughts moving away from this place and time.

"What is it, India?" South asked.

She was not surprised he had caught her mood. He seemed to have little trouble doing that. She raised her face slowly to his and let him see she was now in earnest. "Will you tell me about the prison barge?"

He may have gauged her mood, but her question took him unawares. "What do you want to know?"

"You don't mind?"

"I will tell you if I do."

She nodded. "Very well. When did it happen?"

"Ten years ago. I was in the Peninsula then. Napoleon had taken Madrid after the rebellion. King Joseph had fled. There were skirmishes almost daily in the Atlantic and Mediterranean. The ship I was on had the misfortune to be captured by the frogs."

"You weren't ransomed and returned?"

"No. There were too many uncertainties at that time. We were moved to a barge and kept there while diplomats haggled over our fate."

"You said it was eight months."

"Yes."

"That is a very long time."

"Yes."

His succinct answers revealed more to India than she thought he meant to. "Did you regret your decision to serve?"

"No. Only that my father and I exchanged bitter words over it. He did not want me to go. There was no reason for it, you see, except that it was what I wanted and I was determined. I think he sensed I was prepared to defy him, and that was when he gave in. He did not have to. In that way he was far wiser than I gave him credit. Had he opposed me to the end, we might have never reconciled. I came late to this understanding, but with eight months to reflect on my father's actions, I was finally able to see he was possessed of no less good judgment than Solomon."

India watched a faint smile lift the corners of his mouth. She guessed the reason for it. "You told him so, did you not?"

"As soon as I saw him."

"He agreed with you."

"Of course," South said. "Then he called in my mother so she might hear me say the same. Apparently, my imprisonment had not given her so fine an opinion of her husband. I do not think she was prepared to forgive him if there had been no release."

"You are her son," India said simply. "I think it must always be thus for a mother and her son."

South shrugged. "Perhaps. It is true that she is persuaded she is in the right of everything where I am concerned."

"You do not sound convinced of the same."

"She is my mother, India. Not my conscience. And yes, I have had occasion to tell her so, though not in quite that straightforward a manner. With Mother, one is best served by practicing a bit of roundaboutation."

"And you are very good at that, my lord."

He smiled. "Yes. I am."

She returned his smile, albeit a gentler version than the

one she had given him earlier. "Tell me how you were released," she said. "Was it finally the work of the diplomats that aided you?"

"No. I might be there yet, waiting for an agreement. In the end, there was only one way to guarantee my freedom and that of every other prisoner on board. I escaped."

India's eyes widened fractionally. "Escaped? How was that possible?"

"Mr. Tibbets died," South said. "He was one of the men sharing leg irons with me. The guards had to unshackle us to remove his body. When the linking chain was lifted, I was able to move for the first time without the cooperation or permission of another man. The guards were not prepared for an assault. After so long a confinement, it is understandable that they would miscalculate the strength of their prisoners."

South set aside his spoon and picked up his cup. He wrapped both hands around it, threading his fingers together, and raised it toward his mouth. "I was able to overpower one of them. Mr. Blount, the man who shared shackles with Mr. Tibbets and me, took the other. We had planned for months for just such an occasion as this. It is but one way to pass the time, you understand, and it gives a man purpose to plot his escape."

South's half-smile mocked him. He drank from his cup. "We had imagined being able to take the keys from the guard and free everyone held in the same area. We would then move to other parts of the ship until we had taken it over. It was a reasonable plan given how many of us there were and how few were assigned to guard us."

India waited for the explanation of what had gone wrong. That something had was there in the gravity of his expression and the sober gray eyes that would not quite meet hers.

"One of the guards was able to fire his pistol," South told her. "Mr. Blount went down—mortally wounded, though I did not know that then. The shot alerted other guards. We could hear the shouts and their running approach toward us.

There was no time to effect the escape of all, so I went alone."

"The other prisoners must have urged you do so," India said.

South nodded. "Yes, they did. In very strong terms."

India searched his face. "You have regrets that you listened to them?" she asked gently.

He glanced up from contemplating the contents of his cup. "Regrets," he repeated, his voice slightly hoarse with emotion. "Yes. Always."

"But you . . ."

"I escaped, India," he said flatly. "Many of them did not. Seven men were hanged for having some part in my defection. A score more died from disease or despair."

"And how many were saved?" she asked. "The story does not end there, not with your escape. That is but the beginning. You went back, did you not? You returned for them, and those that survived in your absence were rescued because of it."

"You would have me be a hero, India. Is that it?"

"I would have you be what you are," she said. "Are you telling me you did not return?"

"No," he said. "I did. But you should not make too much of it. I had an obligation to those I left behind. It was my duty."

"You are a man of integrity, my lord. The obligation you had was to yourself, to act in an honorable manner. Perhaps it is as you say: you are no hero—yet it is not every man who risks his life and still asks, years later, what more could I have done. I do not believe you should reproach yourself for what you could not accomplish."

South sat back in his chair and regarded her over the rim of his cup. "Have I acted honorably toward you, India?"

India's brows drew together, and a small crease appeared between them. "I do not know what you mean," she said slowly, feeling her way. "It is not the same thing at all."

South's study remained considering. "Not the same," he murmured. "I wonder if that is . . ." His voice trailed off.

He set down his cup and returned to his rapidly cooling porridge. "You're frowning. Did I burn your porridge after all?"

Her frown actually deepened. "What?" India's glance fell to her bowl. "Oh. No. It is just that . . ."

"Yes?"

She pressed her cup to her lips and drank. "Nothing," she said. "It is nothing." If he did not intend to pursue the question he put to her, then she would be wise not to raise it, but she wondered what had provoked it. Did he believe he had not acted with honor toward her? Was it because he had taken her from London without her permission? Or shared her bed at her own invitation? "Tell me the rest," she said after a moment. "How did you get off the barge?"

South was not surprised when India did not press him to make any other explanation. He doubted that she believed he had acted in any way dishonorably, but it revealed much more about the way she thought of herself than how she thought of him. "There was time enough for me to take a coat and hat from one of the unconscious turnkeys. I put them on and slipped out in the confusion that came with the arrival of the rest of the guards. I made my way topside and threw myself in the water before I could think better of it."

"How did you know which way to swim? Could you see land?"

"Not then. I just struck out. It was when no boats from the ship were released to pursue me that I realized just how far from shore we were. They assumed, quite correctly, that I couldn't swim such a distance."

"Then how . . .?"

"Mere chance," he explained. "Some would say a miracle. A Portuguese fishing boat came upon me and hauled me in."

India's dark eyes narrowed. "How long were you in the water before they found you?"

"A day and a night."

She found she simply had no words to properly express

herself, nor any voice with which to say them. She could only stare at him. That he should explain so plainly, without bravado or extravagance, made India's emotions that much more deeply felt.

"The Portuguese took me to shore. Fed me. Hid me. Three days passed before I was strong enough to leave. I made my way north, found a packet boat, and stowed myself on board. That boat was stopped by one of His Majesty's frigates when it tried to run a blockade."

"You escaped again."

"It was not so much an escape as merely being found."

"And then the frigate returned to rescue the men on the barge?"

He shook his head. "No, that would have meant a full engagement. I asked to be allowed to have use of the packet boat instead and fly the French tricolor. When we arrived in the waters where I had last known the prison ship to be, our presence aroused no alarm. We were taken for a supply ship and given permission to come alongside the barge. By the time our ruse was discovered, we were in position to take the ship."

India knew he would not give her the details of that fight even if she had wanted to hear them. The truth was, she did not. "Did you leave the navy afterward?"

"No. Not immediately."

"But you had already served with distinction. You were honored, weren't you, for your escape and rescue?"

"Yes. Though that is neither here nor there. I remained until we had cleared the way for Wellington's entry into Spain." South saw that small vertical crease appear between India's brows. "It is like seeing a play through to the final act," he said. "Even when you have a wish to slip quietly into the wings before it is done."

"And did you have such a wish?"

"On occasion. As is often true, it was never the same after the rescue. It set me apart from the others, though I would not have had it so. I could not put it in the past, because I was not allowed."

"You were regarded as a hero," India said softly. South's brief, darting glance revealed again how discomfited he was by the thought of it. She imagined he must have abhorred the public expression of praise for his deeds. "And you only meant to do your duty."

"Yes."

She nodded. "I know it is not the same thing at all, but there are times I would rather be Ursula again, the gentlewoman attending on Hero, than Hero."

He chuckled at her wordplay. "If it is not the same thing," South said, "then it is not so very different."

"Perhaps." India finished her tea and set her cup down. "Is it why you choose to work for the colonel?"

South lifted an eyebrow in question.

"I mean, there is little chance of you being acknowledged for what you do at his urging."

He smiled. Trust India to come so pointedly to the heart of it. "That is as good a reason as any. Though I must tell you, the colonel has never urged me to do anything. No matter how it is couched, there can be no mistaking what he says for anything but a command."

"Does your family know?"

"No." He paused. "Does yours?"

India had been spooning her porridge. His carefully timed question made her head snapped up. "You must know that I have no family," she said.

"Why must I know that?" he asked. "I know only that I could not find any."

She merely shrugged.

South reached across the table and laid his hand lightly over her wrist. He held her glance. "Are we at another impasse?" he asked. "Did you think I would not return to the matters that brought us here? I have answered your questions, India. Not because I needed to. Certainly not because I found any pleasure in it. I answered them for no other reason than because you asked."

India swallowed. Her appetite had fled. She slipped her

hand free of South's and pushed her half-eaten bowl of porridge aside. "What do you want to know?" she asked.

"Your name," he said. He saw that he had surprised her. "I reasoned some time ago that the difficulty in discovering much about you lay in the fact you were no longer using your name. You selected India Parr for the stage, did you not?"

India stood and cleared her things from the table. She expected South to raise some objection, but he did not. He let her go, let her busy her hands with the mundane tasks of scraping and washing. "I was called Diana," she said finally. "You will allow that it is not terribly different from India. A letter moved here and there, another changed."

He nodded and continued to wait.

India unpinned the apron protecting her gown and began to fold it neatly. "Hawthorne," she said. "Diana Hawthorne."

"Hawthorne is nothing at all like Parr."

"No," she agreed. "It is not."

"Was Cotswold your home?"

"Cotswold?" At first she did not understand. "Oh, because of my position there as governess. No, I was sent there from Devon. That is where I grew up."

South came to his feet and skirted the table. He took the apron India was creasing with her fingertips out of her hands and laid it across the back of a chair. Placing his hands gently on her shoulders, he turned her around and nudged her toward the adjoining room. He pointed to the settee. "Sit. I will get your shawl."

He was gone no longer than a minute and India was sitting exactly as he had left her. South produced a dark-green Paisley shawl and placed it around her shoulders.

"Did you think I meant to faint, my lord?" she asked when he placed a bench directly in front of her and sat. "I assure you, I would not have."

He was in a better position to judge her pale features than she had been. "Let us call it a precaution," he said.

She nodded and looped the tails of the soft woolen shawl under her breasts. A strand of hair had fallen across her cheek, and she brushed it back. It was then she noticed how cold her hands were. She settled them on her lap, threading her fingers together to keep them still. "Are you familiar with Devon?" she asked.

"I can admit to little more than having ridden through that countryside on my way to Land's End."

"It is rich farmland for as far as the eye can see. Each little plot is carefully tended. Neat hedgerows stitch the fields together as if the landscape were a verdant quilt. The scale of everything is diminutive. Where London sprawls, Devon nestles. The hollows are filled with tiny cottages, and villages stay confined to boundaries of the woods and meadows. The people are plain and steady, hardworking and proud. So much in Devon is small, my lord, except the heart of its inhabitants. The people in the West Country have enormous hearts."

"That is good to know."

India smiled faintly at South's carefully polite tone. "I mention it because it is part of my story. I lived in one of those little cottages. My father had been in the king's regiments years before, and now he had a piece of England that was his own. You might not imagine that farming would suit him, but it did. My mother was a midwife. It was a skill she had occasion to learn following the drum. That had been her life for many years."

"Before you were born," South said.

"Yes. My parents were settled in Devon when I was born."

South nodded. "They are older?"

India changed the tense of his question. "Were," she said. "They were older. They are both gone now."

"How long ago?"

"A dozen years. I was eleven."

A faint frown changed the line of his mouth as South considered not what she had told him, but what she hadn't. "Together?" he asked. "You lost both your parents at the same time?"

"In a fire."

South realized he had not fully prepared himself to hear what she might have to say. "I am sorry." He held her gaze because to look away would have been cowardly. "Was it your home that burned?"

She nodded. "There was nothing left. Nothing. I was gone from the cottage that evening. I had been invited by the vicar and his wife to spend the night because I was to attend the fair with them the following day. My father could not take me, and my mother was anticipating there would be need for her services as Mrs. Doddridge's time was nearing." India hands unfolded, and she absently fingered the fringe on her shawl. Her smile was rueful. "I have not thought of Mrs. Doddridge in years," she said. "My mother confided that she was set to deliver twins. I cannot say whether she did or not. I only know that my mother was not there to assist with the birthing."

South watched India shake her head slightly, rousing herself from her reverie. He waited patiently to see where her thoughts would take her next.

"I sometimes wonder, if I had not been away, if I might have saved them," India said. "I slept more lightly, I think. I might have been able to do something. I asked the vicar about it, but he told me I should not dwell on what might have been. I needed to accept what was."

"There is not much in the way of comfort there for a young girl."

"No," India agreed. "It is not."

"There were no brothers?" South asked. It seemed unusual that she would grow up as an only child in a farming family. He had always imagined that the sturdy stock of the West Country—the spirited descendants of the Saxons and Vikings—would have a brood. Though no particular number defined that term, he knew it was greater than one. "No sisters?"

"No. None. There was only me. Diana Hawthorne. Daughter of Thomas and Marianne."

South thought he might have been able to touch her loneliness. It seemed that tangible to him. He caught her eye. "If there were some other way," he said. "If I could spare . . ."

India's short laugh was without humor. "Never say that you wish you could spare me this. You brought me here to open these wounds. If I must feel the pain, then you can look on it."

"I will look at whatever you want me to see, India. And yes, if I could spare you, or better still, take it upon myself, I would. But you know it is not true that I brought you here to open wounds when I had no knowledge of any."

"Didn't you?"

"You have secrets," he told her. "They are not necessarily one and the same."

India drew in a breath and released it slowly. "Perhaps you are right," she said wearily. "It is only that it has been so long since I spoke of it."

"Why is that?"

She stared at her hands for a long moment before she raised her palms in a helpless gesture. The same helplessness was reflected in her dark, lonely eyes. "I suppose," she said slowly, "because there has been no one to listen."

India had to hear herself say it aloud before she could comprehend what it meant. Had she truly allowed herself to become so isolated? Why hadn't she fought more? she wondered. Offered a struggle? When had she lost hope and embraced acceptance?

A small shudder slipped down the length of her spine. A sound, something between a hiccup and sob, escaped her lips. She covered her mouth with her fingertips, and her eyes darted away from South's implacable study. There was the press of tears at the back of her eyes and an ache in her throat.

"India?"

She shook her head quickly. If she spoke now, even if she only tried to speak, there would be tears, and they were something she did not want him to see. As weak as she had been, she had not often cried. To give in to tears seemed an act not of grief but of surrender.

South's fingers plowed through his hair and came to rest at the back of his neck. He massaged the tension that was like a thick cord under his skin. The action kept him from reaching for India and making an offer of comfort that she was certain to reject. He was on the point of getting up, solely for the purpose of moving about the room, when India turned to him again, her face pale, her expression oddly defiant.

"Let me say the rest," she said. There was a slight quaver in her voice, which India fought to control. "I would be done with this."

"Of course."

She nodded once. "After my parents died, there rose the question of what was to become of me. There were neighbors who would have seen to my care, been glad of it for the help I might have given them. The vicar and his wife, though they had three children of their own, would have also accepted me."

"As you say, the people of Devon are goodhearted."

"Yes. They were everything kind to me. It seemed as if the choice of where I should live would be mine, for no one had an opinion that one place was more suited than another." India smoothed the muslin fabric of her day dress over her lap as a way to dry her damp palms. "That changed when Lady Margrave expressed an interest in having me come to live with her. You were perhaps not aware that she has an estate near Devon. Not Marlhaven—that lies northwest of London. I am speaking of Merrimont. The property has been in her family for centuries and was never encumbered by entailment. She visited often, even after her marriage to the earl of Margrave."

India took a shallow breath, steadied herself, and continued. "You will no doubt wonder how I came to her attention. It is because of her son. She has but one child, and she would deny him very little. When she came to Merrimont, he often accompanied her unless he was at school. Lady Margrave permitted him to make the acquaintance of the village's children, though she made the initial selections.

Some of us would be invited to the estate for tea and cakes, and those who comported themselves well were allowed to return.''

"You were one of those?" asked South, though he knew the answer. He had no difficulty imagining her as she had been then, perched on the edge of a chair, politely accepting her cup of tea and a sweet. Her gold-and-platinum hair had likely been paler then. It would have framed her thin, solemn face like a halo. She would have been careful not to swing her legs or speak out of turn. She would not have given in to her curiosity by letting her eyes stray or asking impertinent questions.

India nodded. "My mother was firm that Lady Margrave would find no fault with my manners, because she knew my failure would reflect poorly on her. I suppose I understood that, too. I practiced sitting and standing and speaking and serving. I could make a curtsy without wobbling and eat a cake without dropping a crumb."

It was as if she were being prepared for the stage even then, South thought. "Did you go often to Merrimont?"

"Yes. Sometimes there would be three or four of us invited for an afternoon. On occasion I was the only one." India saw one of South's dark brows lift slightly in question. "Lady Margrave's son," she said. "He liked . . . he liked to play with me."

The pause was almost infinitesimal. So was the pressure India placed on the tips of her laced fingers. South missed neither. "He is older than you?"

"Five years."

Now South's single raised eyebrow was notched another degree upward. "India." He said her name flatly, with no inflection. "I did not become interested in girls five years my junior until I was twenty-three, and even then I found them silly, vain, and tiresome."

India did not blush. The effect of South's words on her was precisely the opposite. Color drained from her face, leaving her eyes the dark focal point of her features. "You did not know me," she said with quiet dignity.

South was quite certain India had never been silly, vain, or tiresome, just as he was equally certain she was being deliberately disingenuous. This was not a battle worth waging, South decided, at least not at this time. Rather than press her with questions about the young lord of the manor, South chose to let India continue in her own way. "Forgive me," he said. "You are right, of course. I did not know you. Go on." When he saw she was not to be so easily appeased, he added, "Please."

India pressed her lips together briefly, holding back the uncharitable thought that came immediately to mind. "Very well," she said. "As I told you, when my parents died Lady Margrave came forward and asked that I be made her ward. That she would petition to take that responsibility caused a nine days wonder. Until then, I thought I would be living with the vicar."

"You wanted to go with her?"

"I don't know." India saw his skeptical look. "No, I am telling the truth. I *didn't* know. My parents had just died. I had not properly begun to mourn them. I did what people told me, what they said was best for me, because I didn't know any differently. And no one asked what I wanted, Matthew. I was *eleven*. My opinion, if I'd had one, would have counted for nothing. Even the vicar said that I was fortunate to be given this opportunity. People whispered that I was *blessed*. Can you understand my confusion? My parents were gone from me forever, and I was told Lady Margrave's interest made me *blessed*.

"So, no, my lord, I didn't know if I wanted to go to Merrimont or the vicarage or to any of the other homes that would have had me. The clearest memory I have from that time is that I wanted to die."

South heard the quiet defiance that framed her last words. Her eyes were luminous with unshed tears. They hovered on the rim of her lower lashes, then slipped down her cheeks. She seemed unaware when they began to fall. He was not sure that she saw him any longer, though her gaze never wavered from his.

South extended his hand across the small space that separated him from India. "Take it, India," he said. "Take my hand."

She didn't move.

"Please," he said. "Let me . . ."

Her fingers unfolded slowly. They trembled. The tips brushed his, caught, grasped, and then she had him like a lifeline and was in his arms, holding on, being held, tortured sobs wracking her body and shaking him and the bench. She cried with the abandon of a wounded eleven-year-old, and South sank to his knees on the floor and took her with him, cradling her woman's body and her little-girl's heart.

Between the sobs there were inarticulate murmurings, phrases that could hardly be heard, utterances that made little sense at first. South strained to understand the broken words that spilled from her lips like a mantra, and when the meaning came to him, he was chilled.

"Me, too . . . why . . . why didn't . . . kill me, too?"

Chapter Eleven

South held her, rocked her. He felt India's desperation in the fingers that clutched his frock coat, and the cheek pressed hard against his chest. If she could have worked her way under his skin, he knew she would have done so. It hardly mattered, he thought, when she had already worked her way into his heart.

He whispered words of comfort against her hair, though he knew she couldn't hear him over the sound of her own weeping. He didn't ask her to hush, or admonish her. He let her cry until she exhausted herself, and when her body lay quiet next to his, he simply let her rest there.

India pulled away slowly, averting her head so she could knuckle her eyes free of tears. South produced a handkerchief and pressed it into her hand. She accepted it, blew her nose hard, then balled it up in her fist. "I don't cry prettily," she told him, pushing a tendril of hair back from her damp cheek.

South caught her chin and turned her face toward him. "Are you truly a vain and silly chit after all?" he asked her gently. "Or is it that I have given you reason to think so little of me?"

India offered him an embarrassed, watery smile. "I think it must be the former."

"That is all right then," he said with mock gravity. He felt a measure of relief when he saw a bubble of silent laughter part her lips. It would be all right, he thought. When she could laugh at herself, she could heal. "I have some experience with vain and silly chits, you see."

"Tiresome, also?"

"Oh, yes."

"How very regrettable for you, my lord."

He sighed. "I often find it so."

Her tremulous smile deepened, and for a moment it graced her eyes. India leaned forward and brushed his mouth with hers. "Thank you," she whispered. The look of vague bewilderment that crossed his features touched her. It came so easily to him, she thought, he was hardly conscious of what he had done. She took his hand and placed it between her breasts, covering it with her own. "For holding my heart so carefully."

For South it was further proof that she was outside all his experience. He had to clear his throat before he could talk. "Do you want to lie down? I will not press you with more questions now."

India knew it only meant a short reprieve. He would press her later. She drew a shaky breath and released his hand. "No, I will finish. There are things that must be said."

"Very well." He extended his hand to help India to her feet, but she shook her head. South realized she intended to remain sitting on the floor, and he did the same, turning as she was so his back rested against the settee's curved seat.

India hugged her knees close to her chest and watched the fire as she spoke. "It is hard to describe Lady Margrave's disposition toward me once I came to live under her care. She was not overtly attentive, yet she seemed to know all that I did. I was regularly brought before her to give an accounting of myself. She wanted to know my progress in the schoolroom and about my lessons on the pianoforte. She would study my watercolors and my stitchery and comment on my deportment. They were not pleasant interviews, though I cannot say that she was unkind or unreasonably critical. Perhaps it was only that I sensed she was performing a duty and that she regarded my presence as the fulfillment of an obligation.''

"What obligation did she have to you?" asked South.

"None at all. It is toward her son that she felt obliged. It seemed to me that Lady Margrave was rarely of a mind to deny him anything.''

South considered that. "Then he was the one who suggested you should come to live at Merrimont.''

India nodded. "To show charity,'' she told him. "That is how he explained it to me. He would be earl some day, he said, and he was preparing for that responsibility. I was to be his first good work.'' There was the faintest hint of irony in her tone as she said this last. "I was never in expectation that Lady Margrave would come to have fond feelings toward me. Had I been of her blood, I would have been the poor relation whose presence is merely suffered. In truth, our connection was more tenuous than that, and what she was, was indifferent.'' India glanced sideways at South and saw he was frowning. "I would not have you pity me, my lord. I wanted for nothing.''

"That is because you asked for nothing,'' he said flatly.

India ignored him. "I was fed and clothed and educated. In the main I lived at Merrimont, but I often went to Marlhaven and sometimes to London with Lady Margrave. There were times when she was desirous of my company, though not my conversation. I did not mind, because I liked to travel and Lady Margrave was not demanding.''

"What of the earl? He was ultimately your benefactor, was he not? Did you come to his attention?''

"Not in any significant way. He was at Marlhaven or at the London residence on all of the occasions I visited with her ladyship, and I was introduced each time, but beyond a few perfunctory inquires as to my health and well-being, he expressed little enough interest in my presence. I remember that I was relieved because I found him to be a rather frightening individual. He was always stiff and terribly correct, and when he spoke it was as if his voice were coming from a very deep well. The earl was not a large man, so those stentorian tones were all the more surprising. In later years he was often ill, so there were occasions when I was brought directly to his bedside. At the countess's request, I read to him, though I could not say that he cared particularly for my company. Still, he suffered it with more grace than he did that of his own son."

"No love lost there?" asked South.

"None."

"And it was always so?"

India smoothed the fabric of her gown over her knees. "I cannot say how it was before my arrival."

South made no comment, his mood thoughtful.

Watching him out the corner of her eye, India continued. "I do not recall any topic on which they agreed. I have witnessed other people take opposing views for the sheer challenge of the debate, but that was not the case here. This was ... different. Mean-spirited, I suppose. I was glad of being ignored by them when they were at loggerheads, which they often were."

Nodding slowly, South asked, "Even at the end?"

"Oh, yes. Especially then, I think, though I do not know what they argued about. I was careful to make myself scarce except when Lady Margrave insisted that it be otherwise. That was not often as the earl lay dying."

"I see. And when did he die?"

"It's been seven years."

South considered that. "About the same time you left to make your way as a governess."

"Yes."

He gave her an arch look. "Would you have me believe those events are not related?"

"You may believe whatever you like," she said coolly. "But it is a fact that it was never Lady Margrave's intention to present me to Society. Indeed, it would have been inappropriate for her to do so, since I had neither birth nor breeding to recommend me. She was clear from the beginning that I would be prepared for a gentlewoman's position, and you will allow that employment as a governess suits that admirably.''

The line of South's lips was derisive. ''Lady Margrave could have presented a monkey to the *ton* and had it embraced by the fold. She could have made a good marriage for it if such had been her desire. I think you come unreasonably to her defense, India. She sent you away when you were but sixteen.''

''I was ready to leave. In truth, I desired it.''

South shook his head. There was more, and India was still reluctant to tell him the whole of it. He was in equal parts frustrated and intrigued. ''You were still in mourning for the earl.''

''An observation only. I did not mourn him as I did my own parents. There was perhaps only a modest feeling of mutual respect between us. I do not believe I was showing a lack of proper regard by leaving when I did.''

''The countess found the position for you?''

''Yes. She arranged everything.''

''And the new earl?''

''Margrave was in agreement.''

''Then he was finished with his charity toward you.''

India hesitated. ''He wanted to see how I would manage on my own, I think.''

South had the sense that she had chosen her words carefully. India spoke of herself as if she were Margrave's experiment, not his mother's ward. ''Did he consider your turn with the Olmsteads a rousing success or failure?''

''I am not certain. Perhaps a bit of both.''

''I don't understand.''

''My failure to keep the position put me in need of his charity again. He enjoyed that, I believe.''

South's expression was frankly skeptical. ''You merely believe that to be true?'' he asked. ''Or you know it to be true?''

''He enjoyed it,'' she said flatly.

"So in that way it was a success."

"Yes. He would have had me return with him to Marlhaven. I went to London instead. It was not the defiant act you might think, my lord. I had the countess's sanction and the promise of a quarterly allowance from her. Whether she remained my guardian or became my protector is of no importance. It did not alter the nature of our association or our feelings. In return she asked that I keep myself distant from her son."

One of South's brows kicked up. "I can only wonder that it took her so long."

"What do you mean?"

"I mean that she should have taken note of her son's interest in you much earlier and acted upon it."

South's point of view raised India's faint smile. "Her ladyship was desirous that I not tempt Margrave. It was my unsettling influence that she wished to discourage. I was no longer a child, Matthew, much as you might wish to think that I was. And he was twenty-two."

"When you left for London, mayhap, but I am speaking of your earliest days at Merrimont. It matters little what Margrave said you were to him. There was no charity in his heart, and you would be hard pressed to convince me otherwise. His interest in you was . . ." He stopped, searching for the right word. *Unnatural* came to mind, but he refrained from using it. He chose something more vague and less offensive. "It was not at all the thing."

India's bubble of laughter had an edge of hysteria to it. She pressed the back of her hand to her lips to stave it off. "Forgive me," she said after a moment. "It is only that no one has said as much before."

South thought he had said very little—too little in fact. "I have not the clear sense of it yet, India, because even now you are wont to shield Margrave. That alone strains my understanding when I am uncertain that he has ever shown you any real kindness."

"He could be kind, my lord."

"I'm sure he could. But was he?"

"At times."

"When it served him in some manner. Is that right?"

It was, but she was loath to admit it.

South observed the flattening of India's mouth with distaste. "What is his hold over you, India?"

She paled a little. Her fingertips whitened on her knees. "You are mistaken."

"I am not. I can almost see the words rise in your throat, and then they are choked back and swallowed. He does that to you."

She shook her head.

South heaved himself to his feet, unable to sit beside her another moment. He didn't blame her for not looking up at him when he towered over her. "I will have the answers, India. It is not enough that you tell me what you want me to know. There is more, and I will have all of it from you. I thought that was understood between us. Apparently, it is not." He turned then, not waiting for her reply, and went through the kitchen to the back door. His greatcoat was hanging on a peg, and he lifted it and threw it around his shoulders. "I have to see to the horses," he said roughly. "I have left them unattended too long."

India felt the rush of icy air as the door was thrown open. The floor vibrated under her when it was slammed shut.

South stayed away until late in the afternoon. The setting sun laid a transparent blanket of mauve light over every crest of snow and across the cottage's steeply slanted roof. South kept the cottage in his sights and let Griffin pick his way through the trees. Smoke curled from the twin chimneys, and icicles dripped from eaves like pink frosting on a gingerbread house. It should have felt more welcoming, he thought as he neared. His heart should have been lighter. Instead, he could not shake the sense of foreboding. It had been with him since he left the cottage, and taking Griffin hell-bent-for-leather across the snowy fields had done nothing to ease it.

South cursed softly and saw his own breath. He was surprised it was not blue. Those were the kind of words he had left to describe the fool he had been. He had pushed her too hard when his intention had been the opposite. He had known from the very beginning that it would take time. No matter what she said, she did not properly trust him yet. The secrets she had were not ones that could be uncovered in a single evening or the course of a single day. Margrave's presence, or that of his mother's, was very real.

South returned Griffin to his stall, rubbed him down and brushed him, and laid a wool blanket across his back. "I may be sleeping with you and the grays tonight," he said. He patted the thoroughbred's long black nose. "She's likely to put me out, and I cannot say that she should be faulted for doing so." Griffin nuzzled his master's flat hand. "You will leave a warm bed of hay for me, won't you?" The stallion merely regarded him dolefully, and South had to reconcile himself to the fact that he could not delay his return any longer.

The first thing that struck him upon entering the cottage was the tantalizing aroma of stew simmering in the hearth pot. Here was a talent India had not honed under the watchful eye of Lady Margrave. It was her mother, the midwife and follower of the drum, who had taught her how to cook and bake over an open hearth. He stomped his feet inside the doorway, removing the last bit of snow clinging to his boots, then returned his caped greatcoat to the peg. India's pelisse hung beside it. His eyes were drawn to the damp hem and the shallow pool of water that lay on the floor at his feet.

So she had been out as well, and not so long ago from what he observed. South realized he should not have been surprised. If she had felt even a modicum of his fierce restlessness, then she deserved to give it its due. He wondered if she had left with a destination in mind or simply wandered as he had.

"India?" He stepped toward the table and looked into the adjoining room. She was not there. The crimson fabric she had held out for his approval and admiration only yesterday was draped across one arm and the seat of the settee. Pins, thread, and a pair of scissors lay on the stool. Oddly shaped pieces of bleached cotton material were arranged on the braided rug, and South recognized them as part of the practice pattern India was putting together. He called for her again, and this time heard her above stairs, stepping from her room into the hall.

"I am here, m'lord."

It was then that South knew some measure of relief. India's pelisse, the scattered pattern and fabric, the simmering stew, and even her light tread on the floor above him had not been enough to convince him of her presence. He had needed to hear her voice. It shocked him how much he had needed to hear her voice.

South went to the foot of the stairs as India began to descend. She cradled her sketchbook in one arm and had a pencil tucked behind an ear. "I came to get this from my room," she said.

He nodded because it was all he could reasonably do. His vision was filled with her: her pale corn-silk hair, the impossibly dark eyes, the oval face with its beautifully defined cheekbones and chin. She hovered on the lip of one step, almost as if she floated there, wraithlike in her plain ecru day dress and kid slippers. A faintly bemused smile touched her lips.

"My lord?" she asked.

He raised his hand, palm out, and stopped her; then he closed the distance between them, taking the steps two at a time until he stood just below her and their eyes were on the same plane. He searched her face, uncertain of what he wanted or needed to say. He, Matthew Forrester, the Right Honorable the Viscount Southerton, who was rarely without a speech or a quip at the ready, had nothing prepared.

He heard the words at the same time she did. "I fear you will never be moved again to say that I have held your heart carefully. Can you forgive me, India?"

"Oh, Matthew." She touched his cheek with her free hand. His skin was cool beneath her palm, ruddy with color from the outdoors. "Did you think I was angry with you? I am not. There is nothing to forgive."

"But I—"

She shook her head. Her thumb brushed the corner of his mouth. "You were impatient with me. It is understandable. I have given you reason enough. Indeed, I should be glad if impatience were the worst of all that you might feel toward me." India's fingers drifted from South's face and along his arm. She found his hand and took it. "It occurred to me you would not return. I thought perhaps you would go to the village and send Darrow back to sit with me."

"I would not do that. Not without telling you."

"That is what I hoped, but then it was so long that your were gone, I became worried."

"Is that why you left?" he asked. "To search for me?"

"How did you—"

"Your pelisse," he said. "It is wet all along the hem."

"Aaah."

"Your gown and slippers are not, though."

She flushed. "I was changing when I saw you coming from the stalls."

"You didn't want me to know you had gone out?"

"I had given my word I would not leave. I thought you might believe I had attempted to break my promise."

South's gray eyes took on a shrewd glint. "Is that the only reason, India?"

"What do you mean?"

"Was it only worry that sent you out the door and into the cold?" he asked. "Or was it fear?" Her hesitation was enough answer for him. "You did not want me to know how frightened you were. Why is that, India?"

At first she shrugged. Then she saw he meant to stand his ground patiently, blocking her path, until she gave up the truth. "Our supper will be ruined," she told him. Her eyes darted toward the hearth. "There is nothing quite as vile as burnt stew."

"You said the same about the porridge."

"You will not want to make comparisons."

He squeezed her hand lightly. "Tell me, India."

Her sigh was a mix of impatience and defeat, and she did not meet his eyes directly. "I would not have you think me a coward," she said. "I want you to know I can be as brave as you." Her voice was almost inaudible now. "I want to be worthy."

If South had any doubts that India had mastered the talent of rendering him speechless, they were now put to rest. He knew himself to be fortunate to maintain his balance on the stairs. It was as if she had the power to shift the very ground beneath his feet.

India glanced at him, her expression vaguely defiant in the aftermath of her confession. "What is it?" she asked. "What are you thinking?"

South continued to regard her, his head tilted slightly to one side. "I am thinking, my dearest India, that if there is worth to be measured, then I am the one who will come up short."

"That is nonsense."

He chuckled. "You asked what I was thinking, and I told you. You might refrain from pronouncing it nonsense."

She was not deterred. "Well, it is. There is nothing you fear, and it is quite the opposite with me. There is nothing I don't."

South's features lost their edge of humor and took on a solemn cast. "It is only a fool who fears nothing."

"I didn't mean that you were—"

"I know," he said gently. "It is not that I fear nothing, but rather that I have some sense of what is worth fearing. One learns to assess a threat over the course of a lifetime, but not without knowing security and well-being." South paused to let his words sink in, then asked, "When was it that you last remember feeling safe, India?"

His question raised her slight smile. "Not so long ago as you might expect." It was all she needed to say. India saw South's gray glance shift from her to the room at the top of the stairs. The centers of his eyes darkened a fraction, and the irises seemed to turn to smoke. It was difficult to remain looking at him when his attention returned to her. There was such a wealth of understanding there, and the faintly wicked promise of something more, that India's instinct was to shy away from it. She shrugged instead. "Yes, well, there you have it."

"Indeed."

"You are amused."

South's features remained gravely set. "Not at all."

"Yes, you are. You are thinking that if that is where I feel safe, then it presents no inconvenience to you to keep me abed all day."

"Now I am amused." He slipped his arms around her waist when she made to dart past him. "Look at me, India." Her eyes came back to his. "Whether it is in my bed or when we are together just as we are now, I am glad to know that you feel safe—because you are. It is a beginning. The rest—when you can know that you are safe outside of my presence—that will come in time." South saw that India wanted to believe him but her fears were too firmly established to be erased by a few words from him. "You will not always need me, India."

It was on the tip of her tongue to say she did not need him now, but she backed off from the thought because she was no longer certain it was true, or that it had ever been. In a very short time, she had come to realize that he was in some manner necessary to her existence. It was what she had sensed on the occasion of their first meeting at the theatre and again in her home. It was in part why she had not fought him when she woke at the inn, and why she had not tried to escape since. And now he was telling her she would not always need him.

India's teeth caught her lower lip and worried it gently. It was difficult to hold what seemed to be opposing thoughts in her mind long enough to examine them. A small vertical crease appeared between her brows and remained there until she had worked it out. "You mean I will be free to choose," she said quietly.

He nodded. "Yes. That is exactly what I mean."

The crease appeared again. "But then I may not choose you."

"I know." His smile was edged with irony. "I do fear that end, India. Even so, it remains a risk worth taking."

She leaned into him and laid her cheek against his shoulder. Her face was turned into the curve of his neck. "That is what makes you a brave man and names me a coward."

South smiled. His lips brushed her silky hair, and for a moment his hands tightened at the small of her back. "I am not so brave that I would eat your burnt stew."

India sniffed, though it was not entirely because she needed to catch the aroma of the simmering hearth pot. "You better take this," she said, thrusting her sketchbook against his chest. He had to release her from his embrace to grasp the pad, and then she was free to dart past him.

Their supper was saved. They ate in companionable silence at the scarred kitchen table. South found a bottle of red wine to open, and they shared it glass for glass until it was empty. Afterward they retired to the sitting room, where India reclaimed her place on the braided rug so she might continue cutting her pattern and South stretched out on the padded window seat with a book.

India glanced at him, her lips pressed tightly around half a dozen pins. "Wh-are-you-rrearring?"

South looked up, one brow lifted in a perfect arch. "It is perhaps fortunate that your particular dialect was also spoken by my mother and sister. No, I beg you. Do not swallow those pins. Nothing good can come of that." His grin was unabashed, but he did hold up the book to shield himself from her severe look. "It is *Castle Rackrent*. A Gothic novel, of all things. North recommended it to me this summer past when we were a fortnight at Battenburn."

India finished setting the last of her pins in a cushion before she spoke. "You are a friend of the baron and baroness?"

"I would prefer the term acquaintance. I was one of many invited there to celebrate the anniversary of Wellington's victory at Waterloo. Do you know them?"

"Mr. Kent would count the baron among his most reliable contributors."

South's dark brow was lowered only a fraction. "And not the baroness?"

"No."

"I see. Then you have had occasion to fend off Battenburn's advances."

India bent over her work again. "More than one occasion."

South's response was something between a grunt and a growl. He set *Castle Rackrent* sharply on his bent knees and opened it.

India tamped down her smile. South had little familiarity with feeling helpless, and even less liking for it. He had the look of a man who wanted to land someone a facer. "Your friend North is married to Lady Elizabeth Penrose, is he not?"

"Yes. He met her at Battenburn."

She nodded and continued basting the sleeve and bodice of the muslin pattern piece. Her fingers worked nimbly over the material. Occasionally she looked at her open sketchbook, keeping the vision of the end product in her. "You escorted her to Lady Calumet's ball. That was not long ago, I believe."

South laid his index finger on the page to mark his place and looked over at India. For all that her question seemed casual, he doubted it was so. "Yes, I did. Several weeks ago."

"That is unusual, is it not? To escort the wife of your friend?"

"I hope I can count Elizabeth among my friends," he said. "But I take your point. It is perhaps unusual, but certainly it is done. I can only say that my escort was desired by the lady and that it had the approval of her husband. I was unaware until now that it caused comment."

"How can that be?" she chided. "The presence of the Gentleman Thief assured there would be talk. Until that night, Lord North's name had been linked to his. It seems to me that you desired some comment among the *ton* to clear his name."

South's smile was wry. "You are either sharply intuitive or well informed."

"Why can I not be both?"

He chuckled. "Of course. But tell me, who is your source?"

"Margrave." India looked over at South and saw no trace of his earlier amusement. "You did not know he was there?"

"Only after the fact. We were not introduced."

"He knows you."

"What?"

India nodded. "He knows you. That is what he told me."

"That may be, but I have never met him."

"He said differently."

South frowned. "I think he is mistaken."

"Margrave said you would not remember him. It was a long time ago. Your Hambrick Hall days, in fact."

South closed *Castle Rackrent* slowly as he attempted to think back. "It *was* a long time ago," he said. "And Margrave is younger by five years. He had not inherited his title yet, I take it."

"No. He was Newland then. A viscount."

"Newland." South repeated the name thoughtfully; then he shook his head. "No, I don't remember."

"Poor Margrave," India said with mock regret. "I think he hoped you would. He was a member of the Society of Bishops."

"Then I probably knew him by yet another name. As sworn enemies of the Bishops, we in the Compass Club had our own favorite moniker for them. You know, the sort of names only rude boys can think of. Like Sniveler. And Slacker. The Archbishop of Canterbanter. Grendl. Muckrump. Beanboy. Knucklenose."

"Beanboy?" India asked.

South nodded gravely. "Flatulence."

A bubble of laughter parted India's lips. "You *were* rude boys."

South's slim smile was mischievous and unapologetic. "If we were rude, we were also essentially harmless. The Bishops were mean and meant to be."

India sighed. "Yes, then it is easy to see why Margrave became one of them." She was silent a moment, considering. "I think I would have called him Adder."

"Like the snake, you mean."

"Yes. Exactly like the snake. He would blend well into his surroundings. Without particular care one might even cross his path too closely. He is always watchful and prepared for just such a misstep and he would strike without hesitation." India regarded South frankly. "If you could but bring a boy like that to mind, then he would be Newland."

It was not only India's description of young Margrave that raised the hair at the back of South's neck, but that she offered it with so much detachment. "Was he all those things, India?"

"Oh, yes. At times."

"And is he still?"

"I do not think an adder can change his markings, do you? He is what he is."

The problem was, South could recall a few boys who would have fit her description. It would not have surprised him to learn that Margrave had eventually become the Society's archbishop. "I am sorry," he said. "I cannot put a face to him."

She shrugged. "It's of no account. Really." India bit off a dangling piece of thread and deftly made a knot at the end. She smoothed the material over her lap and surveyed her handiwork.

"Perhaps if you drew him for me," South suggested. "As he was then."

India's head snapped up. "No!"

Her vehemence startled him. "Very well," he said, his voice measured and calm.

India plucked the pencil from where it rested behind her ear and laid it on top of her costume sketch. As if she still could not trust herself, she closed the book and pushed it away with her foot so that it rested completely out of her reach. "I could not draw him."

"India. It's all right. I was making no demand."

Her voice came more softly this time. "I could not."

South said nothing. He set his book aside and continued to study her, his eyes narrowing. Her face had lost the wash of pink color that had brightened it earlier, and she had drawn in her lower lip, not worrying it this time but biting down hard.

India did not glance in his direction as she spoke. "He is the one who draws me," she said quietly. "Margrave is an artist, you know. Not a slapdash sketcher as I am, but a real artist with talent for oils and portraiture. He has studied in Paris and Florence and Amsterdam, and I think if he were not the Earl of Margrave he might have chosen to take his livelihood from it. He cannot, naturally. It is not done."

India wrapped a bit of white thread around her finger, unwound it, then wrapped it again. She toyed with it in just that way as she went on. "So he paints in private. He always has. There are but a few of us who have seen his work. His mother, certainly. Perhaps his father. I do not know what he showed his teachers. Beyond that small group, I am unaware of any audience."

The absent circling of the thread around her finger stopped as she glanced at South. "That might change, my lord. You should know that. I believe that when you took me away from London, Margrave's hand was forced. If he cannot find me, he will find some way to hurt me. I think it will be the paintings."

"Tell me about them."

"It will give you disgust of me."

South shook his head. "That is not possible."

"You are wrong."

"You said he paints portraits."

"Of a kind." She began to wind the thread again. "He does not only make a study of faces."

"And you are in many of his paintings."

"I am in all of them."

South was careful to school his features. "All of them?"

"I think so." The tip of India's finger turned bright red as she pulled the thread tight. "I am not always in the foreground, but I have never seen one in which I could not find myself."

"Then he uses other models."

"Yes, but not when he is painting me. I have never posed for him except alone."

South thought back to that morning when India had gone through her contortions to dress modestly under the blankets. He remembered her desire for darkness in the room and how she had refused to pull back the curtains. She had not wanted him to see her. "Adder," she had called Margrave. Watchful. Prepared to strike. What would it have been like to have those cold, black snake's eyes wandering over her? How had she borne that? South asked the question because he had to know the truth from her even if he had arrived at it on his own. "Have you posed nude for him, India?"

India jerked as the thread cut into her skin. A drop of blood appeared, and she quickly lifted her finger to her lips and nursed it.

"India?"

Her eyes closed briefly, and she responded with the faintest of nods.

"Where are the paintings?"

"At Marlhaven and Merrimont, I suppose. In his London home. In my home."

"I have been to your home," South said. "I did not see them."

She tore the loosened thread from her finger and tossed it aside. Her laughter was short and humorless. "Given their nature, I do not display them, my lord."

"I understand. But on two occasions I have been in your home uninvited. I didn't find them either time."

India's tone was rife with sarcasm. "Then perhaps you should apply to the Gentleman Thief for help. I assure you, they are there."

"The locked rooms," South said softly, more to himself than to India.

"Pardon?"

"The locked rooms," he repeated. "I didn't force an entry there."

"How unreasonably civil of you."

South did not think it was possible for her voice to be any icier. "You know why I was there, India."

"The colonel's work. Mr. Kendall's murder."

He nodded. "In part. I was also trying to satisfy my own curiosity. I thought there might be something that would point to your protector, but Margrave had not yet returned from the Continent."

"That would not have mattered. I told you, Lady Margrave is my protector. Not her son."

"You merely receive an allowance from the dowager countess. Her son is still your protector."

"No. You are wrong, my lord." India took a deep breath and released it slowly. "You do not yet understand. I am his."

India rested the back of her head against the lip of the copper tub and closed her eyes. She cupped her hands and sluiced her shoulders with water that was only a few degrees below painfully hot. Those few degrees made all the difference. This was blissful.

Steam rose from the surface of the water, and firelight was trapped in the curling ribbons. Beads of perspiration collected on India's forehead and above her lip. A delicate opalescent glow colored her complexion. The caps of her knees were visible above the waterline, and she idly flicked water across them when she finished splashing her shoulders.

South had done this for her: found the tub, hauled the water, warmed and poured it, then disappeared so she could enjoy it alone. India had not been able to thank him properly. She doubted he knew how dear his gesture was to her. She had done nothing but spin him in circles since making his acquaintance, and the worst he had done was lose his patience.

How did he think there would ever come a time when she would not need him? India could not imagine it.

She thought of how well he had accepted what she'd told him. He hadn't blinked an eye, though in retrospect she considered it was possible that she had stunned him. It was certain that for a moment she had left him speechless.

The memory of him sitting there on the window seat, his handsome features perfectly still, his glance hooded, his long legs stretched in front of him and crossed at the ankles, his arms folded across his chest—it still had the power to stir her. What had seemed relaxed about him was not. He was as alert and watchful as Margrave, and it should have made her apprehensive, yet it was not that way at all.

She had the sense he was challenging her in some manner, as if he knew she was more than she had shown him, that she was capable of more than she knew herself. The fact that she was resourceful on occasion—resourceful enough to attract the colonel's attention—was not enough for South. He was carefully preparing her to become the woman he feared, the one who was free to make choices because she did not need him.

It was not the gilt cage that she had first thought he'd planned for her. This one had the door wide open, and she was the one reluctant to step through it.

India's reverie ended with the sound of South's movement on the stairs. Her eyes flew open, and she sat up quickly, drawing her knees closer to her chest. Water splashed over the side of the tub, and a few droplets sizzled on the stone apron of the fireplace. She swiveled her head as far as she could to observe his progress on the steps.

"May I?" South asked politely when he reached the halfway point.

"I am hardly in a position to stop you."

"But you are, India. You only have to say no."

There it was again, she thought, the quietly issued challenge. Her choice. If she said yes, it was an admission to herself that she desired his company, even vulnerable as she was to his watchful eyes. "I do not want to do that."

South didn't move. One of his brows kicked up instead.

India realized he wanted better confirmation than she had given him. "Yes," she said. "You may come down."

He managed not to grin at the regal tone she affected. "I left my book here," South told her. He gave the tub and India a wide berth as he went to the window seat. *Castle Rackrent* was no longer lying on the padded bench. South's attention was caught by a damp spot on the floor. He stepped back and found the angle that illuminated the shallow puddle in the firelight. It was clearly a footprint. A dainty footprint. His eyes darted to the next one. And the next. He followed them across the floor to their source.

India was up to her chin in the water and looked as if she wanted to go deeper still. The smile that hovered just above the steamy surface was a shade guilty. Her eyes darted to the stool she had pulled up to the tub. Two towels were folded neatly on top. On top of them lay *Castle Rackrent*.

South made no attempt to school his features now. His appreciation of her predicament was simply too great. "I did not realize you have an interest in Gothic novels."

"I am not certain I do," she said. "I have never read any before. I should have asked you, I know, if I might borrow it, but you had already gone to your room and I thought you were readying for bed and I did not want to disturb you so I took it upon myself to . . ." Under South's amused grin, India's voice trailed off to nothingness. "Do you mind terribly?"

"Not terribly," he said. "But I do mind."

"Oh." India actually swallowed a little water as she slid still lower into the tub. She forced her chin up. "I suppose you will be wanting it now."

"Yes, indeed." He continued to eye her with cool interest. "You are not going to drown yourself, are you? There is hardly room enough for me to dive in to save you. I could break my neck."

"I could break it for you."

He laughed. "I do not doubt it."

India sighed. "Very well. You may take your book."

"Would you prefer I close my eyes?"

"I would prefer you wait until I finish my bath."

"Of course." South sat down on the window seat. "I should have thought of that. Pray continue."

It was difficult to be severe with him when he was so bent on mischief. India felt sympathy for all the nannies South had so expertly disposed of with his heart-stopping smile. She needed to prove to herself that she was made of sterner stuff. Sitting up carefully, India lifted one arm out of the water, shook her hand off, then reached for *Castle Rackrent*. Before South could stop her, she was dangling it over the tub. "It is quite heavy, you know," she told him. "It could easily slip from my fingers."

South jumped to his feet. "You *are* diabolical."

She smiled sweetly. "You were entertaining some doubt, I collect."

"No longer."

"Good." She swiveled her arm away from the water and held the book out to him. "Please, take your Gothic novel."

South took a step toward the tub. "Would you prefer I close my eyes?"

"Most assuredly not. I cannot think of anything more certain to land you in the drink. I will trust you to be quick about it."

He was. South took the proffered book and stepped back a respectful distance.

India glanced in his direction when he did not move toward the stairs. One of her eyebrows lifted in mock admonishment. "You are hovering, my lord."

South looked down at himself. His feet were definitely planted. He only felt as if he were floating. That was what India did to him with her arched eyebrow and coolly remote smile. He had tried—and failed—not to notice that her naked shoulders reflected the translucent gold and orange flames of the fire or that a diamond drop of water was sliding slowly from the hollow beneath her ear along the line of her slender neck.

"You're beautiful," he told her.

India looked away from his darkening eyes. "Don't."

"I understand why he wants to paint you."

"No, you don't."

South stood there a moment longer, taking in the stubborn tilt of her chin and the unyielding set of her mouth. She would not explain herself now, even if he pressed her. He had already learned that nothing helpful came of that. South started for the stairs, pausing only briefly at the bottom. "Will you come to my room tonight, India?"

"Yes."

He waited for her to meet his eyes. When she did not, he merely nodded once and continued slowly up the stairs.

India did not move until she heard South open and close the door to his bedchamber. Even then, she rose only a few inches higher in the tub. It was enough that when she looked down at herself she could see the white curves of her breasts above the water and the rosy aureoles below it. Deeper still, she could make out the pale length of her thighs and calves.

She would have to tell him, of course. She could not bear for him to call her beautiful again. The hushed and almost reverent tone he had used should never have been directed toward her, but reserved for something that inspired awe. Far from being flattered, India had merely felt ugly and undeserving. It was not South's fault, she knew, but hers. He did not know what Margrave had done to her body, how it had been made hideous by his admiration so that even she could no longer abide looking at it.

So, yes, she thought. She would have to tell him. But when? Tonight? India shook her head in response to her silent question. She was too selfish to do it this evening, when the promise of his loving her was the last thing she had heard in his voice. *Will you come to my room tonight, India?*

He meant to take her into his bed, his arms. He would press his body against hers so that she could feel the heat

of his skin and know the planes and angles of his lean frame.
There would be his mouth next to her ear, then again at her
throat. His palms would be filled with her breasts and the
curve of her hips. His knee would separate hers and nudge
the sensitive inner side of her thighs. She could feel him
hard and hot against her belly, and he would come into her
because it was what she wanted.

No, she would not tell him tonight. Perhaps in the morning, she thought, when darkness could no longer shield her,
and the memory of his loving would be bittersweet. She
could tell him then.

She was brave enough for that. She hoped.

Sighing deeply, India found the sponge trapped between
her hip and the tub. She rubbed it with the sliver of scented
soap Mrs. Simon had bought for her in the village. The
fragrance of lavender filled her nostrils. She leaned back
once more and closed her eyes and remembered how South
liked to bury his face against her hair.

With that vision keeping her warm, India sank slowly
beneath the water.

Chapter Twelve

India set her candlestick on the bedside table and stepped out of her slippers. The floor was cold enough to make her hop immediately onto the bed. South was waiting for her with a cocoon of blankets as soon as she lay back. She snuggled into the curve of his body, giving up a contented little sigh and shiver as she did so. His wicked smile was imprinted in her mind as he leaned over her to extinguish the candle. Her arms looped around his shoulders.

"You warmed my side of the bed," she whispered. "Thank you."

South's smile deepened. He very much liked the idea that she had appropriated part of his bed as her own. "Your side? I was not aware you had a side here."

India stopped rubbing the cold soles of her feet against his legs. "I did not mean—"

His lips unerringly found the fullness of hers, and the kiss he meant only to silence her lingered long past the first sweet moment. Slow and measured, in the end they were both drugged by it. South raised his head and felt the faint tug of her mouth as he parted from her. His voice was husky.

''I was teasing, India. You may make any claim here that you wish. Indeed, I hope you do.''

The firelight's dim glow allowed her to see the arched eyebrow that gave South's features such a deliciously wicked cast. ''I think you have something specific in mind.''

''Mmmm.'' He bent his head and brushed her lips again. ''Perhaps you are right.''

India stretched under him, liking the weight and warmth of his tautly muscled frame against her. Her fingers threaded in his hair, and she held his head still when he would have drawn back. ''Then I claim you, my lord.''

The soft growl at the back of South's throat signaled his surrender. He felt the slight pressure of her fingertips against his scalp, and he lowered his head until his mouth was a hairbreadth from hers. If she said anything at all, he thought he would be able to know the shape of her words before he heard them.

She said nothing, though. What she did was kiss him.

Her mouth nudged his open. The tip of her tongue made a damp trail on the sensitive underside of his upper lip. It flickered along the ridge of his teeth, then probed more intimately, teasing, tasting, and finally engaging him in a deeply carnal kiss.

India's fingers drifted from his thick hair to his nape, where she could ease the fine cords of tension in his neck. Her hands slid still lower, resting lightly on his shoulders, his upper arms, then his back. His muscles shifted under her touch, his skin grew warm. Her thumbs traced a line on either side of his spine until they rested in the small dimples at the base, just above his buttocks.

There had never been a moment since entering his bed that India was not aware of his body's response to her. South's erection had pressed hot and hard against her hip when she had first nestled against him, and he could have opened her thighs and taken her then, whether she was prepared to accept him or not. The fact that he did not lent her courage now.

When she felt him grow even more rigid against her belly,

she sucked in her breath to make room for her hands to slip between their bodies. She made a cradle for his penis with her palms, then drew them along the length of his heavy erection.

South thought he would come out of his skin. He reared back as she repeated the motion, then thrust himself against her hands. His eyes closed. He tried to hold back, but his hips ground against her anyway. Her fingernails lightly scraped the underside of his scrotum. The words he uttered against the base of her ear were unintelligible.

"Let me," she said. "I want to . . ."

She could do whatever she wanted, he thought. Here was torture he did not properly know how to resist, even if it were his desire to do so. It was not. "Yes," he said. "Yes."

Emboldened now by South's hoarsely whispered encouragement, India wriggled out from under him and pressed him onto his back. He helped her raise the hem of her voluminous nightgown as she rose to her knees. It bunched around her hips as she moved across his body to straddle his thighs. He would have raised it higher, but she pushed his hands away. She ignored his throaty chuckle and caught the material in her fists instead. He fell perfectly silent as India lifted the filmy batiste fabric past her hips and waist, higher still over her breasts and shoulders, and finally over her head. She let it dangle at the end of her fingertips before she dropped it over the side of the bed.

For a moment, her body was limned by the firelight. The contours of her slender frame were given the clear, sharp detail of one of her sketches. Instead of the dark definition of a pencil, the tilt of her head was outlined in golden light. It was the same with the slope of her breasts and the curve of her arm.

South's glimpse was only fleeting. There was no opportunity to enjoy the sight of her before she bent over him and drew up the blankets. Her body was in deep shadow once more, but now it didn't matter, because he could feel the shape of her as she stretched out along his length: her breasts, her hands, her thighs, her mouth.

All of her was beautiful, though he refrained from saying so. It surprised him to hear the words anyway, more so to realize they hadn't come from his lips but from hers.

"You are," she whispered against his lips. "I thought so from the first."

For once South was glad of the darkness, because it hid what he was certain was his ruddy blush. He pinched her lightly on the backside to let her know what he thought of her outrageous compliment.

India was not deterred. She merely wriggled against him, the consequence of which was for South to press his fingers against her buttocks to hold her still.

"I think you are a witch," he said.

"Then I am glad of it." India kissed him again at her leisure, touching her mouth to the corner of his, making her way along his jaw, nibbling at his earlobe. She worked her way down his throat, across his collarbone. She kissed his shoulder and spread more across his chest. Her body slid down his; her hands lightly grazed his skin. He had to give up the grasp he had on her bottom and let his own fingers glide along her back as she slipped lower. He made out the crown of her pale hair just before it disappeared under the covers.

"India?"

She found him with her mouth and hands. South's heart tripped over its own beat, then hammered hard against his chest. Blood surged hot in his veins, and he felt its rush from his brain to his groin. He was touched as if by a fine madness, lost to coherent thought, driven forward by carnal instinct. This was the heady power of lust, hers and his, and he had only to feel it.

The hot suck of India's mouth, the light pressure of her fist at the base of his penis, drew a short, harsh groan from South. Under the covers, his fingers dug into her silky hair as if to give himself purchase. Her tongue laved his flesh. Her hand squeezed. Each foray imitated the thrust of his body in hers, and she did for him here what he had done between her thighs, taking him deeply and wetly and with small murmurs that were equal parts frustration and satisfaction.

"India." He said her name softly, huskily. "Stop. You must . . ." He felt her shoulders stiffen. "You must stop." Her mouth lifted slowly. Her lips lingered near the head of his engorged shaft. South pushed back the covers, laughing a little desperately when India's head poked out. "Come here."

Uncertain, she pushed herself up on her forearms and inched herself up his body until she was stretched along his length again. "I have repulsed you," she whispered, her breath hitching.

There was a faint roar in his ears, and South had to strain to hear her. It was more difficult to comprehend her meaning. "No!" Then more gently, "No. Can you not feel all evidence to the contrary?"

She certainly felt the pulsing outline of his erection against her belly. "That? It signifies nothing. You were in such a state when I came to bed."

South thought he would choke in an effort to hold back his laughter. It occurred to him that she meant to kill him in exactly this manner, and that all men should die so happily. With just such an end in mind, South cupped her bottom, lifted her, and, hearing no protest from India, eased himself into her. "I was in such a state *before* you came to bed."

"Is it the Gothic novel that makes you so?"

In response, South's hand snaked upward and grasped the nape of India's neck. He pressed her head down and kissed her hard. When he was quite certain she was breathless and would have no more sauce for him, he told her, "*Castle Rackrent* is absorbing, my dearest India, but hardly arousing. And well you know it." South did not miss the flash of her siren's smile or the way her body contracted around him. He laid his palm against the side of her face; his thumb brushed the underside of her chin. "You did not repulse me, India," he said softly, solemnly. "Let us leave it at that."

She nodded. Turning her face into his hand, India kissed

the heart of his palm. She felt him shudder under her, and
then the vibration became her own and the frisson was
traveling up her spine and across her shoulders. She felt it
in her fingertips as she pressed them into the mattress on
either side of his shoulders and raised herself up. Her body
began to slowly undulate, lifting, falling, sliding, rocking.
She pressed her pelvis against him. The pulse in her throat
beat out the the rhythm of her most intimate contractions.
Leaning toward him, India offered her breasts to his hands.
He cupped them, brushing his thumbs across her nipples
until they hardened to small pink stones. Her pale hair fell
forward over her shoulder and lay lightly across the back
of his hands. Her breasts swelled under the exquisite caress
of his fingertips.

She looked down at herself and was moved by the sight
of his hands on her body. Here was the proof that it did not
have to be ugly, she thought. There was some part of her
that had always known it must be so, though she had never
been able to embrace it as the truth. It crystallized the difference between understanding and believing.

"What is it?" he asked.

India smiled faintly, ruefully. She shook her head,
deflecting his question. The curling tips of her hair swung
across his hands, and she moaned softly as her nipples
scraped his palms. She closed her eyes as his fingers trailed
from her breasts down her rib cage. She sucked in her breath,
held it, then released it slowly when his touch finally passed
over her abdomen.

South slipped his hand between her parted thighs. The
little heart nestled in the folds of dewy flesh pulsed against
his fingertips. He stroked her once. Twice. He teased her
with the tip of his nail. She cried out as the hood of her
clitoris was pushed back and the pleasure became too intense
to bear. He eased his caress, rubbing more gently now, flesh
against flesh, each stroke deliberate and unhurried, paced to
the tempo of her breathing and the rhythm of her slowly
undulating hips.

He stared up at her, his throat arched, his chest rising and falling in a slightly uneven cadence. There was the faint sough of his breath in the quiet room. He felt the hot strings of tension being pulled taut, first in him, then in her. South grasped her hips, and his fingers dug into the soft flesh of her buttocks. He urged her body faster and harder over his. He bucked. She rode. India gripped him with her thighs, a look of fierce concentration coming over her features as she brought him to climax.

He gave a hoarse shout as he spilled his seed into her. India held him tightly. She leaned forward and pressed a kiss in the curve of his neck, breathing deeply of his masculine scent. The smile that shaped her lush mouth and branded his skin was one of delight and triumph. Her small white teeth nipped his flesh.

South slapped her bottom.

She merely wriggled it against him.

Entirely spent, he was unable to fathom that she could rouse a single sensation in him, yet it was undeniably a prickling he felt under his skin. One of his dark brows arched. "You are feeling very full of yourself."

"No, m'lord. Full of you."

Still joined to her, South swiftly turned India on her back and nestled his hips firmly in the cradle of her thighs. He caught her wrists and lifted them to either side of her head; then he kissed her hard on her damp and parted lips. At first he thought it was only his kiss that had quieted her laughter; then he realized she was far too still under him, her breathing fixed and measured. "What is it?" he asked. "No, do not shake your head at me. Tell me."

"If you would but release me."

South loosed his hold on her wrists and began to move away.

"No," she said quickly. "It is enough that you let me go."

He stayed where was, resting his weight on his forearms. "Better?"

She nodded.

For a moment he thought she might say more, but then

she seemed to reconsider the wisdom of it. South let it pass, loath to disturb the peace between them. There was still the matter of India's own satisfaction to attend to. Her body shifted restlessly beneath his, seeking it. Her movement was enough to raise his roguish smile.

"Lusty wench," he murmured against her ear.

"Yes," she whispered. "It must be so."

His smile deepened because she said it as if it startled her. South slipped from between her thighs and turned onto his side. India whimpered softly at the loss. "Shhh," he said and turned her toward him. He stroked her hip, then the curve of her thigh. He drew her leg across his so that she was parted for him again. He caressed the soft inner side of her thigh. Her hips jerked as his hand drew closer, and she sucked in her lower lip. He pressed the heel of his hand against her mons and felt her press back. She was silky here, too. Warm and wet. His fingers found the hard little nubbin of flesh, and he deftly manipulated it until he felt her breathing change. She reached for his arm as if to shake him off; then her hands found purchase in the sheets instead.

She closed her eyes and whispered his name. She called him Matthew as her body rose, fell, and finally shattered against his.

South washed himself at the basin, then sat on the edge of the bed and passed the damp flannel to India. The candle on the table was once again lighted, and the flame flickered as his hand passed near it. He did not suppose for a moment that she would allow him to perform the intimate task of washing her. It was odd, he thought, what she would permit and what she would not. While his back was turned at the basin, she had reached for her nightgown and dragged it under the covers with her. He had heard her shifting first one way then another, and he gave her time to put it on, not turning around again until she was quiet.

The cloth was cool, and India averted her head as she drew it between her thighs. She should not have given him permission to light the candle, but he had asked politely and it was no longer in her to deny him that. It had been a revelation making love to him this time, and she was certain now that that was what they had done.

Made love. It was more than coupling. More than mating. There was a wildness to it that made it primal, but it was never without tenderness, never without joy. Yes, they had made love.

India returned the cloth to the basin when he held it out to her. She watched him put it back on the commode, supremely unconcerned by his nakedness. He turned and caught her starting at him.

"Does it bother you?" he asked. "Should I put my night-shirt on?"

She shook her head. Why should he? she thought. He was beautiful. She did not say as much to him again, but it was there for him to see in her eyes. India was not shy about feasting on him as he skirted the foot of the bed and came to stand on the other side. She raised the blankets for him. "I have never seen a naked man before."

One of South's brows kicked up. "Never?"

"Never."

"Margrave?"

"No. There has never been . . ." She hesitated. "You know I was a virgin."

South slipped into the bed and turned on his side. He propped himself on an elbow and regarded India frankly. "Yes, and I also know there are ways for a woman to pleasure a man that do not require her to relinquish her virginity. When you took me in your mouth, I thought perhaps you had some knowledge of that."

India's chin came up a notch. "I believe it is not uncommon to have knowledge of things for which one has no experience."

He smiled. The flush that colored her cheeks was at odds with her cool tone. "A fine riposte," he said. "And true enough. Are you angry that I spoke so baldly?"

"No."

South touched his forehead to hers and looked her straight in the eye, playfully trying to judge her truthfulness. "I liked that you wanted to pleasure me in such a fashion." He kissed her lightly on the mouth. "I shall look forward to pleasuring you in the same manner."

India blinked.

"Is it that you have no knowledge or no experience?" he asked, rocking back on his side again.

"No experience."

"I see."

India's smile was rueful. She turned slightly and laid her hand on his chest. "No, you don't, but it is kind of you to pretend." She was reluctantly glad of the candlelight because it left South's features open to her. The centers of his eyes were darkening, almost eclipsing the gray irises. She said softly, "This is an idyll, isn't it?"

"An idyll?"

"Yes."

"I had not thought of it in such terms." Because he did not want to. An idyll was brief, a romantic interlude that by definition must have an end. "Idylls should evoke peace and contentment. You will allow that has not always been the way of it between us."

"No," she agreed. "But there have been moments." Like now, she thought. She was filled with the sweetness of being next to him, lying in his bed, her hand covering his heartbeat, and fairly drowning in the whispered huskiness of his voice. India's sigh was wistful. "I have been wishing I had some talent for storytelling, but my profession requires only that I use the words of others. I should like to lay my account before you slowly, make it last weeks, even months, and little by little over that time I would make you fall in love with me. It is foolish, I know, but mayhap we would not have to leave here then."

India saw he meant to say something, and she shook her head quickly, staving him off. "I have come to realize I am not possessed entirely of a practical nature. There is a bit of a mad romantic in me, though I am not so adventurous as you. You will want to leave Ambermede soon and be about the business of finding Mr. Kendall's killer. There is also poor Mr. Rutherford to think of and the matter of Lady Macquey-Howell and Señor Cruz. I will return to the theatre with some suitable explanation for my absence, and Mr. Kent will find fault with everything I do for a fortnight. In the end, though, he will forgive me and allow me to return to the fold.''

India's hand drifted from South's chest and lay in the space between their bodies. ''You and I will not meet often, and then only by chance. I think the colonel will have no more use for me. It will be the same of you.''

South said nothing for a moment. He pushed himself upright in bed and leaned back against the headboard. His fingers plowed furrows through his inky hair. ''You have given this a great deal of thought.''

''Yes.''

''And you believe you're in the right of it.''

''I would not have said it otherwise.'' India waited to see if he would present some argument to the contrary. He did not. Neither did he look at her. Instead, he stared straight ahead at the opposite wall, though there was nothing there to hold his interest. She could not fathom what he was thinking; his eyes remained remote, the line of his mouth implacable.

India reined in her disappointment. There would be tears when she was alone, but not for anything would she have him see them now. ''I thought I would wait until morning to tell you the rest, but I find I cannot. It should be said and said quickly, so there will be no mistaking what has really been between us.'' At first she thought he had not been listening; then she saw the muscle working in his cheek and the slight affirmative nod. Brushing back a few strands of hair that had fallen over her cheek, India picked up the threads of the story she had abandoned hours earlier.

''I told you that when I left my position at the Olmsteads and made for London it was with Lady Margrave's blessing. That was true. It is also true that in return for her support she asked that I keep my distance from her son. What I did not explain was that he would not keep his distance from me. Even the countess eventually realized that I was not the corrupting influence she would have liked to believe. Her hold on him became increasingly tenuous, while I could find no respite from his presence. He followed me to London just as he had to the Olmsteads' home.''

South looked at her sharply. ''You did not tell me he had followed you to the Olmsteads'.''

''No, I didn't.'' India made no apology for it. Still lying on her side, she plumped the pillow under head and settled more deeply under the thick blankets. He had ice water in his veins, she thought, to be so unaffected by the bedchamber's persistent chill. ''Margrave visited the Olmsteads for several weeks while I was there. He managed the trip on the pretext of learning more about Mr. Olmstead's successful wool enterprise. It was Margrave playing at being a most progressive landlord and earl, yet his visit had but one true purpose: to see for himself how I was faring.''

''What he saw,'' South said, his voice carefully neutral, ''was Mr. Olmstead sniffing after your skirts.''

India ignored that, though it was an accurate enough picture. ''I acquitted myself rather well, considering my employer's single-minded pursuit. I thought I had made a successful show of proving that I could defend my honor. Still, Mr. Olmstead was not easily turned aside, and I had already determined that I must leave, when he was met with an accident.''

South's dark brows knit. ''What sort of accident?''

''A fall from his horse.''

''Was Margrave still in residence?''

''Oh, yes. He was witness to Mr. Olmstead's fall.'' India did not have to say more. She saw the shadow of a frown cross South's face, and the almost imperceptible tightening of his lips. He was quickly putting his own construction on what had come to pass between Margrave and her former employer. ''You are thinking I should have told you this before,'' she said.

"It is but one of my thoughts." There was a certain roughness in his voice that spoke of his frustration with her. "Is this what you meant by stringing out the tale? All along you've dropped crumbs for me to follow, when you knew what was at stake. Kendall. Rutherford. Prinny. To what purpose, India? To extend the idyll? You cannot make me fall in love with you."

For a moment she could not breathe. She wondered if he had heard the slight gasp that preceded it. She spoke carefully, each word measured. "I did not tell you, because I was not prepared to believe it myself. You were asking me to accept that the attempt on the Prince Regent's life had nothing to do with his politics or his suitability as our future king, and everything to do with his attentions to me. Perhaps you do not find it a fantastic idea, but I do. You made the same connection to Kendall, even though his work for the colonel places him at risk from other fronts. And you would have me agree it is the same with Mr. Rutherford, though he had amassed tremendous gambling debts that were as likely to lead him to a bad end. You even questioned my information about Lady Macquey-Howell and the Spanish consul."

"I asked if her life was in danger. You said that it was not." South glanced down at India and saw that her features were not troubled, merely expressionless. "You have changed your mind."

She drew in her lower lip and nodded. "It is because of Mr. Olmstead," she said finally. "And what I have reluctantly come to believe is true about his fall from his horse."

"That it was no accident, you mean."

"Yes," she said. "Exactly that. I had never considered it before. Never once. Margrave could be cruel. I have always known that. I could accept that he might hurt someone if the mood were upon him, but murder? I could not imagine that. I think it was too painful to get my mind around. Perhaps it is because I must bear some of the responsibility. Part of the fault lies with me, you see."

"No, I don't. I have never thought that."

India ignored him. "Mr. Olmstead was a bruising rider. I did not make that judgment myself. Margrave confided as much to me, and he would know. The day that Mr. Olmstead took his fall, Margrave had challenged him to a run across the fields. It was in aid of proving which of them had the better mount, but that is just a man's stratagem for proving who has the better seat. They marked a route that met their requirements for a spirited challenge and made their wagers. It was a stone fence that eliminated my employer from the race. Margrave cleared the jump and Mr. Olmstead did not."

India raised her eyes to South and found he was still watching her closely. "He might have broken his neck in the fall," she said. "The physician who set his broken legs said he was fortunate not to have done so."

"You know this all because you were a witness?"

She shook her head. "I had it from Mrs. Olmstead," India said. "And she had it from her husband. It was odd, she told me, that he should lose his seat there. He had made the same jump hundreds of times with no mishap. She thought he and his mount could clear the fence in their sleep."

South understood why India had not given that day's mishap more than a cursory thought in all the years since. "Then Mr. Olmstead himself made no claim that it was anything but a bad bit of luck."

"That's right. I have no proof to say that it wasn't, but Margrave did not know I had already decided to leave Chipping Campden. If your suspicions are correct, then he may have been acting to make certain Mr. Olmstead could no longer—how did you so eloquently put it?—oh, yes, sniff after my skirts."

The line of South's lips tightened a fraction at her needling. Knowing that he deserved the barb was not the same as liking it. "It seems you have gotten your mind around the problem now."

India's accents were clipped. "Yes. I have."

"What else do I need to know?" he asked, rising from the bed. He padded to the armoire, removed his dressing gown, and shrugged into it. "You mentioned Lady Macquey-Howell earlier."

Nodding, India turned on her side to face him. "I cannot say with certainty, but if I follow your logic, then it is possible her life may be forfeit."

"At Margrave's hand?"

"Yes."

South belted his robe, frowning. "Why would his mark not be Señor Cruz?"

"The Spanish consul has never been my admirer," she said frankly. "Lady Macquey-Howell has."

"I see," he said. And this time he did. "Margrave knows?"

"I think so. There is not much that escapes his notice. She often sent me letters. They were most . . . effusive. I only replied once, in response to her first overture. I was firm, but not unkind."

South turned to the fireplace. He picked up the poker and prodded the logs. When the flames began to crackle and lick at the wood, he added more. "You met with her?"

"Before the letters began she came to my dressing room on several occasions. She was escorted each time by her husband, but it was clear to me at the outset who harbored the real interest."

"Then Lord Macquey-Howell acts as his countess's beard."

"Yes. He seemed to be . . ." Her voice trailed off as she sought the right word. "Helpless. Mayhap resigned. His lordship has little influence over his wife. She is most certainly in command, and he can do naught but follow her lead."

"Most necessary if he is desirous of protecting his reputation." South did not return to the bed. He repositioned the wing chair so that it captured some of the heat from the fireplace but also allowed him to see India on the bed. She still lay with her head against her pillow, propped slightly by the arm she had slid beneath it. "You did not encourage her?" he asked as he stretched out in the chair. Even from the distance that separated them, South felt India stiffen as though affronted. "It was not my intention to insult you. I asked the question because I know you were keeping Mr. Kendall aware of the countess's affair with Señor Cruz." He paused, reconsidering what he'd said. "You knew from the beginning it was no simple affair, didn't you?"

"Yes. Of course I knew. But in answer to your other question, no, I did not encourage her. Mr. Kendall did not begin asking about Lady Macquey-Howell until some weeks after her last visit to the theater. When her letters began, there was little in them that provided information he would have found useful."

"Then she was not your source."

"Only rarely."

"Margrave?"

"Sometimes. More often it was Lady Margrave. She maintained a steady correspondence with me whether she was in town or at one of her country homes. Her letters were often filled the latest *on dit*. She kept me apprised of her coming and goings, the social events she attended, what occupied the thoughts of the privileged. There was always news of Marlhaven and Merrimont: the success or failure of the harvest; how the livestock and the tenants fared. None of it was primarily for my benefit, you understand, but for her son's. They had become estranged—though that was more on his side than hers—and she hoped rather desperately that he would someday pay more than the rare duty call on her."

Because of South's attention to the fire, India could feel the room was finally warming. She sat up, propped the pillow behind the small of her back, and neatly turned down the heavy blankets so they lay across her lap. "She knew he would read the letters she sent me. Even though he never responded to her, I think she imagined it kept them close."

"This estrangement," South said thoughtfully. "Did it begin when you left Marlhaven for employment with the Olmsteads or when you left the Olmstead home for London?"

"The latter. After Mr. Olmstead's accident, I would not return with Margrave to his home. That was when he became suspicious. He had not given me any funds that I might sustain myself in London while I looked for employment, and he knew I could have saved very little during my stay with the Olmsteads. When I went on to London, he went back to Marlhaven and confronted his mother. I have never known the details of what happened between them; indeed, I have never cared enough to ask. I think it was then that Lady Margrave learned the limits of her influence. I know that soon after, her directive to me changed. I was no longer charged with keeping my distance, but keeping him safe."

"An odd request."

India nodded. "I found it so. I was prepared to refuse and accept the consequences of having no funds and no prospects; then Margrave arrived in London on my heels, and he has not been far from me since."

"He will not let you go?"

She hesitated. "It is not precisely that. You might not credit it, but I have made my intention to leave him clear on three separate occasions. I actually did go once. In Paris. Each time it ends in the same way. Margrave elicits my cooperation by trying to kill himself." She said this last without inflection. It was another circumstance of her life to which she had yielded. "Twice he tried to hang himself. In Paris he almost blew his brains out."

The pity of it, South thought, was that he had not succeeded. "You were the one who stopped him?"

"The hangings, yes. Because I had not yet left. Both times it was a narrow thing. In Paris I steeled myself to leave no matter what Margrave threatened. This time it was the concierge who found him. The pistol shot alerted the other tenants in our building. He was lying in a pool of his own blood. The pistol ball glanced off his skull. It was three days before I learned of it, and by then he was being cared for in a Paris asylum. I could not leave him there."

South did not imagine for a moment that India could have done anything else. He rubbed the underside of his chin with his knuckles, his look contemplative. "Lady Margrave's charge to you begins to make more sense. He may have made a similar threat to her, even attempted to carry it out."

"The same has occurred to me."

"So you became his protector."

"After a fashion."

"He's mad, India."

"Quite possibly."

South wondered that she could say it with such composure, but then he reminded himself that she had lived with the truth of it for a very long time. "Have you always known about him?"

"That he is not well?" she asked. Seeing South's nod, she went on. "No, not in the beginning. I was only a young girl when we first met. The visits to Merrimont, remember? I knew he had a particular interest in me that was more frightening than flattering, but I did not understand it then." Her short laugh was without humor. "I do not know if I understand it yet. The pictures he drew of me, even in those early days, were not complimentary. I went back each time I was invited, because I did not want to disappoint my parents. It was such an honor to be selected that I could not tell them how I much I hated it, or that I was sick each time the countess's carriage arrived to take me there. The other children had no complaints, so mine would have sounded very odd. I did not realize that Margrave never cornered them when we played hiding games, nor did they have to show their private parts to secure their release."

India saw South's eyes narrow a fraction, and for a moment his knuckles stopped rubbing the underside of his chin. She thought his mouth moved around an indecently vulgar curse, but he gave it no sound. What she did not observe was his pity, and for that she was glad. Pity would have weakened her somehow, weakened her resolve to tell him the whole of it. She did not need that, not if she was going to prove to herself that she had a measure of courage worthy of South when she wasn't onstage.

"You will have wondered about the paintings," India said with credible indifference. In contrast, there were her fingertips running along the neat fold of the blankets, creasing it carefully again and again where it crossed her lap. "All of the paintings are brilliantly executed. I can say that without fear of being contradicted, because I know something about Margrave's talent. All of them are disturbing, though that may be a point of debate. As one of the subjects in each of his works, I am understandably inclined to find them so.

"You know that I have posed for him without benefit of my clothes. He insists upon it. I have not always done so willingly, but there are opiates, and he uses them without compunction. I have found it is far safer for me to comply than to resist."

Now South did swear loud enough for her to hear it. She blinked at his choice, but he seemed totally unaware of having spoken. India went on. "I do not mean to give you the impression that his collection of paintings is large. He does not work at it every day. A humor takes him and he will paint for a week, almost without rest, then not again for months. It has always been thus."

Quite suddenly, she fell silent and remained that way for some time. South had little choice but to eventually prompt her. "Tell me about the paintings, India."

Her entire body jerked as she came out of her reverie. She forced herself to face South, though she was no longer certain she saw him clearly. Darkness was encroaching at the periphery of her vision. The deep breath she took was only marginally helpful. "Sometimes I am bound. Shackled. He has painted me on a cross." She held up her hands, palms out. "Nailed to it as our Lord was. No, do not look away. It is not at all helpful if you look away."

South nodded and raised his eyes to hers again. There were no scars on her palms or evidence of old abrasions on her wrists. Margrave did not work from reality but from some image that existed only in his mind's distorted eye.

Still, South wondered, what was it like for India to see herself nailed to a cross or shackled in irons?

"He paints me with scars across my back. Whipped. Beaten. On my knees. He makes my hair like a flame as though I am set afire. My body is made into a trellis for delicate climbing roses. The petals blush with the palest of pink hues, and they become my flesh and my flesh becomes them. But the thorns are sharp and they cut my breasts and my belly and my thighs, and my skin weeps bloody teardrops. He covers me with jewels and puts men at my feet, and they worship me and curse me and then they take me. You can smell the lust and feel the terror, the depiction is that true. There is nothing that has not been done to me in Margrave's paintings. There is nothing that can be thought of that I have not been made to do."

India drew another shallow breath. "I told you I had knowledge but no experience. Now you know the why of it."

South was leaning forward in his chair, his gaze set on India, his complexion almost the same gray shade as his eyes. He started to speak, but she held out her hand, cutting him off.

"There is one painting I would have you see." She said it quickly before her courage was lost. Throwing back the blankets, India extended her legs toward the edge of the bed and slid off the side. She walked toward him, drawing close enough that South was forced back in the chair; then she stepped closer still, coming to stand between his splayed legs. Her fingers tugged on the light fabric of her nightgown until it was bunched at the level of her thighs.

South's head was tipped back, his eyes still directed upward to her face. India shook her head slowly. Her hair swung in the same rhythm over her shoulders before it lay still. "Here," she said, drawing his attention lower, to where her fists were closed around her gown. "I am the canvas."

South's glance fell as India drew the nightshift over her head. He did not follow its path to the ground. He looked instead at where she had directed his gaze, and once there, could not look away.

In the seconds between India's announcement and her removal of the gown, South had had a premonition of what she meant to show him. The reality was shocking. It was also beautiful . . . and erotic.

Margrave had indeed made India's slender torso the trellis for his pale pink roses. The thorny vine climbed from between the shadowed juncture of her thighs, across her groin and left hip, then delicately upward along the inner curve of her waist until it ended at the underside of her breast. Each small leaf along the path was like an emerald embedded in her flesh. So perfectly realized were they that they seemed to flutter as if caught in a light breeze.

Belatedly South understood it was the trembling of India's body that made them move.

The fire lent its light to the pale blush of the rose petals, tipping them with gold. There were three exquisitely imagined roses along the vine, and a half-dozen more buds. The arrangement was an impossibility in nature, but the form here, as Margrave had laid it across India's skin, was nothing save perfection. It was just as India described: the fine pink petals had become her flesh, and her flesh had become them.

South raised one hand toward her, then hesitated only inches from her flat belly. He glanced upward, catching her darkly intense eyes, asking for permission before his fingertips grazed her skin. She nodded once, faintly, and still he hesitated. He had meant to press his thumb against one of the blood red tears dripping from the point of a thorn; then his attention was caught by the diamondlike sparkle of the one that lay on the fan of India's lower lashes. South's hand ceased to hover above her belly, but was lifted higher until it was level with her face. He cupped her cheek, and his thumb took the tear from her lash. When it was replaced by another, he took that, too.

South stood and shed his dressing gown, laying it across India's shoulders. A pair of his trousers was folded across the back of a chair, and he picked them up and stepped into them. India had not moved by the time he returned to her. He helped her into his robe and belted it loosely around her waist before he drew her into the wing chair with him. She sat across his lap, her head against his shoulder. There were no more tears, but she could not still her body's trembling.

"It does not repulse me, India," he said quietly. The effect was just the opposite. South found what Margrave had done to her as arousing as it was unsettling. She must know it was so. He might be able to school his features, moderate his voice, but there were certain responses his body made that he could not control or hide. "Did you think it would? Or is it that you are ashamed by what has been done to you?"

"Yes," she whispered. "To both those things."

"It was done against your will."

The flat intonation of South's voice did not make it a question, but India answered anyway, her voice small and choked. "Yes."

"Oh, India." Feeling as if his heart were being squeezed, South turned his head so his lips touched her forehead. "I am sorry for that. I am sorry that you suffered for it then and suffer for it yet." His fingers sifted idly through her hair and grazed the nape of her neck. "Margrave used the opiates you spoke of to make you compliant?"

"I was not made compliant," she said. "I was made senseless."

South nodded. He might never know if Margrave had drugged India to make her submissive or because he wanted to spare her the physical distress. "I have watched tattoo artists ply their trade in many ports, and I have never seen it done painlessly. Men who go quite willingly to have it done often wince under the needle, and it is usually only an arm they offer up. How long did it take Margrave to make the design?"

"I don't remember. A sennight, perhaps. It might have been longer."

"When?"

"Three years ago," she said. "In Paris. After he recovered from his injury."

"Aah, yes. The pistol ball to his head. A miracle that he survived."

India's attention was caught by South's dry, mocking accents. She raised her head from his shoulder so that she might see him better. "Some said it was exactly that."

"I'm sure."

"You do not think so?"

"What I am is unconvinced that divine intervention was at work." With little in the way of pressure, South brought India's head back to his shoulder. "Do you know why Margrave chose roses, India?"

"Purity."

"The thorns?"

"Pain."

"And the significance of the blood-red tears?"

"Passion."

South's gray eyes took on a flinty cast. The set of his mouth remained cold and forbidding. "He told you all this?"

"Yes. Margrave likes to explain his work, what it means, how he has come to conceive it. He wants me to understand it." She shook her head slightly. "I think there can be no understanding, at least on my part. Everything he does is beyond my comprehension, no matter how carefully he explains it to me."

South considered it doubtful that Margrave's explanations were truly meant for India. "He needs to hear himself say it," South told her. "He convinces himself that what he does is a reasoned course of action. In that manner, Margrave is removed many times from a sense of his own madness."

India had never thought of it in such terms before, but upon hearing South's construction, she immediately recognized it as the truth. "How can you know?" she asked, a bit awed that he should grasp so quickly what had always eluded her. "I have never been . . ." Her thought remained unfinished as a shiver slipped under her skin.

South ran his hand along India's back, massaging away

the chill and easing the tension between her shoulder blades. "Margrave justifies what he does," South told her. "He does not explain. There is but a fine line separating the two things, and men who are in many ways more in command of their faculties than Margrave are accomplished at it. One need only visit Parliament to know the truth of that." He smiled faintly as he felt the small vibration of her chuckle under his palm. It eased him a little to know that she could still laugh. He was not certain that he would do the same any time soon. "It is really an insignificant observation that I make, India. There is no reason that you should have known it, especially given that you were Margrave's prisoner."

It surprised her that he used that word. She had never called herself such, though she knew it to be true. The freedom that she had enjoyed was nothing more than an illusion she needed to embrace. "That is the intent of it all, you know."

South frowned, not understanding. "What do you mean?"

"The reason Margrave placed the tattoo upon me, the significance of the design he chose. The final *P. Purity. Pain. Passion.*"

"*Prisoner,*" he said flatly, finishing it for her. "Of course."

India closed her eyes. South's hand at her back was warm, soothing. The pressure of his palm made the satin dressing gown slide most pleasurably against her skin. "Do you know why I chose the stage?" she asked.

South was certain India's question was not the non sequitur it appeared to be. He was equally certain he was not meant to guess at the answer. It left him with one response. "Tell me," he said.

It made her smile, this careful, tempered reply of his. There was a gentleness in his hold on her, in his voice, in the manner that his fingers threaded through her hair, all of it at odds with the heaviness of his heartbeat and the tension she could feel in the line of his body. She could only imagine how difficult it was for him to sit with her now, when what he must want to do was ride hard to London to find the Earl of Margrave. What she would tell him now would not make it any easier.

"I chose the stage," she went on, watching South's features in profile, "because I realized I could escape him there. Not only his presence, but his influence. He cannot touch me when I stand behind the footlamps. No one can. Even Mr. Kent is at my mercy. He controls every aspect of the production until his actors take to the stage, and then he is helpless to do anything but watch."

"It is the same with Margrave," South said.

"Yes. The very same." She saw by the faint downturn at the edge of South's lips, then the deepening of a crease at the corner of his eye, that he was trying to work the puzzle out. A muscle jumped in his cheek as his jaw came tightly closed. "Margrave resents it when I am out of his reach," she told him.

South's frown deepened. There was something here that was just outside his reach. "Yet he has been on the Continent while you were becoming the toast of the London stage."

"Was he?"

"What are you saying? That he has been here with you all this time? I have watched you, India. I've seen who comes and goes from your residence. Doobin. Your dresser. The servants. Kent." His head swiveled sharply. "Is it Kent?" he asked. "Are you telling me that Kent is Margrave?"

India sat up. "No," she said. "He is not Kent, m'lord. He is Mrs. Garrety."

Chapter Thirteen

He waited in a stand of trees and watched the flicker of light in the upper window. It was cold, and he stamped his feet in place and blew on his cupped hands to ward off the piercing chill. The ride to Ambermede had been a hard one, almost without pause. Snow squalls made the journey doubly trying, preventing him from seeing the road ahead or even much of what was under his mount's hooves. He had persevered because it was not in him to do otherwise.

A slim beam of moonlight penetrated the canopy of pine boughs and slanted across his gloved hands as he raised them to his face. He took a single step backward and was swallowed by shadow again.

It was a precaution only. It did not seem likely that anyone would have a purpose to go to the window and peer out. More doubtful was the chance that he might be seen. The lateness of the hour suggested that Southerton and India were sleeping and that the winking light he saw behind the curtains was merely from the fireplace. The suggestion of movement in the room was but a trick of the light and wind-rattled windowpanes. Still, he would wait until he was certain of their absolute slumber before he let himself inside.

* * *

Feeling South's restlessness, India removed herself from his lap. He did not try to stop her. He came almost immediately to his feet and crossed the room, putting some distance between them. He stood at first with his back to her, facing the fireplace, his arms braced on the mantel, his head slightly bowed. It was no easy thing for India to wait for the moment he would turn on her. She drew out the sash of her belted dressing gown, wrapping it around her fingers.

"You might have told me at the outset," South said finally. He glanced backward over his shoulder. "Did it never occur to you to do so?"

"Just the opposite."

"Yet you said nothing."

"To what purpose? I suspected him of nothing. I was charged with protecting him."

"At all cost?" South demanded. He pushed away from the fireplace and turned on his heel to face her. "He is dangerous, India."

Her chin came up and she stared hard at him. "You speak from the superior position of hindsight. Until these last days I have always thought he was only dangerous to himself or to me. Why do you think I asked you not to pursue trying to discover the identity of my protector? I believed I understood the consequences much better than you. When you abducted me from the theatre, it was the same. I supposed that Margrave would find a way to hurt me, perhaps himself, but that he would try to hurt someone else? That he was capable of murder? No, I did not think that."

India's features softened, becoming less challenging and more earnest. "Revealing the truth about Margrave's disguise merely seemed to make him a pathetic creature. It occurs to me now that I was protecting myself as well. I must be no less pitiable, I thought, since I am unable to leave him. It is only that I did not want to seem so in your eyes."

South shook his head. "India. No, it is not—"

She raised her voice slightly, cutting him off. "Yes, South, it *is*. You must know it to be true. I would be with him now if you had not removed me from London. And I will be with him again."

"Absolutely not."

India was having none of it. She set her head at an angle, one brow arched. "You have no say. I will make amends for my culpability. If Margrave is indeed responsible for Mr. Kendall's murder—and I believe now that he must be— then I must do this thing. You have been persuasive in your arguments, my lord, and you cannot take them back now. You still think Margrave killed Mr. Rutherford, do you not?"

South had little choice but to answer honestly. "Yes," he said finally, reluctantly. "Or at least that he caused the murder to be done."

She nodded, satisfied. "And the attempt on the prince regent?"

"Yes."

"You agree Lady Macquey-Howell is also in danger?"

He sighed. "Based on what you have told me, yes."

"Then you know you are at risk as well."

"Me?"

India's eyes narrowed as her regard of him became shrewd and assessing. She wondered if she could believe he had not already considered it, and decided she could not. "You must realize that Margrave will come to learn that I am with you. Indeed, I think you are depending upon it. From the beginning, your plan in removing me from London to Ambermede was twofold. You hoped that I could be persuaded to give you information that would point to the murderer, but barring that, you hoped that my presence here would flush him out."

She felt the edge of the bed behind her, and now she sat down, made a little off balance by this new understanding of her circumstances. "That is it, isn't it? It has never been about my protection, not entirely. You and the colonel have used me to bait the hook."

South was silent for a long time. "Not the colonel," he said at last. "He knew of my plan only after the fact. And then he was against it."

India nodded faintly. "That is something, at least. He will not have wanted you to come to the same end as Mr. Kendall and Mr. Rutherford. I cannot say that I approve of it, either."

It was then that South realized that India's concern was not for herself but for him. He found it as humbling as he did disturbing. "You should be furious with me."

"Do you think I am not? You have deliberately placed yourself in the adder's path. Margrave will try to kill you, and if you are no better than those who have come before you, he will succeed. I regret I did not understand it so well at the outset, but then you thought you had reason to keep certain secrets. Now you must allow me to protect you."

South made a vaguely dismissive and impatient gesture. "India, you said yourself that I used you to bait the hook. Do you care so little for yourself that you cannot be angry with me for that?"

India's brows drew together as she frowned. "You have a most curious mind, my lord. It is not that I care nothing for myself but that Margrave's anger does not place me in the same jeopardy as you. If we are not successful in stopping him, my life with him will only be more confined and difficult. Your life will be at an end. It is not the same thing at all."

"I mean to keep you safe," he said quietly.

"I know that. It is what places you at the greatest risk." India took a deep breath and let it out slowly. "That is why I must return to London quickly. It is too isolated here. If I cannot deflect Margrave's attention from you, you will be far better protected with your friends to guard your back."

"No."

"No? I do not understand." India watched in some amazement as South simply gave her his back. Just as if he had not heard her at all, he padded to the armoire and rooted through it until he found his nightshirt. He pulled it over his head, then removed his trousers from under it. After making certain the fire was burning hot, he returned to his side of the bed and slipped under the covers. For a moment she could not speak. Twisting slightly so that she might see him better, India concluded that he would be quite grateful if she remained silent. There was nothing about his obdurate expression that invited conversation. "I am not afraid of you, you know, so it is no good looking at me like that."

"I am not looking at you."

Indeed, he was not. He was lying on his back, staring at the ceiling, and there was nothing contemplative about his pose. India snuffed the candle between her thumb and forefinger before she removed South's dressing gown and joined him under the blankets. She turned on her side toward him and propped her head on her elbow. "I will not be ignored," she said. "Perhaps you are used to giving commands and having them obeyed, but it is not enough to tell me no. I deserve an explanation." She saw by the faint lift of one dark brow that she had startled him. "I think you are arrogant, my lord, and do not like to be questioned."

It was probably a fair observation, South thought, though he was loath to admit it. His eyes shifted briefly to India, and he sighed. "Do you think I can allow you to return to Margrave knowing what I know now? When you speak of going back to London, that's what you mean. Returning to the stage, to your home, to *him.*"

"Yes," she said softly. "But it would not be for long. You have not the evidence you need now to arrest him. There is no proof that he has done any of the things you believe. I certainly can offer none, and I do not think you mean to take the life of a man who has not been judged guilty of a crime or even accused of one."

"Do not mistake my resolve, India. I can easily kill Margrave for what he has made you bear."

She shook her head. "No. You mustn't. To acquit yourself you would have to tell what was done to me at Margrave's hands, and it still might not be enough. Do you think I desire that all of London should know what he did, or that you should be called to defend your actions on my behalf? Until recently his mother was legally my guardian, while you can make no claim at all to me. I am nothing to you, my lord. No relation. No wife. I am not even properly your mistress. Do not set yourself on a course to avenge me. No one is served by that.''

"You would prefer that I pretend the motive for the murders is political, not personal.''

"Is it not what you and the colonel thought at first?''

"Yes. It was only Rutherford's murder that made me consider another possibility.'' South's cheeks puffed a little as he released a long breath. "I suppose it is good that people believe he has fled the country. Even his family would be hard pressed to accept his murder was in any way connected to politics.''

"You must concentrate on Mr. Kendall's murder,'' India said. "Or how Margrave arranged the attempt on the prince regent's life. And there is still Lady Macquey-Howell to consider.''

A small, rueful smile edged South's lips as he considered what India was trying to do. "I am not unaware of your real purpose, India.''

Her response held every nuance of innocence. "What do you mean?''

"There is but one reason you want me to assign the Earl of Margrave political motives for the murders, and it has nothing to do with what people would think of you if the truth were known. If that were to come to pass, you would simply withdraw from the scandal and retire in quiet and content obscurity. Perhaps the Cotswold Hills again or somewhere near Ambermede. I do not think you would be at all sorry to leave London.''

South glanced at her. Even with her features in shadow, he sensed he had engaged her full attention. "I believe you mean to protect me still, India. Not from Margrave this time, but from myself. From acting with anything less than a clear head when I come face-to-face with him. That is what you meant when you said I shouldn't avenge you. You are afraid that sort of passion will cause me to act rashly.''

She hesitated before asking, "Won't it?"

"Yes." He turned on his side and faced her. There was a glint of white teeth as his rueful smile widened. "It would. And it was good of you to realize it, though unnecessary. The colonel has said as much to me in the past."

"He has?"

"Oh, yes. He has never minced words about my romantic streak."

"Romantic? You mean reckless, I think."

"He would say they are not so different. I accept his caution because it is meant well and because I know he loves me like a son." South felt India's stillness, and his voice dropped, nudging her with its quiet intensity. "But that is not how you love me, is it?"

"I . . . mmm . . ." How was she supposed to answer that question? she wondered. "I think . . ."

"Is it so very hard for you to say?"

"I have never heard the same from you, m'lord."

South's chuckle vibrated from deep within his chest. "You take a perverse pleasure in keeping me in my place. M'lord this. M'lord that." He reached out and laid his hand lightly on the curve of her neck. His thumb brushed her chin, then the lower line of her lip. "I know you mean to remind me of the disparity in our stations, but the distinction is far more important to you than it is to me. It is not that I am unaware of society's opinion on such things, but that I am indifferent to it. You will recall that I count West as one of my very good friends and have done so since we were at Hambrick. It has never mattered that he was a bastard, and I shall remind him of it in the event he becomes too high in the instep."

"You would not," she whispered.

"You may depend upon it. West will." South traced a line from the underside of India's chin to the hollow of her throat. He felt her swallow hard. "You have not yet said that you love me, India. I have not forgotten, you know."

"Can it be so very important? Surely it is another complication."

"Hang the complications."

The laughter that came to India's lips was tinged with uncertainty. "Mayhap if you went first."

"I already have."

Now she frowned deeply. "No, you haven't. I would remember a declaration of that nature."

"Did I not say, 'Myself am moved to woo thee for my wife'?"

India felt a queer little curling in her stomach, part excitement, part unease. It was not so different from the first time he had said those words to her. On that occasion, her knees had simply gone out from under her and she had dropped into the chair beside her. For his part, South had seemed supremely unaffected. It seemed to India that little had changed. "That signifies nothing. You were reciting from the *Shrew.*"

"For want of better lines myself."

"You offered them in jest."

"I offered them as a warning."

"A warning?"

"Of my intent to marry you."

India's heart hammered against her rib cage. She could not quite catch her breath or a coherent thought.

"India?"

She shook her head quickly and covered her mouth with her hand as her small, nervous laugh ended in an abrupt hiccup. "Oh."

South frowned. "Are you unwell? Shall I get you a glass of water?"

India managed to draw in a ragged breath. Smelling salts were more in order, she thought. Or burnt feathers. "No," she said. "I am fine."

"You do not seem fine." He pressed her gently onto her back and swept her hair from where it had fallen over her shoulders. "Is it because you cannot imagine yourself married to me?"

"Oh, no," India said softly. "It is because I can."

"Then?"

She searched his face as he bent closer. "Then . . . nothing. You mustn't speak of it again. I do love you, you know." Her smile was a shade rueful. "There, I have said it. You have accomplished what you set out to do, and made me say the words."

"No, India. You are wrong. I did not speak of marriage to force your admission."

"Then why speak of it at all?"

"Because I *do* love you, and it seems the very essence of what is right and natural that marriage should follow."

"You are mistaken, m'lord."

One of South's dark brows lifted in a perfect arch. "Do you hear yourself, India? You mean to put a distance between us where none has to exist."

"I will not argue with you on this count. Apply to your friends and family if you wish to entertain debate. They will give sufficient evidence as to the foolishness of a marriage between us." She felt South draw a breath and prepare to resume making his point. "No, m'lord. I am adamant. You told me once that I cannot make you love me. Do you remember? It was—"

South put a finger to his lips, cutting her off. "Of course I remember," he said. "And I know what construction you put on my words, but that does not mean you were right. There was part of that sentence that was left unsaid. You cannot make me love you, India, *because I already do.*"

India fell silent as South's huskily voiced words echoed in her head. "I wish it did not matter so much," she said finally, softly. "But I find that it does. I do want to be loved by you."

South's response was simple. "You are."

She believed him. Even as comforting warmth unfolded inside her, India was compelled to say again, "It does not mean we should marry."

"It means exactly that, but I appreciate you have reservations."

"They are not reservations. They are firmly held convictions."

He shrugged as if the difference were of no account. "The special license will be there when your convictions are not."

The warmth turned to tingling. The sensation was not without a certain amount of alarm. "You mean for me to snap at that bit of bait," she said. "Well, I will not."

Shrugging, South fell onto his back and pulled the blankets up to his chest. "Good night, India."

India murmured something unintelligible under her breath as she turned on her side. She plumped the pillow with her fists until it raised her head at just the right angle; then she brought her knees toward her chest. "Good night."

South's breathing quickly became steady and even. India's did not. She stole a glimpse of his profile through the fan of her lashes. He seemed supremely unaware of her regard, or at least indifferent to it. Wondering if South was truly sleeping, India edged closer. Her knees bumped his hip, and she waited to see if he would stir. He didn't.

She sighed. It was borne home to her that she did not possess South's well of patience. Forgoing the dubious comfort of the pillow, India sought out the curve of South's shoulder instead. She lay one hand on his chest, near the open collar of his nightshirt, and finally surrendered to the inevitable. "What special license?"

"The one I applied for and received when I went back to London."

India gave a start, which brought her head up. The light but insistent pressure of South's hand at the back of her neck brought it down to his shoulder again. "You did not properly know me then," she said. "Why would you do such a thing?"

"Because of Elizabeth and North." He felt India's confusion as a near-palpable thing. "Their marriage was arranged under the most trying circumstances," he told her. "I cannot say more than that. When I saw them at West's after the funeral, I was of the opinion that they were miserable together. I had reason to regret even the small role I played in helping to bring about the marriage. Then, a day later, Elizabeth was gone."

"Gone? What do you mean?"

"She left North. At first he would have had us believe that she had gone to her father's estate at Rosemont. We knew better. It is the personal matter I spoke of, the one that kept me overlong in London. I could not leave without knowing where she was or that she was safe."

"Of course you could not. She is your friend. And North is like a brother. You did exactly the right thing."

He tipped his head to the side and laid his mouth against India's brow, kissing her lightly. "You might wish I had not," he said. "It was being witness to North's distress that prompted me to acquire the license. It can make little sense to you, but it was then I understood how swift and unpredictable were affairs of the heart. He loves her, you see. And I do not think she could have been so miserable at West's if she had not loved him. When I left, North had gone to her at Stonewickam. That is where his grandfather resides and where Elizabeth fled. He will have brought her back to London by now."

"You seem very certain. Perhaps she will not return with him."

"She will. North is our soldier and he knows something about winning a campaign."

Recalling the Compass Club charter, India smiled to herself. *"For we are soldier, sailor, tinker, spy.* Is that it?"

He nodded.

"And what do sailors know?"

"They know that having a special license at the ready is as important as a lifeboat when a man goes overboard."

When India lifted her head this time, he did not try to stop her. She studied his shadowed features, the glint of silver in his eyes, the faint upward tilt of the corners of his mouth. "Is that you, Matthew? Have you gone overboard?"

"Heart over bucket."

She smiled. "Then I suppose I shall have to save you."

South opened his arms and gave himself up to her sweet rescue.

* * *

It was the creak of floorboards below stairs that woke India. She bolted upright and prepared to vault out of the bed. A hand on her shoulder stayed her.

"I heard it also," South said quietly. "I will see what it is, and you will remain here."

India recognized that South was not offering a suggestion. With some reluctance she folded herself back under the covers.

Gratified that there would be no argument, South slipped soundlessly out of bed. He found his trousers on the floor and stepped into them, then tucked the long tails of his nightshirt haphazardly into the waistband. From the bottom of the armoire he removed a pistol and checked the priming. Satisfied that it would fire, he carefully hefted it in his right hand. Turning, his bare toes nudged India's nightgown. He picked it up and tossed it to her. He did not have to tell her what to do with it. She was pulling it over her head before it had properly settled in her hands.

"It is probably nothing," he said.

India's head came through the opening, and she stared pointedly at the pistol in his hand.

"In the event that it is." South gave her a swift, roguish smile and left the room. He had little doubt that she would not remain long in bed when he was out of it. At the top of the stairs, he stopped and cocked his head to one side, listening for the same sounds that had disturbed him earlier. India had woken when she heard the floorboards creak, but South had been alert to noises earlier than that. His first thought when he heard the rush of wind through the door was that Darrow had returned. He put it out of his mind when there was no announcement of the same. Darrow would not have had any reason for stealth. He knew such a manner would have raised South's suspicions, not quieted them.

South's tread on the stairs was light but not without sound. He tried to time each step so that it accompanied the intermittent gusts of wind that buffeted the cottage. His hand remained steady on the banister, easing the distribution of his weight.

"You may as well announce yourself with a cry from crow's nest," West said dryly. "Land ho! Avast, ye maties! Or whatever it is one cries from the mainmast."

South stopped in his tracks, one foot on a step, the other hovering above the next. "Bloody hell, West. I might have shot you."

West regarded the pistol in South's hand, unconcerned. "Not if you were aiming."

"If that is evidence of your wit, pray do not strain yourself."

West shrugged. It was an awkward gesture given the fact that he was laid out on the settee as if it were a stiff hammock, his head propped at one end, his feet at the other. He sat up slowly, stretching as South finished his descent. West reached for the oil lamp on the end table and turned up the wick. "I apologize for waking you. Not at all what I meant to do. I thought I could come in from the cold and get a few hours' sleep before daybreak."

"You didn't stop on your way here?"

"No. I came straightaway from London."

Both of South's brows rose. He ran a hand through his hair and managed to suppress a yawn that would have cracked his jaw if he had given in to it. "Then I take it you are not here to look after your recent inheritance. That business cannot have been so urgent."

"No. I may go there later. Have you been to the estate?"

"I rode past it yesterday morning." Had it been so recent? It seemed days ago that he had taken Griffin out across the snow-covered fields. It was inevitable that his meandering journey would take him past the Westphal keep. The duke's holdings were vast, and the cottage at Ambermede sat on one small corner of the property. "Your brother is in residence, I believe."

Save for a softly issued grunt, West showed no interest. "Unless it is your intention to shoot me still," he told South, "you might put down the pistol."

South looked down at his hand. The pistol was indeed leveled in West's direction. Grinning but unapologetic, he set it on the table beside the oil lamp and pulled up a stool. "Is it Elizabeth?" he asked.

West shook his head. "No. She is back in London with North. I have not seen them yet, but East says they are indecently happy."

"That is good, then."

"It may be, yes."

South smiled faintly. Trust West to be suspicious of romantic entanglements. South had always supposed it was part and parcel of growing up a bastard, but now he wondered if that was strictly true. West had always held something of himself back. In his own way he was as insular as India. "Why have you come, West? If it is not that you mean to wrest all of the Westphal keep from your brother, then what is it?"

West pointed to where he had placed his satchel against the opposite wall. Beside the leather bag were two canvas cylinders, each some thirty inches long. They were tied with brown string in the middle to keep them from unrolling. "There," he said. "I came across them in the course of some work I am doing for the colonel. When I showed them to him, he sent me here to you."

South shifted on his stool to get a better look. "What are they? Maps?"

"No. You need to see them for yourself." South started to rise, but West leaned forward and laid one hand across his forearm. "I will get them." He rose from the settee and crossed the room. "Miss Parr is sleeping?" he asked.

She was probably at the top of the stairs listening to their exchange, South thought, but it would be ungallant of him to admit as much. "If we have not awakened her." That reply at least did not reveal that she had been in his bed. Belatedly South realized that West should not have known whom he brought to the cottage. "Did the colonel tell you it was Miss Parr I had here, or did I make some misstep?"

"It was the colonel. Offered quite reluctantly, I assure

you. I had no notion of it. You can be a deep one, South.''
West bent and picked up both cylinders, one in each hand,
and carried them back to where South was sitting. ''I did
not know what to make of these. The colonel thought you
might.'' He placed one in South's open palm but did not
release it. He glanced once in the direction of the stairs,
then back to his friend. ''Perhaps it is better that you heard
me come in. I think it would have been more difficult in
the morning.''

''Because of Miss Parr's presence, you mean.'' When
West nodded, South's eyes shifted toward the stairs again.
If she was there, she was being astonishingly quiet. Had
she guessed what West was handing him? South thought it
unlikely. She could not know the shape and texture and
weight of the thing in his hand. He did, though, and his
fingers trembled.

South took the canvas from West and laid it crosswise
on his lap. He plucked at the string, inadvertently tightened
the knot, and ended up sliding it off one end of the cylinder.
He started to unroll it, vaguely aware that West had taken
a step backward.

''Oh, God.'' South spoke the words under his breath, part
prayer, part curse, as the painting was unfolded before him.
The colors were so vibrant that his first reaction was to
blink. There was the deep sapphire blue of a damask-covered
chaise longue, and the brilliant metallic gold and platinum
threads of India's hair lying resplendently across its curved
back. Rich velvet drapes the color of rubies hung in the
background, and their heavy folds swept the floor. India had
one slender arm extended toward them, as if she might
draw them back and let a narrow beam of sunshine enter.
It reminded South that there was no source for the light in
the room Margrave had painted. No lamp. No candles. No
fire.

Instead, it was India herself that was the wellspring of
radiance. She was stretched naked along the length of the
chaise, one leg raised, an arm flung above her head. Her skin
had the luster of mother-of-pearl. Her eyes, slumberously

hooded, hinted at the dark glow of polished onyx. Her back was slightly arched, her moist lips parted. The tip of her pink tongue could be seen teasing the ridge of her teeth. India's pale breasts were raised, the nipples puckered. Between her thighs her pubis glistened with the evidence of her arousal and the spendings of the men who had already taken her.

India was not alone in the exotic, jewel-toned room. Margrave had placed three men with her. Two stood at the edge of the room with only their naked backs presented to someone studying the painting. The third man stood at the foot of the chaise, his cock rampant, his knees slightly bent as he leaned forward. In the next moment he would grasp India's ankles and pull her toward him, raising her hips just as he fell to his knees. Her long legs would wind around him and he would push himself into her. Hard. Grindingly hard.

Closing his eyes was no escape from the vision Margrave had made so brutally real. Swearing softly, South shoved the canvas off his lap, opening his eyes in time to see West pluck it out of the air and roll it up quickly.

"Do you wish to see the other?"

"Should I?" Glimpsing West's troubled expression, South knew he should not have asked the question. This was not a decision a friend could make for him. He held out his hand. "Give it to me."

West's hesitation would have been imperceptible to anyone but the colonel and a fellow member of the Compass Club. That he should act in any way that did not suggest confidence would always catch their attention. It did so now.

"It's all right," South said. "I want to see it." It was a lie, of course. They both knew it. South suspected his own complexion was ashen. West was good enough not to remark on it.

West placed the second rolled canvas in South's extended hand. This time he did not offer South a modicum of privacy by stepping back. He looked away instead.

Uncertain what he would find, except that it would twist

his gut, South unrolled the painting. He gave it only a cursory glance. That was all that was required to know it was Margrave's work. The vibrant colors were there. The mysterious light that made India's nude body the focal point of the painting was also present. She was in a different room this time, a colder place than before. It might have been a temple. The graceful Doric columns, the polished floor, and something that was probably an altar were all cut from the same green-veined marble. India's wrists were cuffed in gold chains, and she was stretched tautly between two pillars. Behind her was . . .

South rolled the canvas up himself and returned it to West. "Where did you get them?"

"I stole them."

Which was not precisely an answer. "Can you say more?"

"I can tell you I got them from one of the ambassadors."

It was enough. South only needed to know that the paintings had moved from Margrave's collection to being privately owned. "They are not the sort of works of art likely to be reported missing."

"That's what I thought." West returned both paintings to where they had previously stood against the wall. As he considered what he must do next, he rubbed the back of his neck with his palm. Strands of dark-red hair were lifted from his collar to lie lightly at his nape. "You will not credit it, South, but what I am uncovering appears to have something to do with the Bishops."

South's head jerked upward. His first thought was that he could not possibly have heard correctly. "The Bishops? Are you speaking of the Society?"

"I am."

Shaking his head slowly, South glanced toward the rolled canvases again. "But not the Hambrick Hall boys."

"No. At least I hope it doesn't end there. Men are at work here, not children." West's voice dropped fractionally. "Not yet."

South nodded once. "What do you require of me?"

West returned to the settee. He sat in one corner, slightly

slouched, his long legs stretched out before him. "I would like to ask Miss Parr about the paintings. Will you permit it?"

"If she does, but it may not be necessary. I know something about them."

"She told you?"

"Yes." South saw that if West was surprised, he was careful not to show it. "She had some concerns the paintings would be shown publicly."

Now one of West's brows lifted. "She would be ruined."

"Yes."

"Forgive me if I overstep, but are you . . ." West paused, searching for an inoffensive word that might describe South's relationship to India Parr. ". . . *involved* with her?"

"I intend that she will be my wife." Once again South gave his friend full marks for his neutral expression. "It remains uncertain if she will have me."

A dimple appeared at the corner of West's mouth as his lips quirked. "Then she is a woman possessed of her own strong opinions."

"She says they're convictions."

West's dimple deepened momentarily, then he sobered. "Have you shared your intentions with anyone else?"

"No one aside from Miss Parr. You are the first. I would ask you not to say anything to East or Northam. The colonel, also."

West did not inquire as to South's reasons. He merely said, "They would not believe me. I am unsure if I believe it myself." When South offered no reply, West went on. "Did Miss Parr tell you who the artist was? The paintings were unsigned, but I believe they were done by the same person."

"They were. His name is Margrave."

"I do not know him."

"He is the Earl of Margrave now. It is another connection to the Bishops, West. You will want to know that. He was at Hambrick Hall for some of the same time we were, and a member of the Society. He was Viscount Newland then."

West's brows creased as he tried to call up a countenance to accompany the name. "Younger? Older?"

"Five years younger."

"One of the altar boys, then." West's face cleared and green eyes glinted with satisfaction. "Allen Parrish," he said. "The one they called Lingam. Do you not recall? The Bishops would have had everyone believe he wore an ebony phallus on a chain around his neck and that it lent him mystical powers."

Since a lingam was a stylized phallic symbol of Indian origin, the name was entirely appropriate. South had a fleeting picture of a rather frail-looking boy with pointed features and dark eyes. "Parrish," he said, more to himself than to West. "Yes, it fits."

"What's that again?"

South came out of his reverie. "Parrish. Parr. I had not made that connection before. India did not stray far from her origins."

West's confusion did not lessen. "I'm not sure I understand. What are you saying about their names?"

South made an airy, dismissive gesture. "Merely exercising my gray matter," he said. "It really has no bearing on the paintings."

It occurred to West that he might challenge South's last assertion, but he could not believe anything would be accomplished by it. "What else can you tell me about the paintings?"

"India tells me they have little enough reality about them."

"She did not pose for Margrave?"

"She posed. Not always willingly." South ran his fingers through his hair and considered his words carefully. Providing little in the way of elaboration, he retold the aspects of India's story that pertained to West's inquiry. For his part, West confined his questions to those things he absolutely needed to know to continue his own assignment.

At some point during South's dispassionate, factual recitation, West had leaned forward and rested his forearms on his knees. He stopped regarding his friend's coldly cast features and stared at the floor instead, forcing himself to listen with his head and not his heart. When South finished, West went to the drinks cabinet and poured himself a whiskey. "You?"

South nodded.

West poured a second glass, then carried it and the decanter to South. "Does Miss Parr know how many paintings Margrave has done?" he asked when he had returned to his seat.

"She never mentioned a particular number, only that the collection was not large." He pointed to the paintings. "However, it is most assuredly more than two. There were no others where you found those?"

"No. None with Miss Parr. I would have taken them as well."

"What do you intend to do with them?"

West had been anticipating the question but was not looking forward to the answer he must give. "I have to keep them, South. It is not possible to do anything else until my assignment is finished."

"I understand." He did. India, he knew, would not. "And then?" he asked. "What will you do with them?"

"Destroy them, if that's your wish."

It wasn't. "Return them to India."

"Of course."

"She should decide what happens to them."

West nodded. "You will assure Miss Parr that I will keep them safe? No one will see them."

South knew he could take West at his word. "I will tell her."

Leaning back, West took a swallow of whiskey. "I've seen the marble room, South. The pillars. The altar. They exist."

A muscle jumped in South's lean cheek.

"There is perhaps more reality than Miss Parr has allowed."

"No," South said. "I don't believe—"

A noise at the top of the stairs interrupted him. He turned. West's eyes lifted in the same direction. Neither of them spoke. Their first glimpse of India was when her slippered foot touched the edge of uppermost step. A slim ankle encased in white silk stockings appeared next, then the scalloped edge of her mint green day dress. She rested one hand on the banister to steady herself and completed her descent with the splendidly regal air of someone to the manor born. South and West both came to their feet, and India acknowledged each of them in turn with a coolly tempered smile.

South extended a hand toward her, his fingers slightly curled to beckon her closer. "Miss Parr," he said by way of greeting her. "Come. I would have you meet my good friend."

India crossed the room to South's side, her chin lifted the merest fraction, her dark eyes reflective and remote. She did not take his hand, but neither did she step away when he placed it casually at the small of her back.

South wondered how much of his conversation with West India had missed while she was changing clothes. He understood her desire to present herself without the vulnerability of bare feet, nightdress, and robe. At what point had she left her place at the top of the stairs to return to her room? When she realized West was in possession of Margrave's paintings? Or during his own recitation of her treatment at Margrave's hands?

She looked lovely, he thought. It was hard to reconcile this vision of her beside him, perfectly composed in her rather sweet and virginal calico dress, with the woman in the paintings, whose naked passion had been detailed as something hovering between pleasure and pain.

"His Grace, the Duke of Westphal," South said, ignoring West's flash of annoyance at this reference to his title. "Your Grace, may I present Miss Parr, an actress of extraordinary talent?"

West recovered himself enough to put aside his drink and take India's hand. He raised it to his lips. "Miss Parr." His gallantry was meant to jab a little at South, but there was nothing unpleasant about India's soft and fragrant skin against his mouth.

"Your Grace." India made a demure inclination of her head.

With some reluctance, West released India's hand. "It will be intolerable if you insist upon that formality. I am West."

India gave him the butter-wouldn't-melt smile that South knew so well, and said, "As you wish, Your Grace."

South chuckled, appreciating West's frustration. "It's no good, West. She will have her way."

West sighed. To no one in particular, he said, "The old duke should rot for this trick he's played me. Damn me if this inheritance doesn't sit on my shoulders like a lodestone, attracting trouble like iron filings."

A measure of India's composure slipped. Her wide, owlish blink in West's direction deepened South's smile.

"You will have to be patient," South told India. "He has no appreciation for his acquired station. It will take considerable work on your part to put him in his place and keep him there."

India's mouth flattened at South's thinly veiled barb. She was aware that West's interest had been engaged and that his intelligent green eyes were shifting from South to her and back to South again. In other circumstances she would have sparred with South, but with West looking on, she refrained.

West chuckled softly. "Thought for a moment she might land you a facer, South. I should have liked to see that again." He pointed to the settee. "Won't you sit, Miss Parr? May I get you a drink? Sherry, perhaps?"

India sat, but she declined the offer of a drink. It was not yet three o'clock in the morning, and while she did not begrudge them their whiskey, she could not imagine joining them. As soon as South and West returned to their seats, India came to the matter that had brought her downstairs.

"I was listening, you know," she said without apology. "You have some paintings, I believe."

"Yes," West said. "Two." He pointed to them.

"May I?" She saw immediately that neither man was comfortable with her request. "Now you are being ridiculous," she said, including both of them in her admonishment. "You have looked at them, have you not?" She started to rise, but South stayed her and retrieved the paintings himself.

"You do not have to do this," he said, holding them out to her.

"I do. His Grace has questions, I believe." India chose one of the paintings, slipped off the twine, and unrolled it. She looked at it only long enough to assure herself it was one of Margrave's, then did the same with the second. What had been unimaginable minutes ago seemed perfectly reasonable now. Returning them both to South, she said, "I will have that drink, if you please."

"Of course." He headed for the drinks cabinet.

"Brandy," she said. "Not sherry."

South set down the sherry decanter and chose the brandy. His smile was still a trifle grimly set when he gave India her drink. "You have seen those paintings before?"

She nodded. "Not for some time. The one with the chaise was done in Paris. That would make it at least three years old. The temple painting was completed in the last eighteen months." India turned to West and spoke frankly. "I overheard you say that you have seen that place. I can only tell you that I have not. Nor the room with the chaise and the velvet drapes. I had always supposed those backgrounds to be a fantasy of Margrave's, not so different from a stage."

West frowned slightly and rubbed his unshaven chin with his knuckles. "You may be more correct that you realize, Miss Parr, though the theatre is decidedly different than the one you know." He shook his head slightly, regretting that he could not say more even as he regretted having said so much. "Forgive me, Miss Parr, but I must know if you are acquainted with the men in the paintings."

Out of the corner of her eye, India saw South's fingers tighten on his glass. She thought he might protest the question, but he held himself in check. "No, Your Grace. I am not. You will understand when I tell you that I have thought of them as no more than props. Margrave has never said if they exist in flesh-and-blood form.''

"How many paintings are there?''

"I can estimate only. They could number forty.'' India heard South's sharp intake of breath but remained attentive to Westphal. "Will you allow me to destroy the paintings, Your Grace? I wish to burn them.''

"I cannot.''

The answer was not unexpected. The pressure India felt against her chest was enormous. She looked to South now, applying to him for help.

It pained South that he could not do this thing for her. "West assures me he will keep them safe, India. No one will see them, and when his assignment is concluded he will return them to you.''

"I thought they were safe,'' she said on a thread of sound. "And now His Grace has two. It is as I feared: Margrave is making them public.''

West shook his head. "No, Miss Parr. I found these in a very private collection. I took them because you were the subject of both, and I recognized you from the theatre, but there are others. Many others. And they do not feature you.''

India covered her mouth with her hand, and for a moment she thought she would be sick. South encouraged her to drink, and she raised her glass with fingers that trembled slightly. "Are they also Margrave's work?'' she asked.

"I cannot say,'' West said. "I think not. There are many dissimilarities in the styles.''

India wished she had not crept into the hallway after South had gone below stairs. She wished she had returned to his bed or her own instead of dressing as if for afternoon tea. She wished . . .

Her head came up sharply and her nostrils flared. "Do you . . .'' She stood. Nerveless fingers could no longer hold the glass, and it fell to the floor, splashing brandy on her gown and at the edge of the braided rug.

South leaped to his feet beside her and he spun toward

the stairs, alert now to the same danger as India. He closed the distance to the steps in a few strides, West on his heels.

"Get your pelisse, India," South told her as he started up the stairs. "And wait for us outside."

She wanted to argue, to insist that she could offer a pair of helping hands, but South was taking the stairs two at a time and West was rounding the newell post to follow in the same direction. They had no time to reason with her or she with them, so she let them go and went to retrieve her pelisse.

Stepping out into the crisp night air, India considered it a fitting irony that Margrave's paintings might be destroyed by fire after all.

Chapter Fourteen

It was a trap.

South realized it only after he and West were firmly caught. Flames crawled up the drapes and across the bed's counterpane, licking at the ceiling and scorching the bedposts. West used his jacket to beat at the fire. South found a blanket that had not yet been touched, and did the same. For a while it seemed as if their efforts only fanned the conflagration. Fingers of fire leaped to the mantel, and smoke rolled out from under the armoire. The occasional unpredictable gust of wind found its way through the open bedroom window and made the flames dance and spin toward South, retreat, then do the same in West's direction.

At one point, both men were pushed back by the heat and smoke to the door. They came at the fire again, this time with fresh blankets from the adjoining bedroom and buckets of snow that West hauled from outside. On this round, it was the fire that retreated.

Standing in the doorway, West surveyed the damage. Most of what the fire had done was superficial, scorching but not incinerating what was in its path. The curtains and bedcovers were a minor loss. The mattress still smoldered.

Wisps of smoke curled along the length of the mantel and between cracks in the floorboards. "Are you all right?" West asked, glancing sideways at his friend.

South nodded. "You?"

West idly ground out the glowing embers on the blanket at his feet. "Fine," he said. "What do you make of it?"

It was then that South knew precisely what to make of it. West's simple question forced him to examine all the separate elements and find the whole. The window had been closed when he left the bedchamber, and India would have had no reason to open it. South crossed the charred floor to the mantel and ran his hand along the edge. His fingers came away blackened, but there were hints of an oily residue. The gusting wind was not the only reason the fire had leaped with such abandon. If he took the time to investigate, he was certain he would find traces of lamp oil all along the path the flames took.

"India," he said softly, more to himself than to West. "He's come for India."

"What?"

But South understood he had no time to make explanations. He sprinted from the room and managed the steps in a few jumps. Not breaking stride, he went for the cottage's back door and flung it open. Heedless that he was barefoot and without a coat, South ran outside. "India!" He knew he was calling in vain, that even if she were close enough to answer she would be restrained from doing so. South cupped his hands around his mouth and tried again. His voice rose hoarsely into the cold night air. "India!"

West came up beside him and took his arm. South shook him off. Far from being discouraged, West stepped directly in front of his friend and eyed him levelly. "Tell me, South. What is it you think you know?"

South reluctantly lowered his hands. "It's Margrave. He's taken India. I'm sure of it. The fire was deliberately set to get her out of the cottage. If we had followed . . ." He left the rest unsaid. His gaze went past West's shoulder and to the wood beyond. "I have to find her."

West had heard enough. "Not dressed like that," he said. South might be oblivious to the cold at the moment, but it couldn't last long. He pointed back to the cottage. "Inside." His terse command did what the bitter cold had been unable to. West watched South gather the threads of his senses and acknowledge how hopelessly unprepared he was to track India's trail. He waited for South to turn and head for the door before he followed in his friend's footsteps.

West needed only to get his coat. He left South to find suitably warmer clothes and boots for himself and went to ready their mounts. He didn't know why he was surprised to find the animals gone, but he was. "Bloody, bloody hell," he swore under his breath. For good measure he kicked the stall door.

He was halfway back to the cottage when he saw South step out, carrying a lantern. West immediately shook his head and called to him, "It's no good. He's made off with our horses. Even the grays are gone."

South felt as if he'd taken a blow to his midsection. He actually rocked back on his heels under the imaginary force of it. His recovery, though, was swift. "Griffin will return to me."

West nodded. "As will mine. Margrave cannot possibly manage Miss Parr and the horses for long. Miss Parr alone will make the journey difficult for him."

South was not so certain about India. "Margrave has drugged her before, West. Even if he has not done as much already, the threat of the same may be enough to encourage her cooperation." Raising the lantern, South surveyed the ground for some hint of the direction Margrave had taken. He began walking to where the horses had been stabled, West at this side. "India told me only tonight that she thinks my safety would be served if she returned to London and Margrave. I do not think we can assume she is making it hard for him to get her away."

West frowned. "Is she aiding him, do you mean?"

"No. But neither will she resist him." South's mouth flattened in a grim line. "At least, I hope she doesn't. He's capable of hurting her in ways you can't imagine, West. Leave it at that.''

West did, though questions hovered on his lips. ''Throw your light that way,'' he said, pointing to the stand of trees.

South did, and they clearly saw the path of trampled snow that wended its way toward the pines. ''It looks as if he tethered the horses together.''

Thinking the same thing, West nodded. ''If I were him I'd let them go one at a time and make it more difficult for us to determine the path he set for himself and Miss Parr.''

South agreed. Without a word passing between them, they began walking the trail. It would be impossible to follow on foot for more than a few miles, but the hope they would come across their mounts more quickly this way prompted their pedestrian pursuit.

It was daybreak before West's mount crossed their path, and another hour before one of the grays came meandering toward them. Without bridle and saddle, the horses could not be ridden far, and already Margrave's trail had grown colder than the crusty snow. The divergent paths, some of which led to a better traveled road, made it no more than guesswork to know which route Margrave had taken. South finally had to acknowledge there was no point in going farther.

Glancing at West, he realized he had come late to the decision to turn back. ''You should have spoken up, West.''

''No. You had to determine the point of return. I would not have you regret we gave up too quickly.''

''I have not given up at all.''

There was no mistaking the grim resolve in South's tone. West nodded, understanding. ''What can I do?''

South shook his head. ''It is for me to do.''

''But—''

Holding up a gloved hand, South cut his friend off. ''It is for me to do,'' he repeated firmly.

West was having none of it. ''Would you absolve me of all responsibility, South? Or hadn't you yet considered that I must have led Margrave to you?''

"Considered and dismissed," South said. "It's more likely he got wind of my destination when I left London. He couldn't touch me while I was there, for fear of not being able to find India, but once I took to the road, he had to have eventually realized my destination. India accused me of wanting him to follow, and the truth is, she was more in the right of it than wrong. I did not know it was Margrave then that I was trying to draw out, but that didn't matter. I knew enough to understand that India's presence would bring her protector in pursuit."

South could see his breath mist in the air as he exhaled. "A poorly laid trap, as it turns out."

West wondered if that was entirely so. His own presence had probably cost South his chance for capture. "That's why you came downstairs armed with the pistol," West said. "You were expecting Margrave."

South shrugged. "It occurred to me."

Cursing softly, West curled his hands into loose fists at his sides. "So you are determined to do this alone?"

"Yes."

"Even North asked for help from his friends."

"It is not the same thing. Elizabeth was not abducted. She fled. There was no prospect of danger in looking for her, either to Elizabeth herself or to one of us. That is not true in India's case. Margrave will have her only for himself. If he cannot, then I believe he will make it impossible for anyone to have her."

"He would kill her?"

South did not answer immediately. He stared straight ahead, his eyes little different in their coloring or coolness from the silver-gray snow clouds on the horizon. "Yes," he said finally. Numb to every kind of feeling, his voice held no inflection. "I think there can be no other way for him. His mind will make sense of it. His sickness is so profound, he can justify any action he takes."

"He will try to kill you first."

"Most likely."

West felt a shiver chase a chill down his spine. "This is not something you can talk your way out of, South."

South smiled, though his grave features were little changed by the effort. "We'll see, won't we?"

India came to consciousness slowly. There was nothing about what she saw that was familiar, nothing about what she felt that did not hurt. Groaning softly, she tried to lift her head. The few degrees she was able to manage gave her a restricted view of the snow-covered ground. When her head fell back, she recognized the smell and textured silkiness of a horse's hindquarters.

Her first coherent thought was that she should throw herself from the animal. On the heels of that came the realization that she had no idea how to go about it. When she tried to move her arms and legs, she discovered she had not the free use of them. Her thighs were pressed tightly together; her arms lay flush to her sides. Every part of her body save her head was securely trussed in a heavy blanket. Secured in that ignominious manner, she had been thrown over the horse's back. Now each forward motion of the mount jarred her belly and made her head pound.

"Coming around, are we?" Margrave asked. Though it was a question, there was nothing in his tone that indicated he had a particular interest in the answer.

"Allow me to rise," India said.

"You will have to repeat yourself, I'm afraid."

She did not fault him for his lack of comprehension, only for what he had done to make it so. To India's own ears her words were almost unintelligible. It was always thus after one of his opiate treatments. Her mouth was invariably so dry and her tongue so thick that words could not be formed easily around it. "Let me up," she said, forcing emphasis into each consonant.

"In time." Margrave reached behind him to make certain she was still situated properly on his mount's back. "But now is not the time."

"I cannot bear this," she said. It did not matter to India if he understood her. The panic in her voice was clear enough.

"Yes, you can," said Margrave. "This and so much more. You will see, India. You only think you cannot bear it. It is a lie you tell yourself and would have me believe."

There was nothing for it but that she close her eyes. Her head swam. Splashes of color appeared behind her eyelids, fading and reappearing, shifting and coming into new focus in a kaleidoscopic display. She thought she would be sick, but it was only fear that made her stomach clench and caused beads of sweat to form on her brow. She could feel tendrils of hair clinging to her damp cheeks and neck and had no means to brush them away.

"Please," she said, though she had promised herself she would not beg.

"Very prettily said," Margrave told her. "I shall look forward to hearing it again from your lips." One corner of his mouth edged upward in a parody of a smile. "And I will, you know. Often."

India surrendered consciousness again.

The next time she woke, she was in a closed carriage. The blinds were drawn over the windows, but it was of little matter. She could tell by the unrelieved darkness at the edges that it was hours past nightfall. Her slight movement attracted the attention of her companion. She felt Margrave lean toward her from the opposite seat. His shadowed features came into focus, and when he spoke she smelled the sweetness of peppermint on his breath. It meant that he had been smoking. The cloying fragrance of his cheroot still clung to his clothes.

"I know you're awake," he said. "Come. Sit up and talk to me. I would have some conversation. It has been deuced unpleasant of you to sleep for so long. You do it just to spite me."

"You drugged me." Her tongue was no longer thick in

her mouth, but the dryness had not vanished. "It is not at all the same as sleeping."

He shrugged. "Now you are splitting hairs."

"Is there water?"

"No. But I have a flask of brandy. Would that serve?"

She nodded.

Margrave saw the movement, but he wanted to hear her say it. "You will have to speak up."

"Yes."

"There is more, perhaps?"

"Yes, please."

"Very good." He reached inside his frock coat and removed a silver flask. "This was my father's, you know." He held it out to her. "Here. Take it. There is no drug in it."

In the darkness, it was impossible to accept the flask without touching him. He wore gloves, and the leather was butter soft around his elegantly shaped hands. The contact sent a chill through her that she could not completely hide. She could only hope that he would attribute it to the cold. "Thank you." India sipped the brandy, letting it wash over her tongue and all around the interior of her mouth before she swallowed. "Where are we going?"

"Marlhaven."

Not to London, then. India had hoped it would be London. That would be where South would look first. "Your mother is expecting us?"

"I have not written her of our intention to visit, but never fear that she will turn us away. Mother will be happy for the company."

India knew it was a partial truth. The countess would be glad of her son's visit. She would merely suffer India's presence. Heart thudding softly against her breast, she stoppered the flask and made to return it to Margrave.

He pressed it back. "Keep it," he said. "You will have want of more before the night is gone."

It occurred to India that she had no idea how far they had traveled from Ambermede or how close they might be to

Marlhaven. "Will we arrive at your home tonight?" she asked, setting the flask beside her.

"Hardly. It will take us all of tonight and the next before we get there."

That meant there would be stops, India realized. Time enough, if she were careful, to leave a message with an innkeeper or guest that would eventually find its way to Southerton.

Margrave sat back again, at his ease in the close confines of the carriage. He took off his polished beaver hat and placed it on the seat beside him. He ran one gloved hand through his gold-and-ginger hair, lifting the curls away from his scalp so they settled lightly around the crown of his head. "I know what you are thinking, Dini," he said in bored accents. "Shall I tell you?"

"If it pleases you."

"It does. You are always so certain I cannot read your mind, and yet I do so time and again. Now, for instance, you are supposing that our journey will present you with some opportunity to get a message to the viscount. It is not clear what you want him to know. Mayhap only that you are safe. Or that you will be going to Marlhaven. I imagine you thought it would be London." Margrave's slim shoulders lifted in an indifferent shrug. "It matters not at all, because Southerton will never receive any communication from you. Do you understand, India? Your Lord Southerton is dead. His friend Westphal, also. Two points of the compass have been eliminated."

"You are lying."

"Am I? There is very little conviction in your voice." Margrave casually crossed his arms in front of his chest. "Shall you miss him? I am speaking of Southerton, of course. Westphal cannot be well known to you, since he only recently arrived."

"You saw him come to the cottage?"

"Answer my question first; then I shall answer yours. There must be that agreement between us."

"Shall I miss him?" she asked, repeating Margrave's question. "Only in the way one misses a toothache."

Margrave's bark of laughter held genuine amusement. "That is too bad of you. I do not believe you, naturally, but it was a good attempt to make me think otherwise. I'm afraid I have known you too long to be so easily gulled. There are nuances to your voice that do not escape me. Perhaps it was unfair for me to put such a question to you when you can be doing nothing less than reeling from the pain of it."

India would have welcomed the drugging comfort of laudanum. If Margrave presented her with a bottle now, she would thank him for it and drain it dry. She was not certain that she believed his assertion that South was dead, but neither could she detect the lie in his tone or manner. The Earl of Margrave might have made a success of the stage if the circumstances of his birth had been different and India had not found refuge there first.

Carefully modulating her voice so that it revealed more indifference than interest, India reminded Margrave of his promise to answer the question she posed. "What of Westphal's arrival? You were there, I collect."

"Yes. For some time, actually. Do you know, India, that when you left London I had not the least notion where you had gone? You had a megrim that evening. I got the cab for you; do you remember?"

"Yes."

Margrave nodded. "And then you disappeared. I did not realize it, of course, until I went to your home. The servants were surprised to see Mrs. Garrety arriving before their mistress. It was the first indication I had that there had been some trouble. Did you go willingly, Dini? I have wondered about that." When she did not answer, he chuckled softly. "No, you will not answer, will you? I have not yet fully explained myself to you."

Margrave placed one foot on the opposite seat so that it rested near India's knee. "I suspected Southerton. He was the natural choice to have spirited you away. I can say that it was most confusing when he returned to town so quickly and you remained gone. Oh, and what a merry chase he and his friends led me those nine days. After the old duke's funeral, they would congregate for the odd moment and then scatter. I thought it had something to do with you, you see, but that was not the case at all. It was Northam's wife they were trying to find, though I did not understand that until quite late. I followed him all the way to Battenburn in expectation of finding you, and all along he was only trying to help his friend.''

India was glad of the darkness that covered her bittersweet smile. She remembered South's long absence from Ambermede with a certain poignancy. Every day that she teased Darrow with a bowl of broth while heartier fare was bubbling below stairs, was followed by a night spent alone in her room, her thoughts occupied by South's inevitable return and his intentions toward her. It would have eased her mind had she known then the reason for his delay. That he was helping his friend would have comforted her. She wondered if South knew how she had exhausted herself before his return, or how few defenses she had had at her fingertips when she saw him again.

You will ease yourself with me, she had said. *And I with you.*

''You are very still of a sudden,'' Margrave said.

India did not have to see his dark predator eyes to know they were now narrowed on her. She had never accustomed herself to his stare. There was nothing natural about his assessment, only things unnatural. ''I am merely listening,'' she said quietly. ''Pray continue.''

Margrave cocked an eyebrow. It sounded almost as if she were ordering him. That was a trifle unsettling. ''Very well,'' he said. ''When I came to know the real purpose of South's activities, I merely bided my time. He would return to you, I thought. Or return for you. Northam found his wife at Stonewickam.''

''Yes. I know. It is North's grandfather's home.'' India wondered how Margrave had learned of it. She had imagined the Compass Club as being a circle of friends who would act with discretion. Margrave could not have heard it from any of them. He had to have briefly made his way into one of their homes. "Have you been posing as a tradesman again, Margrave? Did you perhaps win the confidence of a servant?"

He lightly applauded her. "You know me well in your own right, Dini. One does what one must." Margrave threaded his fingers together in a loose fist. "When it was clear that Lady Northam was found, I knew that wherever Southerton went next, it would lead to you."

"Then you have been near Ambermede for some time."

"Yes. I stayed in the village. I met a very nice woman there. A widow, I think she said she was."

India's stomach clenched uncomfortably. Her mouth flattened, and she pressed the fingertips of one hand against her temple. The steady rocking of the carriage no longer had the power to soothe. She lifted her head from where it rested against the leather squabs, and tried to concentrate on what she was hearing. "You made the acquaintance of Mrs. Simon?"

"Aaah, yes. That was her name. Very helpful, she was. There was also Southerton's man, of course, but he was a closed one. I think he was most anxious to leave the village and return to the cottage. Mrs. Simon, though, was of a mind to give the viscount and his ladybird time alone." Margrave nudged India's knee with the toe of his boot. "Were you South's ladybird? Or was the widow given to foolish romantic notions?"

India did not believe for a moment that Mrs. Simon had called her Southerton's ladybird. Margrave's intention was to goad her. He had left it until too late. She was too weary and sick at heart to be provoked into rashness now. "I was with Lord Southerton much against my will," she said. "The widow's notions are her own."

Margrave was thoughtful. "I doubt that it was against your will, Dini. According to the widow, you nursed South's manservant in his absence. It seems to me it would have presented an opportunity to leave, yet you did not."

India shrugged. "You will believe what you will, Margrave. It is not for me to contradict you."

"Did you become his mistress?" Margrave asked. Before she could say anything, he cautioned her, "Have a care how you answer. There are ways for me to learn the truth."

India's head began to pound in earnest, and she blanched at the thought of Margrave touching her so intimately. "You want to know if he lay with me. The answer is yes. He did."

"Lay with you? Surely, an odd turn of phrase. Did he not imagine himself in love with you, India? Or you with him? Is that not what occurred between you?"

She said nothing.

"Now you disappoint," Margrave said. "I think when we arrive at Marlhaven I will paint you with him. It will be a good exercise for me. I have never tried to capture tender feeling in my work. And perhaps we will add another rose to your vine. This is the fourth time you have tried to leave me. The roses should number four now, as should the tears."

South sat alone in his study, an unopened bottle of wine on the table beside him and an unopened book in his lap. He had taste for neither. Another day of combing London had not gone well, and there was still no news of India Parr from any quarter. His mother had called him home and demanded to know if what her dear friend Celia Worth Hampton had said was true, namely, that he had taken up with the opera dancer and was going to make her his wife.

South had corrected his mother on the only point he could. "India Parr is not an opera dancer," he had said. That distinction seemed to have provided little in the way of calming effect. His mother had reached for her smelling salts and called for a glass of sherry to be brought to her—and it was not yet eleven.

That afternoon North denied that he had said anything to his mother about India Parr, though he had learned some of what had passed at Ambermede from West. Elizabeth had walked into the room then, all grace and good cheer, and

South had immediately come to understand how things were passed from friend to friend, then to wife, and finally to mother-in-law. The Dowager Countess of Northam had made straightaway to his own mother to apprise her of every detail. South could only be thankful that she did not know many.

From Eastlyn there was no sympathy. The marquess was still entangled in a false engagement and a promise of marriage he believed had never been properly made. He was becoming used to the gossip surrounding his activities and was not at all sorry to have South on the verge of the same.

The disappearance of India was another matter entirely and no cause for levity. To a man, his friends had proposed to help in the search. South declined all offers. He had no place left to tell them to look.

He had been to the theatre, to her home, even to Margrave's London residence. He had gone to the boarding house were Margrave had rented a room for Mrs. Garrety. There was a new tenant there. Upon giving up his identity as India's dresser, Margrave had ceased to pay rent on the room.

South had been to visit Mr. Kendall's family, to question them again about the woman for whom he may have developed a tendre. Neither his sisters nor his mother remembered anything they had not told him before, and South knew his visit accomplished nothing but upset.

It was the same when he renewed his acquaintance with the Rutherfords. They wanted no part of his questions. Any evidence that existed linking Margrave to Mr. Rutherford's murder continued to elude South. More important, India was nowhere near his grasp.

He paid a visit on Lady Macquey-Howell and made discreet inquiries. Of her financial arrangements with the Spanish consul, South said nothing. He would not compromise that investigation by alarming her. He did, however, discover that the countess had taken a new lover. South reasoned it would go a long way to keeping her out of Margrave's jealous and jaded eye.

There had also been no information forthcoming when he visited Margrave's estates at Merrimont and Marlhaven. At Merrimont he could only speak to the housekeeper, and while she was clearly uncomfortable with his questions and protective of the earl and his mother, South never suspected that her answers were less than honest. She remembered Miss Diana Hawthorne quite fondly and had no notion that the young girl who had been fostered at Merrimont was now a much admired actress on the London stage. South did not take it upon himself to apprise her of that fact.

At Marlhaven the reception was considerably cooler and more tempered. The dowager countess graciously deigned to receive South, but her civility was tested in the interview that followed. Although she found his questions disagreeable in the extreme, she made no effort to have him ejected from her home. South did not know that he would have been so solicitous if their positions had been reversed. Once again, he left without intelligence that would help him find India.

South had pinned some hope on Doobin, and there the situation became complicated. The boy was no longer with Mr. Kent's theatre company, and no one South spoke to seemed to know where he'd gone. Though the reason for his dismissal was theft, South suspected Margrave's fine hand at work. It took South two days of searching the garbage-strewn alleyways of Holborn to locate the boy, then the better part of an hour to convince him to return home with him. Doobin was not so trusting as he had been, certain that Southerton was to blame for India's disappearance. Since he was not far off the mark, South had had to do considerable explaining to bring the thing about. Bribery had figured largely in the outcome.

The lad had known little that was of help to South, but having him safe in residence, if sometimes underfoot, was a salve to South's troubled conscience. It was a small thing to do for India, he knew, but a necessary thing to do for himself. The child did not deserve to suffer at Margrave's hands for the loyalty and friendship he had extended to India.

South did not turn his head as the door to his study was gently pushed open. No one but Doobin would have come in without first receiving an entrée from him. "What is it, Doobin?"

The fact that South knew it was him was a trifle alarming. Doobin's tongue cleaved to the roof of his mouth. "I've come for your boots, my lord. Mr. Darrow says it's for me to polish them."

"That is very good of Darrow," South said. "But I am still wearing them."

"I mean to take them off, my lord, and return them directly."

"I see." South felt a reluctant smile tug at the corners of his mouth. It had been a long time since his lips had been drawn in that shape. "Well, have at them."

Doobin crossed the room quickly and dropped to his haunches in front of South. He lifted the viscount's boot and took it firmly by the heel. "I'll have this done in a trice, my lord. Just see if I don't. I aim to make Mr. Darrow pleased that I'm in your service now."

Darrow would be mortified that Doobin had disturbed South here, but South vowed it was something they would work out between them. South would only suggest to his manservant that he not be too hard on the lad. He was a particular favorite of India's, after all.

Doobin removed South's right boot without difficulty. The left one presented more of a challenge. The boy's efforts were punctuated with soft grunts and the occasional curse. In the end, South had to set his unopened book aside and help.

"Thank you, my lord." Holding the boots aloft, Doobin made a slight bow. "I shall be quick about."

"Very good," South said. He wriggled his toes in his stockings and stretched out in the soft leather chair, his entire body curved in a comfortable slouch. When Doobin made to pass him, South caught the boy's wrist. "A moment, if you please."

"Of course, my lord."

"Have you seen Mrs. Garrety since you've been under my roof, Doobin?"

"Mrs. Garrety?" He was genuinely surprised by the question. "No. Why would she come here?"

"Perhaps to find Miss Parr. Mrs. Garrety was very close to her."

"Oh, yes. Like a flea she was. Always nipping at Miss Parr. Trying to get under her skin." Doobin shook his head. "I haven't seen her since Miss Parr left London. My ears are glad of it, too. She boxed them regular. There's a bit of ringing yet in the left one."

South hoped again that he would get the opportunity to lay Margrave out. Perhaps he would box the earl's ears first. "Miss Parr told me once that you collected all the cards that were given to her."

"Yes, my lord. I have them still."

"Were there many women who came calling?"

"Not many. Not backstage at the theatre. It's not a proper place for a lady, though I can't see how it can be proper for Miss Parr. She is a lady through and through."

"She certainly is."

"Lady Macquey-Howell came to the greenroom on occasion. A few others. Is it important? I can show you my cards."

"Perhaps later. Did Miss Parr receive many guests at her home?"

"I can't say if it were many. I have the cards she gave me."

"Do you recall if there was one from the Dowager Countess of Margrave?"

The gap between Doobin's front teeth was clearly visible as he smiled broadly. "I remember that one quite well. I was at Miss Parr's when her ladyship visited, though I wish I had been gone. They had quite a row, you know."

"You saw her?"

"From the upstairs hall. I was taking my lessons with Miss Parr in her sitting room when Lady Margrave called. Miss Parr went down to greet her, and I peeked to see her.

I know I should not have, but Miss Parr was unhappy about the visit. I wondered about the person who could upset her.''

"Can you describe Lady Margrave to me?"

Doobin's brow puckered as he gave the matter his fierce attention. "She's very tall, my lord. For a lady, that is. She stood eye-to-eye with Miss Parr, and there's not many that can do that. She wore a velvet bonnet with ostrich plumes that kept dipping and swaying when she spoke. She had a habit of bobbing her head, you see. They quite took my notice, so I don't remember the color of her hair. She has the face of a horse, though. *That* I recall. Put me in mind of a particular one I saw in Tattersall's once. It was an Arabian, I think, with a long black mane, rather like those plumes on her ladyship's bonnet. The Arabian was quite beautiful with its narrow nose and great dark eyes." He paused and admitted a trifle sheepishly, "Though there is something different about it on a lady."

"Indeed," South said dryly. He knew the kind of features Doobin was trying to describe. He imagined a rather elongated face and wide, flaring nostrils. Perhaps Lady Margrave's cheeks had become a bit jowly. "Then you would not say Lady Margrave was beautiful, even in her younger days?"

Doobin could not imagine the woman in her younger days. "She's what they call handsome, my lord. That's how I hear the gents at the theatre describe one such as she."

South nodded, his attention turning away from the boy. Somewhat absently he thanked Doobin. Minutes passed before he noticed he was alone in the room.

Colonel John Blackwood sat in his favorite chair, his feet propped comfortably on a padded stool. He tapped the bowl of his pipe against an ashtray, knocking the residue of a previous smoke loose before he packed it with his special blend of tobacco. "I cannot talk you out of it?" he asked casually, not sparing a glance in South's direction.

"No, sir. I have come close to tearing London apart looking for her, with no success."

"Oh, I would say you have made a success of tearing London apart. It certainly has come to my ears that you have done so." Without giving South time to insert a defense of himself, the colonel went on. "What has it been? Three weeks or four, since you returned from Ambermede?"

"Three weeks and three days," South said. He could have stated the number of hours but refrained from doing so.

"It has come to my attention from a variety of directions that you have disrupted the theatre at Drury Lane on at least three occasions with interruptions of their rehearsals, that you've bedeviled the families of both Mr. Kendall and Mr. Rutherford with questions they cannot answer and would not wish to if they could, that you have been seen wandering the alleyways of Holborn, that you've been to see Lady Macquey-Howell and may have inadvertently alerted her to the investigation by the Foreign Office, and finally that your own mother is becoming increasingly anxious as to the fitness of your mind. This last news I have heard directly from your father, who seems not to have the same concerns but nevertheless was pressed upon by your mother to voice them. I will leave it to you to guess who apprised me of the rest."

South opened his mouth to speak, but the colonel was not yet through.

"That you could have accomplished so much upset in so short a time and still have it not come to the notice of the wags or the gutter press is truly a remarkable feat. Add to that the fact that you have already been to Marlhaven and made a nuisance of yourself with the countess in asking after her son and demanding to know the whereabouts of Miss Parr, and you begin to see that my waking hours are filled with some news of your latest enterprise."

South tried again to speak and was summarily cut off when the colonel jabbed his pipe in the air to emphasize his final points.

"Your friends have each applied to me to insist that

they be allowed to help. Now that North's affair with the Gentleman Thief is satisfactorily concluded and Elizabeth is at her ease in Society, it seems to me that Northam, at least, might be spared to assist you."

South came to his feet. "And make Elizabeth a widow, sir? No, I will not have that on my conscience." He remembered all too well sitting with Eastlyn and Westphal in North's Merrifield Square home, listening to Elizabeth lay the tale of the Gentleman Thief before them. She had simply shined under the attentions of her husband, her almond-shaped eyes alight with mischief and wit. They had toasted her, and she had raised her glass to them in turn. "The Compass Club," she had said, just as if they were heroes.

It had almost been more than he could bear to accept her good wishes and praise when he knew very well that he was no hero at all. He had sat there making light of North's recent injury and Elizabeth's well-intentioned hovering, using humor to deflect the envy that was in his own heart. Envy, he thought, because he would not allow himself to give in to grief.

"It appears that North and his countess have their happy ending," South said. "I would not have it altered on my account. Furthermore, sir, when my friends come to you with the particulars of my latest intrigues, you may tell them I want no more skulking in my shadow. They are worse than any nursemaid I have ever had for listening at doors."

The colonel raised one black eyebrow. His spectacles glinted in the firelight. "Then you are set on the matter."

"Firmly set, sir. India is not in London. Margrave has either taken her abroad—a possibility for which I can find no evidence—or he is hiding her at one of his estates. I have good reason now to suspect it is Marlhaven."

There existed another possibility, but because South did not mention that India might already be dead, the colonel did not raise it himself. South's despair was almost palpable, yet it did not exist in any manner that was familiar to the colonel. South's handsome features were not haggard or drawn, but set hard as stone, obdurate and implacable. The

amusement that could set light into his eyes was rarely
visible. Instead they were most often cold and unyielding.
The colonel had good reason to know why the Countess of
Redding was concerned for her son. His own concerns,
like those of South's best friends, were only a trifle more
moderate.

"You have already been to Marlhaven," Blackwood
pointed out. "And the dowager countess would have no part
of your presence once you explained the reason for it. Why
will a second visit end differently?"

"Because I intend to take a page from Margrave's book,
sir." South picked up his wineglass and drained it. "My
own mother won't recognize me. I sincerely doubt that his
will."

"Of course you must go," Elizabeth said. Sunlight was
trapped in the gold highlights in her hair as she sat at the
window in the downstairs drawing room. She looked to her
husband and dear friends with something like disappointment in her dark-amber eyes. "I cannot understand your
hesitation. It has been more than a sennight since he left,
and there has been no word. If any of you were in danger,
South would not hesitate to come to your aid." Elizabeth
gave her husband a sharply wry glance. "Indeed, did he not
just do that very thing to clear your name, North? Perhaps
you have forgotten it was South who risked bringing suspicion to himself by accompanying me to Lady Calumet's
ball. He might have been caught, prowling about as he was.
And to what purpose except to make certain the *ton* no
longer suspected you were the thief in their midst. It really
is not to be borne, North, that you would let him go off to
Marlhaven alone."

North cleared his throat, a bit uncomfortable with his
wife's level stare. "South was adamant that he did not
want our help," he said. "Told the colonel we should stop
following him."

"What does that signify?" Elizabeth turned her attention

to her two guests. Good manners dictated that she deal
with them politely, but she had spent enough time in their
company to know that civility would not serve her now.
"East? What does it matter that South has not applied to
you for help? When has he ever done such a thing? And
you, West? You were the one who told me how South turned
the tables on the Bishops at Hambrick Hall. Did he ask you
for assistance then? That is not how I remember the tale.
And he knew very well the trap that had been laid for him.
He willingly put himself at the mercy of their tribunal while
all of you listened at the door." She drew in a deep breath
and let it out slowly, then said gently, "The very least you
could do for him now is listen at the door. I do not think
that is an unreasonable request."

No member of the Compass Club spoke for a moment.
They exchanged glances with one another, not in a way
that ignored Elizabeth's dressing-down, but in a way that
communicated they had heard every word of it.

West spoke first. "He will not thank us for it," he said
to no one in particular.

"Thank us?" East said. "It is quite possible he will never
speak to us again."

North's mouth twitched. "That would be a point in favor
of going to Marlhaven."

East considered that, the line of his own mouth set wryly.
"It's as good a reason as any. I have never believed South
was made to properly pay for that bit of business at Hambrick. It would serve him a good one if we were to rush to
his aid now."

West leaned back in his chair and eyed his friends. "He
did write our charter," he said. "*North. South. East. West.
Friends for life, we have confessed. All other truths, we'll
deny. For we are soldier, sailor, tinker, spy.* Amends must
be made for bad rhyme."

Elizabeth smiled, encouraged now. She knew them all
too well to suppose their amusement lessened the import of
their decision. They would go to Marlhaven, and at the very
least, they would listen at the door.

* * *

India stood at the window of her receiving room and looked out over the moonlit garden maze. In the spring the yews would be neatly clipped to bring symmetry and order to the elaborate design. Now they were covered with a cap of glistening snow, and the path from the starting point to the stone benches and fountain at the center was not easily visible, even from India's vantage point.

It had been many years since she had wandered through the maze. It had been a place of solitude on the occasions she had visited Marlhaven. Margrave had been distracted by his father's illness and his mother's demands and had not made a nuisance of himself by following her. She had sometimes carried a book with her; more often it was her sketchpad. She would set it on her lap by the fountain and let her hand fly across the paper, putting down in broad charcoal strokes whatever her mind could imagine.

What had she imagined then?

India pressed the flat of her hand against the cool window-pane. Her smile was faint and wistful. Whatever she had seen in her mind's eye, it had not been this. If there had been a castle and tower and damsel needing rescuing, then there had also been a someone to mount the rescue. She had not been so foolish as to place dragons before her without drawing the dragonslayer.

In life, it was an entirely different matter.

Behind her, India heard a key being turned in the door of the adjoining bedchamber. She did not bother to leave her place at the window. In all the time she had been at Marlhaven, only Margrave or his mother had come to her suite. The countess's visits were unpredictable in both their frequency and their duration. Permission was granted at her son's whim, and there was no accounting for it. India had learned very quickly that Lady Margrave was as much a prisoner at Marlhaven as she herself.

"I have brought you dinner," Margrave said, entering from India's bedchamber. "Shall you have it here?"

India straightened, nodding dully, and closed her eyes. "On the table, if you will." She hoped he would not stay this evening to watch her eat and drink. She had spent the better part of the morning prying floorboards loose under her armoire. The hiding place would be the repository for her food for at least a sennight. The worst that would happen was that the mice would become fat and glassy-eyed while they dined on rich sauces and opium.

"It is shepherd's pie tonight," he told her. "I remembered that you like it, and asked Mrs. Hoover to prepare it especially for you."

"It was kind of you to think of it."

Margrave's dark eyes narrowed as he studied India. She remained at the window, her shoulders slightly hunched as she hugged herself. Her head was bowed, and her long platinum braid had fallen forward over her shoulder, exposing the nape of her neck. She looked heartbreakingly vulnerable, and yet . . . "If you are cold," he said, "you should come away from the window."

India had enough of her wits about her to recognize that Margrave's suggestion was not that at all. She took a step backward and turned on her heel slowly, opening her eyes before she was facing him. Her pupils were wide, her gaze a trifle vague. She moved away from the candlelight and into the shadow that was cast by the large easel and canvas.

"Will you join me this evening?" she asked. "There is enough for two."

Still watching her closely, Margrave shook his head. "I have already eaten. Mother begged me to join her, and it would have been churlish to refuse. She asks for very little these days save for the pleasure of my company."

"Of course." Careful not to press, India sat at the small table and lifted the cover on the shepherd's pie. Her mouth watered almost instantly. It would be difficult to resist tonight's fare. Shepherd's pie *was* a favorite, and she was very, very hungry. Conscious of Margrave's watchful gaze, she served herself a generous portion, then picked up her fork.

"He will not come, India," Margrave said suddenly.

India gave him no reaction. As if he hadn't spoken, she tucked into her food, taking as large a bite as she dared to satisfy him.

"He cannot come. You understand that, don't you? He is dead. Burned in the fire. Just like your parents."

In her lap her hand tightened into a fist, but the fingers around the fork remained light in their grip. "Yes," she said. "I remember. You have said so before."

Margrave's darkly remote glance shifted from India's plate to the bottle of wine on her right. He made his decision without warning, picking up the bottle by the neck and placing it under his arm. "Perhaps a different wine," he said. "I am not certain this one will suit your palate."

Eyes on her plate, India merely nodded. It wasn't until she heard Margrave's retreating footsteps in the corridor that she permitted herself the small luxury of a triumphant smile.

Chapter Fifteen

There was no servant at Marlhaven who was not afraid of the earl. No one ever said as much to South, yet there was no escaping the truth of it. Fear existed in the very air one breathed.

The large estate was understaffed. There were insufficient grooms for the stables, not enough maids of all work for the house proper, and the footmen numbered only six. South learned this state of affairs was the result of a relatively recent purge by the dowager countess. Normally, a country home with the size and splendor of Marlhaven was a veritable hive of worker bees serving the queen. In addition to footmen, grooms, and maids of all work, there would be laundresses and lamp boys, groundskeepers and gardeners, maids for the upstairs and maids for the downstairs, a first groom of the chambers, and first and second butlers. The cook had survived, but with only one of her helpers and the dairymaid. The baker and confectioner were both gone, as was the pantry boy.

There was work enough for all those people, and rooms enough to do it in. Marlhaven had vast galleries and drawing rooms. There was a breakfast room and a morning room, a dining room for the family, another for entertaining guests, and still another built to accommodate the King and his entourage if a visit of that nature were ever to come about. The grand public rooms also included an excellent library and the splendidly appointed master's study.

Like other country homes, Marlhaven was a repository for artwork, and all of it required care. Portraits of Margraves past crowded the gallery and lined the main entrance and staircase. Landscapes depicting the pastoral pleasures of hunting and fishing occupied prominent places in the dining room and study. Tapestries hung in the library and in many of the private apartments. Nor was the art limited to what crowded the walls. It was intrinsic to the house itself, from the magnificent setting amid a fairy-tale woodland to the impressive gardens that enhanced the home's Elizabethan architecture. Art existed in the woodwork and ceilings and intricately inlaid floors. The three-dimensional expression of it could be seen in the elaborately carved mantels and again in the polished marble columns that stood like sentinels in the palatial drawing rooms.

For centuries artists and artisans commissioned by the family had contributed their considerable talents to imbue Marlhaven with grace and grandeur, and had circumstances been different, South could have found much to admire about the house. What he noticed, however, was that nowhere was the artwork representative of the current Earl of Margrave's peculiar personal tastes.

South's arrival at Marlhaven was timely, coming as it did on the heels of the dowager countess's elimination of better than half of her staff. With so many positions vital to the maintenance of the estate gone, it required only the passage of a few weeks before the rashness of her act bore consequences. There were simply not enough hours in the day for the remaining servants to see to all the tasks that were laid before them.

So it was that in spite of their best efforts, things fell by the wayside. Linens were not changed with the same frequency, and bedchambers were not aired. Cobwebs appeared in dark corners. Dust lay in the scrollwork on the wainscoting. The silver lost some of its polish, and the oil lamps were no longer collected, filled, and trimmed daily. It was not possible to sweep all the floors or beat the carpets, or even visit all of the rooms where the work was to be accomplished. The chambers and halls at Marlhaven numbered one hundred twenty-seven.

South was hired when the dowager countess rescinded her order to the estate's steward and allowed for the reappointment of some positions. It was now South's job to carry coals from the coal house and see that there was always a sufficient supply of full buckets for the fireplaces and ovens.

It was hard and honest work, suitable for the man he had become. He walked with a slight limp and stooped carriage, his shoulders permanently hunched as though he were braced for the cold. His dark hair was covered with a shaggy wig that had been liberally woven with wiry gray strands, and he wore spectacles high on the bridge of his nose. Complaining of rheumatism, he often hid his youthful hands under gloves. When that was not possible, he was careful to keep his fingers stiffly curled. It was Doobin who taught him how to paint shadows under his eyes and emphasize the creases at the corners so that they would hold up under some scrutiny. South had thought himself skilled at such deceptive practices until India's young helper had shown him how much he had to learn. He altered the tone and volume and cadence of his speech until he affected the accents of an old salt he'd served with from Liverpool.

In the end, just as he promised the colonel, South was unrecognizable to his own mother.

On the morning of his fourth day at Marlhaven, South sat on a three-legged stool by the kitchen's large hearth and warmed himself. Occasionally, he stirred the simmering kettle of chicken stock with a long-handled spoon given to him by the cook. Mrs. Hoover determined that if he was going to avail himself of the heat before lugging in another pail of coal, he may as well make some use of himself.

South did not attempt to make conversation with the cook.

Except to give orders, she rarely spoke to anyone, though she often looked as if the silence pained her. In that respect she was like most of the other servants at Marlhaven. It was such a contrast to South's experience in his London home or his family's estate that it struck him as singular from the very first. As a boy he had often escaped notice of his nannies and tutors by hiding in the warren of rooms where the servants lived and carried out many of their tasks. He had never noticed the maids or footmen lacking for something to talk about or being reluctant to do so. South had on occasion learned more about what was happening in his own family from eavesdropping outside the scullery or wash-house than he had from his parents.

It was very different at Marlhaven. The way the servants were given to glancing over their shoulders at odd moments, South suspected they were in almost constant anticipation of being interrupted or spied upon. Without any apparent edict to do so, they went out of their way to perform their duties without being seen or heard. What work could be accomplished by their reduced numbers was many times completed hours before first light. The housemaids used the backstairs whenever possible and walked out of their way to avoid an accidental meeting with the master of the house.

The threat of dismissal was suspended above every one of the servants like a guillotine blade. Reestablishing a dozen positions in the household did not lessen their worries or calm their fears. Both emotions were palpable. South believed there would have been a mass exodus if they believed their lot could be improved elsewhere.

A comely chambermaid stepped into the kitchen and retreated just as rapidly when she saw the cook had work to be done. South heard Mrs. Hoover cluck her tongue disapprovingly and mutter something under her breath. He chuckled loudly enough to get her attention but pretended to be oblivious to her sharp look.

"There's something amusing you?" she asked, dusting off her floured hands.

South shrugged his narrowly hunched shoulders.

"That's what I thought." She eyed the soup pot. "Have a care not to let the vegetables scorch on the bottom."

Under her watchful gaze, he gave the soup a vigorous stir.

"Better," she said. Picking up a muffin still hot from the oven, she held it in her hands a moment as though undecided what to do with it. Somewhat reluctantly she thrust the thing at South. "For you. It will warm your insides."

"Thank you," he said in the gravel-filled voice he had perfected. "It's kindness you are."

Suspicious of any sort of flattery, Mrs. Hoover merely pursed her lips.

"And a most excellent maker of muffins."

She gave him an arch look and went to check on a second batch of muffins.

"It seems to me," South went on, "that the good countess does not know your worth."

"What do you mean by that?"

"She would see to it that you had help enough in the kitchen so that you might devote yourself to these." He swallowed the large bite he had been cheeking. "Food of the gods."

Mrs. Hoover could not quite hold her rather sour, put-upon expression any longer. Her mouth twitched.

It was not a smile, South thought, but a good beginning. He took another bite and once again spoke around it. "I have never tasted the like before."

"These were a favorite of his lordship's." She set down the pan she had removed from the oven. "I made them often for him when he was a boy. I thought he might like them again."

"No doubt he will appreciate your efforts." He noticed that the cook did not look at all certain of the same. "But what of Lady Margrave? Surely you mean to please her palate as well. You have something particular for her?"

"The soup is for her. She takes little else these days."

South had observed the same. While there was almost no discussion among the servants of how things fared at

Marlhaven, their careful and quiet activity spoke for them. He learned that the trays of food prepared by Mrs. Hoover never went to the dining room but were delivered to the private apartments in the east wing. It was there that the earl accepted them because none of the servants had been allowed into the corridor in weeks.

"She is not well?" South asked.

The cook glanced over her shoulder in the manner that was peculiar to so many among the staff. "I fear it's the melancholia again."

"I see. She is given to bouts of it, then."

She nodded quickly. "Since her husband died. This is the worst it's been." Mrs. Hoover pressed her lips together suddenly, quite certain she had said enough.

South finished his muffin and stirred the soup. "There's no physician?"

Mrs. Hoover hesitated, then said, "His lordship cares for her. He will not have it any other way."

South watched the cook spread flour across the breadboard and bend to her kneading. Cords of muscle stood out in her forearms as she pressed the heels of her hands into the dough. She folded it, gave it a quarter turn, and pressed hard again. "I've heard melancholia can account for peculiar notions. That must be the way of it with Lady Margrave."

The cook frowned deeply, but she did not look up from her task. "What notions?" she asked brusquely.

"The dismissals."

Mrs. Hoover glanced over her shoulder a second time. "I don't know what accounts for the notions you've taken into your head, but the dismissals were his lordship's idea."

South saw her mouth clamp shut and knew he would not pry another word out of her. The creases deepening around her bow mouth and widely set eyes spoke eloquently to her fears, and for the first time since returning to Marlhaven, South understood what he had not grasped before. The dowager countess's staff was not entirely worried about what would become of them but rather what would become of her.

And still, after three days of shuttling coal between one place and another, making himself almost perfectly inconspicuous so that he might hear what they would never reveal to a stranger, South had yet to catch a single word spoken of India Parr. It was as if the staff at Marlhaven had no knowledge of her existence.

The possibility that Margrave had kept India's presence a secret disturbed South. The possibility that she was no longer at Marlhaven terrified him.

Lady Margrave preceded her son into India's suite. She walked with stately grace, her carriage erect, her head held high. Her sharply defined features were what one noticed first. She had high, finely arched cheekbones and a strong chin. The long oval of her face was accented by a bold nose with slightly flaring nostrils and eyes that were as dark as coffee. Her mouth was firmly set, but age had turned the corners permanently down, and delicate lines were etched across her wide brow. Her hair was no longer as light a color or as fine as it had been in her youth. Now threads of gray mingled with the flaxen shades at her temples and at the crown of her head. She resisted temptation to hide them under turbans or lace caps in her own home, preferring to address these signs of advancing years with an excess of dignity.

At the entrance of mother and son, India stopped her rocking chair and set her feet flat on the floor. She was a trifle unsteady as she came to her feet. "Good evening, Lady Margrave. M'lord."

Margrave removed his hand from where it rested at the small of his mother's back. "Mother desired the pleasure of your company tonight, Dini. I told her that she might visit for a while. Would you like that?"

India nodded. "Yes. I should like it very much."

Margrave smiled encouragingly toward his mother. "See, Mother? Did I not say she would approve?" His eyes darted to India. "She frets that you are still angry. She thinks you blame her for your being here."

"I have never been angry with her, m'lord." She said nothing about blame. If she exonerated Lady Margrave, then the matter of responsibility would be placed squarely on her son's shoulders and he would never accept it. India had no desire to raise his ire this evening with talk of fault. "Come, my lady, we will sit in the other room. I think you will find it quite comfortable. I have the piece of embroidery you were working on during your last visit. Perhaps you would like to do that."

Lady Margrave nodded faintly.

India closed the distance between them and cupped her elbow. "This way," she said. Looking around her ladyship toward Margrave, she added, "I would like a moment of your time, please."

"Of course." He cooled his heels in India's bedchamber while she situated his mother in the adjoining room. Looking around, he made a note that she would need more coals this evening and fresh linens in the morning. An exchange of the books he had brought her also seemed to be in order. He stopped thumbing through the pages of a historical novel when India reentered the room. He set it down with the others on her bedside table. "You are looking well this evening, India."

She went immediately to the heart of the matter. "Your mother is not."

Margrave cocked an eyebrow at her. "Is this what you wish to discuss? My mother?"

"You are making her insensible with your opiates, my lord. I am afraid you will do her irreparable harm if you do not give her respite."

"Obviously, the same cannot be said of you. You would do well to proceed cautiously, India. I have no liking for these challenges."

India knew it was a risk to broach the subject with him, yet she could not watch Margrave make an addict of his own mother without saying a word. She held her tongue now because pressing her point could only go badly for her.

Margrave smiled thinly when India made no reply. He raised his hand and touched the side of her face, brushing back a tendril of pale hair and tucking it behind her ear. "You do well to keep your thoughts to yourself. I think I know best how to deal with Mother. Go now. Entertain her for a few hours. I will return then with your coals, and mayhap we will work on our new painting. I have some ideas, India, that I think you will like."

It required considerable effort not to blanch. It was knowing how much that reaction would satisfy Margrave that helped India not to give in to it. She merely inclined her head instead. There was nothing about the gesture that granted permission. It was intended only to acknowledge that she had heard him.

Margrave understood the difference. He let his hand fall away from her face. "Enjoy your time with Mother," he told her.

India watched him go, waiting until the key was turned in the lock and his footsteps receded before she made her way to the adjoining sitting room. Lady Margrave was seated by the fire, her embroidery hoop in hand. She had yet to start a stitch. India dropped to her knees beside Lady Margrave's chair and placed her hand gently on the older woman's forearm. "Shall I start it for you?" she asked. "Perhaps if you watch . . ."

With a rather grave air, Lady Margrave turned her head and looked down the length of her nose at India. "Have you none of your wits about you, my dear?" she asked. "I doubt we can succeed if I must think for the both of us."

India blinked. Her mouth parted, then snapped shut.

The dowager countess smiled faintly. "It is gratifying to know that I could persuade you of my incapacitation. I believe my son is similarly convinced, but I suspected you would be a harsher critic."

"Oh, no. You are in the wrong of it there. Margrave

is the one you must prevail upon, and you have done so admirably.''

''I think it helped that you were willing to speak to him on my behalf. He is not used to you being my champion.''

India stood, uncertain of Lady Margrave's meaning. ''I have never spoken ill of you to your son.''

Lady Margrave's dark eyes became a shade pensive. ''No, of course you have not,'' she said softly. ''That has never been your way. I suspect you have, in fact, spoken very little of me.''

''That is true.''

The countess nodded, expecting no other response. She put aside the embroidery hoop. ''I dislike needlework, you know. I always have. I find that its effect on me is quite the opposite of what one hopes for. Restive rather than restful.'' She paused and indicated the chair opposite her. ''Is it the same for you?''

''No, my lady.'' India lowered herself into the wing chair but did not push herself deeply into it. She sat perched on the edge, her hands folded quietly in her lap. ''Needlework relaxes and clears my mind.''

Lady Margrave's sigh had a wistful quality. ''We really have so little in common.''

India said nothing. It seemed the countess made the observation in the manner of one speaking to herself rather than with the expectation of a reply from her companion.

''Do you think he's listening?'' the countess asked suddenly. Her eyes darted toward the door.

''No,'' India said. ''I would have stopped you at the outset if I thought we would be overheard. Margrave is gone.'' She saw Lady Margrave's slight shoulders relax. ''How is it that you've managed to avoid taking the opium?''

''I know you were not hopeful that I heard anything you said to me on my previous visits, but that I am in command of my faculties is proof that I did. Your words came back to me at odd moments, often just as I was waking or preparing to close my eyes for sleep. And when I sat down to take the meal Allen brought me, it was your voice inside my head telling me to eat and drink sparingly. I have hidden my food when I could and purged myself when my son left me no other choice."

India nodded. She had also purged following a visit from Margrave in which he joined her for the entire meal. The difficulty was hiding the evidence of her sickness. Her concern for Lady Margrave was more basic, however. The countess's face was thinner than it had been only a week earlier. "Are you receiving enough nourishment? Weakness may be as debilitating as Margrave's tinctures."

"I am fine," she said stoutly. "Can you say the same?" Before India could answer, Lady Margrave held up her hand. "No, I can see very well that you cannot. Those shadows beneath your eyes are very real, my dear, and that dress hangs perfectly dreadfully from your shoulders. Has Allen commented?"

"No."

"How like him. He sees only what he wishes to see. You could lie abed three days without moving before it would occur to him that you were dead."

India's brows rose at her ladyship's plain speaking and dark humor.

"I have shocked you," Lady Margrave said.

"No . . . that is, I am not used . . ." India surrendered the truth. "Yes, you have shocked me. I have never been certain how well you understand Margrave's attachment to me."

"I imagine I understand it far better than you. Certainly I understand it differently." She shook her head slightly when she saw India would raise a question. "We cannot know how much time we have. Tell me what plan you have to remove us from here."

"Do you have the ear of any of the staff?"

"No longer. I have spoken to my steward, Mr. Leeds, on but two occasions since Allen's arrival. Once, to dismiss more than half the servants at Marlhaven, and a second time to make arrangements for the restoration of a handful of positions. Neither time was I permitted to be alone with him." Lady Margrave touched her hair a trifle self-consciously. "I was forced to dismiss even my personal maid. My son will not hear of her returning to my service.''

India sighed. ''He told me I could not depend upon the servants to come to my aid, but I thought he meant only that he intended to keep them from me. I had no idea he had taken steps to reduce their numbers. The estate cannot possibly be managed.''

''I have told him as much. Mr. Leeds said the same, of course, but he could not make too fine a point of it. He knows Allen would have pressed me to let him go as well.'' Lady Margrave's fingertips dug into the arms of her chair, but her voice remained steady. ''My son has never had the least concern for Marlhaven. He has always been content to allow me to manage this home and Merrimont and to take his living from the profits of the two estates. Mr. Leeds will do what he can to make certain the tenants are assisted and the house does not collapse over our heads. It is a daunting task, but there are those retainers I believe he can depend upon for support.''

''Mrs. Hoover in the kitchen,'' India said.

''Yes. And Mrs. Billings, my housekeeper. Smythson has always been reliable. He still oversees many things.''

''Why have none of them come to your aid? Or sought help on your behalf?'' Both questions had plagued India, but on the few occasions she had had opportunity to ask them, Lady Margrave was in no condition to supply the answers.

''Because they are afraid of my son,'' she said simply. ''Not entirely for what he might do to them, but for what they fear he might do to me.''

India waited because for a moment it looked as if the dowager countess might say more. It was only when Lady Margrave cleared her throat that India went on. ''Since it appears there is no means to get a message out and no reason to suppose we could rely on their assistance if we did, it remains for you and me to manage the thing ourselves.''

''I am in complete agreement.''

''You understand we will have but one opportunity. If

we fail, Margrave will never permit us to be together again. He is most suspicious of me plotting my escape, and I must justify my every thought to him."

"I understand."

"I doubt we can accomplish our escape without injury to Margrave. I must know I can depend upon your resolve."

The dowager countess said nothing for a time. Her fingers bit more deeply into the damask chair covering; her face remained a mask. "This injury?" she asked finally. "It will not be fatal?"

India's eyes widened. "No! Never. I could not . . ."

Lady Margrave leaned forward and patted the back of India's hand. "It's all right. I needed to be certain and now I am. You have never lacked for heart the way my son has." She sat back and lifted her chin a fraction. "I can do whatever you require."

"I require only that you distract him. I must have time to retrieve my weapon."

"Your weapon?"

"I have pried loose a floorboard from under my bed. It will serve, I believe."

Lady Margrave took a deep breath and released it slowly. Now she was the one to take India's measure. "You must hit him squarely."

"I know."

"You make me afraid for you. He will beat you soundly if you do not succeed."

"He has never beaten me."

"You have never tried to hurt him. Not physically."

India could not restrain her shudder. She reached behind her and removed her shawl from where it lay across the back of the chair. Placing it around her shoulders, she asked, "And you? What will he do to you?"

"Do not concern yourself with me. Whatever he does, the blame for it cannot be laid at your feet."

"But . . ."

"I mean it, Diana. You should not think beyond what you must do to succeed. How much longer do you suppose we can survive in these apartments without going mad? We should be no different than Allen then. Could you bear that? God help me. I still love my son, but I could not bear to be like him.''

India shook her head. ''I could not, either.''

Lady Margrave came to her feet, her hands clasped together. There was a gentle rippling movement in the bombazine fabric of her dark-plum gown as she took a step toward the fireplace. She stared at the flames, unable to face India directly and pose her question. ''Do you blame me?'' she asked quietly.

''Blame you?''

The countess raised her hands almost helplessly. ''For what he is. For what he has become.''

''No,'' India said. ''Not for that.''

''Then what?''

''It cannot be important now.''

''I would not have asked if I did not want to hear the answer.''

India hesitated. ''I was your ward. I thought you would have done more to protect me.''

''I sent you to the Olmsteads.''

''He followed me.''

''I supported you in London.''

''You paid me to watch over him.''

''I did not know how to keep him at Marlhaven.''

''He showed you some of his paintings.''

The countess nodded. Her knuckles whitened as she pressed her hands together. ''They terrified me.''

''And yet you were no part of them. I was the one he made pose. Can you begin to imagine how it was for me?''

''I have always tried not to.''

Her reply had the power to make India's breath catch at the back of her throat. ''Did you think so little of me or love him so very much?''

''You do not understand.''

''No,'' India said. ''I do not. I never have.''

''And I cannot explain it to you.''

India was struck by the weariness framing the countess's words. There was an edge of defeat in her tone, and the look of it in her slumped shoulders and bowed head. India accepted that she would learn no more. "Perhaps we should apply ourselves to our needlepoint," she suggested. "Margrave will want to know how we passed our time together."

Lady Margrave nodded and returned to her seat. She picked up the embroidery hoop and examined her stitches. Her nostrils flared slightly as she vented her disgust with a heavy sigh. Still, she plucked the needle from where she'd left it in the taut fabric and made a neat stitch. The proof that she found no pleasure in it was in the line of her tightly clamped jaw and the muscle that twitched in her cheek.

They worked in silence for several long minutes before Lady Margrave said, "Will you want to make our escape tonight?"

"I think we must."

"Do you have the strength for it?" the countess asked. "I could not help but notice that you were unsteady on your feet earlier."

"I would not have Margrave think I am grown tolerant of the opium. It was for his benefit only."

Lady Margrave's dark eyes narrowed a fraction as she studied India's carefully schooled features. "I do not think I believe you."

Under the countess's scrutiny India felt herself faltering. "It was a touch of light-headedness only. I am fine."

"You are certain you will be able to thwack him?"

India smiled faintly. "Oh, yes."

"Good."

South climbed the servants' stairs to the east wing, a bucket of coal in each hand. HIs progress was slow and deliberate. He had accustomed himself to the idea that someone might be watching him. It was a consequence of working at Marlhaven, he was learning. One adopted the manner of the staff whether one wished to or not. After a full sennight spent in the company of the servants, he had come around to their way of thinking. The Earl of Margrave had a disconcerting habit of appearing in odd places at unlikely moments.

Thus far, South had managed to avoid him. On occasion it had been a narrow thing. There had been the morning Margrave had come to the kitchen just as South was leaving. Had Mrs. Hoover not shooed him away from her soup kettle, he would have come toe-to-toe with the earl. Margrave's visit to the underbelly of the great house was a curiosity to South. He was not certain his own father knew where the kitchen at Redding was, and he could say the same for any number of his peers. The kitchens were purposely built far from the dining rooms so the cooking odors would not assail the family and guests. If the food arrived cold—and it often did—then so be it. At least the delicate olfactory senses of the aristocracy were not offended.

South's cynical smile turned into a grimace as one of the pails he was carrying hit the lip of a step and jarred his arm all the way to the shoulder. A few coals were thrown out of the pail and bounced on the stairs. Swearing softly, he set the buckets down and retrieved the bits of coal, tidying up as he went.

Bending over his work, he had a sudden vision of the picture he made, his long, loose-limbed frame hunched in the narrow stairwell, small dustpan and brush in hand, sweeping up the rear servants' passage and making a bloody good job of it lest he be let go like so many others before him. The thought of what his friends would make of it made South's sardonic smile return. He hooked the dust pan and brush on his leather apron, hefted the pails, and continued up the stairs.

There had been a second incident where his path had almost crossed the earl's. He had been leaning on his shovel in the doorway of the coal house when he saw one of the grooms leading a striking cinnamon-colored Arabian from the stables. He watched their progress across the yard and realized the mount had been prepared for the earl. Hoping to learn where Margrave's morning ride might take him, South left his shovel in the doorway and started to follow.

Margrave surprised him, though, coming from the rear of the manor and walking briskly through the crusty snow in South's direction. Not wishing to tempt fate by testing the strength of his disguise, South had ducked his head. It wouldn't have mattered. Margrave passed within two feet and never noticed him. South had stood there for some time, watching Margrave accept a leg up, then marking the earl's route to the northeast.

South had waited until moonrise before he left his bed in the airless cupboard near the kitchen and walked the same route, following the Arabian's trail for miles in the cold before admitting to himself it led nowhere. There was no hunting lodge or trysting cottage, no vacant tenant's house or crofter's shed where Margrave had secreted India away. The earl's morning ride had been without any purpose in regard to India. It had been meant only for his own pleasure.

That realization managed to work its way under South's skin as nothing else had. There was no one to rail against. No one save himself to curse. He was alone in a way he had never been before, and he would have felt exactly the same surrounded by his friends at White's. This aloneness was not about who was with him, but who was not.

It required no special talent on his part to bring her laughter to his ears or her hesitant smile to his mind's eye. She was by turns sassy and shy, confident behind the footlights, cautious in front of them. He heard her softly accented voice say his name. He was never "my lord" to her now. Matthew, she said. The sound of it was carried on the back of the wind.

Was she frightened? he wondered. Or merely resigned. When she heard his voice, what was it that he said to her?

You cannot expect that I will always save you, Hortense.

The echo of those words, the first words he had ever spoken to her, left him with an ache in his chest where he thought he was only numb. Hidden in a moon shadow cast

by a stand of trees, Marlhaven an ominous silhouette in the
distance, South finally surrendered to his grief and wept.

Straightening as he reached the top of the stairs, South
also pulled himself back to the present. He paused and peered
down the long hallway. A phalanx of brass sconces lined
the walls and provided arcs of candlelight the entire length
of the corridor. South's explorations in and around Marlhaven had been largely accomplished at night after most of
the staff had retired, but this area remained unknown to him
because of Margrave's presence. During the day, the position
he held had not afforded him opportunity to visit the upper
floors of the east wing. Although he carried coal into the
house, it was the duty of the liveried footmen or chamber-
maids to distribute it among the 127 rooms that required
heating.

This evening, however, there had been no one save him
to answer the ring when more coals were needed. Although
it seemed to pain Mrs. Hoover to do so, she had warned
him to step lively and sent him on his way. The earl, she
whispered, had no tolerance for sloth or infirmity.

South knew he was supposed to leave the coal buckets
at the top of the stairs and remove himself quickly from the
corridor. It had never been his intention to do so. He started
down the wide hallway, pausing at each closed door, listening just a moment for voices and movement.

The presence of a hallway in this wing struck South as an
oddity. There were additions to the house and improvements
made over the centuries, but the east wing was original to
Marlhaven and was likely to have served as the family's
private apartments for much of that time. Hallways were not
common to Elizabethan structures. People moved through
adjoining rooms and connecting doors, not along an outside
corridor. Privacy in the bedchamber and lady's boudoir was
provided by great four-poster beds with their heavy curtains
drawn around. South wondered at the costliness of carving
up the rooms to add the hallway, and what purpose had been
served by it. He could think of only one from Margrave's
perspective: to keep others out.

South counted five doors along the hall. He knew there were more than five rooms on the other side, but that each door probably represented the entrance to a suite. If India was a prisoner in this part of the house, then he would have to find the proper entrance to her suite, and finally the room where she was being held. Getting her out could prove as difficult as getting in. In this case, one entrance meant one exit. South understood the nature of Margrave's trap on this occasion.

The metal pails clattered loudly as South dropped them on the hardwood floor. The noise was meant to bring Margrave out, and it was successful within seconds. South barely had time to tip one of the pails and scatter coals before the earl was stepping out from the door at the far end of the hall. Kneeling, South bent quickly to his task of cleaning up the mess just as he had on the stairs.

"Bloody hell," Margrave said, striding down the hall. "What's this? What's happened here?"

"Beggin' your pardon, my lord." South kept his head bent as he gathered the coals. Margrave's foot came down on South's hand as it curled around one of the bits. The action was intended to hurt, and South could not pretend that it didn't. He grimaced under the grinding weight that Margrave applied to his knuckles.

"Where's Smythson?" Margrave demanded. He eased the pressure on South's knuckles but did not remove his foot. "Why isn't he here?"

"I don't know, m'lord. I was the only one who could come wi' the coals."

"Weren't you instructed to leave them at the end of the hall?"

"Aye. But which end? I was thinkin'."

Margrave was unamused. "Stupid old man." He ground his foot again, harder than he had done before. "Clean them up."

South could not accomplish the task single-handedly, and he could not ask the earl to remove his foot. He picked up as many coals as he could reach with his free hand and awkwardly managed the dustpan and brush to sweep some of the soot. It was only then that Margrave stepped back. South's fingers uncurled slowly around the bit of coal cutting into his palm. His hand tingled with the rush of blood. In his hurry to answer the earl's bidding, the gloves he usually wore to haul the coal had been left lying on the stool by the kitchen hearth. He'd had nothing to protect himself from the heel of Margrave's grinding boot.

What he wanted to do was grab the earl by the ankle and upend him in the hallway, smash his face with a well-planted fist, then push a bit of coal into the space he'd make by breaking most of Margrave's teeth. It was a tempting and satisfying picture. The problem was that it would not necessarily lead him to India. If she wasn't behind any of the doors in the east wing, Margrave might never reveal where she was after he'd been attacked.

South flexed his fingers, shook out his hand, and proceeded to finish his work. There was not a moment when he was unaware of the earl's hovering. Upon completing his work, he sat back on his haunches and awaited direction.

"Leave the pails here," Margrave said, his voice clipped. "Go. And inform Smythson that you are not to be sent here again."

South stood slowly, bobbing his head slightly as he rose. He did not come to his full height. Rather, he remained stooped, his posture stiff as though every bone ached when he tried to unfold his hunched frame. Behind his spectacles, South's eyes remained respectfully downcast. His weight shifted from one foot to the other. "Yes, my lord. Of course."

Brushing his blackened palms on the apron, South began to back away. He came very close to bumping one of the coal pails again. Margrave's sharp intake of breath halted him in his tracks.

"Go," Margrave repeated, impatience rife in the single word.

South turned sharply on his heel and hurried away as quickly as the limping gait he'd perfected allowed him. He

disappeared into the servants' stairwell and descended half
the steps before he stopped and waited. He stood there
for several moments, listening for Margrave's approaching
footfalls. When they didn't come, South knew he had not
been found out. The earl had no reason to follow him.
Quietly, with the utmost care, he began retracing his steps
to the top of the stairs.

As he approached the rise, he stopped again and slid
sideways into the shadow against the wall. He looked down
the corridor and saw that Margrave was still standing beside
the coal pails. He looked as if he had not moved at all. His
head was bent as he studied something in the palm of his
hand.

Watching him, South was first struck by how slight a
figure he was. It had not seemed so earlier when he had
brought his weight to bear, nor a few days ago when Margrave had strode from the house wearing his heavily caped
greatcoat and polished beaver top hat. The earl had a presence about him; South would give him that. He held himself
perfectly erect, the manner more haughty than merely proud,
but also with a certain grace that South had seen in India
as well. He was self-possessed in a way she was not, and
there, perhaps, South thought, was the chink in his armor.

It was difficult at first to see Margrave as Mrs. Garrety.
South had to look past the straight Roman nose and reshape
it with putty and paint to imagine the aquiline beak at the
center of the dresser's face. In his mind's eye he placed a dark
mole on the earl's right cheek and gave it three frighteningly
aggressive hairs for good measure. He added deep frown
lines to the corners of Margrave's mouth, and a wig of
coarse gray hair. He could see the hunch in the earl's back
and the sharp, jutting elbows that were used so effectively
to remove the rabble from India's dressing room.

Margrave had expressed his disapproval without once
clucking his tongue or using the shrill tones he affected as
Mrs. Garrety, but South had no difficulty recalling them.

He thought about his interview with Marlhaven's dowager
countess several weeks ago and the description Doobin had

given him later of Lady Margrave. South knew now there had been nothing wrong with his instincts. The woman he met—indeed, the woman he had spent almost an hour with, making inquiries about India—was not the countess but her son.

Margrave had not meant his disguise to look like his mother. He knew South and Lady Margrave had never met. It was enough that he had simply fooled South into thinking he *was* his mother. As the dowager countess, Margrave had expressed a precise mix of disdain and contempt, doubt and concern. The remarkable performance sent South from Marlhaven believing that India and the earl must be in London. He remembered thinking then that Lady Margrave might be moved to protect her son, but she would not do so at the expense of India's well-being.

The slim smile that shaped South's lips was grim. He had been well and truly gulled. There was little solace in the realization that he was not Margrave's only victim, merely one who had managed to live long enough to discover it. Mr. Kendall had not been so fortunate. Neither had Mr. Rutherford.

Margrave's movement in the corridor caught South's attention anew. He watched the earl manipulate the object that was resting in his open palm and take a step toward the door at his right. It was then South understood that Margrave held a key. He watched the earl use it in the lock, then pocket it. Margrave pressed the toe of his boot against the door to nudge it open before he picked up a coal pail in each hand and entered the suite.

South stepped out of the shadows and finished climbing the stairs.

At the sound of Margrave's key in the lock, India and the dowager countess exchanged startled, apprehensive glances. For a moment, their hands were still over their needlework. They caught themselves simultaneously, their eyes returning to their embroidery hoops, and resumed the stitching that had occupied them for the better part of the evening.

Margrave entered from India's bedchamber. He paused in the doorway and looked on the scene before him with a somewhat jaundiced eye. "Such domesticity. Mother, how is it that India can persuade you to spend your time in such a manner when you despise it so?"

"I do not despise it," she said slowly. Her expression was vaguely puzzled, as though she were searching for the proper words. "I find it tedious, Allen. There is a difference, you know."

One of Margrave's slim, dark brows lifted in a perfect arch. "I had not realized such," he said, his tone plainly sardonic. He raised the pail of coal in his hand to draw attention to it. "I have placed one beside the hearth in your bedchamber, India. Have you need of another here?"

"Yes, please."

Nodding once, Margrave entered the sitting room. He added several coals to the fire before he set the pail down. He did not choose a chair for himself; rather, he stood beside the fireplace, his shoulder against the mantel. "You have had a pleasant visit?"

It was Lady Margrave who answered. "Yes, Allen." Her expression shifted again, this time displaying a weary, slightly distant smile. "Quite pleasant."

India did not look up from her needlepoint as she addressed Margrave. "We have been discussing the theatre," she said. "That is, I have been discussing it. Your mother has been kind enough to listen to me."

"Oh?"

"I think I should like to return to the stage. Would you consider such a thing, my lord?"

"No," he said not unkindly. "I don't believe I would."

There was a momentary pause between stitches; then India nodded. It was not an unexpected answer.

"No argument?" he asked.

"I think not," she said. "I find I haven't the stomach for it."

"Have a care, India. You will begin to bore me."

"That would indeed be unfortunate."

"Yes, it would."

India glanced up and saw that he meant it. There had been no humor in his tone; certainly there was none in his darkly piercing glance.

Margrave pointed casually to the easel that stood near the window. A large cloth draped the framed canvas, hiding his work from view. "Have you shown Mother our latest effort, India? I think it is as good as any I have ever done."

India set her embroidery hoop aside and came to her feet. Momentarily light-headed, she touched her fingertips to her temple. "May I have a word with you, my lord?"

"I believe you are."

"Privately." Her eyes darted to the dowager countess, who remained bent over her embroidery. "Please."

Margrave did not immediately respond. He regarded India with no small amount of suspiciousness. "I think not. You may speak freely in front of Mother."

Before India could protest, Lady Margrave stood and offered them both an apologetic if somewhat vapid smile. "If you will excuse me." Without waiting for permission, or even acknowledging that permission was needed, the countess made a gravely dignified exit.

"She cannot be left alone long," India said. "I do not believe she is at all well."

"Then say what you must quickly." He cocked his head in the direction of the bedchamber, listening for his mother's telltale movements. Had she enough wits about her to try the outer door? he wondered, or would she make a comfortable nest for herself on India's bed? "I will hold you responsible if she comes to harm."

India took a shallow, fortifying breath. "I do not wish Lady Margrave to see the painting," she said. "You suggested it with no purpose save to punish me."

He shrugged. "I do not trust you, India. You cannot expect that I should. If you do not want Mother to see our painting, then you should mind your tongue and your tone."

India felt the sting of tears. She blinked them back.

The edges of Margrave's mouth curved upward in a dryly appreciative smile. His light applause was the perfect ironic accompaniment. "Very good. Tears are often overdone, but never by you. As always, you choose your moments judiciously."

India made an impatient swipe at her eyes. "Let us go, Margrave."

"You grow tiresome." Straightening, the earl stepped away from the fireplace. "Mother? You may return. India is quite finished." There was no reply and no swish of skirts. "Mother?"

Ignoring Margrave's accusing glance, India started for the bedchamber. She was brought up short by his fingers tightly circling her arm just above the elbow. She stayed her ground and did not try to shake him off. It was not a battle she could win.

"I will see to her and you will remain here."

Nodding, India waited for Margrave to release her. He did so with some reluctance, then brushed past her and stepped through the doorway into the bedchamber. India had a glimpse of him being halted in his tracks before she hurried to follow.

Whatever diversion the dowager countess had created, she thought, it was exceeding expectation.

Chapter Sixteen

India came to a halt just behind Margrave. He quickly threw an arm out to the side to prevent her from moving around him. Looking over his shoulder, India saw why he meant for her to go no farther.

The dowager countess's diversion was not of her own making. It was South's presence that had changed things. India's heart hammered hard in her chest, and for a moment she forgot to breathe. He was here and he was whole. Her eyes drank him in, seeing past the roughly cut hair and lined face of the old man to the sharply intent gray eyes and familiar ironic smile. She would love that face when he *was* an old man, she thought, and it did not seem the least bit odd to her that she should think that now. If only for the span of a few heartbeats, it was as if she were alone with him. She did not want to give that up. It would be painfully hard when the reality came upon her.

India glanced from South to the door of her bedchamber. "How did you get in?"

South casually rested his shoulder against one of the corner posts of the bed. "It was left unlocked. I don't suppose he was expecting a visitor."

"No," she said, matching his gently wry tone. "I don't suppose he was."

Her perfect mimicry deepened his smile. He recognized, as she did, the nuance of intimacy in their exchange. They might have been sharing a private joke, something silly and without consequence, the kind of humor that made lovers smile and annoyed everyone else.

It had exactly that affect on the Earl of Margrave. The arm he had flung out to the side stiffened, and when India pushed at it, she found he would not be moved. When she ducked to go under it, he blocked her path with his body.

"Let her come to me," South said with perfect affability. "Or I swear I will kill you."

Margrave frowned. The broad accents of the man he had met minutes earlier in the hallway were absent now. The subservient posturing and cowed manner had also disappeared. This man stood taller and possessed an easy grace that had been no part of the coal tender's bearing, and he had just threatened to do murder in a tone so pleasant and friendly that it must be taken seriously.

"You." The single word had the import of an accusation as Margrave saw what he had not been able to before. His slight smile did not touch his eyes. "My compliments, Southerton. I am not usually gulled by so simple a disguise, but then, my own experience has taught me that one never looks too closely at the servants. It would seem I am hoist by my own petard. You played your part admirably."

Though South acknowledged Margrave's recognition with a faint, mocking bow of his head, his position remained unchanged. "Release her, Margrave."

The dowager countess stood uneasily at the foot of the bed, her hands clasped tightly in front of her. Unnoticed until now, she regarded her son with imploring eyes that were made liquid by the increasing tension in the room. "Please, Margrave. Do as he says. You must let her go."

One of the earl's brows kicked up. "You, Mother?" he asked softly. "You would betray me also? Or has he made some threat against you?"

"Lady Margrave is free to leave," South said, indicating the door with a turn of his hand.

The countess made no move to do so. "Please," she repeated, her full attention on Margrave. "He means to do you harm."

Margrave laughed lightly. "He means to kill me, Mother. It is rather more than threatening to blacken my eye or bloody my lip."

While the earl's attention was elsewhere, India made a second attempt to push past his braced arm. He was able to hold her back with little effort. Frustrated, she changed the angle of her approach and shoved hard at his shoulders, forcing him to take a single staggering step out of the doorway. Taking advantage of the small opening she was afforded, India darted through it. She was brought up short by the handful of skirt that Margrave caught in his fist. He drew her back against him and captured her waist in the crook of his arm.

Seeing that India was in no real danger yet, South stayed his ground. He watched her take a steadying breath, then relax in Margrave's hold. In consequence, there was an almost imperceptible easing of the earl's grip. South was careful not to catch her eye or show his approval of her tactics.

"What is it you hope to accomplish, Margrave?" he asked. "Do you imagine you have some ownership of India?"

That struck a chord with the earl. "She is mine." He nudged India with his arm. "Tell him, Dini. Tell him that you have always been mine."

"I have always been his," she said simply.

Lady Margrave's knuckles whitened as she pressed her hands even more closely together. Her voice was taut. "Do not humor him. It is not natural that he should make you say such things." She sat suddenly on the edge of the bed, her head bent and her shoulders sagging. "*He* is not natural."

India did not feel Margrave's start of surprise next to her own. What she did notice after recovering herself was that his arm had dropped away from her waist. She bolted out of the circle of his reach and threw herself into South's protective embrace. She laid her cheek against his shoulder and heard the soft murmur of his voice next to her ear.

"You have saved yourself," he whispered.

Tears blurred India's vision. Was it true? she wondered. Had she saved herself after all? She thought of the loose floorboard under the bed that she had intended to use on Margrave's skull. Perhaps she could be satisfied with merely being out of his reach, but she doubted it. "I meant to thwack him, you know."

Though South pressed his smile into India's hair, his eyes were cold as they regarded Margrave over the top of her head. "I shouldn't be at all surprised if you still get your chance," he said softly.

India's cheek rubbed against the rough fabric of South's frock coat. Coal dust smudged her pale skin. "He told me you were dead," she said, her voice hoarse with emotion. "I didn't want to believe him. I didn't. But then . . . it was so long . . . and I . . ."

"I know." South breathed deeply of the fragrance of India's hair. "I know."

"You came for me."

"Yes. Always."

"Touching," Margrave said, sarcasm rife in his tone. He jerked his chin in his mother's direction. "Mayhap you find this display natural and more to your liking. He's had her, of course. As soon as she was out of my sight, the little harlot spread her legs for him. Didn't I always say that's what she would do if I wasn't with her? She is not so different than her mother, is she?"

The countess's head snapped up. "That is quite enough. You go too far, Allen."

Margrave's dark eyes narrowed. "I think the laudanum is not so efficacious as you would have had me believe. There is more than a bit of trickery afoot. Tell me about this subterfuge, Mother. Was it something you thought of on your own, or did India persuade you to defy me?"

India turned in South's embrace and faced Margrave. "You will let her be. There is no reason she should answer to you."

Margrave's response was dry. "Is it the presence of your lover that gives you such courage, India? You have not always shown this temerity. I cannot say that I am in any way admiring of it."

India's cheeks flushed with color, but she did not avoid his scornful glance. Holding her hand out to the dowager countess, she said, "We are going now."

The earl took a step toward them, his attention slipping sideways toward his mother. "Shall you tell her, Mother? Or shall I? What sort of feeling will India bear you then? I wonder if she shall love you less or more than I."

"Have off," South said sharply. "Unless you mean to afford me the greatest pleasure of laying you out."

Margrave merely smiled.

India's brows furrowed. Her eyes darted between Margrave and his mother, then to South. "Tell me what?" she asked. "What is it all of you think you know that I do not?"

The earl shrugged and raised his hands with an air of helplessness. "Do you see, Southerton? She is curious. She *wants* to know."

South shook his head. "India, take the countess out. I will follow shortly."

India understood she was being given a directive. Only minutes ago it had been her intention to do the very thing South was telling her to do. "No," she said. "I will not."

It was Margrave who laughed. "You must admit that she does not fail to amuse," he said to South. "Though I understand you will find it less so since she is now defying you. Tread carefully, Southerton. You may discover that the wrong response will send her flying back into my arms."

"I am in no fear of that," South said. "Even so, India may alight wherever she wishes."

"I am not moving at all," India told them. It was not entirely true. While her intention was to remain firmly rooted where she stood, she felt herself becoming light-headed again. It seemed to her that the room wavered; then she realized it was she. Thrusting out a hand, she refused the attentions of South and Margrave as they each took a step toward her. She pressed three fingers to her temple, managed a deep breath, and found herself grounded again.

"It is because of the opium," Lady Margrave told South. "She has taken little nourishment these past weeks to protect herself from its effects. She warned me of the consequences of such a drastic course, but I do not think she heeded her own advice."

India started to protest that such was not the case, but her effort went unnoticed by everyone in the room. Without signaling his intention in any way, South's long stride put him within striking distance of Margrave. He jabbed sharply at the earl's midsection with his right fist, making Margrave gasp for air and begin to double over. South followed this with a hard left to Margrave's elegantly defined chin. The blow actually lifted the earl off his feet. He landed lightly, but off balance, and stumbled backward. South struck again, jabbing with his right. The breath that Margrave was trying to recover was lost, and his knees folded. He dropped to the floor, grunting softly and clutching his middle.

South stared down at the earl's bowed head and slumped shoulders and wondered if he could trust him to remain there. He felt no particular satisfaction in what he had done, yet knew that he was prepared to do it again. And again.

South's features were without expression, which of itself was telling. The heat of the moment had subsided into a hard, bitter coldness. What was left was more dangerous than what had come before.

Stepping back, South began to turn toward India. He was conscious of her sudden movement, the leap in his direction, but he had no time to understand the reason for it. The blow to his head was delivered with mind-numbing accuracy. He staggered forward into India's outstretched arms. She could not support his weight, and he felt himself falling, folding just as Margrave had, his knees buckling under him. It seemed to happen slowly, as if he were drifting down through black water, buoyant and leaden at the same time.

India dropped to her knees beside South, but not in time to stop him from receiving a second blow to his head, this time when it came in hard contact with the floor. She tore off his roughly cut wig and ran her fingers along his scalp, feeling for an open wound while her eyes were raised accusingly in Lady Margrave's direction.

Her hands shaking, the dowager countess stared at what she had wrought. At first she felt no connection to what she saw. The fact that she still held the board she'd removed from under India's bed was in no way relevant to the fact that Southerton lay crumpled on the floor at her feet. That India's dark eyes found fault with her did not make sense. Even her son's sardonic chuckle had no impact.

She came to herself suddenly, her mouth opening in horror at what she now understood she'd done. "I'm sorry," she whispered. The words were lost as her nerveless fingers let the board slip between them and thudded to the floor. "I'm so sorry."

Margrave gingerly worked his jaw from side to side. "Your apology is hardly flattering, Mother. One might suppose you meant to use that board on my poor pate." He glanced at India and cocked an eyebrow. "Your idea?"

India ignored him. She cradled South's head in her lap and continued to sift through his thick hair with her fingertips. She felt him stir ever so slightly.

"Of course it was your idea," Margrave went on. "You have been bent on leaving here from the beginning. I do not think you have ever considered Marlhaven your home, Dini. Merrimont, either."

"They have never been my home," India said quietly.

"That is really too bad of you." Margrave clucked his tongue softly. It was an admonishing affectation he had often used as Mrs. Garrety, and he knew that India would recognize it as such. That she was annoyed by it pleased him. It was proof that she was not as immune to him as she would have him believe. Southerton be damned, he thought.

It was he who had the power to work his way under her skin. "You have always been welcomed here."

India merely shook her head. Even at the outset, she had been more prisoner than guest. It seemed to her that these past weeks Margrave had simply ceased to pretend it had ever been otherwise. She would not sanction his alternative view of the past now.

"It *is* your home," he said, slowly climbing to his feet. He brushed off the knees of his trousers and straightened the line of his frock coat by pulling on the sleeves. "I mean that." His attention was pulled to his mother, who shuddered with a sob she could not restrain. Margrave snapped, "Have done with it, Mother! Your tears grow tiresome."

The countess made no attempt to swipe at her damp eyes, though she did press her lips together to stop their trembling.

Margrave sighed. "That is a poor effort." He watched his mother's tears begin to flow with renewed vigor. "Sit down! This is intolerable."

As if deflated, the dowager countess sank slowly into a nearby chair. "I'm sorry," she said again. Her words were for India, not her son. "Can you forgive me?"

"Do not speak of it," India said wearily. She lightly brushed South's lean cheek with her knuckles and watched the even rise and fall of his chest. She removed his spectacles. "It is understandable that you would act to protect your son. Indeed, I held out too much hope you could do anything else." Margrave's deep chuckle strained her taut nerves. "Something amuses you, my lord?"

Margrave ignored the sweetness in India's tone that lent it bite. He spoke only to her question. "Certainly I am amused. You have misunderstood Mother. Her apology is not for what she has done in these last few minutes but for what she has done these last twenty-three years." His dark eyes swiveled to his mother. "Is that not correct? It is an apology for a lifetime of wrongs."

Two small creases appeared between India's brows. She searched Lady Margrave's drawn features. The countess avoided her eyes, glancing down at the hands folded in her lap instead. ''My lady? What does he mean?''

It was as if Lady Margrave had not heard. She fidgeted with the folds of her gown, smoothing them across her knees, picking at an imaginary loose thread.

Watching her, Margrave shook his head, one corner of his mouth edging upward. ''I do not believe she will speak of it, India. I suppose you will have to hear it from me.''

Though she was curious, India doubted she would believe anything Margrave had to tell her. She realized belatedly that something of her skepticism must have shown on her face, because the earl's slim smile became wry.

''It does present a dilemma, does it not?'' he mused aloud. His eyes fell to South. ''I suspect you can count on no help from that quarter. Pity. I think he knows rather more than I should have thought anyone could.''

''He knows you are responsible for Mr. Kendall's murder.''

''Really?''

India dismissed out of hand the amusement she heard in the earl's voice. She knew she had piqued his interest and his concern. She looked down at South's perfectly still features. It had been several minutes since he had last faintly stirred. ''Mr. Rutherford's also,'' she said. ''The attempt on Prinny's life as well.'' Beside her she heard the dowager countess's sharp intake of breath. ''You have been found out, my lord. I am no longer the only one who knows what a monster you are.''

He laughed outright. ''A monster? I am hardly that. The theatre has given you a penchant for melodrama, my dear India.''

Lady Margrave pressed one hand to her mouth as if to stifle a second sob. Her face was without color, and her nostrils flared widely as she drew in a steadying breath. She spoke haltingly through her fingers. ''Is this true?''

Uncertain to whom she was speaking, or what she was wanting to confirm as truth, neither India nor Margrave answered.

The countess's hand fell away from her face. Her voice rose shrilly. "Is this true?!"

India noticed that Margrave actually flinched. His cheeks flushed with high color while his narrow smile remained eerily in place. India reached out to Lady Margrave, laying one hand over hers. "My lady, have a care. You will make yourself ill."

"I *am* ill." Her eyes implored her son. "Does she speak the truth, Allen? Are you responsible for the attempt on the Prince Regent's life?"

"Mother," he said placatingly, "have you forgotten a man was hanged for the assassination attempt? I have never heard that my name was in any way connected to that sorry bit of business."

Lady Margrave was not pacified. "You have not answered my question. Were you responsible for it?"

Both of Margrave's brows rose at her tone, but he nevertheless answered, "I was not."

"Liar," India said. "I do not know the particulars of how it was accomplished, but I know you lie. You thought Prinny wanted to make me his mistress. You have always thought others wanted me. Kendall. Rutherford. You would have liked to kill South at the cottage at Ambermede, but your need to get me away from him was stronger. And Westphal was there. I think you were not prepared to challenge them both."

The countess continued to stare at her son. "She is telling the truth, isn't she? You *have* done these things."

Margrave was not listening to his mother. "Prinny *did* want you for his mistress. Do not deny it, India. I saw how he looked at you. I saw how they all looked at you. It never seemed to matter that you were without station or consequence. You drew them to you. Always." He said nothing for a moment. His eyes drifted away from India as he retrieved a memory. "Olmstead," he said quietly. "He wanted you. Mother arranged for your position there knowing all the while that your position would be a reclining one."

Agitated, Lady Margrave came to her feet. "That's a lie. I sent her away for her own protection."

Margrave's mouth twisted. "You sent her away for *your* protection."

A strangled sound came from the back of the countess's throat.

"You do not deny it, Mother."

"You are without conscience."

"The pot calling the kettle, and all that." He waved one hand, dismissing her, and looked down on India. "Your viscount has been out rather long, India. Perhaps some smelling salts are in order."

India leaned over South protectively. "You will not touch him."

"As you wish. It is a large knot at the back of his head, I collect."

It was, but India did not confirm that was the case. "Neither South nor I require your assistance, my lord."

"You may well speak for yourself. I am not certain Southerton would agree." Margrave bent and picked up the board that his mother had dropped. He turned it over in his hands, idly examining it, then gave it a decisive swing over India's head. He laughed as she instinctively ducked to avoid the blow. The board had not come within six inches of her scalp. "Did that raise a few hairs at the back of your neck, India?"

India lifted her face to him and spoke quietly but distinctly. "You disgust me."

"Oh? More than Olmstead? More than Prinny? You would have me believe they disgusted you as well."

"Stop it," Lady Margrave said. She carefully lowered herself to her knees beside India and searched South's pale face. "What can I do? There must be something. A damp cloth, perhaps, for his forehead."

"Hold him," India told her. "I will get it." There was the small stain of blood on her gown where South's head had lain. She rose and turned toward the commode. Margrave stopped her, placing one hand at the crook of her elbow. "You will allow me to attend to him, my lord."

"Why? I intend to kill him, you know."

India did not flinch from what she saw in his eyes. "And I will see to his comfort until then."

Margrave smiled. "As you wish, India. As always, I can deny you nothing." He let her go, watching her as she poured cool water into the basin and chose a cloth to dampen. She wrung it out, then carried it back to South and handed it to the countess. His mother folded it carefully and laid it across the viscount's brow. Margrave tried to remember if she had ever been so gentle with him. Yes, he thought, she had, but it seemed so very long ago that he could not bring the place or time to mind. Still, he could recall her light touch on his brow, the sweet sound of her lullaby in his ears. She must have loved him once.

The earl set the board down, leaning it against the fire-place, out of reach of his mother. "Does it disturb you, India, that Southerton has accused me of Kendall's murder?"

"No longer." She knelt again. It was not South's hand she sought, but Lady Margrave's. The countess's skin was cool, and her fingers trembled slightly in India's light grasp. "I have had time to accustom myself to the truth of it. At first I did not want to believe it."

"You championed me?"

"After a fashion."

"You surprise me."

India shrugged. "I did not do it for you. It seemed that if it were true I must bear some of the responsibility. I was not prepared to do that."

"And now?"

"Now I understand that while you did all of the things South says you have, it does not make me guilty."

"Is that what Southerton told you? That you are not culpable?" He did not wait for her to respond. "He's wrong, India. Everything that has been done has been done for *you*."

"It has been done for *you*."

"No."

India lifted her face. Her eyes glittered with the strength

of her icy condemnation. "Yes," she said. "It was been done for no one save you."

Margrave did not hesitate. He brought the flat of his hand hard across India's cheek. The downward sweep of his palm was swift and powerful. India was knocked sideways. Lady Margrave cried out as India was torn from her, and she caught her son's arm to stop him from delivering a second blow. He shook her off easily.

Not so the second pair of hands that grabbed him.

South brought all the pressure he could to bear and used Margrave's efforts to pull away to help himself rise. Jerked into a sitting position by the earl's wiry strength, South was able to get his feet under him, then stand on his own power. Without signaling his intention, he let Margrave go suddenly. Off balance, Margrave shot backward, falling against the fireplace.

India pulled the countess out of the way as the earl picked up the board and swung it fiercely in South's direction. South jumped back and ducked. The board whistled through the air as it swept just over his head. He charged then, running like a bull at Margrave's midsection, throwing him back against the wall. The board was hurled from the earl's hands and came within a hairbreadth of hitting his mother. India pushed the countess into a chair and picked up the makeshift weapon just as South plowed his fist into Margrave's belly.

Margrave doubled over, making retching noises as he simultaneously tried to suck air into his lungs. South stepped lightly away and sent a second punch, a roundhouse this time, straight for Margrave's jaw. The contact crunched bone and tore flesh. Spitting blood, the earl staggered sideways, then collapsed to his knees. He swiped ineffectually at the air in search of South's legs. South danced easily out of his reach and, out of the corner of his eye, saw India's approach.

He grinned when she didn't hesitate. Her timing was as impeccably sharp as it was onstage. She delivered this blow as though it were the exclamation point at the end of her finest line.

India hammered the plank across the back of Margrave's head and sent him crashing forward. He thumped to the floor, then lay still. India raised the board again, poised to strike, but South stayed her hand this time.

"It is enough," he said gently. "There is no need for an encore."

India let the board fall and launched herself once more into South's open arms. He held her closely, stroking her back and placing small, healing kisses on the crown of her head. She sagged against him, eyes closed, when his fingers sifted through her hair. India was content to remain exactly as she was, firmly in the circle of South's embrace, with the steady, reassuring beat of his heart under her palm. He let it be so for several minutes; then he lifted her just enough to set her on the edge of the bed and drew back. He searched her face.

"I'm fine," she said, looking up at him. "Truly."

South nodded, accepting her assessment but making one of his own anyway. That she had lost weight was noticeable in the fine, sculpted lines of her face and the loose fit of her gown. The bones of her wrists were more pronounced, making her seem delicate, yet he had watched her swing that plank with the skill and strength of a batsman, so he knew fragility was more illusion than fact. The vagueness he had glimpsed earlier in her dark eyes had vanished. They were sharply focused on him now and engaged in their own assessment. "I'm fine," he said, a glimmer of a smile playing about his mouth. "Truly."

India felt herself returning that small smile. "Yes," she said. "You are. Very fine indeed."

The thought that he might actually blush made South avert his gaze. The shift brought him around to Lady Margrave, who had remained seated throughout this last altercation with her son. She did not return his regard. Her attention was all for the unconscious earl. It surprised South that she had made no effort to go to him. "He is not dead," he assured her. "You can see that he breathes."

"Yes." The countess's lips merely moved around the word. It was virtually without sound.

South dropped to his haunches beside Margrave and checked the earl's head for injury. The lump at the back of Margrave's skull was little bigger than South's own. "India? Would you give me the cords that hold back the drapes?"

India started to rise, but Lady Margrave put out a hand and waved her back. "I will get them," she said. "It is the very least I can do." She caught South's small start of surprise. "Do you think I mean to play you some trick? I assure you, I do not." She stood, went to the window, and removed the gold braided cords that gathered the drapes on either side of the leaded glass. She gave them to South. "Tie them tightly. You would not want him to loose himself easily at any time."

South expected the dowager countess to return to her chair. Instead, she remained at his side while he bound her son's wrists and ankles, then gave her approval in a regal nod when he was through. Lightly massaging the swelling at the back of his head, South came to his feet. Puzzled by her actions, he regarded Lady Margrave with a slight frown. "No doubt it is that I am lacking in the upper works that makes this a poser, my lady, but if you sanction my actions now, then why did you clobber me earlier?"

"He is my son," she said simply. "It is not easy to always know the best way to protect him. It has occurred to me that he is safer secured than he is facing you again."

That was true, South thought. It would not take much provocation on Margrave's part for South to kill him. India's blow had struck him down, but it may have also saved his life. Nodding, South cupped the dowager's elbow and led her back to the chair. She seemed grateful for the support. She took his hand, squeezing it once as she sank into the deep cushion of the wing chair. South allowed her to hold on to him a moment longer before he gently removed his hand and returned to India's side. He did not sit with her but held out an arm. His fingers curled, beckoned.

India stared at South's extended hand, knowing that he meant her to take it, yet finding herself reluctant to do so. She shook her head slowly, her eyes asking him for understanding. "Not yet," she said quietly. Her gaze slid sideways to where the dowager countess sat. The older woman's hands were folded tightly in her lap, the knuckles waxlike in their bloodless state. "I believe there are some things in want of being said." Her voice dropped to a mere whisper. The tenor of it was hoarse. "Is that not the truth . . . Mother?"

The countess did not so much startle at this form of address as appear undone by it. Her shoulders slumped. She seemed to withdraw into herself, becoming somehow smaller than she had been only moments earlier. Pained eyes downcast, her head drooped forward as though it had become too heavy for the slender stem of her neck.

Out of the corner of her eye, India saw that South had no reaction at all. She glanced up at him. "You knew."

"Yes." She had not accused him, but neither was it a question. There was no purpose in withholding the truth from her any longer, nor any kind way of revealing it. "Yes, I know."

"Have you always?"

"Always?" South shook his head. His voice was gentle. "No. Not so long as that. It is only something that occurred to me recently, and I had no proof of the truth of it until today. Even if Margrave had not hinted as much, you have your mother's eyes."

India looked in Lady Margrave's direction. The dowager countess's head remained bowed, and India could not reacquaint herself with the eyes that South said were so like her own. India's gaze slipped slowly from the countess, past South, and finally rested on Margrave's trussed and unconscious figure. She watched a droplet of blood gather at one corner of his mouth, then fall. It pooled with another spattering of blood on the floor.

It was not the sight of the blood that made India shudder, but the inescapable realization that she was connected to it. Bile rose in her throat, and she choked it back. The taste of it made her want to gag, and for a moment she thought she would disgrace herself by being sick.

"India?" South took a step toward the bed and was stopped by the stricken eyes she raised to him. He saw that the full knowledge of what it meant to be Lady Margrave's daughter had been borne home.

"He is my brother." She forced the words past the acid at the back of her throat. This had to be said, too, and the effort of it made her moan softly. Closing her eyes, India pressed her balled fists against her middle as she hunched forward.

South was immediately beside her. He slipped an arm around her back and drew her against him. He rocked her gently on the edge of the bed. Over the top of her head, he saw Margrave stir. Had South's arms not been full of India, he would have planted the earl a second facer.

"Oh, God." India's words were muffled against South's woolen coat. "My brother."

"Your half-brother." It was not South who made this distinction, but Lady Margrave. "Allen is your half-brother."

This minor difference did nothing to settle India's roiling stomach. She could not warm herself, even in South's close embrace. The chill she felt went to the marrow of her bones, then her soul. She pressed her face into the curve of South's neck and would have clamped her hands over her ears if such a thing were possible. The manner in which he held her kept her from doing so. She made a halfhearted struggle against him, but he didn't release her, and in truth, she wasn't certain she wanted him to. If there were things that must be said, then it followed there were things that must be listened to. Hadn't she been the one who wanted to know what everyone else did? South would have protected her from the truth. She knew that now. It had been Margrave's intention to punish her with it. He'd meant for it to cripple her. It was his last, best revenge, a consequence of his hatred that reached beyond her to his mother. He had caught them both with a single blow.

India felt her breathing calm and tension slowly seep away. She knew that South felt it, too. His embrace loosened. He raised his head, and his cheek no longer rubbed against the corn-silk softness of her hair. "It's all right," she said, as much to herself as to him. "I'm all right."

"I know." He said it because he wanted it to be true, not because he was sure it was.

India pressed a shaky smile into his neck. "No. Really. I am."

"It takes your breath away, doesn't it?" It was Margrave who spoke. He rolled onto his back, then struggled into a sitting position. Hands tied behind him, he used his bound heels to push himself across the floor until he rested against the far wall. His mouth was swollen, and a thin line of blood marked his face from the corner of his lips to his jaw. "Doesn't it?" he repeated.

India turned her head and stared at him. She said nothing.

"That's precisely what happened to me when I learned you were my sister. My *half*-sister. The distinction seems noteworthy to our mother, even if it does little to lessen the impact. Of course, I was very young when I learned the truth. Nine, I think." He glanced at the countess. "Is that right, Mother? Was I nine?"

A breath shuddered through Lady Margrave. "Yes."

"You must speak up," Margrave said. "There is a ringing in my ears. A result of the blow, I suspect. Did you say yes?"

"Yes."

Margrave nodded and returned his attention to India. "I was nine. Just as I thought. And you were four. You were living with the Hawthornes. Thomas and Marianne. Just as you always had. You didn't know me then. There was no reason that you should. You knew no life outside Devon, and I imagine you were content with the prospect of growing up there in the shadow of Merrimont. You might have passed your entire life without knowing of your connection to that place. Mother would have had it so. I was the one who did not think it was fair."

India sensed that South meant to interrupt Margrave. She made a small negative shake of her head, stopping him. "I want to hear," she said. "I want to know all of it."

Lady Margrave came to her feet. She lifted her chin and made to compose herself. "Then you shall hear it from me."

"By all means," Margrave said sardonically. "Your version of the truth is no less entertaining than my own."

Ignoring him, India regarded the dowager countess. "Tell me."

Lady Margrave's hands unfolded and fell to her sides. "Allen overheard my husband and me arguing about you. There was a question of whether you should continue to live with the Hawthornes. The earl did not approve of the arrangement and wanted you to come to Merrimont and eventually to Marlhaven. As I was the one who made the arrangement with Mrs. Hawthorne, I was of the opposite opinion."

India slipped her fingers through South's. "My mother was the midwife present when you gave birth to me." That she chose to name Marianne Hawthorne her mother was quite deliberate. Lady Margrave's response was to press her lips together briefly and shield the pain in her eyes by staring for a moment at the floor. "You gave me to her," India said. "You gave me away."

The countess looked at India again and nodded this time. "Yes. That is exactly what I did. I hated him, you see. And I wanted to punish him. I could think of no more complete way to do that than to make certain he never saw his child."

India frowned. "I don't understand. If Margrave is my half-brother and you are mother to both of us . . ." Her voice trailed off as she thought this through. "You *are* mother to both of us, aren't you?"

Margrave gave an abrupt laugh. "Oh, she is that, my dear sister. There is no denying that we can claim this whore for our mother."

India's fingers tightened against South's. It was the only indication that she had heard what Margrave said or had given it any heed. "If your husband was Margrave's father," she said, "then who is mine?"

The countess shook her head. "It is not what you think. You are not my bastard child." She took a steadying breath. "My son is."

India's glance shot to Margrave. "Did you know?"

He shrugged and made a show of a modest smile that was chilling for all its pleasantness. "Not immediately upon discovering you were my sister. That understanding came later. In the beginning I believed as the earl did. I was his heir. You were his unfaithful wife's bastard. I learned the truth long before he did. Mother's letters from her lover laid the story out for me. You will be happy to know, India, that I told him the truth before he died. I would not be surprised to learn that's what killed him in the end. It seemed to me that he quite gave up when I informed him of the turn in the tale."

Lady Margrave spun on her heel and stared down at her son's twisted smile. The madness was there in his eyes. She had seen it before. It was not the fevered brightness of someone who no longer shared the reality of others; it was the cool, penetrating darkness of someone who lived for shifting the reality. She had always thought he looked a great deal like her, but when she studied his features now, she could see only that he was in every way his father's son.

"You killed the earl," she said. "And it was not your last words that put him in his grave. What did you use? Arsenic? Foxglove?"

South heard India suck in a breath, but he saw that Margrave was unmoved by the accusation. "Do you know it for a fact?" he asked Lady Margrave.

Not turning away from her son, she answered South's question. "I know he did it. Can I prove it?" She shook her head. "He was afraid my husband would discover the truth on his own and disinherit him. He never believed me that I would not tell. Why would I? I had deceived my lord husband for all the years of our marriage. I had everything to lose and nothing to gain by revealing what I had done. I had made him believe the child of my lover was his own, and denied him the child he had fathered. Do you think he would have forgiven me for that?''

This last question hung in the air, not meant to be answered by anyone. India traded glances with South. Margrave simply stared at his mother.

Lady Margrave used the toe of her shoe to nudge aside the board that both she and India had wielded earlier. She took a step closer to her son. ''Why were you so afraid of her?'' she asked him. ''There was no reason she had to be any part of your life. It was *your* father I loved. It was *you* I looked after, coddled, gave every advantage. It was never enough. There was no filling that part of you that was soul-less.'' She turned around and faced India. ''He would have killed us both,'' she said. ''I think he would have let you linger, but you would not have thanked him for it. He meant a quicker end for me, and it would have been a kindness, though I do not believe he has thought ahead to what he would have done without us. In our own way we've kept him alive. Do you see, India? He lived for us—most especially you—just as his father did for me. When my husband forced an end to my affair, Allen's father killed himself. Can you understand that I thought my son might do the same? They share so many of the same qualities.'' Her voice began to trail away, and her eyes lost their focus. ''So many of the same desires.''

India felt a chill creeping along the length of her spine. South's fingers squeezed hers gently, then released her hand. He came to his feet. Aware that the dowager countess might perceive this small change as a threat, he stayed at the bedside, well away from her, and counted the steps it would take to reach her if such were necessary. ''There is no one here who doubts how much you have loved your son or your son's father. Though he may deny it, even Margrave knows the truth. It cannot have been easy for you to have accepted a loveless marriage. Was it your idea? Or your lover's?''

Lady Margrave said nothing. She looked uncertainly at South, as though she did not comprehend the question.

"The necessity of it must have occurred to you both,'' South said. "It would have been difficult to continue as you had without an acceptable match for one of you. You both must have feared that eventually there would be talk. So it was agreed that you would be the one to marry. Perhaps your lover helped arrange the match. As he planned to share you with another man, he certainly had an interest in your attachment. Somehow, you settled on the Earl of Margrave. You may even have felt some affection for him in the beginning, though one can only imagine the strain that would have placed on you.''

South stood with his feet slightly apart, his hands clasped behind his back. He gestured with his fingers for India to move toward the door. "For a time, it seems the marriage worked splendidly. You gave birth to your first child, and your husband never suspected he was not the father. Even after he learned of your affair, he did not question his son's legitimacy. I suppose it was too terrible a consequence to consider. He must have decided there are some stones better left unturned.''

India stood slowly and absently smoothed the front of her gown. She waited until South casually took a step away from the bed before she slipped behind him. She hovered for a moment at his side, then began walking toward the door as he continued addressing Lady Margrave.

"He insisted you end your affair.''

Watching India, the countess seemed to collect herself. "I did end it.''

"Did you? Or did it end when you found you were pregnant with your husband's child?''

"He forced himself on me.'' She saw the hesitation in India's step and knew she was understood. "I would not let him have the satisfaction of knowing it was he who got me with child.''

"But your lover knew the truth," South said.

"Yes."

"And he killed himself."

"Yes." She regarded India, her eyes imploring. "You must understand. I couldn't keep you. You were always a reminder of that rape, and a more painful reminder of what I no longer had."

India shook her head. "What I understand is that you thought only of yourself and your revenge. You sent me to the Hawthornes and then you took me away again."

"No! That was Allen's doing. He is the one who forced it. He wanted to meet you. He wanted to know his sister. I couldn't refuse him."

"He was nine years old."

The countess's hands curled into fists. Her voice wavered as it rose in pitch. "I couldn't refuse him!"

Using his back and shoulders to brace himself against the wall, Margrave climbed to his feet. "She's afraid of me," he said. "She always has been. Afraid of what I might say or do . . . or become. She didn't want to bring you to Merrimont. The earl had asked her to do that, remember? He would have accepted you as a daughter. That was the argument I overheard. He had long since forgiven her and wanted you to live with us. It was Mother who was opposed to the idea."

"So you asked her."

"In a manner of speaking."

India knew the boy he had been. The adder. He would have threatened his own mother. If the dowager was right, he had been moved to kill the man who had been for all intents his father. "That was the purpose for the teas at Merrimont," she said. "You wanted me there."

"Can you doubt it?"

"And when my parents died, you . . ." She stopped abruptly, and her hand flew to her mouth. Above her fingertips, India's eyes widened. "You set the fire. You were responsible for it just as you were at Ambermede." She turned to South, her eyes darkening with the horror of what she knew to be the truth. "He killed my parents," she said, her voice hollow. "South. He killed my parents."

"I know." Seeing that she would not move toward the door now, South went to her. "He couldn't let anyone else have you, India. Even then. It is a trait he shared with his father." Over the top of India's head, he watched the countess's features become still as stone. "Isn't that what you meant, my lady? Your son shared the same obsession with his sister that your brother shared with you."

The dowager's keening cry was abruptly cut short by the gold cord Margrave wound around her throat. He twisted it in his fist, garroting her. She clawed at her neck and kicked out behind her. Her struggle only tightened her son's hold. "Have a care, Mother. You'll hang yourself." The very calm of his voice set the countess on her feet. She gasped for breath, choking, and looked to India and South for rescue.

South put India to his side and slightly behind him. The fact that she accepted this place told him what he needed to know about the state of her own mind. This last revelation had left her reeling. He measured the distance to Margrave and calculated how much time he had before the earl strangled his own mother. "What do you want, Margrave?"

"I want to leave."

"Then go. But release the countess."

Margrave shook his head. "You'd never let me pass."

"I give you my word."

"Give me India."

"No."

"My feet are still bound. I need her to untie them."

"Release your mother, and your hands will be free to do the thing yourself."

Margrave's passionless eyes sought out India. "Come here."

She stayed her ground. "No."

He turned his fist so the cord was pulled taut and then ordered India a second time.

India hesitated, then a took a step, but it was in the direction of the door. "I'll open it for you," she said.

"South's offer is made in good faith." Before Margrave could call her back, she flew across the last few feet and flung the door open, then fairly vibrated with the shortness of her stop. "Oh! You!"

Somewhat guiltily the three men on the other side of the threshold straightened. They looked past India to survey the scuffling scene in the bedchamber. South had used the distraction to wrest Margrave's hold away from his mother. The countess was on her knees, her hands at her throat, while Margrave tried to tear away the forearm South pressed against his Adam's apple.

"It seems we missed our cue," North said amiably.

East stepped into the room. "Indeed we did. Most unfortunate."

West made a show of sighing as he regarded his friend. "You really cannot expect that we shall always save you, South. Now. What is to be done?"

Epilogue

Like a golden serpent, the braided cord wound its way around India's neck. Flexing its muscles, it coiled tightly. With each undulating ripple and slither, it bit more deeply into her skin and finally closed her air passage. She opened her mouth to draw in a breath, but no part of it reached her lungs, and her scream was a silent one. The pressure created in her chest was unbearable. Her heart thudded loudly and made her deaf to every sound but the roar in her ears. There were jagged flashes of light at the back of her lids, all of them crimson now. She tore at her throat, gasping.

"India!"

She flinched from the weight on her shoulder, arching her back, then rolling onto her side. Still clawing and heaving for breath, India curled into a protective fetal position.

"India!"

The weight landed again, heavier this time, gripping and insistent. She could no longer throw it off, nor could she endure its prodding. Tears stung her eyes, and her throat swelled with an ache she could not swallow.

"India." Gently now, South pulled her toward him. His hand slid under hers, and he tugged at the flaxen braid curled

around her neck. It slipped through her fingers, though not
without effort. Her next breath was drawn harshly, and then
there was a wrenching sob that tore at South's heart. He
turned her into his chest and let her weep against his nightshirt. She lay with one arm flung across his abdomen and
the other burrowed under his pillow. Her tears dampened
the cool cotton comfort under her cheek. South untied the
ribbon that held her thick plait together, and let his fingers
unwind the platinum-and-gold cords of hair.

"India." He whispered her name this time. His breath
lifted delicate strands of hair. He breathed in the scent of
her. The fragrance of lavender salts from her bath still clung
to her skin. There was the hint of womanly musk in the
warmth of her body. He kissed the crown of her head. Her
hair tickled his lips, and he pressed his small smile there.
"A dream, India. It is naught but a dream."

She felt the heat of his arm across her back, proof of the
security of his embrace. She needed it just now—especially
now, when the dark memories stole into her dreams and
became nightmares. At first she had worried that he would
grow weary of this disruption to his sleep, yet he had never
once suggested an alternative to their arrangement. To be
fair to him, India had broached the subject. Before she could
finish laying out her proposal, South's arch look from under
that single raised eyebrow made her fall silent. She had not
mentioned it again.

"They are fewer and farther between," South said. He
pressed one corner of the sheet into her hand so that she
might dry her eyes. "It has been more than six weeks since
the last. Did you know that?"

She hadn't. Somewhat self-consciously she asked, "Do
you keep an accounting?"

"India." His voice gently chided her. "Do you really
think that?"

"No." Easing herself out of South's embrace, India sat
up and leaned against the headboard. She wiped her eyes,
then tucked the blankets around her. "It is just that it does
not seem so long ago to me."

"I imagine not." He plumped a pillow under his head and turned on his side to see her better. She was already leaning toward the nightstand to light the lamp. Where once she had insisted upon the cover of darkness, India found in the aftermath of her nightmares that she wanted light. He waited for her to settle back before he spoke. "I remember the last time because Elizabeth and North had come calling in the afternoon. Remember? Elizabeth confided to you that she was pregnant."

"Yes." India recalled it quite well. It was impossible not to feel something wonderful in the wake of Elizabeth's joy. Northam had looked rather dazed by his good fortune, and South had had rather too much amusement at his expense. It had been a pleasant day passed in the company of friends, and India was unconvinced it lay at the root of her previous nightmare. "You do not think it was their visit that precipitated . . ."

She stopped because South was shaking his head. "No," he said. "That is not what I think at all. It is merely that I recall they were here some six weeks ago. Have you forgotten it was also the same day a post from Lady Margrave arrived?"

India *had* forgotten that. It had come just as they were sitting down to tea. India had ignored it until later that evening, when she and South were once again alone. "There was a post from her ladyship today."

"I know." He could not fail to notice that India did not refer to the countess as her mother. It was still a difficult transition for her to make. South did not press her to think about it differently. If it were to happen at all, India would come upon acceptance in her own time. "Darrow told me."

She smiled faintly. "There is nothing that gets past him."

South's own grin was lopsided. "No. Nothing does."

India became quiet, thoughtful. Her brow creased. "Is it her missives, do you think?"

"Not precisely. More likely they simply cause you to reflect on all that has happened. You speak little of what she writes, and less of what you think of it. You would have me believe it does not distress you any longer; then you have the nightmares. It would seem that what you try to hide from me, you cannot hide from yourself.''

She considered that. ''I am not certain I like you knowing me so very well.''

Treading carefully, South said, ''I assure you, I do not. Women, by their very nature, are unfathomable.''

''What poppycock.'' India's lip curled in amused derision. ''Did the marquess tell you that? Given the muddle East made of his odd engagement to Sophie, one can see how he might arrive at that conclusion. Simply because *he* did not have sense enough to understand what was before him, *she* must be incomprehensible. It is very badly done by men.''

South laughed. ''You have me there.''

She ran her fingers through his thick hair and ruffled the strands at his nape. ''Promise me there will be no repetition of such inane utterances.''

''I swear it.'' He would no doubt have occasion to think it many times, but he would bloody his tongue before he said it aloud in India's presence. South took her hand and rubbed the pad of his thumb back and forth across her knuckles. ''What did Lady Margrave write?''

India welcomed the light pressure of his hand against hers, the knowledge that she was not alone in this. ''You would have it out of me, then? There is no moving you from the subject?''

''Is that what you wish?''

The choice was hers. He always gave her the choice. ''No,'' she said at last. ''I want you to know. She has invited me again to Marlhaven.''

''I see.'' He had suspected it might be something of that nature. ''There were previous invitations?''

India nodded. ''She extends it each time she writes. I am sorry I did not mention it before.'' She hesitated, worrying her lower lip. ''I don't think I'm prepared to make that journey just yet.''

''Did you believe I would press you to do otherwise?''

"No," she said quickly. "I knew you wouldn't. It's simply that telling you would have forced me to consider it more often. I wanted to put it from my mind, not examine it." India smiled ruefully. "But it seems that you are right. Putting it from my mind is not so easily accomplished. There are the nightmares to plague me." She touched her throat, rubbing the hollow lightly with her fingertips. "I dreamed Margrave was choking me. At first it was his mother that he had in his hands, just as he had her at Marlhaven, but this time there was no rescue. You did not come for me. Neither did your friends. He killed Lady Margrave and then he came for me."

South did not like to think how close they had come to just that end. That was the stuff his own nightmares were made of. He closed his eyes briefly, suppressing the shudder that India surely would have felt.

Enough time had passed that they were able to think more clearly about Margrave's obsession with India. It was neither love nor hatred that compelled him to take the actions he had, but rather a twisted combination of both those powerful emotions. He found himself at once drawn to her and repelled by his own desires. The fact that she was his sister only seemed to intensify his jealousy and possessiveness. There was no escaping the fact that if the truth of her parentage had been known by the late earl, India would have been publicly recognized as his daughter. Instead of Lady Margrave's pregnancy being concealed, it would have been celebrated.

India was heiress to a fortune.

It was not greed alone that tortured Margrave's heart and mind. He had never shown particular interest in the title or wealth that had been his. It was the fear that he might be exposed as a bastard that eroded rationality. From his early days at Hambrick Hall, when he witnessed how bastards like West were treated by the Society of Bishops, Margrave determined he would set himself apart from that stigma. Later, when he discovered that he was the offspring of an incestuous relationship, Margrave's fear turned to something that was icy and forbidding, and India became the object of all that fascinated and frightened him.

There were no self-imposed limits for Allen Parrish, Earl of Margrave. There was nothing he would not do to secure his ends. With no moral compass to guide him, the law offered no deterrents. He existed for India, and in his confused mind she existed for no one but him.

His peculiar madness had allowed him to justify all that he had done. With the Compass Club, India, and his own mother for an audience, Margrave had offered a rambling, ranting confession. It was a disturbing soliloquy, even more difficult to listen to than it was to deliver. There was a certain relish in the earl's voice that made the hair stand up at the back of their necks.

First, there had been the fire. Killing India's parents had seemed a perfectly reasonable solution to the problem of how to bring her back to Merrimont and keep her there. He had not been able to anticipate the consequences of having India at the estate, or the trips she would make to Marlhaven. While he was away at Hambrick Hall, he imagined that she was becoming a favorite of his mother. More important to him was his growing suspicion that she might usurp his place with the earl. To prevent that from happening, Margrave determined that he would have to eliminate the man he now knew was not his father. Poison presented the simplest solution, just as Lady Margrave had come to believe.

The earl's death was meant to remove a rival, but it did not entirely provide the outcome Margrave had hoped for. He had not foreseen that his mother would send India away. He did the only thing he could: he followed her.

Margrave had described in detail how he had removed the lecherous Mr. Olmstead as an opponent by raising the height of the stone fence so that his mount could not make the jump. With Olmstead incapacitated, Margrave believed India would come back with him to Marlhaven. Instead, she ran to London.

He followed again, this time making himself necessary to the theatre company where she had found work. As Mrs.

Garrety, he had entrée into every aspect of India's life. It was he who insisted she take the name Parr because it was the diminutive of Parrish. As a secret benefactor of Kent's troupe, he was able to influence productions, locations, and India's progression from small roles to leading actress. Each time she tried to rebel or in any way end the arrangement, he manipulated her into staying with an attempt on his life.

Margrave had not understood how his mother had struck her own bargain with India. He never knew that in some ways he had become as much watched as he was the watcher. It was no easier for India to call a halt to her agreement with the countess than it was to finish with Margrave. She was too neatly caught.

For all that they knew about each other, there were aspects that were secret to both. During the earl's chilling recitation, it became clear to South that India was correct: Margrave had had no knowledge of her involvement with the colonel. That secrecy had been a death sentence for Mr. Kendall. Margrave could not imagine another reason Kendall was so often in the company of India, save that he desired her. With so many disguises at his disposal, and a gift for mimicry, it was Margrave who fashioned himself into the woman that Kendall met before his death. The earl retained wits about him enough to hire footpads to deal the fatal blows. In a similar fashion, he had dispatched Mr. Rutherford, removing the man's heart for no other reason than that it offended him.

About the assassination attempt on the Prince Regent, Margrave was less clear. He seemed to have difficulty collecting his thoughts, and the expression of them was sometimes incoherent. Listening to him, South had wondered cynically if the madness had taken control of Margrave or if Margrave controlled the madness.

In the end, they all heard enough to know that whatever was to be done about him required a private reckoning. It was not for the dowager countess's sake that this decision was reached, but rather for India's. A public accounting of the earl's crimes would have raised as many questions as it answered. Lord and Lady Macquey-Howell's marriage would have been exposed for the odd convenience that it was. That the object of the lady's love was another woman and not the Spanish consul would have provided a feeding frenzy for the *ton*. Better to let them scavenge for other food this season.

South saw that some color had returned to India's complexion. It was her eyes that remained as darkly troubled as the course of her thoughts. "What are you thinking?" he asked.

One corner of her mouth lifted slightly in a plaintive smile. There was no chance that she might prevaricate. He would have the answer from her and know if it was true or not. "The paintings," she said. "I was thinking about the paintings."

"They are destroyed."

"The ones we found at Marlhaven."

"And the ones West discovered."

"There might be others. I can't be certain and neither can you. Margrave does not even know how many there were or what became of them all. I wish I did not know that some of the paintings left his hands. I will always wonder who among the *ton* has seen me posed so vulgarly. No one could suspect it was done against my will or that the composition of all of Margrave's work was but an invention of his mind." India's voice dropped to a whisper. "You must wonder the same from time to time. It can be no easy thing to be married to the whore in those paintings."

"India!" His voice was like a whip, and South felt her flinch beside him. He did not regret his sharpness in the least. "I am not married to the woman in those paintings. She does not exist. You are not her."

"I am not India Parr, either. She is someone I created."

"She is someone you became."

India wondered at the subtle distinction South made. Did he mean she had grown into the woman she wanted to be? The actress he knew was resourceful, a woman of considerable courage and cleverness. She felt neither of those things now. "And what of Diana Hawthorne?" she asked quietly.

Without any more encouragement than a slight tug on her hand, South drew India beside him. She lay turned into him, her head on his shoulder, one leg resting warmly along his. "You have not abandoned her," he said. "Is that what you think? I do not believe she has ever been separate from you."

"But I never *was* her."

"Of course you were."

"And Lady Diana Alexandra Parrish?"

"A name only. She is not even the woman you were meant to be. If Lady Margrave had had her way, you would have never known the truth." He was silent for a moment, allowing India to consider that. Then he added, "It does not change the fact that you know the truth now. The countess *is* your mother."

India was not prepared to embrace that knowledge yet. "There were times I believed I might be the earl's daughter, but never once did I imagine I might be hers. Even then, the prospect of being related to Margrave was too horrible to contemplate. I tried never to consider it for long. Reciting lines, memorizing passages—all of it helped to put aside the uncertainty." She shivered slightly, then lay still. "Do you think I should accept her invitation?"

"I think you should make up your own mind on the matter."

She sighed. "Sometimes it is far simpler to be told what to do."

"Now, *there* is a trap I would do well to avoid."

Smiling gently, India laid her hand over his heart and moved closer. The strong, steady beat was cupped in her palm. "She is not well, South. Perhaps some allowance should be made for that."

South remained neutral. "Perhaps." He did not inquire into the nature of Lady Margrave's illness. He suspected it had everything to do with the loss of her son. Margrave's confession had taken its toll on his mother's will. By the time he finished, she had looked as if she wished he had snapped her neck when he'd had the opportunity to do so. What she felt for him was as confused as what Margrave felt for India. No one who heard what passed between mother and son that day doubted that the dowager countess was a little mad herself. While the earl required—and South insisted upon—the security of an asylum, Lady Margrave was best attended to in the privacy of her home. The countess's long-time and loyal retainers made certain that she presented no harm to herself or to others. South would not have entertained the notion of India's visiting Marlhaven if he did not think it was safe for her to do so. "Is the invitation for both of us?" he asked. "I would go with you, you know, if that is your wish."

She had thought he would insist. "She does not expressly say so, though I cannot believe she means to exclude you."

"I can believe exactly that. She blames me for what has become of her son."

"That is only because she cannot accept responsibility herself. That he is alive at all is your doing."

"That he is in an asylum is also my doing," he said gravely. "I understand her anger. It is no easy life for him there."

"She can visit him."

"And the visits cannot be without heartache for her."

"He might have been transported."

"No." South's voice was firm. "We have discussed this before, India. Transportation was never a possibility."

She lifted her head and searched his face. South's resolve was in the set of his jaw and the steely color of his eyes. He would have seen Margrave hanged for his crimes— or killed him himself—before he would have supported transportation to Van Diemen's Land. It was necessary to South to know where Margrave was. Though escape from the penal colony on the other side of the world seemed impossible, he was unwilling to trust that Margrave could not accomplish it.

"He cannot leave the asylum?" India wished she had not

asked the question. She had not meant for her fear to surface in the tremor of her voice. It was not how she wished South to know her.

"He cannot leave," South said. "Ever." He raised his hand and cupped the back of her head. "Do you believe me, India?"

She did. Her hair softly rubbed his palm as she nodded.

"Good." He drew her head down and kissed her full on the mouth. Her cheeks were flushed with color by the time he released her. "That was good, too." He grinned when India gave him a light pinch just above his hip. "Have a care."

She smiled to herself and then slid back into the natural cradle of his body. He would protect her. She knew that. It did not negate what was his greatest gift to her: the confidence that she could stand alone off the stage. He had never once doubted that she would have managed to escape Marlhaven on her own. Coming for her had been about his need to do something, he'd told her, not because she needed him. She was not certain that was entirely true, but she loved him dearly for saying it.

She'd told him yes in advance of a proper marriage proposal. The rest of the Compass Club understood the import of her words before South had registered their meaning. Love had made him dull-witted and slow, they said as money exchanged hands. As always, there had been a wager. He should be grateful, they assured him, that she had not thwacked *him* with a plank. It was kinder that she lifted the special license from his pocket and merely waved it under his nose. He had once promised her that it would remain there until she was ready—and it did.

The constancy of South's word was something she could depend upon. He had told her there would be no great uproar when he revealed the fact of their marriage to his family and no great scandal when the *ton* learned the same. His father was in anticipation of just such an event, given South's efforts to find India. Even Lady Redding had been girding herself for that end. She was determined to conduct herself

with a style and graciousness that was the equal of Northam's
mother when she had faced a similar situation with her own
son.

"Never underestimate the competition between friends,"
South had advised India. "My mother will escort you about
London so often that you might begin to think you married
her."

It had not been as bad as all that. Though the Countess
of Redding could be a formidable presence, the presence
she made was on India's behalf. It helped that she knew
something of India's background. While the *ton* learned only
that she was the ward of the late Earl and the Countess of
Margrave, at India's insistence, South's parents were told
more in the way of the truth. That went a great way to
endearing their daughter-in-law to them.

South's friends drew her into their circle. She met the
colonel a second time and discovered that in spite of the
progression of his illness, he was almost as formidable as
South's mother. Having a slight acquaintance with Lady
Redding, John Blackwood genuinely appreciated India's
candor in saying so. He laughed long and hard, then complained at length that her marriage to South had removed
her from the theatre. She let him go on because there was
no polite way to stop him, but she had never been comfortable with praise for her talents. She had learned to accept
the applause but not the attention. South had understood that
the theatre had been a refuge for her, not a means to bring
notice to herself. When she assured him she did not miss
it, he believed her.

It was important to her that he should.

Doobin was as much a reminder of the theatre as India
ever would require. She found pleasure in seeing what he
was becoming under Darrow's watchful eye. He had found
any number of ways to make himself invaluable, starting
with the service he had provided to the Compass Club when
they set off to Marlhaven. Without Doobin's help, Northam,
Eastlyn, and Westphal would not have so easily found their
way to where their friend was confronting Margrave. It was

the description of the disguise Doobin had helped South fashion and a rough sketch of the same that assisted them.

Upon coming to Marlhaven, their intention had not been to upset the routine of the household. They'd meant to reacquaint themselves with Margrave while not exposing South's presence. Their tenuous connection to the earl through Hambrick Hall was reason enough for their visit. When they were left to cool their heels in the library and Margrave did not appear in spite of the housekeeper's repeated assurances that he would do so, they determined that their arrival may have already been left until too late.

It was then that they had surrendered all pretense of pleasantness. The housekeeper was pressed into giving up the location of Margrave's private rooms in the great house, though she adamantly refused to escort them there. Recognizing her fear for what it was, Northam showed her Doobin's sketch of South. The catch of her breath was audible, and the implication was clear: she could identify the shabby old man in the pencil drawing. What she could not tell them was where he might be at the moment.

A wider search eventually brought them to Mrs. Hoover in the kitchen. The cook was willing to tell them that South had taken coals to Margrave's suite and had not yet returned. Her willingness to tell them anything had much to do with the pistol Eastlyn casually waved about her kitchen. In spite of his considerable diplomatic skills, the marquess was not always a patient man. Westphal, at least, had kept his blade in his boot.

They had understood the servants' reluctance to assist them. They shared many of the same fears for the safety of India and Lady Margrave. As for South, they consoled themselves that he was at his best talking his way out. They would know at what point their intervention was required.

A different outcome was unthinkable.

Sometimes India wondered if South had actually heard them in the corridor. He denied it when she asked him, and his expression gave nothing away. Still, she remembered how he had motioned her toward the door when it had not seemed so urgent that she remove herself. He might not have been so willing to let her out of his sight if he had not known his friends were there. Perhaps it was only that he was so much a part of them that he suspected their presence. The links of those boyhood friendships were forged in steel.

North. South. East. West. Friends for life we have confessed. All other truths, we'll deny. For we are soldier, sailor, tinker, spy.

South's fingers stilled in her hair. "What was that?"

"Hmmm?"

"Did you say something?"

India smiled. She had not realized she'd spoken any part of the rhyme aloud. "I was thinking of your friends."

"I can't say I much approve of that. You're in my bed."

"I'm in *our* bed, and I can think whatever I like."

Growling playfully, South turned India quickly onto her back and pinned her to the mattress. She did not try to resist, or feel a moment's need to. Those urges had long been dispelled from her mind. She had even made peace with South's finding her tattoo in every way exotic. There was no more effort expended to hide it from him. That had ended on their wedding night when he made love to her in front of the cheval glass.

The memory of his loving—of watching him make love to her—sent a delicate shiver through India. It was as if she were possessed of a second sight that night, one that allowed her to see herself though his eyes, then to finally see herself as she was. When he had whispered that she was beautiful, she did not shy from it, and their time together since had not lessened the impact of those words or her ability to find pleasure in them now.

When he released her wrists, India shimmied out of her nightdress. She let it sail over the side of the bed, then helped him out of his shirt. They came together quickly, with the sort of urgency that still could surprise her with its fierceness. The need was mutual. They shared desire with a rivaling intensity.

She looked down at their bodies as they came together.

He had taught her that. Her hips lifted as his thrust forward, and she closed her eyes, all sensation now, feeling him so deeply inside her that she could not imagine he would leave her. He did, though, and it was wonderful, too. The sliding of his thighs against hers, the heat of his skin, the curve of his palm on her breast: all of it made her aware of her body in a way that was powerfully erotic.

It was no different for South. He ached with this hunger to have her close, then closer. There were nightmares that plagued his sleep as well. Sometimes he dreamed of losing her in the warren of rooms at Marlhaven. Trapdoors opened on a stage that existed only in his mind, and always India fell through them while he watched helplessly from the audience. It was she who comforted him on those occasions, holding him against her breast and giving him ease with her body when his need to have her erased every other thought.

Spent, they lay in a tangle of limbs and sheets while their hearts settled and their breathing calmed. He nudged her gently from her sideways sprawl and fit her against him until they were like spoons in a drawer. Reaching over India's shoulder, South turned back the lamp so that only a flicker of light remained. He thought she would sleep almost immediately, but she did not so much as close her eyes.

"India?"

It was as if he had asked an entire question with only that slight inflection of her name. "I think I shall go to Marlhaven after all," she said quietly.

"You are certain?"

"No, not in the least." She took his hand in hers, threading her fingers through his. "But I find that when I try to put all that has happened behind me, it follows me everywhere, and when I put it in front of me, it blocks my path. I suspect the answer is to learn to keep it beside me."

"Like me."

"Yes," she said. "Exactly like you."

South pushed aside the heavy lock of hair that lay against her neck. He kissed her there. "Shall I go with you?"

"If you like."

"Then I shall."

She smiled and gave his hand a gentle squeeze. In time her eyelids fluttered and eventually closed. Her lashes lay still in a dark arc against her cheek. The clasp of her fingers relaxed. South listened to the cadence of her breathing change and felt the subtle shift in the press of her body against his. It was no small pleasure he enjoyed, watching her fall asleep. "You may no longer need me to save you, India," he whispered into the near darkness. "But you cannot expect that I should fail Hortense."

Where his palm rested warmly on the slight swelling curve of India's abdomen, their child stirred.

The Compass Club returns!
Please turn the page for an exciting sneak
peek of East's story,
ALL I EVER NEEDED,
coming from Zebra Books in October 2003!

Dear Reader,

The Compass Club stories all begin at Hambrick Hall, an exclusive, though entirely fictional, school in London. The four boys who make up the total membership of the club remain fast friends into adulthood. Like all friends, they connect and collide and go their separate ways, coming together again when the need is there. The adventures of Northam, Southerton, Eastlyn, and Westphal do not happen one after another, but more or less at the same time. (How convenient, uncomplicated, and boring life would be if my friends would put their lives on hold until I get through *my* crisis!)

The books are independent of each other, yet you might experience a sense of deja vu as you read certain scenes. That's because there are some events that are played out again, though from a slightly different direction. Sometimes it's North's, sometimes South's, sometimes ... well, you get the idea.

All the best,

Jo

Chapter One

June 1818, London

There was a fluttering across the tip of Sophie's nose. She batted at it idly, too weary to open her eyes and identify the cause. A moment passed before the tickling visited her again, this time between her honey-colored brows. She frowned slightly, creasing the space just above her nose. When it came a third time it fluttered across her cheek. It was when the sensation flickered along her jaw from ear to chin that Sophie was roused to action.

She slapped herself lightly on the side of the face and was rewarded for her effort, not by trapping an offending insect, but by the echo of oddly familiar laughter. It struck her with more force than her hand had against her cheek. She *knew* the deep throaty timbre of that laugh. Even when heard in concert with his three friends she had always been able to distinguish which thread of sound was his.

Lady Sophia Colley blinked widely and stared up into the amused countenance of Gabriel Whitney, the eighth Marquess of Eastlyn.

"May I?" he asked, letting his hand sweep over the

expanse of blanket where Sophie sat. "It is a tolerably fine day for being out of doors and settled in the heart of nature's bounty."

The garden at No. 14 Bowden Street was hardly the heart of nature's bounty, but Sophie felt certain the marquess knew that. She wondered if he thought she was unaware of the same. Perhaps he believed her naiveté extended to all manner of subjects. Sophie rose as far as her knees, quickly pushing the rucked hem of her dress to modestly cover her ankles. "You might find the bench over there more to your liking."

East glanced over his shoulder to the heavy stone slab supported by two frighteningly plump cherubs. He raised one eyebrow. "I don't believe so, no. I would not find it in the least comfortable." The eyebrow relaxed its skeptical arch. "But if you are opposed to sharing your blanket, I will avail myself of this patch of grass."

Before Sophie could protest that she had no objections, or rather that she would voice none, the marquess simply dropped to the ground, folding his legs tailor-fashion and resting his elbows lightly on his knees.

"Please, m'lord," Sophie said quickly. "Your trousers will be stained."

"It is good of you to warn me, but it is of no consequence."

"You will allow that your valet's opinion might be contrary to your own."

He smiled. "You are right, of course." East moved to the blanket where he repositioned himself in the same manner as before. He pointed to the book at Sophie's side. "What were you reading?"

Sophie could hardly make sense of the change of subject. She had to glance at the book to prompt her recollection of it. "It is my journal."

"You keep a diary, then. A worthy endeavor."

"Yes, I like to think so."

"Though perhaps not so interesting as woolgathering. Deep contemplation beneath an apple tree has much to rec-

ommend it. Or so North says." His rich baritone voice
softened to a confidential tone. "I believe he has been
inspired by Sir Isaac Newton's success."

Sophie's eyes darted into the boughs. Was it too much
to hope that an apple would fall directly on the marquess's
head? Barring that event, was it too much to hope one would
fall on hers?

Following the direction of her gaze as well as her errant
thoughts, Eastlyn casually remarked, "They're puny green
things now, but if you will invite me to return in the fall
when they're beautifully ripened and it takes no more than
a hint of wind to nudge them from the branches, I can
promise you that one of us will be most satisfyingly thumped
on the head, thereby putting a period to all awkward moments
between us."

Sophie was sure she did not like having her thoughts so
easily interpreted by his man. On the other hand, it was
somehow reassuring that he also found this encounter awkward. Sophie eased herself back against the rough bark of
the trunk and let her legs slide to one side. Strands of softly
curling hair the color of wild honey fluttered as she moved.
She lifted her face and regarded the marquess with a certain
solemn intensity. If the eyes that returned his amused gaze
could arguably be described as too large for her heart-shaped
face, there was no argument from any quarter that they were
remarkably sober.

"I've been in anticipation of your visit, my lord."

He nodded, equally grave now. How like Lady Sophia to
place her cards before him. She did not dissemble or play
coy as most young women in the same circumstances would
do. Even as her lack of pretense raised her in his estimation,
he was also reminded that she was not so very young, at least
not by the standards that were often set for a marriageable age
among the *ton*. She was more of a certain age, one somewhere after *la jeune fille* and before ape leader, mayhap in
her twenty-third year. He was heartily glad of it, if the truth
be known. Had she been younger he would have had to

tread more carefully, taking special pains not to trample a heart already foolishly attached to him.

Lady Sophia was hardly foolish. On short acquaintance, it was perhaps the thing he liked best about her—if he was taking no note of her singularly splendid eyes. It was not their studied seriousness that had drawn his attention on their first meeting, but their coloring, which was in every way the equal of her hair. He supposed the color they approximated was hazel, but it was far too dull a descriptor to be leveled at these features. If her hair was honey shot through with sunlight, then so were her eyes. Sophia's radiance, though, came from within.

This last is what made her so totally unsuitable. She was very nearly angelic with her too-perfect countenance. The heart-shaped face, the sweetly lush mouth, the small chin and pared nose, the large and beautifully colored eyes, and finally the softly curling hair that framed her face like the Madonna's halo . . . it was all rather more innocence than East believed he could properly manage. In principle he was in favor of innocence in females. In practice he found it was tedious.

He waited for Sophia to gather the threads of her thoughts, loath to interrupt her now that she was earnestly giving him her full attention. This was to be an odd encounter, prompted by even more peculiar circumstances. A sennight ago he, Eastlyn, discovered that he was rumored to have made a surprising declaration. It seemed that from among all the young women counted as suitable to be his wife, Lady Sophia Colley was the one he had chosen.

"I have heard the rumors of our engagement," she said. "I want you to know that I recognize they have no truth to recommend them. My cousin has admitted that you have not been in correspondence with his father, nor had any meeting with him in which you might have sought permission for my hand. Harold and Tremont would be happy if it were otherwise, but wishful thinking on their part cannot make it so. I am afraid they did nothing to dissuade people from believing as they will, and for that I am heartily sorry.

The earl would count himself fortunate to have such a marriage arranged for me. I hope you will understand and go gently with such remarks as you might make to others. If they have caused you embarrassment by failing to deny any link between my name and yours, I apologize.''

A crease appeared between Eastlyn's brows. He let his chin drop forward and rested it on his steepled fingers. "Surely it can't be your place to apologize, Lady Sophia.''

Since she did not think either Harold or Tremont had the stomach for it, even if they had the vocabulary, Sophie couldn't imagine who else was in a position to make amends. "I am not without responsibility, m'lord. I did not deny the rumors, either.''

East raised his head and let his steepled fingers fall. He plucked a blade of grass and rolled it absently between his long fingers as he leveled Sophia with his thoughtful gaze. "You had many opportunities, did you?''

"I . . . that is, I . . .'' Sophie was unaccustomed to fumbling for words. She did not thank the marquess for having that effect on her.

"I am not mistaken, am I?'' East continued. "You are not often away from home.''

He was scrupulously polite. Sophie could allow him that. He was kind to couch his observation that she was not the recipient of many invitations. "I am away as often as I need to be,'' she said.

"I see.'' A hint of a smile edged his mouth. "Almack's?''

"On occasion.''

"The theatre?''

"When there is something worth seeing.''

"The park?''

"When there is some*one* worth seeing.''

He laughed. "Which is to say that you rarely take your constitutional there.''

Distracted by his laugh, Sophie nodded faintly. She looked past his watchful eyes and focused on a point beyond his shoulder. A swallow alighted on the stone bench behind him and paced the length of it looking for crumbs. Since Sophie

had permitted Harold's children to take tea there only yesterday, the swallow was fortunate in his choice of picnic spots.
"Perhaps I am about town more often than you suspect and
it is only that I am outside your notice."

Eastlyn started to deny it but caught himself abruptly
when she held up a hand. Her smile was slight, but genuine.

"You must not be gallant, my lord, and deny such a thing
is the most reasonable explanation. I am fully aware that I
am an unlikely female to command your attention. It will
ease your mind to know that our initial introduction aside,
you are not the sort of someone I would go to the park to
see."

It did *not* ease the marquess's mind. In point of fact he
was not insulted, but she had tweaked him rather sharply, and
while he thought he should avoid hearing her explanation, he
simply could not. When he left the Battenburn estate this
morning, he was in expectation of a wholly different meeting
with Lady Sophia. Though he had cringed at the possibility,
he had forced himself to consider the prospect of tears and
how they might be dealt with swiftly but with some compassion. The exercise had been a waste of gray matter, he
realized now. Far from being near tears, the eyes that met
him were frank and reasonable. Except for one brief lapse,
Lady Sophia remained composed. Perfectly so.

"You would not go to the park upon hearing I would be
there?" he asked. "Even if I were driving my new
barouche?"

"Do not feign disappointment, my lord. It is badly done
of you. You can naught be but relieved that I bear you no
affection."

He was. Or at least he thought he was until she placed it
so baldly before him. He wondered if she was entirely correct
in assuming his disappointment was feigned. "There you
have me," he said slowly, regarding her with new interest.
"But you must allow that I am curious. What makes me so
beneath your notice?"

"Oh, no." She shook her head and the halo of hair waved
softly about her face until she was still again. "You misun-

derstand. It is not at all that you are beneath my notice, only outside of it.''

''There is a difference, I collect,'' he said dryly.

''Certainly. The former suggests you are not worthy of my attention. I meant to say that you simply do not fix my attention.''

''You are not making it any more palatable, you know. I cannot recall when last I was so deftly cut to the quick.''

Sophie searched Eastlyn's face for some sign that she had indeed done him an injury. His fine features remained impassive during her scrutiny, giving nothing of his thoughts away, no hint of amusement or distress. Still, it was Sophie's conclusion that he was teasing her. Any other outcome would have been difficult to imagine, no matter what emotion he affected. Her words could not have truly pricked him. The Marquess of Eastlyn must know he was recklessly handsome.

''Are you quite all right?'' Eastlyn asked. It seemed to him that Lady Sophie had become several degrees more sober, if such a thing were possible. The wash of pink in her cheeks was gone now; even her mouth was pale. He was moved to look behind him, suspecting that whatever had caused this change in her countenance must be at some distance beyond his shoulder. East saw nothing but the garden wall and the stone bench, neither occupied by any member of her family likely to induce such alarm. ''Shall I get you something? Water? Spirits?''

His offer of assistance forced Sophie to collect herself. It required rather more effort than she wished it might. ''I am all of a piece,'' she said calmly.

One of Eastlyn's brows kicked up and he made a survey of her face, flatly skeptical of her assertion. ''You are certain?''

''Yes.''

Eastlyn regarded Lady Sophia's perfectly cast features with some consternation. Her expression was now one of absolute composure, yet East had the distinct impression she was no longer aware of him in any substantive way. It was just as she had said earlier: he was unable to fix her attention.

Devil a bit, but it bothered him. It was not an admission he particularly wanted to make, and having made it, not one that he wanted to dwell overlong on. In what way could it possibly matter that Lady Sophia Colley was as uninterested in him as he was in her? Surely that was the best of all circumstances. Everything was made so much simpler by her easy acceptance of their situation. She did not blame him for any part of it, though she must suspect it was someone he knew who gave the rumor its sharp teeth. She was not in anticipation of a real offer of marriage, or even a sham engagement to satisfy the rumor mill until one of them was in a position to make a dignified exit. He would have insisted that she be the one to cry off, of course, and lay the blame for their dissolution at his feet. His reputation would not suffer unduly. Lady Sophia would not be so fortunate if she were cast as the one who had done the injury.

It was all moot. There would be no engagement, in truth or in fiction, and that was certainly as it should be. Eastlyn did not welcome the prospect of carrying out his work while observing all the tedious conventions that an affianced couple must needs endure. There might be less pleasurable ways to pass part of one's life, but they didn't come immediately to East's mind.

That is why it surprised him when he said, "You know, Lady Sophia, in some quarters I am considered a desirable partner."

Sophie drew in an uneasy breath and released it slowly, suddenly afraid of the direction of his conversation. "Have you truly considered the consequences, my lord, if I were to agree?"

ABOUT THE AUTHOR

Jo Goodman lives with her family in Colliers, West Virginia. She is the author of twenty-two historical romances (all published by Zebra Books), including her beloved Dennehy sisters series: *Wild Sweet Ecstasy* (Mary Michael's story), *Rogue's Mistress* (Rennie's story), *Forever in My Heart* (Maggie's story). *Always in My Dreams* (Skye's story), and *Only in My Arms* (Mary's story), as well as her Thorne Brothers trilogy: *My Steadfast Heart* (Colin's story), *My Reckless Heart* (Decker's story) and *With All My Heart* (Grey's story).

She is currently working on her newest Zebra historical romance, the third of a four-book series set during the Regency period. Look for East's story in October 2003. Jo loves hearing from readers, and you may write to her c/o Zebra Books. Please include a self-addressed stamped envelope if you would like a response. Or e-mail her at jdobrzan@weir.net.

BOOK YOUR PLACE ON OUR WEBSITE AND MAKE THE READING CONNECTION!

We've created a customized website just for our very special readers, where you can get the inside scoop on everything that's going on with Zebra, Pinnacle and Kensington books.

When you come online, you'll have the exciting opportunity to:

- View covers of upcoming books
- Read sample chapters
- Learn about our future publishing schedule (listed by publication month *and author*)
- Find out when your favorite authors will be visiting a city near you
- Search for and order backlist books from our online catalog
- Check out author bios and background information
- Send e-mail to your favorite authors
- Meet the Kensington staff online
- Join us in weekly chats with authors, readers and other guests
- Get writing guidelines
- AND MUCH MORE!

**Visit our website at
http://www.kensingtonbooks.com**